There are no mistakes, only detours.
--Ledorian proverb

Star Trails Tetralogy: Volume II

A Dark of Endless Days

Marcha Fox

Kalliope Rising Press
Burnet, Texas

This is a work of fiction. Names, characters, places, and incidents are products of the author's imagination or are used fictitiously and are not to be construed as real. Any resemblance to actual events, locales, organizations, or persons living or dead, is entirely coincidental.

Kalliope Rising Press
P.O. Box 23
Burnet, Texas 78611

ISBN 978-0-9980789-7-7

Publisher's Cataloging-In-Publication Data
(Prepared by The Donohue Group, Inc.)

Names: Fox, Marcha, author, illustrator.
Title: A dark of endless days / Marcha Fox.
Description: [Revised edition]. | Burnet, Texas : Kalliope Rising Press, 2012. | Series: Star trails tetralogy ; Volume II | "Revised 2012." | "Interior design and illustrations by the author." | Interest age level: 13 and up. | Summary: "On a hostile planet like Cyraria, terralogists (planetary engineers) are in high demand and Laren Brightstar is one of the best ... Plunged into a web of political intrigue for his failure to lend his planetary engineering skills to a wannabe despot, Laren Brightstar finds himself on a planet cursed with lethal weather extremes where survival can never be taken for granted ... Protecting his family becomes impossible as old debts come due, leaving his teenage son, Dirck, to complete the daunting task Laren began to assure the family's survival."-- Provided by publisher.
Identifiers: ISBN 978-0-615-67124-6 | ISBN 0-615-67124-1 | ISBN 978-0-9980789-1-5 (ebook) | ISBN 0-9980789-1-3 (ebook)
Subjects: LCSH: Families--Juvenile fiction. | Engineers--Juvenile fiction. | Planets--Juvenile fiction. | Survival--Juvenile fiction. | Outer space--Juvenile fiction. | CYAC: Families--Fiction. | Engineers--Fiction. | Planets--Fiction. | Survival--Fiction. | Outer space--Fiction. | LCGFT: Science fiction.
Classification: LCC PZ7.1.F69 Da 2012 (print) | LCC PZ7.1.F69 (ebook) | DDC [Fic]--dc23

*To the muses
whose relentless promptings brought
this story to life and the physics professors whose instruction allowed
me to do the necessary math.*

System Description

Type: Binary
Location: Scorpius
Designation: Xi A & B
Class: F5-IV Subgiants

ZETA (Xi A)
Surface Temperature: 6800K
Mass: 2.88×10^{30} kg
Radius: 1.131×10^6 km
Luminosity: 1.95×10^{34} erg sec^{-1}
Absolute Magnitude: 2.9

ZINNI (Xi B)
Surface Temperature: 6500K
Mass: 2.66×10^{30} kg
Radius: 1.213×10^6 km
Luminosity: 1.87×10^{34} erg sec^{-1}
Absolute Magnitude: 3.1

HABITABLE PLANET (Cyraria)
Surface Temperature Range: -53C/-64F to 101C/214F
Mass: 6.8×10^{24} kg
Radius: 6.5×10^3 km
Rotational Period: 26 hours
Axial Inclination from Ecliptic Plane: 3°
Gravitational Acceleration: 10.735 meters sec^{-2}
Orbit: Lemniscate
Circuit: ~14,000 days
Standard Galactic Year: 400 days

    Zeta
        Semi-major Axis: 2.02×10^8 km
        Eccentricity: .333
        Period: 6880 days
    Zinni
        Semi-major Axis (Zinni): 1.99×10^8 km
        Eccentricity: .326
        Period: 7120 days

PLANETARY SATELLITE (Nifeir)
Radius: 2144 km
Mean Distance: 1.46×10^5 km
Composition: Nickel (Ni); Iron (Fe); Iridium (Ir)

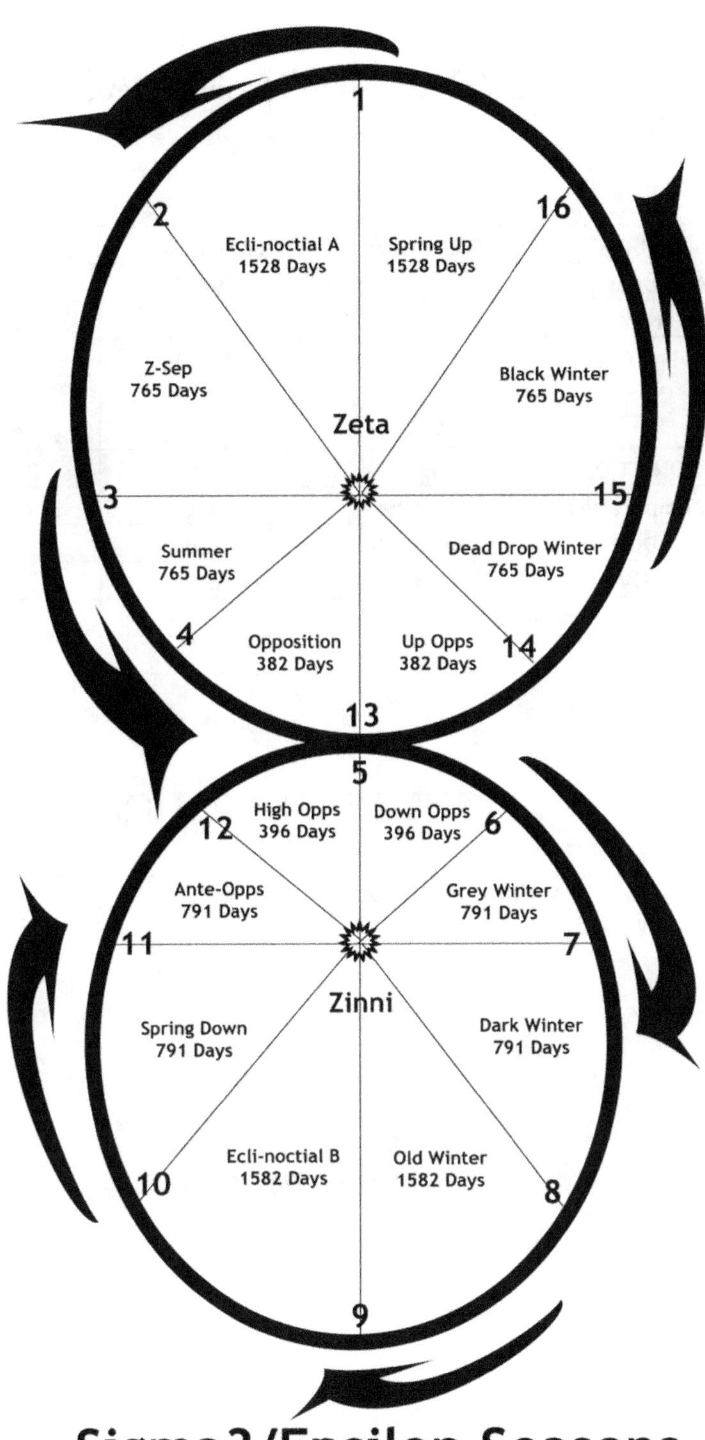

Sigma3/Epsilon Seasons
45 Degrees North Latitude

CYRARIAN CALMANAC

45° North Latitude

CURRENT	Sub-season	Sequential	Remaining
Anteopps 779		779/791	12
NEXT	**Sub-season**	**Sequential**	**Remaining**
High Opps		0/396	-12
	Peak (HO 132-264)	0/132	-144
CONDITIONS	**Max**	**Min**	**Probability**
Temperature	43°C/109°F	39°C/102°F	99%
Dust	Med-High	Med	87%
UV	High	High	100%
Pressure Vortices (PVs)			12%
Quakes			32%

LIGHT DISTRIBUTION

ZETA ξα	⍟	ZINNI ξβ	⍟

LEGEND
Rise/Set ♁
Circumpolar (CP) ⍟
Sub-Horizonal ✪

Visit www.StarTrailsSaga.com for additional information pertaining to the *Star Trails* Universe

Prologue

Of the numerous planetary hellholes Laren Brightstar had seen during his career as a terralogist, Cyraria was by far the worst. Genour in one hand, glass of sediment-laden water in the other, he considered how perhaps with major climatical engineering it could eventually fit galactic requirements to sustain human life.

Perhaps.

For now such a statement was not only presumptuous, but potentially homicidal.

The primary sun, Zeta, hovered above the distant horizon, dusted with Cyraria's persistent orange haze. As if its influence wasn't scorching enough, its companion contributed an equally malefic heat load from the opposite direction, disallowing any relief of shade. Officially named Incineraria, a name derived from its unfortunate influence, it was commonly referred to as Zinni, as if the whimsical nickname could lessen its effects. It currently traced a lopsided circumpolar path, circling like a bird of prey patiently awaiting the demise of its next meal on the ground below. Meanwhile, Zeta, recumbent for now, awaited its turn to rise when Zinni later descended to a similar declination, but likewise refused to set.

Together the pair would blast Sigma-3/Epsilon with unceasing light and unspeakable heat, day and non-existent night, for nearly two standard galactic years. The season was suitably called High Opps, culminating as the planet passed between its two host stars, searing what was already desolate waste with temperatures far beyond what humans could withstand without advanced technological intervention.

Of which the Brightstars currently had none.

The ballome offered some protection, but the climatic extremes exceeded the capabilities of its gel insulation and control systems at both ends of the temperature scale.

Laren was familiar with ballomes, typically used as experimental outposts in remote locations, and knew their systems and vulnerabilities well. The structure's heat load maximum of 66C/150F degrees was inadequate against what would reach an ambient temperature of 101C/214F or more during Peak High Opps. With little effort, he could name at least two elements that would melt in that range, more if he considered the effects of continuous exposure. Cyrarian seasons were long, ranging between 396 - 1582 days, Opposition mercifully the shortest, thanks to the mechanics of elliptical orbits.

Nonetheless, extremes during those 132 days of Peak Opps' could kill them. The cold season could, too, except the ballome's deficiency was less and not as threatening, being nearly two galactic standard years in the future. He'd already decided that by then they'd either be dead or living in better conditions, anyway.

Considering his current options, he wiped the sweat from his forehead with the back of his hand, realizing he'd left his sweatband inside, and took a reluctant sip of water. The only thing that could possibly save them was the fact he possessed numerous science and engineering skills, though construction was typically accomplished by robotic crews. Furthermore, there was the issue of finding, much less fabricating, needed components. Advanced technologies required sophisticated manufacturing facilities and exotic materials which he could never hope to find, leaving him with only the most fundamental principles of chemistry and physics at his disposal.

Given enough time, he knew he could do it, but whether enough remained before one of his enemies, of which the weather was only one, moved in for the kill, was his greatest concern.

His thoughts stopped abruptly when his wife, Sharra, hugged him from behind, head resting affectionately on his back, a stark reminder that the people he cared for more than life itself were at risk, thus denying him the luxury of surrendering to the inevitable and saving himself a lot of time and trouble.

"Good morning," she said a little too cheerfully. "Been up long?"

He crossed his arms on top of hers and stifled a sigh. Telling her he'd been awake the entire night certainly wouldn't be compatible with her belief that he'd take care of them, regardless of what environmental adversaries imposed on their humble abode.

"Not long enough," he said evasively, then turned, kissed her on top of the head, and activated the rear door palm lock, which obediently responded by disappearing overhead. Sharra close on his heels, he ducked back inside, where the cool contrast bespoke a chilling reminder of what needed to be done. A glance at the integrated calendar and almanac embedded in the curved wall held no surprises, only motivation, with a forecast for continual daylight, atmospheric turbidity factors, a.k.a. dust levels, and four lunar cycles of 36 days each remaining until it would be forever too late.

He entered his sons' sleeproom without further comment, managing again to avoid his bondling's questioning gaze. If she saw his eyes, she'd know, and having her worry, too, wouldn't help a thing.

Like his mood, the boys' sleeproom was dark, the glare of everlasting suns mostly masked by photo-sensitive plastiglas that darkened during programmed sleep hours. What little remained was occluded by heavy storm shutters, designed to protect the window from sand storms. They hadn't had a serious one yet, but they were coming, an inevitable part of the approaching season. Even nature protested the throes of Opposition. Groundquakes hadn't arrived yet, but were inevitable as Zeta and Zinni competed for Cyraria's mass during its semi-circuit passage between them.

What a planet, he thought grimly. *Calling this place a hellhole was an undeserved compliment.*

He sighed, digesting the import of their situation while his eyes adjusted. A quote surfaced in the stillness from what seemed eons ago, as if to taunt him: *If you can fix it, do; if not, pretend you can.*

Flashes from his side trip to Esheron with his brother, Jen, a short time before both families left Mira III, taunted him on a regular basis. While he'd vowed to oppose the encroaching political issues in whatever way he could, he had no idea he'd be living in conditions like this, where simply taking care of his family would be an ongoing battle with potentially lethal consequences.

According to Ledorian belief, visualizing the end result set the Universe in motion to deliver thoughts from the spiritual to corporeal plane. That was all well and good in theory. The problem was that the only vision he could muster under these conditions bespoke a horrifically bleak outcome.

Would his negative thinking manifest as well?

Probably.

He shuddered at the thought and tried to focus on what he *could* do, or at least attempt. *If you can fix it, do...* Yeah, right. In these conditions, the "pretend" part wouldn't end well, yet that was exactly what he had to do.

The shadows in the room gradually took form, revealing little Deven sprawled in his cyll with a peaceful look only a six year old could achieve, while the boy's teenage brother, Dirck, hair soaked with sweat, was breathing loudly, mouth agape, as if drawing his final breath.

Whether or not his older son would be any real help was beside the point. The boy's trek toward manhood had to continue, for reasons far more ominous that Cyraria's hostile clime. Indeed, preparing him for what was inevitably to come was top priority.

He mentally thanked the Benefics for the c-com he'd received on Esheron, a device which could serve as a repository for information he didn't have time to convey, should his worst fears for his personal safety materialize. It wouldn't guarantee success in his absence, but would certainly improve the odds. Hopefully, Dirck would catch onto the contingency plan without explicit instructions. The kid was already prone to worry, so didn't need anymore distractions than there already were.

Zeta's rising light cut through an unseen gap in the shutters and cast an eerie streak of reddened light on his son's sleeping face. The man-child reached up as if to brush it off, then turned over restlessly. Laren smiled grimly at its metaphorical irony, then reached inside his son's cyll and shook his shoulder, even while renewed thoughts of futility blared through his head.

"Wake up, Dirck," he said. "C'mon. *Now*. We have work to do."

CALMANAC: High Opps/Peak -144 Days		
Temp: 39C/103F	PVs: 34%	Quakes: 45%

The Mother of Invention

Dirck Brightstar groaned and turned over, the heat far more disturbing than the tone of his father's voice. "I can't," he replied hoarsely, eyes still closed.

"Why not?"

The question was far from sympathetic, but moving was out of the question. Every muscle ached, every breath a dry, suffocating gasp.

"I'm sick, 'Merapa. Really. I hurt. Everywhere. And I think I've got a fever."

His father's next response was prefaced with an exasperated sigh. "Very funny, Dirck. Get up. We have work to do, lots of it, and the best part of the day is all but gone."

"Assuming there is one," Dirck muttered, then gradually opened his eyes, squinting first at his father, then around the room. The heat was neither flu, nor nightmare, nor malfunctioning cyll comfort control, but the unwelcome environment of their new home. His groan was cut short by a pinfly buzzing his ear. He swatted at it without success, then sat up slowly, rubbing his eyes.

The gaze that met his own was less commanding than expected, but insistent nonetheless. "A forced circadian shift to a different time and light cycle isn't fun, but it's not fatal, either. The sooner you get moving and into a new routine, the faster you'll feel better," his father explained almost sympathetically, then abruptly shifted back to command mode. "So get up, get something to eat, and get dressed," 'Merapa ordered. "*Now!*"

Message loud and clear, Dirck stumbled to his feet and into the cramped sanicube to splash some warm, gritty water on his face. Indeed, another miserable chapter of their lives had begun. He straightened up, dripping, to meet the pitiful green-eyed stare in the wall's reflective surface, its distortions matching his attitude.

A haircut. He had to get a haircut. It had a tendency to fall in his face, anyway, plus now it was over his ears. Maybe his little brother, Deven, could stand it like that, but it would drive him crazy, especially in this heat. He wet his hands and raked them through his hair, temporarily getting it out of his face, then shuffled back to his sleeproom and rummaged through a container of clothes he'd brought from Mira III. Nothing, absolutely nothing, would work in this climate. His *naterra* had been persistently cool, so his Academy uniform was out, unispans almost as heavy.

He pulled out an old green and purple anoia uniform comprised of a sleeveless shirt and shorts, wondering if he'd ever play again and if so, with whom. At least the fabric was light, more than he could say for anything else. He pulled it on followed by his boots, trying not to think of how ridiculous he probably looked, not that it mattered. Good thing Creena was gone. She would have laughed herself silly. His heart fell, either from guilt or because he missed her, he wasn't sure which, as he wondered if he'd ever see his sister again.

He pushed his hair out of his eyes, again, mercifully distracted from a replay of his part in her disappearance, when he noticed he was already drenched with sweat. And 'Merapa said they were going to work.

Doing what?

All he wanted to do was sit down and die.

He slunk to the galley and collapsed on a stool where his mother looked up from the sink, then brought him a chunk of genour with a glass of murky water. He stared at the particles swirling within, quickly overcome by a massive, involuntary sigh.

"Oh, 'Merama," he groaned. "How can you stand this horrible place?"

She tucked a strand of reddish blond hair behind her ear and studied his face. "It'll be a lot easier now that you're both home," she said, pausing but a moment as her eyes focused somewhere far away before giving him an encouraging pat on the back. "So eat. Your father's been up for hours. He needs your help."

Dirck's laugh was short and humorless. "Yeah, right. He's going to need a lot more help than that. This place is hopeless. Besides, since when has he ever needed me for anything?"

His mother sat down and took his hand. "Listen. He told me what a good job you did looking for Creena. He said you're a natural pilot, have a very good head on your shoulders, and that your deductive reasoning powers are at least as good as his. But the real truth of it's really pretty simple. There's a lot of heavy, male gender work to be done around here and he can't do it alone. Any more questions?"

For the first time since their arrival, he nearly smiled. *A natural pilot.* Wow. At least the approval he'd felt during their excursion looking for Creena had been genuine.

"I suppose not," he admitted and met her gaze, not surprised by the worry lurking behind her eyes.

"Good. So drink your mud and get to work." She patted his hand and grinned, reminding him how much he'd missed her, but somehow he couldn't return it. Instead, he choked down a breakfast far worse than any they'd had in space, then went into his parent's sleeproom where his father was occupied with his c-com. The device's function, as its full name of *cerebral companion* implied, was not only to remember, but augment, its owner's thought processes. Without looking up, his father motioned for him to sit on the bench beside him.

"The first order of business is to do something about that water," he said. "First, purify it, second, set up a gravity feed system so we have enough pressure for a decent shower."

Dirck nodded numbly, trying to remember the last time he'd had the luxury of a shower that did more than dribble out of the ceiling with less enthusiasm that his overworked sweat glands.

"The next order of business is to design a cooling system," 'Merapa went on. "This heat is a killer and it's going to get worse, far beyond the ballome's cooling and possibly even structural capabilities. Peak High Opps gets the air hot enough to boil water, so you can imagine what long-term exposure can do." His father looked at him for the first time. "Do you understand what I'm saying, Dirck? I mean *really* understand? This is serious, dead serious."

"Yes, 'Merapa," he replied, more from Miran compliance conditioning than comprehension.

"You'd better," his father answered grimly. "They have public Opps shelters, but the nearest one is Cira City and, from what your mother says, they're worse than the immigration shelter she and Devin were in. So, that's out, we stay here. But that means we'll have to dig our own safe, here at the ballome, but not until we augment the cooling capability to withstand High Opps temperatures. From what I know of this planet's crust, we'll be lucky to get down a few meters before hitting bedrock, so keeping the indoor temperature within livable range is more important versus killing ourselves digging a hole."

Dirck only grunted, convinced that death in such circumstances would be more reward than consequences.

"And we need power. With that much energy outside, all we have to do is harness it. Ideally, I'd want a solar dynamic system with something like sodium or lithium fluoride, but we'll be lucky to find the components for a classic heat exchanger. Same for collector panels with a decent efficiency rating. But however we do it, we need more power. A cooling system will require more than we have now, just to run a compressor, unless I can find the components for an acoustical unit, which I doubt. Actually, an evaporative cooler would work well with it so dry, except in all this dust, we're better off with a closed system. And in the meantime, we need to design some growing chambers. We've only got enough genour for forty days and there isn't much left to barter with."

Dirck blinked incredulously, wondering if his father had jumped states, crossing that fine line between genius and insanity.

"'Merapa. You think we're doing all that? With what? What materials? What tools? We have nothing, 'Merapa. *Nothing.* We're not even as high tech as the psetoras on Verdaris. It's hopeless. There's no way."

His father's jaw was set, eyes hard with determination. "What do you mean, there's no way? The key to technology is knowledge, and that we have. You either conquer this environment or it conquers you. It's up to us to take care of your mother and Deven while we wait for Creena to get back with some help. Hopefully soon." He glanced toward the galley, checking whether his bondling was within earshot. "Besides, there are a few other complications," he said, lowering his voice.

Dirck stiffened with caution at the look in his father's darkened eyes. "What?" he whispered back.

"Remember what I told you, about when Jen and I went to Esheron before we left Mira III, and how it involved more than revalidating our *naterra* status?"

"What? That Ledorian Order stuff?"

'Merapa nodded. "Like I told you before, my bloodline qualifies us for membership. Since we were already going to Cyraria, we were called into service."

Dirck stretched his shoulders, popping his neck. "Right. To fight the INTEGRATOR's efforts to enslave systems in the Hostii Interplanetary Organization. Like Cyraria."

"I'm afraid so. Being chief terralogist would have been a great cover. It's going to be a lot harder now."

"So what exactly will you be doing?" Dirck asked, expecting the answer would be among his grandest fears.

'Merapa leaned back, scowling. "I don't know. Especially now. I suspect Troy knows about it, though, and intends to stop us. At any cost."

"Wonderful," Dirck said, recalling the animosity the Regional Governor held toward his father. "Does 'Merama know?"

"Yes and no. She knows about the assignment, but I don't think she really understands all the implications."

"I'm not sure I do, either. Besides, I thought there were choices on Esheron."

"There are."

He met his father's eyes. "So why didn't you turn it down?"

His father's expression shifted to one he couldn't read. "You don't turn down a call to the Order," he said.

"Why not? You didn't have any problem turning down Troy's offer."

"There's no comparison. They're like night and day. Being inducted into the Order is a privilege. An honor. Refusing simply isn't an option. It's not done."

Dirck gritted his teeth and looked around. If something remotely prestigious had occurred since leaving Mira III, it certainly wasn't evident. Even his parents' sleeproom was strictly utilitarian, nothing like the expansive suite they had in their Miran tower, high above the city with a three-hundred-sixty degree view. Here the workdeck consumed most the floor space and stacks of stowage boxes lined the outside wall with barely enough room between them and the dual sleeping cyll to squeeze by. The ballome's single sanicube through an arch to their right connected the room with his and Deven's. A flame of anger ignited in his gut as more hardships panned through recent memory.

"A privilege?" he asked bitterly, spewing the word as if it were poison. "Really? Even when it wrecks your entire life and your family's, too? How can they make you give up everything? *Everything!* Just because some idiot's taking over the planet! What right, what authority, do they have to do that?"

The lines around 'Merapa's eyes deepened like they always did when he was asked a question too difficult to answer. "There's more authority there than you can possibly imagine, son," he said, his voice gentle, not condemning, yet edged with an inflection Dirck didn't like. "We won't always understand why we're expected to perform certain tasks, or even how. But we have to do what we know is right. What's going on here is wrong, in numerous ways. After our excursion looking for Creena, you know as much as I do, maybe more, about the future. Some things we can change and we're expected to, but the seasons aren't one of them. And we don't have much time."

"Time or anything else," Dirck muttered, then cupped his face in his hands, elbows on his knees, and stared at the dull, metal floor. 'Merapa's answer had somehow doused the anger, but his discouragement had escalated. "It's hopeless, 'Merapa," he repeated. "This whole place is hopeless."

Any sympathy his father may have felt before disappeared. "Listen," he said sternly. "Without hope there's nothing. Like they say, *If you can fix it, do; if not, pretend you can.* Remember that. Literally and figuratively. I know we can pull this off, Dirck. We have to. This is the least of what we'll have to do here. Making this place livable is something we can and will do. Are you with me or not?"

Dirck hesitated, not with denial, but to assume his share of the weight. "All right," he agreed, meeting his father's steady gaze. "I'm in. But I want to know one thing first."

"What's that?"

"How'd you get through customs with the lasomag?"

'Merapa's face froze momentarily, then relaxed in a wry smile. He glanced into the living area again and motioned Dirck closer. "In the Space Command I had an Omega-5/NR clearance. That allows access to anything and everything. Source documents, the works. They're usually permanent, but now it's suspended. Why, I don't know, probably because I renounced my citizenship when we left Mira III. Anyway, I managed to get it reactivated while we were out. With an Omega-5/NR, they wouldn't stop me with a lasoclear bomb."

Dirck laughed, choking when his father gave him the Esheronian pinching gesture to shut down. "Do you know how worried I was?" he whispered. "Why didn't you tell me?"

"Because I wasn't sure it would work until I actually got through. Besides, I didn't know if you'd even remember I had it, and if you did, I wanted you prepared for the worst."

"How could I forget something like that? Furthermore, I'm never prepared for the worst," Dirck said, adding, "And with you around, I haven't had to be."

"Yeah." His father laughed humorlessly. "Thanks. I think. But remember, that might not always be the case. We accessed a lot of sensitive information out there, Dirck. If Troy gets wind of it, I'm history. You could be, too. Preparing for the worst is usually your best bet."

"Things couldn't get much worse than this."

"Don't bet on it," 'Merapa replied, grimness darkening his words.

"I didn't know you had a security clearance," Dirck said, shifting the subject. "Do all pilots have one that high?"

"No. Most are on a need-to-know or mission-specific basis."

"So how come you did?"

His father hesitated. "Being a pilot was a cover. Actually, I was doing environmental engineering."

"What's so secret about that?"

"There's a lot more to environmental engineering than terralogy. Planetary systems have tremendous amounts of energy which can be manipulated in hostile ways, either directly as weapons systems or for instigating weather or climatic changes that put the enemy at a disadvantage. Among other things, the project I was working on was developing methods for planetary tomography."

"What's that?"

"Mapping the interior of a planet. In the military, that means finding underground munitions, minerals, tunnels, command posts — that sort of thing."

"Did it work?"

"It worked, all right. But they got a little more than they bargained for."

"Like what?"

"The people on the ground experienced serious physiological and psychological effects."

"It affected their minds?"

"Exactly. They were concentrating on how to control it when I got out. I didn't like some of the things that were going on as a result. I worked on a similar tomography system for the HIO, but it was limited to exploration on uninhabited worlds."

"What didn't you like?"

'Merapa's eyes grew distant and his face clouded. "They started conducting mind control experiments. They would go to primitive worlds and manipulate indigenous populations in weird and immoral ways. In order to prove that the technology was causing the behavioral effects, they had to be bizarre and extreme."

"Such as?"

"Such as human sacrifice. They'd also convince the natives that as stargods they must be obeyed. Since they already had the ability to manipulate weather, they could threaten them with floods, famine, lightning or other extremes. Of course when these threats materialized, the natives were willing to do anything. And did. Anything to propitiate the supposed gods."

"That's horrible! So you knew what they were doing and how?" Dirck asked, eyes wide.

"Yes. I didn't agree, so I voted with my feet and left."

Dirck had always known his father was valuable, but exactly why or to what extent had never made sense before. Now it did, the knowledge tightening into a knot of anxiety. "Does Troy know?" he asked.

"I'm afraid so."

"What about 'Merama?"

"No."

"Why tell me?"

"If anything happens to me, someone needs to know why."

As his father's impromptu confession took hold, Dirck's fears yielded to more immediate concerns. On the positive side, certainly anyone involved in the highest level of Space Command technology could build a water purifier.

It really didn't look that hard. The list of components in the notelog was simple, consisting mainly of pipes and fittings, which the regional government provided free, plus corrugated metal and several meters of plastic sheeting. All they needed to do was fabricate an evaporator tray or series of troughs, then enclose it. Zeta's and Zinni's heat would evaporate the muddy well water, which fortunately was plentiful albeit nasty, leaving sediment behind. The vapor would be directed to cooler space within the ballome's layered composite walls where it would condense, drip into a collector, then into a storage tank. Installing the tank as high as possible would provide the gravity feed needed to improve their water pressure. If there was one thing they had in abundance it was heat, which would increase its evaporative efficiency.

Notelog firmly in hand, 'Merapa got up and went into the living area to summon the transport to take them to the settlement, which Dirck hadn't visited since their arrival onworld. He stood before the ballome's integrated command center, simply said, "comm-net", and the holographic image of the system's control panel bubbled out from the wall.

"Transport to Sigma3/Epsilon," he said, the image morphing into the itinerary display within the vehicle with their coordinates added along with those of the settlement. A map indicated its current location and progress along the way, the estimated time of arrival, or ETA, a few minutes away. The crude, boxy vehicle arrived on-schedule in a cloud of dust and they were on their way, skimming across kilometers of rust colored desolation.

"What a planet," Dirck muttered, mystified by his father's humorless laugh.

They disembarked at the settlement's only stop, a dusty, unpaved thoroughfare surrounded by a handful of simple composite buildings offering the few services available to Sigma3/Epsilon regionists. It looked even worse than Dirck remembered, the comcenter's makeshift sign taking him back to the day they arrived, when they'd gone in there for information on where to find 'Merama and Deven. A blast of anxiety as fresh as the memory shot through him and he quickly looked the opposite way, just in time to see his father disappear inside the supply depot.

The building was hot and stuffy, the paddle fan high overhead having little effect other than to emit an annoying thump with every revolution. Most of the space was taken by plumbing supplies, the rest filled with a potpourri of pumps, motors, collectors and zeta, or solar, cell arrays. It was manned by a stocky, brazen skinned Erebusite over two meters tall, and a young human, not much older than himself. The claim application process for their free supplies was, surprisingly, as simple as palming in, then completing a requisition for the other things they needed, *i.e.* a storage tank, pipe, collector material, and various fittings.

"Guess that's it for now," 'Merapa said, passing Dirck several lengths of pipe.

"No =CC='s, eh?" the human noted upon entering the information into the system. "You must be new here. I'm Win Sendori." He looked from Dirck to his father with penetrating blue eyes. Shoulder length brown hair framed a face accented by high cheekbones, slightly crooked nose and a shallow cleft in his chin. Dirck and his father introduced themselves, followed by a brief and appropriately vague rendition of how they'd come to be on Cyraria.

"That's Crjlx-IM over there," Win went on. The Erebusite stopped, waved a three-fingered hand, then returned to task, reflections from the overhead lighting gleaming on his hairless head. "So what else is on your list?" Dirck turned the notelog so he could see. "Let's see — you'll need an additional =C47C=. Or something worth that in trade."

Dirck's mind was busy scouring the ballome for something worth trading and he could tell his father was doing the same. He opened the container with the tool allowance, quickly noting he had most of them already. "How 'bout we trade back some of this stuff?"

"Sure," Win agreed. "Whatcha wanna trade?"

Dirck plucked out standard and cross-nosed twisters, and a set of star-bolt wrenches and held them up, looking first to his father for approval, which he got with a nod. "How much for these?" he asked.

"Just enough." He called to Crjlx-IM to bring over the corrugated material for the collector tray, then asked, "Whatcha building, anyway?"

"We'll let you know when it works," 'Merapa cut in. "C'mon, Dirck, we have work to do."

Dirck gave Win a *Parents!* eyeroll and followed his father outside with the first load of supplies. The transport arrived a moment later and the two of them secured the collector material to the roof and pipe to the sides, then Dirck returned to get the rest. By then, 'Merapa had strapped the storage tank to the back and everything else fit inside for the trip back.

During the return trip, 'Merapa explained again how they'd put it together, components thumping and banging various objections along the way. When they got home, Dirck started unstrapping the pipe from the transport while 'Merapa set the storage tank on the ground, then carefully removed the collector sheets from the roof before heading for the ballome, carrying as much as he could. Dirck had barely lowered the pipe to the ground, most of it still in place on the other side, when the transport noticed all its passengers had disembarked and took off in a swell of dust.

"*Hey!*" he yelled, coughing. "Get back here!"

His father stepped around from behind the ballome, saw what had happened, and started to laugh as Dirck ran inside to summon it back. It returned what seemed a long time later, pipe intact, allowing them barely enough time to unload the remainder before it took off again.

The work was hot and tedious, both suns monitoring their progress with unmerciful diligence, as they constructed the support structure to hold the weight of the storage tank, then started work on the still itself. It didn't take long to realize they didn't have enough collector tray material, but with it too late to go back to the SD, they called it quits for the day.

They got to it first thing the next morning, but quickly found that connecting it to the ballome's water system would be more complicated than planned. Various other fittings and elbows were required, necessitating yet another trip to the SD, then another when the sizes were wrong, which again took the better part of the next day. At least by then, Dirck figured out how to outsmart the transport while he unloaded it, which was as simple as taking Deven along, then having him stay onboard until they'd finished. The transport emitted a series of raucous alerts in an attempt to convince its last passenger to leave, but nonetheless stayed in place.

Zinni's light was flushed with orange as it dipped toward the horizon and Zeta had begun another ascent by the time Dirck tightened the last connector and opened the valve. He was sweaty, tired and covered with mud, but the thought of a clear drink drove him on. Since results would require zetalight and time, he cylled out when he was done, hoping, and for the first time since his arrival actually looked forward to the following day.

He woke up before anyone else and ran into the galley. Zeta had long since risen, doing its share of the work. He held a pitcher under the tap and pushed back the valve. Almost a liter of clear water spilled into it before the pipes chugged and rattled with air.

"Hey! Wake up, everyone!" he yelled. "Look at this!"

His parents and Deven joined him moments later. Everyone cheered their first environmental victory, exchanged the Miran grip, then split the results in a toast to Creena's speedy return. Even the genour tasted good as they momentarily forgot their other troubles to celebrate their first victory.

Dirck dramatically shook the last drop into his mouth, then reluctantly returned to the present. "So, what are we going to build today, 'Merapa?" he asked. "What's next?"

"First, we need to adjust our work hours. Since daylight is constant, it's foolish to sleep when both suns are at their lowest declination. We need to maximize that time for outside work, while allowing some overlap with the SD's operating schedule. So we need to reprogram our cylls based on less light, not more. As soon as we get that done, I need to get busy on more plans," his father replied, enthusiasm for their success already spent. "The still was easy, and more important to our morale than survival. The success or failure of the next project will determine whether or not we stay alive."

Before Dirck could comment, 'Merapa motioned for him to follow to his workdeck, where a progressing schematic for the heat exchanger glowed from its surface. Dirck groaned at the labyrinth of symbols representing lines and valves, fans, a compressor, and too many other components he couldn't identify.

"How long until Peak Opps?" he asked, frowning.

"Not long enough," his father responded grimly. "Not long enough."

CALMANAC: High Opps/Peak -139 Days		
Temp: 40C/104F	PVs: 35%	Quakes: 47%

Wildlife

Dirck sat at the comcon, staring blankly at the various messages hovering before him, mind faraway in the unexpected quiet. 'Merama had gone to visit Zahra at the comcenter, 'Merapa was working, as usual, and Deven was outside somewhere, doing whatever little kids do.

He was having a difficult time adjusting to the schedule shift, his body clinging to its former rhythms while his mind struggled to function. In such moments, that bad feeling about the heat exchanger inevitably gripped him again, as always, and his stomach tightened on cue with the thought. He could tell his father was worried, too, expressing more than once that a cavernous gap existed between understanding the principle and producing a working model, especially when the preferred components weren't available. There were only 139 days left before High Opps, adequate time for a design study, but not to build the actual hardware.

But they had to try, the results of failure too dire to entertain.

After growing up on Mira III, Dirck could almost comprehend the dark chill of winter, but this heat was like nothing he'd ever imagined. He still hadn't completely figured out Cyraria's numerous seasons due to the complexity of its binary star system. Including High Opps, there were sixteen separately defined periods, temperature extremes matched by wildly divergent lengths of day and night. All this because the planet not only orbited its two stars in a lemniscate or figure-eight pattern, but also rotated on its side, poles parallel to its orbital plane, rather than perpendicular, which was more the norm. Thus, Cyraria had two things working against it, both resulting in climate extremes.

He recalled that 'Merapa had once commented that the lemniscadian orbit was extremely rare and likewise unstable; what the implications of that might be, he didn't know and was afraid to ask, given that things were bad enough already. He did know that the planet's passage between its two suns was a precarious time, not only from heat, but opposing gravity. Fortunately, it only occurred approximately every twenty standard years. Unfortunately, their arrival time placed them there just in time for their latitude's most lethal seasonal band.

On impulse, he brought up Cyrarian Climate Central to see if this time he could figure out how the seasons played out. The combined calendar and almanac, or calmanac, showed the immediate situation, but didn't provide the particulars, which he felt a need to understand. The message board dissolved and a virtual image of the Cyrarian system resolved in the space before him.

Currently the planet was entering the corridor between its two suns, when it was closest to both simultaneously, the equator perpendicular to both. Thus, for their mid-latitude location, both Zinni and Zeta were above the horizon, all the time, in a lopsided circumpolar orbit. That he could follow because he could see it, day in, day out.

He changed the view from the top view of the entire system to what was visible from their location. The path of both would continue to tilt until again, they would rise and set, but only barely; each would linger beneath the horizon for only a short time, and daylight would still be constant. That made sense, too, because he'd noticed that as the days progressed, it was higher on one side of the sky and lower on the other, the difference increasing. Unfortunately, the higher it reached, the stronger its effects. He advanced the animation to Up Opps, when Cyraria began to orbit Zeta, leaving Zinni behind. At that time, both Zeta's and Zinni's respective paths would rise and set, at which point, thanks to their 45 degree latitude, at least they wouldn't be directly overhead. That alone reduced their heat, while one chased the other across the sky, meaning one or the other would be visible at all times.

Ironically, cooling came quickly not long after that, as first Zeta disappeared below the horizon, then Zinni sank lower and lower until it, too, was gone as well as distant, resulting in a period of utter darkness, during which time their lives would depend on staying warm.

Too bad they couldn't save some of Opp's heat for Dead Drop Winter, he thought.

Now that he had a better understanding of the dynamic dance between Cyraria and its two stars, he switched to the end results in the form of specific weather projections.

Anteopps, which was where they were now, was bad enough, with daytime temperatures already 43 degrees centigrade or 110 degrees Fahrenheit and increasing daily. High Opps, when it would reach at least 101C (214F) was incomprehensible. Temperatures were given for ambient, or air temperature. Objects exposed to continual zetalight got even hotter. Sodium was known to melt at Peak Opps and its melting point was documented at over 97C, nearly the boiling point of water. As a prelude, a dribble of sweat coursed from his temple to his chin, and he switched off the image, less than comforted by the confirmation of everything his father had said.

He then covered his eyes wearily with his hands as if to hide from the vicious realities settling on his mind, one of which was how long it was taking Merapa to calculate how much heat energy they'd have to remove to keep the ballome at a "comfortable" 29C (85F). His rising frustration was evident, due to the fact that everything was taking longer than expected. Technical information sources at his fingertips on Mira III now were either inaccessible or difficult to find, forcing him to either draw from memory, or in some cases, derive the data from scratch.

He'd gotten the c-com when he and Jen visited Esheron, and he hadn't downloaded everything he needed before they'd left Mira, due to the fact the dire situation they were in now was entirely unknown. Thus, he had to baseline it with his own knowledge, then command it specifically how to expand the data, which sometimes involved excursions down divergent paths, wasting time and effort. Finding substitutions for the ideal materials and components which met system specifications was the worst part, with such a problem entirely unheard of on civilized worlds. His frustration was contagious and so was his anxiety, no matter how much Dirck believed in him. He'd never seen his father out of his element before, and the prospect was unsettling.

Since there wasn't much Dirck could do other than get in the way or obsess on their problems, which wasn't helped in the slightest by what he'd seen on the comcon, he switched it off, paced the room nervously for several moments, then finally decided to do something useful, such as check the still for leaks. He grabbed his sweatband off the counter, then exited through the back door and climbed up the service ladder they'd constructed from leftover pipe and a network of T-fittings, rails and rungs hot to the touch in spite of being somewhat shaded. He worked his way along, checking all the plumbing joints and elbows, and the seal on the polymeric sheet. The entire system passed inspection, though the covering was already warping from the heat.

He sighed, wondering if it could withstand all it would have to endure, then shaded his eyes with his hand and took advantage of his vantage point to scan the barren landscape, as if to see something he hadn't before. It stretched in every direction with equal desolation, marred by minor differences in terrain. Toward the back of the ballome, he noted what looked like several large outcroppings of rock a hundred or so meters away, and a few dark smudges against the red earth, possibly vegetation. It was hot, but not yet scorching; 'Merapa had been right about working with Zeta down. Maybe he'd take a walk and check it out.

He went back inside, the relative cool reminding him again how much hotter it was going to get. Hopefully, 'Merapa was making progress on the heat exchanger; once the outside temperature exceeded the ballome's capabilities, it would be extremely uncomfortable. Frowning as what he'd seen in Climate Central came back unbidden, the back door slide up and Deven wandered in. The boy went directly to the sink, stood on tiptoe to reach his tumbler, then drew himself a drink and gulped it down.

"Good water, Dirck," he said, smiling.

Dirck grinned back, pride easily aroused, yet knowing humility would replace it soon enough. "Thanks, Dev," he said.

Of course he couldn't have built the still without his father's detailed instructions but the fact he'd had anything to do with it at all was gratifying.

Deven set his tumbler on the shelf and headed back to the door. He took off at about this time every day, and for the first time Dirck wondered where the boy went. He'd usually be back before Zeta rose and the heat set in, but never said anything about his activities. Dirck realized that was partly his own fault, since he hadn't had time to be sociable while he was working on the still. Actually, due to the age difference, he never socialized with him much on Mira III, Creena either, except for recreational fighting, because most of his time was spent at the Academy or with his friends. This would be the perfect opportunity to catch up.

"Hey, Dev—where you going?" he asked. "Okay if I join you?"

The boy hesitated only a moment before breaking into a huge grin. "Yeah! That would be great. I'll show you around."

Dirck could tell his brother had been itching to share his discoveries for a long time. When he and 'Merama first arrived, she'd humored him for a while, until she became engrossed with other things, like food and whether she'd ever see her bondling or other two children alive again.

"Let me get my visor, okay?" Dirck asked.

"Okay. I'll meet you outside."

Dirck returned moments later, the light-sensitive visor in hand that he'd traded the spare spanner for at the SD. On the way by his parents' sleeproom, he stopped.

"'Merapa," he said. "I'm going for a walk with Deven." His father nodded without looking up, apparently communicating with the c-com, and Dirck suspected by the time his mother returned from the comcenter, he wouldn't have the foggiest notion where they were; it happened all the time back home. The main thing was that he'd told him, he decided, and promptly left. His little brother was drawing pictures in the dirt with a stick, grin returning when he saw Dirck, almost as if he were surprised he was actually going. The two started walking, Dirck deferring to the boy to lead the way.

It was hot already, Zinni at perigee a few degrees above the forward horizon, Zeta still low and skirting the one behind. After an initial nasty case of zetaburn, Dirck's skin had darkened to the same shade as his brother's, his hair bleached blond. He set the visor in place, holding back his hair to keep from trapping it in front of his face. He still needed a haircut, now worse than ever, and he made a mental note to ask 'Merama for one when he got back.

Deven turned left after several meters and climbed nimbly over some red sandstone boulders that cluttered a slope where scrubby bushes grew in sparse patches of shade. The sky was dusty gold, Zinni's orange disk casting ghostly shadows only slightly compromised by Zeta's waning light. When both suns were equally high in the sky, shadows were canceled, giving the landscape an odd, dimensionless appearance. Mira III's lack of direct light precluded them entirely, so the concept was similar. Thus, using shadows to estimate time or direction was difficult at best, and impossible at worst, given that both suns looked about the same during this phase of the circuit when they were about the same distance away.

High above their heads, a trio of heliaria darted in erratic paths, their broad wings spread while rotating tails directed their flight. Heliaria were scavenger birds and common to other worlds. What was there to scavenge there, besides dirt and rocks?

Probably regionists, like them.

He shuddered at the thought, eyes fixed once more on the ground, as they continued their trek across zeta-parched ground, dodging rocks and occasional scrawny patches of vegetation. Massive, red and brown rock formations, sculpted to unlikely shapes by sand-laden winds, towered before them. There wasn't much to talk about other than incidentals, but even that ended abruptly when Deven motioned him to silence.

His brother stood perfectly still at the base of a steeper ascent, Dirck beginning to wonder whether or not he should panic, when ever so slowly Deven pointed toward a six-legged lizard about a half meter long, poised on an outcropping a few meters away. Red, orange and green geometric designs painted its body as well as the flimsy collar around its neck. The creature flicked its tail and blinked deep-set eyes, apparently oblivious to their presence.

"That's a yraglian lizard," Deven whispered. "We need to stay back. They smell *really* bad if you upset them. I mean, really, *really* bad."

Dirck nodded, unsurprised that the first native creature he encountered on Cyraria represented it so well.

Deven turned right, then ducked through a short windswept tunnel between the rocks, which opened on a flat stretch of land. A grouping of phynques huddled below, making soft, smacking noises. Hundreds of tiny feet-like roots, capable of transporting the entire plant, wiggled at each base. The phynques had located near a flasher mound and several parades of the tiny insects were marching to their sticky fate.

Dirck stared at them in wonder. Cyraria not only had flora and fauna, but flauna, species with both plant and animal characteristics. The phynques were undoubtedly in that category, and brought back wary memories of Verdaris and Mira III's biodomes. There was something about living plants that creeped him out.

"C'mon, Dirck," Deven prodded. "Let's go."

To his relief, no flora were more than a few meters tall, at least until a bulky, pale green monolith towered through the brush straight ahead. As Dirck drew closer, he could see its surface was not only textured with numerous bumps, but pocked with small holes. Curious, he tipped back his visor a few degrees and stepped closer.

"Don't!" Deven warned, arm extended across his path.

Dirck halted, dead in his tracks. "Why not?"

"It's a spickle tree. Watch."

Deven crouched behind a rock, gesturing for Dirck to follow, then chucked a stone at it, leaving a moist bruise at the point of impact. An instant later, hundreds of spikes launched in their direction, clattering to the ground in a chorus of vain impacts.

"Holy holocubes!" Dirck gasped. He picked one up, frowning as he examined a potentially lethal green shard, about the same length as one of his fingers. "That, that, plant, or whatever it is, could kill you! How'd you know it would do that?"

"My friend told me," Deven said.

Friend? What friend? Dirck hadn't seen a kid Deven's age since the *Aquarius.* "Who?" he asked.

"You'll see," Deven replied with a mischievous smile.

Vegetation thickened around them, including the gnarled, black branches of a large bush tangled with creeping sage. Deven explained that it was an atsna tree, its massive roots useful for getting rid of "that bad taste" everything had on Cyraria. A different plant flowered beneath it, its huge, pink flower shaped like a bowl.

"It's called a bowlbush. When the flower dies, you can dig it up and eat the root," Deven said. "It tastes pretty good."

"How do you know?" Dirck asked, curiosity growing. Where was his brother learning this stuff?

"I told you," Deven replied. "My friend told me."

"Can I meet your friend?" Dirck asked, more mystified than ever.

"Sure," he replied. "That's where we're going."

It wasn't quite as bad as Verdaris, but Dirck still had an eerie, uncomfortable feeling, given some vegetation was openly hostile, with others possibly smarter than humans. The thought that the bowlbush was edible fascinated him. Anything would be better than genour, the desiccated rations they'd lived on since leaving Mira III.

A bush rustled beside them, followed by a clicking sound similar to the noise his 'cruiser made with an unbalanced impeller. Before he could even ask, his brother mimicked the sound and started in that direction.

"Hey," Dirck said, grabbing his arm. "What was that? Where you going?"

Deven turned and smiled, his missing front tooth contributing to his widening grin. "C'mon," he said. "You can meet my friend."

Dirck had grown up on a world where aliens were commonplace and little surprised him. Size, shape, number of limbs or eyes, color, eating habits, and strange odors were all part of an intergalactic society. Dirck really believed he'd seen it all. But even by those standards, Deven's friend was the most bizarre creature he'd ever seen.

It was bulky as well as large, and stood upright as they approached, making it slightly taller than he was, with two massive legs and six arms, each with scoop-like hands. Its bulbous eyes were deep set with multiple eyelids beneath a protruding brow, its mouth wide and probably huge, if opened to capacity. Its tail was almost as long as its body, and nearly as heavy.

But its most outstanding feature was its skin.

At least he thought it was skin. Whatever it was, it rippled in the breeze, like a translucent, gold-spun cloak. Several other layers beneath reflected a rainbow of color. Even dulled by Cyrarian dust, it shone and sparkled. And strangest of all, in spite of its size and odd appearance, the alien emanated a feeling of welcome that Dirck had never sensed in any culture, including his own.

"What is it?" he whispered.

"A bnolar," Deven replied. "I call him Enoch. They live in underground caves and like people, but some people are mean, so they usually hide. But he knows we're his friends and isn't afraid."

The creature resumed the clicking sounds, which Deven seemed to understand. Dirck followed them down a path flanked with atsna bushes, sudden reverence quieting his mind as he watched the two unlikely friends in an unfriendly world. After they'd walked for about a hundred meters, Dirck noticed the smell of sulfur growing stronger. A short time later, they walked through another cluster of rocks to a bubbling fumarole where yellow-tinged mud boiled from thermal energy generated deep within the planet's crust. As if there wasn't enough heat on the surface, he thought grimly, they even had it coming from below. Great.

Beyond the mud pot was the entrance to a cave, the ground around it littered with a dry and scratchy vine Deven called pubescent crawler, warning him that the delicate, air-filled vine emitted an offensive odor if stepped on. Dirck broke off a piece, noting the ground beneath it was cool. The stench was worse than expected, but nonetheless he suspected it could serve as more than a scratchy, fetid vine, given its obvious insulation properties.

Not far from the fumarol, a small spring gurgled in a rock-confined pool. The bnolar scooped up some water with a shallow bowl and handed it to Deven. The liquid looked clean and pure. His brother took a small sip, gave it back. The bnolar set it down by the fumarole and dragged three claw-like fingers through the steaming mud, plucking out several short, fat, sticks.

Except the wrinkled, brown cylinders were moving and undoubtedly alive.

Deven rinsed them in the spring, placed them in the bowl, then set it in the fumarole until the water steamed. A while later, he poured off the water, let it cool for a few moments, then broke one open and, to Dirck's horror, ate it.

"Deven!" he cried. "What are you doing?"

"They're good, Dirck. They're called wiittiins. Here, have one."

"Yuck!"

"They're better than genour," his brother taunted, and with an exaggerated flourish, popped another one in his mouth.

Dirck tilted back his visor and gingerly picked one up. He pulled off the skin, sniffed it, took a timid bite. Deven was right, it had an odd texture, but tasted great. He quickly ate the rest of that one, and reached for another.

Deven and his friend conversed in their curious way a while longer, then Deven indicated it was time to leave so they started back to the ballome.

Dirck's mind rattled with a thousand questions, the heat nearly forgotten. When they reached a space between the towering stone pillars, he could stand it no longer, so picked up his brother and set him on a rock.

"Hey! Whatcha doin'?" Deven protested, squirming to get free.

"That's quite a friend you have there," Dirck said, trapping his escape.

"I know. Isn't he neat?" Deven replied, quickly settled and swinging his feet.

"Yeah, he is," Dirck answered. "Have you told anyone about him?"

Deven frowned. "Like 'Merama?"

"Yes. Exactly. Like 'Merama."

"Are you kidding, Dirck?" he said, eyes wide. "She'd ground out if she knew! She'd never let me leave that crummy ballome again for as long as I live! She'd kill me, Dirck!"

Dirck rested his hand on his brother's knee. "No. Listen. I don't think she would. Your friend has taught you some really great stuff. They need to know about this."

Deven's hair usually covered his eyebrows, but not when he scowled. "No!" he said. "I'll get in trouble. I'll be in time-off until I rot, and die, and smell worse than an yraglian lizard. No."

Dirck sighed with frustration, wondering when he got old enough to start running interference between his little brother and their parents.

"Deven, they have to know. I'll do everything I can to keep you from getting punished, but I don't think you will. This is important. I mean it—they have to know. I'll tell them if you like, or I'll go with you, but we have to tell them. Okay?"

In response Deven's lower lip quivered and eyes filled with tears. "But I promised."

"Promised who?"

"Enoch. I promised him I wouldn't tell. He said if I did, people would come and hurt him and the others."

"'Merapa and 'Merama wouldn't hurt him or anyone else." He stopped, realizing that his father would probably hurt Troy, given the chance, but that was beside the point.

"But I promised," Deven insisted. A tear broke free and slipped down his cheek, leaving a muddy trail.

Dirck reached over and wiped it away with a gentle finger as he struggled for an explanation, vaguely recalling his father's lecture on higher laws, what seemed so long ago.

"Look, Dev. It's like this. We're a family," he said. "Families stick together. If one of us makes a promise, we'll all keep it. And when there's something important, you have to tell 'Merapa and 'Merama. At least 'Merapa. That's just the way it is. There's nothing you can't tell him, understand?"

"Have you always told them everything, Dirck?"

Dirck looked deep into his little brother's dark, trusting eyes, guilt rising like steam from the fumarole.

"I guess not," he admitted.

"What did you do?"

Dirck wasn't sure whether to tell him or not, then finally decided if he shared one of his secrets, Deven might feel better.

"Okay. One time I sloughed classes at the Academy with my friends so we could goof off downtown. . ."

He told him the entire story, holding back nothing, figuring it would make Deven realize the bnolar was mild by comparison. When he'd finished, Deven scuffed his heels on the rock, then looked Dirck squarely in the eye.

"Okay," he said. "I'll make you a deal — I'll tell if you do. But I want you there to protect me."

"Okay," Dirck replied grimly. "As long as you're there to protect me, it's a deal."

Deven laughed, then leaned forward and gave him a hug. "You're a pretty neat brother, Dirck," he said.

Yeah, right, Dirck thought. *I'll be a pretty dead brother after this.*

* * *

*Regional Settlement
Sigma3/Epsilon*

The transport groaned as the antigravity coils activated and the vehicle settled on its heading toward the ballome. Sharra wilted into her seat, staring vacantly out the dirt-smudged window as parched terrain swept by beneath, wondering why the visits with Zahra didn't help anymore.

Actually, she knew.

Jendaks weren't very high on the intelligence scale, but their intuition was startling. Zahra could gather and interpret information from the cosmos in remarkable ways. Sharra had no idea how she did it, but she'd been right consistently enough she put a lot of faith in what she predicted would happen. She even explained how her emotional makeup had changed, now that she was in a different location of the galaxy, something that made little logical sense. How the energy could be that different to have such an effect seemed crazy, yet fit what she was experiencing perfectly.

Today Zahra told her, as gently as possible, that Creena wasn't going to return anytime soon. She had struggled constantly with the fact that Laren had actually sent her away. At the time, it seemed to make sense, but not any more, not if she wasn't going to return soon enough to help. And there was something in Zahra's round, yellow eyes that told her there was more, something too horrific to reveal, and Sharra was afraid to ask.

It felt as if something inside her had died, then settled in her heart as a cold, unyielding lump. The feeling was a new one, such that she'd never known existed until leaving Mira III. Part of it was fear, but not all. She'd been afraid before, yet never like this. She'd thought it would go away once Laren and Dirck returned with Creena. Wherein lay the explanation—they hadn't.

She couldn't tell whether Laren really believed she'd come back with help or not. Dirck either. Only Deven never wavered, continuing his assertion that she would indeed be back. But of course the real question was when? As much as she wanted to believe her younger son, the fear of disappointment remained. She'd sustained herself on that thought before, and the agony when they'd returned without her was almost more than she could bear.

The transport trembled and lilted back and forth as a dust devil's erratic path crossed theirs, Sharra gripping the rail beside her until it stabilized. The whirlwind skipped along spewing sand, oblivious to the brief disturbance, dashing amongst boulders and brush, which suddenly split it in two. One wound down to a wispy cloud, the other leaving sight when it danced behind a rock-strewn rise. Its whimsy mocked rumors of its massive cousins known as pressure vortices, called PVs by the locals, violent tornado-like storms several kilometers across, which swept the ground clean. Weather perils were still hard to grasp, though the heat made a convincing prologue. Laren had repeatedly told her that probability was in their favor and not to worry, that the planet was large and their paths narrow. And with more immediate concerns, like Creena's welfare, not dwelling on PV's had been easy.

She wanted to believe Creena was okay and deep inside it felt right. But, any feelings of comfort defied all logic, the desire for evidence more tangible than a rhyming, telepathic voice only kept at bay by distractions. And then there was the guilt that tweaked her longing from time to time, reminding her that at least she had her bondling and two sons. But her little girl was still gone and she missed her horribly. If they knew how much Creena's absence still bothered her, they'd probably think she wasn't grateful they were home, which wasn't true. But having their family separated, by space and possibly even time, left a void that could only be filled by one solitary event—Creena's permanent return.

While she really wanted to believe that it would happen, every neuron of her logical Miran mind screamed *"No!"* With miracles excluded from the solution set, the outcome was nearly assured to be unpleasant.

Except for that crazy feeling.

Again, she disciplined herself to remember what she had. Feelings stirred, then fear escalated again as the unwelcome thought occurred that there were no guarantees nothing would happen to Laren, Dirck or Deven.

None whatsoever.

The hazards around them were tangible. This certainly wasn't the life they'd anticipated. Laren seemed to have things under control. He always did. But were they really? What if she lost him? Or the boys?

And what was that haunting look lurking in the depths of Zahra's soulful eyes?

Memories of lonely days of worry and hunger closed around her like the darkest of nights. It took a conscious effort to release herself from its grasp, deluging her mind with self-manufactured reassurances that now they were home and would never leave her again. In spite of her best efforts, shadows remained, the sudden need to hold them close consuming what remained of her composure.

She watched impatiently through a thickening wall of tears as the coordinates on the transport's console slowly ascended toward those that represented home. Never had the trip seemed so endless. At last the transport trembled to a stop, heat bursting through its open door.

Sharra swallowed hard and wiped her eyes, emotions rising as she flew from her seat, down the transport's treaded steps, then anxiously toward the ballome.

Confessions and Concessions

The walk back to the ballome was shortened by anticipation, some good, some not. Deven's discoveries had the potential to greatly affect their conditions for the better. Confessing his Miran misdeeds to his father, however, generated a far more dismal scenario.

As soon as Dirck entered the ballome, he could feel something was wrong. Deven did, too, judging by the way he stopped dead inside the door, brown eyes wide. Dirck removed his visor and tossed it next to the comcon tray, their few furnishings resolving from the dim light. His parents were in the living area, their conversation cut short by their entrance. 'Merama's frantic expression instantaneously thawed from agitation to relief. Her eyes closed then an unfamiliar emotion took charge.

"Where have you been?" she cried, green eyes clashing with his.

"We went for a walk," Dirck replied with deliberate, soft-spoken calm. His mother had never acted this way on Mira III. "I told 'Merapa." His father gave him the expected blank stare. "I really did," he added, bracing for what was sure to come.

"Oh, never mind, Sharra," 'Merapa said. "They're home now, safe, so there's nothing to be upset about."

His mother's stare shifted from Dirck to 'Merapa, emanating that look only a bondling could achieve given their mate's ill-thought-out behavior, intentional or otherwise.

"No reason to be upset? Who knows what's out there, Laren! Isn't having Creena missing enough?"

Their eyes met and held, emotions surging between them that charged the room with unseen visions of recent past. Dirck's shoulders slumped, chest aching with regret at his part in her distress. His father started to speak, but caught himself and shook his head. 'Merama just looked back and forth from her bondling to him, eyes filling with tears.

"I'm really glad you're home safe," she finally said, her voice shaky but saturated with relief. "Really."

With that she wrapped her arms around him and then Deven in a firm, emotion-laden hug, gave her bondling one final distressed look, then squared her shoulders with unspoken dignity, and disappeared into her and 'Merapa's sleeproom. The door dropped to the floor with a thud while his father stared after her, expression troubled, apparently debating whether or not to follow. Fortunately for Dirck, he decided against it. All she needed right now was to hear about her baby's adventures with spike-hurling plants and cave-dwelling aliens. His father walked to the galley to get a drink, then stood staring out the ruddy window while Dirck and Deven cautiously crept up behind.

"'Merapa?" Dirck said. "We need to talk."

When his father turned around, it didn't look as if he wanted to hear it, good, bad, or indifferent. He gulped down the rest of his water and set the tumbler down a little too firmly. "Make it quick," he said. "I've had enough distractions already and need to get back to the heat exchanger. You know that."

"I know. But this is important."

'Merapa leaned against the sink basin and folded his arms with an exasperated sigh. "Fine. Go ahead."

Dirck didn't know where to start. Maybe he could wait, do it as a male-bonding activity or something, when they'd both have a good laugh. That certainly wasn't going to happen now. Deven pulled at his sleeve and gave him a look.

"Okay, it's like this," he said, heart accelerating with dread. "Deven and I made this deal. I have to tell you something, and then he's going to tell you something."

His father's expression indicated he was operating somewhere outside his interest range, but Dirck plunged forward before losing his nerve.

"Before we left Mira III, I did some things that were kinda wrong. I guess I'll feel better if I told you about it." A spark of interest ignited in his father's tired eyes.

"Oh? So what'd you do?" he asked.

"Well, me and my friends decided to slough school. We wanted to go into the city and, well, you know. Anyway, my 'cruiser wasn't running...'"

"...as usual," 'Merapa muttered.

"Yeah. As usual." Dirck's laugh lacked enough energy to materialize. "So, well, we really wanted to go. So, I swapped out some parts with yours to fix it." Dirck cringed and held his breath, braced for the worst, and waited.

A thoughtful frown slowly appeared on his father's forehead as he digested the information. "Like what?" he asked.

"Oh, a power cell, the impeller drive, a compressor switch..." 'Merapa's eyes narrowed but he remained silent.

"Keep going, Dirck," Deven prodded, as if he knew that, by comparison, what he'd done was zero on the parental-anger scale. Dirck tossed him a "chill-out, kid" look and went on.

"Well, when we got downtown, the truancy scanner picked us up, and we got caught. So, they were going to contact you from the constable's base, but I told them you weren't my father."

"You *what*?"

"I talked them into believing that Jen was my father, that the datalogs were wrong, so he could pick me up, instead of you."

"Thanks, Dirck," 'Merapa said, sarcasm thick. "Nice gesture. So did Jen bail you out?"

"Yeah. But he made me promise to tell you."

"And you didn't, until now. Right?"

"Uh, yeah. 'fraid so."

"So now I know. And guess what? Jen told me back when it happened, before he even picked you up." His jaw flexed, lines appearing around his eyes. "Except for the part about my 'cruiser. I always thought it was suspicious, all those parts going out at once. *Hmppph.* I never dreamed it was my own son."

And that was all he said.

When his father turned around to get another drink, Dirck and Deven exchanged a look of mutual surprise, then got ready for act two. Except their father seemed more interested in intermission, because as soon as he'd finished his drink, he started back to resume his battle of wits with the heat exchanger.

"'Merapa?" Dirck called after him cautiously. His father stopped and turned, a weary look of frustration lining his face. "Deven has something to tell you, too. And you really need to hear it. It has to do with where we were. It's important, 'Merapa. Really."

Tired and frustrated as he was, his father sat down on a stool, lifted Deven onto his lap and told him to go ahead, impatience well masked, if not gone. Dirck sat on the floor by the sink basin and waited. Deven licked his lips nervously, then tumbled into a detailed account of how he'd started investigating around the ballome, then kept getting farther away each day.

"Then one day I met my friend, just over the hills behind us, and we were both scared," he said.

"Your *friend*?" 'Merapa asked. "You mean there's another family around here?"

"Sort of," Deven replied. "They were here before we were. My friend, he's a bnolar. He lives in a cave, a few kilometers away."

It was obvious that 'Merapa hadn't caught on to the bnolar's intelligence level until much later in Deven's tale, when he started talking about edible and hostile plants, migrating flauna, and the lizard that used flatulence as a tactical weapon.

The story took almost an hour to tell but 'Merapa never prompted the boy to hurry or showed the slightest hint of impatience. When he was done, he thanked him for the information, gave him a hug, then gently set him on the floor.

"So can I go back, 'Merapa?" Deven asked. "Can I still go see him?"

'Merapa cast Dirck a strange look, then looked back to his younger son. "I think we ought to talk to your mother about this," he said. "We need to define some rules for your wanderings, Deven, so that we always know exactly where you are. It's fortunate the bnolar was friendly, and that he was able to warn you about things like the spickle tree before you got hurt. But I think you'd better stay away, at least for now, unless Dirck goes with you. Okay?"

For the second time that day Deven's lower lip quivered as his eyes filled with tears. "Awwwww, do I have to, 'Merapa?" he asked. His father nodded. "But I can go with Dirck?" His father nodded again. "Okay," he sighed, wiped his eyes and started to leave.

"Wait, Deven," Dirck said. "Remember what we brought home?"

Deven's face lit up and he dashed for the back door, coming back with a bulbous tuber that filled his arms.

"What in Wimba's moons is that?" 'Merapa asked.

"Dinner!" Deven answered, grinning.

About then, Sharra came out of the sleeproom, much calmer then when she'd left. "What's that?" she asked.

"A bowlbush root," Dirck answered. "They're edible."

"They are?" She stepped over and touched its rough surface with a cautious finger. "Where did you find it?"

"It's a long story," 'Merapa said. "I say we try it. It can't be any worse than genour."

As it turned out, it was much better than genour, and the sanitized version of the story came out much easier over a good meal. 'Merama could hardly wait for them to harvest some more, plus bring back some atsna nuts which were useful as seasoning, creeping sage, and wiittiins, too. And then she came up with something that brought another surge of hope.

"When I was at the comcenter today Zahra was telling me they're putting a barterboard on the comcon. Regionists can list what they have to sell or trade. It'll include commodities, services and information. The =CC='s are posted electronically. I'll bet if we write up something about these native plants, other regionists will pay us for it." She smiled. "What do you think?"

"I think that's a terrific idea," 'Merapa said. "And now that the still's working so well, we could use water to barter at the SD."

"And there's something else, 'Merapa, that I almost forgot," Dirck continued. "There's this vine out there, too, that works like insulation. It smells raunchy, but only when it's crushed. I was thinking maybe we could use it here."

"Bring some home and we'll take a look at it," his father said. "Insulation would help a lot when we have the cooling system working. Speaking of which, I'm going back to work."

"Come on, Deven, I want you to tell me everything you know about those plants," 'Merama said.

"And I think I'll take some water into the SD and see how much it's worth," Dirck volunteered.

"Good job, boys," 'Merapa said. "You really helped out today. And by the way, Dirck, send Jen a message that he owes me twenty =CC='s."

"What for?" Dirck asked.

"We made a bet a while back, about whether you'd ever confess. Looks like I won."

"Oh."

* * *

Territorial Tower
Cira City, Cyraria

Augustus Troy leaned back in his chair, staring blankly at the barren walls surrounding his workdeck. The office was still too small and much too warm, but somehow tolerable, its discomforts occulted by more important concerns. Such as those performed in dark counsels far below, in the lowest depths of the Tower, where it remained cool, heat exchangers or not.

At least he had quiet, no distractions, and plenty of data. He'd formulated numerous strategic and tactical plans in the past—successful ones—with far less. Actually, simplicity had advantages. Without aesthetic distractions of fine fixtures and holografix, his powers of concentration had greatly increased. And truly he needed them now, as never before. While researchers completed the next phase, it was time for serious tactical moves on other fronts. Complex strategic plans required parallel processing where each path progressed steadily until it was time to converge.

The Director of Remotely Accessed Intelligence, known generally as DORAI, had gathered a tremendous amount of information on the girl from her time spent in the escape pod. As a result, they'd confirmed that Brightstar's daughter was right hemisphere dominant, endowing her with a higher level of intuition and creativity than the norm. This desirable baseline would be further augmented, once they refined the technology to obtain her mindprint. The fact she'd somehow managed to slip from his grasp while in Cyrarian local spacetime was frustrating, but further proved her value. They'd obtained some anomalous signals prior to her escape, which were currently being studied. Her behavior spoke for itself and they knew where she was headed, though it could be difficult to find her. No matter. That, along with any other obstacles, would be dealt with in due time.

The pod had yielded voluminous data, but that was within a controlled environment. Seeing how much influence the Miran compliance training had, versus her innate abilities and intuition, would be important for training purposes later. They needed to know how much resistance to expect to any directives given, once control had been established.

Achieving the correct balance between compliance and intuition was essential for successful intervention. Too much compliance and she would exhibit blind obedience; too much intuition and she'd ignore their directives completely. Properly balanced, she would follow orders appropriately and only question them when her intuition provided superior ideas, all while remaining within bounds of long-term objectives.

At that point, rather than using her as bait, he could use her as poison.

For now, the girl was far from her native environment, culturally and emotionally, the basic scheme the same, to keep not only her, but the entire family, separated by the greatest possible distances, for the longest possible time. Such situations had proven the undoing of many a family, seldom drawing them together as one might expect. Rather, the collective blame ricocheted off the guilt until whose fault it was mattered more than their common loss. Once contention began, disintegration was only a matter of time.

The solitude allowed him a rare sigh, even as he considered his own past, which was the source of his insights. Truly, the most valuable lessons were often the hardest and most painful. If there was one thing Troy knew, it was that families were destroyed by separation. But rather than compassion, he hungered for others to know the pain.

Solemnity deepening, he considered his options. Brightstar had admitted vulnerability by sending his daughter to get help. Nonetheless, he wasn't knocking on his door for help yet, either. While he may be willing to die versus joining INTEGRATION, the remainder of his family probably wasn't as dedicated. Getting them situated in Sigma/Epsilon instead of their original assignment had been amazingly effective. He gloated with malicious pride that, as Regional Governor, he had the power to make their lives as luxurious or miserable as he wanted — whichever best served his purposes.

Learning that Brightstar found power and substance meaningless hadn't been easy. In the process, he'd also come to realize his quarry considered his family members' lives more valuable than his own. Meaning the current approach would work, as long as the man had anyone to care about. Brightstar thrived on challenge and rarely failed. But everyone had a breaking point.

Everyone.

Brightstar was determined to survive and had the ability to do so. But how much primitive misery could the other family members stand before applying pressure for a more comfortable lifestyle, especially after the luxurious affluence they'd enjoyed on Mira III? With a devious smile, he brought up the file he'd accumulated so far on Brightstar's activities since arriving on Cyraria.

The infrared data from the S3 satellite constellation, deployed under the pretense of exploration, didn't show much detail, but in this case it was enough. The emissions indicated that their home already was no ordinary ballome. It had a heat signature that was entirely different than the usual composite-epoxy inflatable structure. Instead of the usual bland and circular footprint, theirs was blotched with hot spots here, and cold spots there. From the =CC= transaction data, it appeared they were bartering water, implying they'd put together some kind of still.

Clever.

But hardly unexpected. Even by taking away nearly everything the man had, Brightstar was still indomitable. Which yielded even further evidence of the ingenuity Troy needed so desperately to conquer the rest of this miserable planet. Yes, someday, through whatever means necessary, it would be his, in spite of its horrific climate with its outlandish extremes.

He leaned back in his chair for a moment, relishing the thought, but idle dreaming was a luxury he could ill-afford. Until that glorious day arrived, there was much to be done, including turning up the heat on Brightstar. He laughed aloud, thanking the approach of High Opps for already doing such an exemplary job. The heat season's approach fit perfectly with his tactics. Brightstar knew what to do to get through High Opps, but did the others? Removing him from the survival equation was a no-brainer, the means already in place, just waiting to be activated.

The man still owed him a substantial sum of money — a debt he had power to collect. And then there was the matter of even more serious offenses, fabricated though they may be. Loaning him his own ship had been a stroke of genius, the telemetry invaluable.

How could he lose?

Troy logged out of the S3 data and into the Planetary Law Enforcement Database, where he called up an increasingly familiar record. There was no question his options were far from exhausted. To the contrary. Things had only barely begun to get interesting. He entered the necessary passkeys and validation commands to gain write-access. It should be a simple matter to bring the man to his knees, once and for all.

Troy smiled again in spite of himself. Commanding a starship was but child's play by comparison. He thought a moment, then brought up the log of the *Cosmos II*, his own ship which Brightstar had used to pursue his daughter what seemed so long ago. Downloading the violations into the PLED took only a moment, then he reviewed his quarry's immigration record. He laughed out loud, remembering.

Yes. This would work. Anticipation burned inside as he polished the entry with a few personal touches, then flagged it *Active* and transmitted it to the local authorities. Again, he allowed himself to gloat, shamelessly this time.

This was what being Regional Governor was all about.

* * *

CALMANAC: High Opps/Peak -130 Days		
Temp: 41C/106F	PVs: 36%	Quakes: 48%

Regional Settlement
Sigma3/Epsilon

Dirck set the flask on the SD workdeck, waiting for Win to finish stocking a bin with zeta cells. Just as he was setting the last one in place Dirck slapped the counter to announce his presence, laughing when Win whipped around so fast his shoulder-length hair wrapped completely around his face.

"Hey," Dirck said. "How much can I get in trade for this?"

Win smiled with recognition. "Dirck! What's goin' on?"

"Nothing much. Still trying to build up our =CC=s. What do you figure this is worth?"

Win picked it up, sloshed it back and forth. "What is it?"

"Water."

"Water?" He looked closer, eyes wide. "*Clear* water? Where'd you get that?"

"Our still. That's what we were working on last time, with all that pipe."

Win set it on the counter, almost reverently, still staring. "So how much do you have?"

"Quite a bit. We get about forty liters extra per day, and it keeps increasing as it gets hotter. Unless our well runs dry, we're in pretty good shape. So how much is it worth, say, per liter?" Win was still staring at it longingly.

"You know how prices go around here. It would depend on how badly other regionists want it. It could be worth anywhere from nothing to, say, a thousand =CC='s. I'd start around ten and see what happens. If you get no business, lower the price. If you get too much, raise it."

"We need enough =CC=s for the parts for the heat exchanger and to improve the power system. If I put together a supply list, can you tell me about what it'll cost? Then we'll know what we're shooting for."

Trouble lines gathered on Win's forehead. "We're not supposed to quote prices. They change too fast. But I could give you a range."

"That would work."

"So what are you doing while your father designs the heat exchanger?" Win asked. "Think he'll be done by High Opps?"

Dirck shrugged. "It'll be pretty tough. While he's doing that, I'm starting a growing chamber. Most of the seeds in the starter kit aren't suitable for this climate. Too hot and dry. I can maybe solve the dry part with an enclosure. Not much I can do about the heat, though, and it's hard finding shade with Zeta and Zinni coming from different directions."

Win nodded. "That's for sure. I've heard growing chambers work fairly well. Genour gets pretty gross after a while, doesn't it?"

"Yeah. We actually had something decent a few days ago, though. We found this plant that tastes great, raw or cooked. It was like a feast."

Win's eyes lit up with that look people get when they've been on genour too long. "Plant? What plant?"

Dirck smiled tauntingly. "Watch the Barterboard. We're putting together the information now. It ought to be posted in a few days."

"You people are the most resourceful regionists I've ever seen," Win said. "You're going to be rich someday, just wait and see."

"I don't know about that," Dirck replied. "But we won't go down without a fight. At least not as long as my father's around."

"Why wouldn't he be?"

Dirck swallowed. "Oh, you never know," he said.

"You never know, all right." Win looked over his shoulder. Crjlx-IM was nowhere around. He leaned forward over the counter, voice lowered. "There's a lot of stuff going on they try to keep quiet, but I get a lot from the datalogs when I log in to order supplies. Let's get together sometime, outside this place, go have some fun, and I'll fill you in."

Something about Win's offer made him nervous, but anything he found out could be advantageous. He couldn't quite admit it, but the desire to go out was appealing, too, as he realized how much he missed hanging out with his friends back on Mira III.

"Yeah, let's do that," Dirck replied. "I could use a break."

"So could I," Win agreed, seriousness clouding his features. "So could I."

During the ride back to the ballome, Dirck traced the decline in his brief surge of optimism directly to Win's comments. He was right. All sorts of things were going on, and he was a fool to pretend they weren't. He'd also tried to ignore the possible significance of his father spending the better part of a day a while back exchanging real-time messages with Jen on the comcon. It wasn't so much the time spent, but his grim expression during the exchange. Whatever they were conversing about wasn't good, and somehow he felt it was more than the weather.

He stared blankly at the advancing coordinates on the console, wondering if Creena would actually be able to get back to Mira III and find help. He couldn't imagine her and whatever weird companions she'd picked up actually getting all the way back to their *naterra*, much less convincing anyone to come to their rescue.

He sighed and shifted his gaze past the dusty window to the rock-littered landscape beyond, remembering days past. He missed her, sort of, and really believed he cared, yet they'd still spent the better part of their lives in a state of contention. There were even times he had to admit he was more disturbed by the disruption of having her gone than genuinely worried about her return. If getting back to normal would happen when she came back, great. And by the same token, if things worked out where survival wasn't an issue, and they lived in some degree of comfort, even remotely similar to what they'd had on Mira III, then, would the truth be known, he probably wouldn't miss her that much at all.

The thoughts were shameful and he could hardly admit that he allowed them to form, even to himself, much less anyone else. He couldn't even identify why she could get him so angry. Sure, it was embarrassing when she got all those NCRs back on Mira III, but it was more than that. Some of his friends were regulars on the Board, too, and that never bothered him in the slightest.

But she did.

A stand of atsna whizzed past below, rocking in the transport's impeller wash, reminding him of when Deven had first introduced him to the bnolar. 'Merama had been quiet and withdrawn ever since, certainly not her usual self.

Not that 'Merapa was any better, his obsession with the heat exchanger putting him in a zone he'd never seen before, either. He sighed with the realization that since their arrival on this despicable world, both his parents had become virtual strangers.

As the transport glided to a stop outside the ballome Dirck's thoughts switched from speculation to reality.

Neither was particularly pleasant.

HE/927-652-A

Cerulean Nimrod
Local Spacetime
HE/927-652-A

An electronic scream ripped through the ship's lower chamber, the obvious tone of an alarm. Creena catapulted from her seat, certain it related to all the unexplained thumping sounds she'd heard since leaving Cyraria. Certainly this wasn't good.

She ran up the circular ramp to the piloting chamber, where she found Aggie interfaced with the console.

"Hey! What's all the racket?" she asked.

The robot scanned her with that cool, mechanical stare she'd grown to dread. "The landing alarm. I told you we'd get here faster than I originally calculated. Strap yourself in so I can complete the deceleration phase."

Creena dropped into the copilot's seat and secured the harness, anxiety switching to enthusiasm. If they were actually there, it didn't really matter what the other sounds were. The point was to find better transportation to Mira III anyway, hopefully in short order, so she could return to her *naterra*, find her uncle to see if he could provide any assistance, and then get back to her family, as quickly as possible.

The straps tightened for an instant as the acceleration buffers took the load, then all she felt was an abbreviated sense of forward motion. As soon as they were at constant velocity again, she shot to the window strip, curiosity burning. The *Cerulean Nimrod* had no datalogs whatsoever, other than which planets were inhabited by humans, the only information the ship's former owners cared about given they were cannibals. Whether this one would be like Mira III, Verdaris, somewhere inbetween, or entirely unique was virtually unknown.

The sight beyond was unlike any planet she'd ever seen. Delicate fingers of white marbled its surface, swirling in atmospheric whirlpools above an orb of purest blue. The occasional golden shadow of a land mass slipped by as well, the overall beauty serene and beckoning. She studied the topography more closely, deciding all that glimmering blue had to be water. Lots of it.

Her father had often commented on how essential water was to life, that it was a bigger driver for successful colonization than any other. She thought of him fondly, imagining him beside her while they shared such a beautiful sight, even more so compared to the barren wastes of Cyraria. The longer she admired it, the more her optimism soared. At long last she was one step closer to home.

Vector disks hummed, sending subtle vibrations through the deck beneath her feet as the ship edged closer. She thought of how she'd had a bad feeling about this planet before, which didn't make sense. Maybe it was only because she'd needed to change course to make contact with her family. Already her desire to complete her assignment and get home was nearing desperation. The consequences, if they goofed up, were beyond consideration. She tried not to think of how much responsibility she had because it always sent her into a pity party, which didn't set well with Aggie. And there was nothing more annoying than a sarcastic 'troid.

"Here's the plan," Aggie stated. "First, we'll set a parking orbit at about three hundred kilometers. From there, we'll be able to scan the surface with our lifeform and technology probes. We'll also monitor their transmissions to see who they consider friends in the intergalactic community. Their alliances will clearly indicate where they stand politically and whether we'll be received as friend or foe. Then, assuming everything checks out, we'll look for a landing bay."

"How long do you think it will take to find help?"

"Not long. If nothing else, most planets have starcruisers leaving on a regular basis, though there may be other stops along the way."

"Hopefully not. I don't want to spend any longer here, or anywhere else, than absolutely necessary. C'mon, let's go."

Aggie guided the ship to the edge of the atmosphere, then signaled for Creena to secure herself once more while she set orbit. As soon as the craft was stable, Creena returned to the window, watching as the terminator dividing night from day crept along the surface, darkening the approaching portion with night. Numerous bright spots, apparently cities, sprung up from the darkness, indicating moderately populated areas scattered across the globe.

Their near capture in Cyrarian airspace still gave her nightmares, but as far as she could tell, this planet was peaceful. There were a few satellites, but only one that looked large enough to be manned. Oddly enough, there were no space stations or other signs of advanced technology. At least there were no obvious landing restrictions or entry points for incoming stellar traffic, either. Every now and then, what appeared to be an intrastellar craft, typically only slightly more sophisticated than theirs, arrived or left the system, some heading for its single moon, but the off-world traffic flow was exceptionally light. Hopefully, they'd be able to contact one on the ground in short order, and hitch a ride to Mira III or some other connection point.

Amidst one of the vast bodies of water near the equator, an enormous moonlit whirlpool of clouds rotated slowly, tiny flashes of lightning sparking its edges. For a moment she remembered the storms on Verdaris and glanced spaceward for any itinerant comets or debris. Nothing but random stars and the concentrated band that comprised the galactic arm stared back.

"Doesn't it seem kind of funny there aren't more ships around? I've only seen a few, coming or going," she mused aloud.

"It's fairly well populated, at least in certain areas," Aggie reported. "The ecology is self-contained, so they may not be into heavy intragalactic trading. There are a few communications satellites in rotational sync, plus several smaller ones at lower altitudes, probably for navigation or surveillance."

Another concentration of shimmering lights came into view, rugged peaks reeling past as moonlight highlighted their whitened crests, casting grooves and crevices in bold relief.

"Why are they white on top?" Creena asked.

Aggie checked the environmental monitor. "It's essentially frozen water. They call it snow."

"So it's cold?"

"The median temperature is just right for human habitation but the specifics vary from location to location. The technology reading is only point two-seven, however. It has an excellent magnetic field and well-defined world grid, which we can use to recharge our systems if we need to, but I don't understand why they aren't using it for power generation. Instead, they have all sorts of antiquated systems including nuclear and other turbine driven ones, to produce electricity. Weird. What a waste of energy. Turn on the comcon, Creena, to see if we can pick up any broadcasts. So far things aren't looking very good."

"What frequency?"

"Use the radio frequency scanner to find the strongest signal."

Creena flicked it on, static hissing as it started its search. Within a few moments, it changed to a high-pitched squeal, then a garbled, patchy buzzing. Gradually, the chatter turned to words, words that, though faint, sounded familiar. And not just familiar — like a landing bay as well.

. . .Flight 659 to tower. . .Over. . .

Static crackled again, Creena pondering what she'd just heard. The bad feeling was creeping in again, but no longer made sense. The protocol was different, but clearly related to air traffic. Again, she bombarded her mind with the numerous reasons why they should land, from the good weather, the satellites, and the landing bay to the fact there simply weren't any other choices. Gradually, her doubts retreated, commanded to silence.

"I don't know," Aggie mused. "That technology rating is dangerously low."

"I think we ought to land," Creena stated decisively. "What could it hurt? If they can't help, we'll just charge things up and go somewhere else."

The 'troid stared at her momentarily until smile radii sparkled from her photoreceptors. "A very logical choice. A *very* logical choice." Creena hardly noticed the compliment, concentrating instead on an incoming transmission.

Tower to Flight six-five-niner. You're cleared for runway one-four. Visibility approximately one mile. Wind, east five knots. Over.

The language was familiar, but the words made no sense. The signal faded back to patchy buzzing, scanner whining forlornly at its loss.

"Check that," Aggie stated, indicating the monitor.

It was a close-up view of the largest satellite, apparently some sort of orbiting laboratory. It was little more than a large cylinder with what was probably a solar array shaped like an "X" on one end, oriented toward the planet's sun.

"What's that?" she asked.

"Looks like space junk to me," Aggie responded. "But three lifeforms are onboard, apparently human. If there were more of them, I'd think it was some kind of prison. Hold on—they're transmitting. Aggie locked onto the frequency and turned on the audio, allowing more unfamiliar words to spill from the receiver.

Houston, Skylab.

Go, Skylab.

Capcom, we have a visual on that NORAD signal. Better patch in Flight on the secure channel.

Roger that, Skylab. Stand by.

The scanner swept the frequencies again, the transmission lost.

"What happened?" Creena asked.

"They went to a different frequency, one that's encrypted."

"Why? Did they know we're listening?"

"I doubt it. Whatever they wanted to say, they didn't want on an open loop. It looks like some ancient version of an orbital spacecraft. Extremely old technology. Pathetic, actually."

As they watched, the craft fired its thrusters. Windows came into view, momentarily reflecting harsh sunlight as it slowly eased to a new orientation. Eventually, three men were clearly visible, squinting intently in their direction. They appeared to be floating freely, something Creena remembered well from the escape pod.

"I wonder why there's no gravity simulator," she mused.

"They're probably processing materials of some sort, but it sure is small for a commercial lab."

"Maybe we should make contact. They don't look hostile."

"There are no weapons onboard but there's not much they could do for us, either. We're better off continuing our ground scan."

"Why don't we go back to where we picked up that first transmission and make contact?" Before Aggie could reply, Thyron's familiar bouquet gathered around her. The vegemal had been incredibly quiet lately, his telepathic wisdom seldom entering her thoughts.

[If you want a helping hand
This isn't where you want to land.]

"Why not?" she responded, trying to ignore the twinge of concern that Thryon's view matched her rejected intuition.

[Humans on that planet are
Not trustworthy very far.]

The twinge expanded to an anxious knot in her chest, but another part of her didn't want to hear it. Thryon's rambling, either, when she'd already decided, quite logically, what needed to be done. Why couldn't he just say what he meant, anyway, instead of talking in riddles? Distrustful as he was, he wouldn't want to land anywhere but Sapphira, where everyone and everything was carnivorous. Suddenly she could understand why Aggie found illogical behavior so infuriating.

[Their eating habits aren't the clue—

"Oh, shut down!" Creena grumbled back, annoyed he'd been reading her mind again, on top of everything else. Snurkles, she was stressed enough without him. "If you can't be logical, then let me and Aggie handle it, all right?"

"Are you talking to that flaky flauna again?" Lime-colored pulsations of binary jealousy surrounded the 'troid's photoreceptors.

"Never mind," Creena muttered. "C'mon, let's make contact and land."

"We need to gather more data. That way we can make sure we come in at the best port, or at least the strongest point of their world grid, so we can recharge."

"What difference does it make?" Creena retorted, impatience in full bloom. "Everything checks out and we can always leave. Let's land and get on with it. You're acting as norfy as the plant."

That apparently did it, because without further argument, Aggie braked hard with the aft momentum disks, acceleration straps tightening against her chest. The dramatic drop in velocity lowered their orbit substantially by the time they'd reached the other side of the globe, the increased density of the atmosphere slowing them even more. Fiery entry plasma pulsed in the window strip as Aggie banked toward the faint signal crackling through the receiver. Textured swirls of fluffy clouds hugged the horizon as the craft made a tight arc over a sparkling polar cap, then proceeded directly toward the strongest signal.

Mountain Home, this is Hill. NORAD has detected what may be another bogey traveling at mach fourteen approaching the border. Please confirm. Over.

Creena turned up the volume from the arm of the copilot's seat.

Copy that, Hill. How 'bout another altitude check? Over.

Mountain Home, altitude is angels one-fifty and descending. Over.

Aggie punched in some numbers on the control panel. "I'm going to take it down to about fifty kilometers and home in on that signal. It should take us to a landing bay."

Creena leaned forward in her seat, still confused by the strange terminology. "Is that frequency the same as before?" she asked.

"No. This one's stronger."

Mountain Home, Hill. Bogey is definitely non-ballistic. It's reversed direction and heading north at mach ten angels sixty-five. That rules out an ICBM or meteoroid. We'll have a fix momentarily. Over.

Creena looked at Aggie, confusion thick. "What in the world are they talking about? What's a bogey?"

The 'troid's attention remained fixed on the instruments as she searched her language database. "They've detected an unidentified signal with an altitude just under twenty kilometers, going ten times the speed of sound."

"Snurkles! What do you think it is?" Creena asked.

Aggie looked at her, long and hard.

"*Us!*"

Worlds Apart

Creena's cheeks colored with embarrassment. "Oh," she said, turning evasively toward the holoscreen for a better view. Meanwhile, Aggie descended some more and circled the landing bay in a dramatic loop. The projection changed resolution, displaying a three-dimensional array of glowing blue crisscrosses below.

Mountain Home, Hill. Bogey at ground zero and sweeping the perimeter. F-16's scrambled for rendezvous.

"I wonder why they didn't pick up the landing request I coded in?" Aggie mused. "They should have validated by now. Maybe I can talk to that guy and find out what's going on. All this voice com is highly unusual. Maybe they took a solar flare hit and their automated system is down." The 'troid matched the incoming frequency with the transmitter and turned toward the remote microphone on the console.

"H-E-nine-two-seven-dash-six-five-two-dash-A, incoming from H-V-nine-four-four-dash-eight-seven-six-dash-A requesting D and D permission."

Nothing.

Aggie checked the comcon, locked the transmitter into the monitored frequency. "H-E-nine-two-seven-dash-six-five-two-dash-A, incoming from H-V-nine-four-four-dash-eight-seven-six-dash-A requesting D and D permission. Do you copy?"

This is Hill Air Force Base. You've intruded on restricted radio and air space reserved for the United States Department of Defense. Identity yourself immediately.

"This is AG4MI," Aggie responded politely. "Onboard the *Cerulean Nimrod,* incoming from H-V-nine-four-four-dash-eight-seven-six-dash-A."

Creena glanced from the image of the ground to the window strip's limited view. In a flash, an air vehicle appeared, only meters away, a primitive yet mean-looking craft with swept-back wings, spiked beneath with numerous missiles.

"Aggie! Look!" she gasped.

Aggie's attention was fully focused on the comcon, so she wasn't too surprised when she didn't respond.

That tail number is invalid, AG4MI. Depart immediately or we'll provide an escort.

"We don't want an escort, we want D and D. You know, galactic standard terminology for descend and disembark? What's the problem?"

"Snurkles, is that guy ever dense," Creena murmured. "Unless he wonders why we're coming in from a planet that's been evacuated."

Is H-V-nine-four-four-dash-eight-seven-six-dash-A a foreign registration? Repeat your point of origination.

Aggie rolled her photoreceptors. "That *is* our point of origination in standard galactic coordinates. *Quadrant Omicron in sector two. Verdaris. The Algonian System.* Like I said, H-V-nine-four-four-dash-eight-seven-six-dash-A."

The pause that followed was so long Creena wondered if they'd lost contact. Meanwhile, five more air vehicles joined the first, surrounding them. The 'troid whirled her photoreceptors toward Creena in disgust.

"That controller must have a burned out memory chip or something."

Creena nodded solemnly, wondering if it was more than simple stupidity. "Maybe Thyron is right, Aggie.

Maybe it isn't such a good idea to land here. I sure don't like the looks of those air vehicles out there."

For the first time, Aggie focused her attention on their escort. "You know, I do believe you're right. Those are definitely offensive weapons, pitiful technology or not."

"I'm getting a bad feeling about this," Creena admitted, squirming. A confusion of thoughts filled her mind, the apprehension too similar to when the pygmies had landed to ignore. "C'mon, Aggie. Forget this place. Let's get out of here."

Aggie, Hill. Proceed with the F-16s and set down as instructed. Any deviation and we'll take offensive measures. Do you copy? Over.

"That's not exactly what I call a welcoming committee out there," Aggie commented off-line. "I'm with you. Hang on while I shift to vertical and break away from that escort. By the time they turn around, we'll be out of the system."

Aggie entered the command and the ship's subtle drone lowered in pitch as it usually did when the antigraviton flow increased, before instituting a vertical climb. Creena gripped the seat and braced for an acceleration that never came. Instead, the whine's pitch slowed and lowered, slowed and lowered, slowed and lowered, until the only sound was the intimidating roar of the escort.

"What's wrong?" Creena gasped.

Aggie ran a status check, then diagnostics. "There's a valve stuck in the cryo line. The antigraviton generator expanded from lack of coolant and jammed. Shouldn't be hard to fix, but for now we're stuck. That's apparently what's been causing those anomalous vibrations."

One of the F-16's cut away from the others, banked to the right and disappeared behind them. By the racket they made, they had to be running some sort of fuel. The impeller on Dirck's 'cruiser was more advanced than that.

Aggie. Set down in the area cordoned off by red flares. Your escort will direct your descent to within five hundred feet of target.

Upon landing you and all passengers are to disembark, surrender all weapons and proceed as directed with your hands above your head. Do you copy?

"I copy," Aggie responded grimly, then activated the retro disks and lowered the ship gradually to the ground, where numerous ground vehicles with red flashing lights were racing toward the designated landing site. The ship set down gently, then all was still. Creena removed her landing harness and walked nervously to the window.

Military personnel in dark green uniforms stood four to six deep on every side. They were human. And young, maybe even as young as Dirck. Some of them looked mean, others as frightened as she was. Each held a weapon that looked like some sort of lasomag. As she searched their faces, a telepathic statement joined her thoughts, increasing her rapidly mounting reservations. Thyron still hadn't given up.

> [Creena, please, it's not too late
> Staying here you're tempting fate.
> The 'troid can fix the cryo line
> And then for us a course define.
> Their weapons cannot harm the ship
> The hardened walls they cannot rip.
> Look outside—we're under siege
> Their cry is not that you're their liege.
> We're not as trapped as it appears
> The ship's our fortress, do not fear.]

A myriad of conflicting feelings welled up again as something told her he was right. Being there was wrong. She should have known from that nagging feeling, the same one she'd had when the Sapphirans landed. Logic was fine in its place, but instinct spanned the gaps when all the facts weren't in. In her excitement and impatience to move on, she'd purposely ignored what should have been obvious from the start.

If Aggie could fix the ship, then they could get away and find another planet that could help her get home. From what she'd seen so far, this one was barely out of the dark ages—they hadn't even progressed beyond the wheel for ground transportation.

"C'mon, Creena," Aggie prodded. "What are you waiting for, girl?"

"I don't think we should go out there. Look at them!"

"They're just scared. I can tell by their auras. They've never seen anything like this before. They're curious about us and afraid we'll hurt them. Once we explain why we're here and show them we're friendly, they'll let us repair our ship and leave. Trust me." Without waiting for a response, Aggie glided for the ramp.

What Aggie said made a lot on sense, but there was no denying what she felt. She lingered a moment, waiting for Thyron's reply but none came, which wasn't surprising. He'd made his opinion known and wasn't one to argue. Typically, when his advice was ignored, he'd respond with a leafy shrug and go back to his corner, which was undoubtedly what he'd done. A compromise came to mind and she ran to catch up with the 'troid.

"Let me code you to *Survival*," she suggested. "In fact, let me go back and get the stungun."

"Do you really think that one little stungun is going to do you much good against *that*?"

"What are they, anyway?"

"Projectile weapons," Aggie replied. "They shoot little metal balls called bullets."

"That doesn't sound all that dangerous," Creena commented, frowning.

"They are when they're going the speed of sound."

"Oh."

"I need to stay on *Mechanical/Communications* so we can get some help," Aggie went on. "If they won't cooperate then you can code me for *Survival*. But as far as I can tell, there's no reason for alarm. They just need to figure out we're not a threat."

"Seems like all those weapons are plenty of reason for alarm," Creena muttered, nonetheless telling herself over and over that what Aggie said sounded reasonable. Why would anyone want to hurt them? They hadn't done anything wrong, only needed some help. The Hostii Interplanetary Organization, commonly referred to as the HIO, had numerous conventions agreed upon by member planets, which allowed for emergency repairs. Which all sounded good, the thought they may not be a member never entering her mind.

Thyron was usually right, too. But how logical was he? His botanical paranoia was rubbing off. On the other hand, she'd still feel better with the stungun. She raced down to her bunk, fished it out, then returned to follow Aggie to the ramp. On impulse, she took her pocket laser from her pocket and dropped it in her boot, just as the 'troid lowered the ramp.

Darkness filled the space beyond. Smoking red markers tinted the air, highlighted by floodlights mounted high behind the army that encircled the ship. Blue lights faded to distant perspective toward where a city sparkled serenely beside the nearby mountains. It was quiet and peaceful, the air cool and dry, unlike the stickiness of Verdaris. A whistling roar shocked the air as the remainder of their escort touched down with a series of abrupt screeches a short distance away.

Aggie glided down the ramp and proceeded across the short stretch of pavement separating them from the crowd while Creena followed nervously. Stars winked from the blackness above, the galaxy's spiral arm still visible as a pale smear overhead.

Aggie proceeded forward, neither impeded nor intimidated by the press of people. No one uttered a word, only stared with strange, startled expressions as Creena followed a few steps behind, moving cautiously forward amid the shuffle of feet and occasional rattle of a shifted weapon.

Just when she was beginning to think that they'd recognized they were harmless, someone yelled, "Hands up!" and she lifted her arms high, clumsily dropping the stungun with a thud. A soldier rushed forward, thrusting the muzzle of a primitive weapon in her face.

"Turn around," he ordered, as another soldier wearing heavy gloves retrieved the stungun, examining it closely.

Great, she thought. *Now they'll really think we're dangerous.*

"Hands high, you hear me?"

Several others clustered around them and she heard his weapon hit the ground. A moment later, rough hands frisked her from shoulders to ankles. She glared at him angrily for being so rude, but said nothing. After that he shoved her forward. People continued to gather on the tarmac, all staring as an eerie silence charged the air. She thought self-consciously of her Code Orange uniform, which was in horrible condition since her adventures on Verdaris. The crowd continued to part as they approached, allowing them to pass, but everyone looked shocked, as if they'd never seen a girl or 'troid before. And truly, amongst the vast crowd, she saw no children, few women and no 'troids. Step by step they proceeded, toward an armored vehicle bedecked with flashing lights.

Her heart pounded in her ears as anxiety and fear fogged her brain. What was going on? Why were they treating her like this? From behind, the soldier shoved her toward the vehicle's open door, which was now only a few meters away. Before she could enter, another strange lasomag crossed her path. A soldier exited the vehicle and yanked her hands behind her back, securing a pair of heavy restraints around her wrists before pushing her inside and strapping her into a seat.

The interior was filled with more soldiers, but in their midst was a man in a different type of uniform, tan but not ornate in the slightest, with several bent bars on the sleeves. Apparently, he was in charge, judging by how the others deferred to his directions. The man didn't look mean, just stern, and maybe a little bewildered. At least he looked as if he had some authority to do something, hopefully to help.

"Uh, sir?" she said quietly, putting on her most compliant Mira III behavior. "Can someone help us send a message?"

He stared at her for several long moments. *"My God!"* he finally answered. "You're only a kid. *A kid!"*

"I know, sir," she replied politely. "I need to send a message.   To Mira III. Using tachyonic transmission capability. You do have that here, don't you?"

The man didn't answer, only stared as if he hadn't understood a word she'd said. Heavy chains clanged and she turned her head to see another soldier securing Aggie to a floor hitch.

"Tell them we're on our way," the man ordered the driver.

"Yes, sergeant," he replied, picking up a handheld device from under the console, which he spoke into as directed.

The door slammed with a heavy thud, the jolt punctuating the situation like an unexpected blow. Gradually her racing heart settled into a heavy rhythm of its own, initial surprise succumbing to the dark intensity of utter and complete emotional shock. Everyone was staring at her, their expressions in some unexplainable way reflections of her own.

She swallowed hard and stared straight in front of her, trying to figure out what to do now. This was definitely not the kind of assistance she had in mind.   Aggie's photoreceptors had dimmed to standby, but she suspected the 'troid was taking it all in, regardless.   Hopefully, she'd come up with something to get them out of this one.

The vehicle roared to life, gears turned and fell somewhere beneath the floor, then engaged. The engine changed pitch, jerked forward slightly then slowly started to move.

Earthbound

The vehicle jerked to a stop beside the door to a cement block house that apparently housed their command center, judging by its ancient antennas, some fixed, some tracking. The man who'd been called "sergeant" waited while she was escorted outside and someone released Aggie from the floor, though the chains remained. With the 'troid too heavy to carry, they allowed her to roll on her own power next to Creena, flanked on all sides by armed guards. Eventually, the sergeant stepped out of the van and approached the door, where he pressed a code into keypad. The lock released and he pushed it open, holding it with his foot as he motioned them inside. It closed hard, trapping them in a pale yellow tiled corridor.

"This is a pretty hostile welcoming committee," Aggie whispered beside her. "They must be scared to death or they wouldn't be treating us like this."

Somehow Aggie's logic couldn't faze the gathering impression they'd made a very serious mistake. When people were frightened there was no telling what they might do. The sergeant unlocked the second door on their right and guards directed her and Aggie into a drab, windowless room. More guards were inside, obviously at the command of an older man who sat behind a grey metal desk on the far side of the room, blue uniform bedecked with medals and ribbons.

The sergeant saluted, then stepped to one side, standing quietly against the wall in deference to the one behind the desk, who was clearly a high ranking officer. His hair was dark but splattered with grey, his eyes a penetrating blue that emanated authority. He stood and motioned for her to sit in the chair directly in front of the desk. She obeyed, leaning forward a bit to keep the restraints from digging into her hands as they directed Aggie beside her.

Again, the absence of technology surprised her. No grafix, information panels, comcons, or anything else that bespoke even moderate advancement, other than what appeared to be a monitor with nothing but green characters shining from its screen. A metal box immediately below it, apparently some sort of data storage device, was connected to a receptacle in the wall by a dangling black cord. She stared at sheets of some unfamiliar material cluttering the workdeck, then maps and charts of the same substance covering the walls. Above them, what appeared to be a timekeeping device, round with a system of pointers, one of which was sweeping a circular arc, was the only thing that even vaguely resembled a technological device. No holographic displays, no 'troids.

She hesitantly met the man's unsettling gaze, cringing when his icy blue stare connected with hers, reminding her of the numerous times she'd been reprimanded for noncompliant behavior at the Academy back on Mira III.

"What's your name, little lady?" he asked, sitting down again. So far he was the only one she'd encountered who appeared even reasonably calm. His voice was deep and resonate, one she was certain could attain significant volume when provoked.

"I'm Creena Brightstar," she said nervously. "And this is my 'troid, Aggie."

"I'm Colonel Jenkins, Creena," he replied, maintaining his steady gaze. "How about we start with some basics, like where you came from and where you got that. . .vehicle?"

Creena's heart skipped a beat. So that was it—the Sapphirans had reported it stolen! How would she ever get home if she wound up on Bezarna, that dreadful penal colony?

"We, well, I guess we kind of borrowed it, uh, sir," she stammered. "We were going to give it back, we really were."

"Borrowed it?"

"Well, yes," she went on, anxious to explain. "You see, they were Sapphirans and were going to take me back to, well, eat, I guess. But Aggie knocked them out with some gas and we took the ship so I could get home to my parents."

Now even Jenkins looked norfed, his eyes wide and mouth slightly agape. Suddenly, he set his jaw and threw a suspicious look at Aggie. The guards moved in closer, but stopped when Jenkins raised his hand and shook his head.

"Maybe you'd better start at the beginning. Just where are your parents?" he asked, voice deepening in a no-nonsense way, like 'Merapa's always did when she was in trouble.

After she'd recounted her story as far as the escape pod landing on Verdaris, their eyes locked again. He still looked either totally norfed or as if he hadn't believed a single word she'd said.

"I found Aggie on Verdaris," she continued. "The Sapphirans landed when they picked up our distress signal, so we, uh, borrowed their ship. We eventually got to Cyraria, but my father told me to go back to Mira III, because they're in some kind of trouble. We couldn't make it all the way back in that ship, so we decided to stop here to either get a better one or find a starship that could take me to Mira III."

It didn't look as if Colonel Jenkins had heard a word. As he stared back and forth between her and Aggie with a look as blank as intergalactic space, Creena knew, without a doubt, they'd made a humongous mistake. Thyron was pretty smart. He'd probably done a lot of traveling with the pygmies and apparently knew something about this planet she hadn't given him a chance to explain. All he'd said was they weren't trustworthy. Why hadn't he told her they were overtly aggressive? She would have paid attention to that.

She jumped back to the present when Colonel Jenkins' chair squeaked in protest as he leaned back, arms folded. "Well, well, a regular little space pirate, eh?" Jenkins shook his head, expression impossible to read. "If I didn't have the living proof out there on the runway, little lady, I'd think you were telling me one devil of a tall tale."

"The only reason we landed was to find a way to Mira III. First, I need to use your comcenter to send a message to my uncle, then find a ship to get me there."

He rested his arms on the workdeck and leaned toward her. "What's the matter with your UFO out there? Why can't you get there in that?"

"My *what*?"

"Your ship. Why can't you go find them in that?"

Creena scowled, confused. "It's too small. It doesn't have warp drive. Can't you tell?"

They both jumped at the sound of an urgent knock.

"Yeah?" he barked, tone entirely different than the one he was using with her.

Another man entered, his uniform considerably more humble than Jenkins'. He hesitated slightly when he saw so many people then walked over beside Aggie and saluted Jenkins.

"Sir, the Pentagon's on the phone." He glanced over at Creena with wide, grey eyes, light brown hair standing up on the top of his head, whether from fear or style she didn't know. His gaze shifted to Aggie, who rotated her photoreceptors in an electronic eye roll. "They want to know what, uh, what's going on. Sir."

So do I, thought Creena.

"Tell 'em it's under control, Carlson. I'll get back with them when we're done here. They can wait."

"Sir, there's a herd of reporters at the front gate. What should we tell them, Colonel?"

"What's the press doing here?" he growled, anger firing his eyes.   "Where's the leak? How did they find out?" Creena swallowed, wondering what the *press* was that would make him so upset. Some kind of weapon?

The man shrugged. "Half the valley saw it land, sir."

Jenkins sighed, suddenly calmer. "I suppose they did. That could definitely present a problem."

"The switchboard's lit up like a Christmas tree," the man continued. "NASA called, too. The flight director said the Skylab crew reported a sighting to Mission Control on their secured frequency at about twenty-one hundred. At first, they thought it was orbital debris, then all three astronauts made visual contact. Then it was gone. Their description matched perfectly."

The communicator chirped and the colonel yanked it from its holder. Creena could hear the female voice clear across the room.

"Sir, the MUFON director's on the line. He wants to know if the reports are true."

"Put him through," he said, then turned back to his subordinate, hand covering the phone. "Lieutenant, get rid of those reporters. Tell 'em we'll have a press conference at oh-seven-hundred. Then contact everyone above the field-grade officers and tell them to be in the secure briefing room at twenty-three hundred. And Carlson?" The man tore his eyes away from Creena and saluted nervously.

"Sir?"

"Keep your pants on, Carlson. It's under control."

"Y-y-es, s-sir!" he said, saluting again before proceeding out the door.

The colonel removed his hand from the receiver and stared at Creena, who looked away evasively. They weren't acting as if she was a criminal, yet she was still handcuffed and none of the guards had left or put away their weapons, either. And why wouldn't they let her contact Mira III? It was obviously a military installation and should have the right equipment. Or would they? She tuned in on Jenkins' conversation, hoping for some clue to what was really going on. Was she a prisoner or what? There was no doubt at this point she was.

"Yes, this is Colonel Milton Jenkins out at Hill. Hi, Lenny. Long time no hear, eh? Yeah, it's true, all right. They're sitting right here in my office. No, I'm not kidding. Do you want to talk to her? Yeah, it's a *her*. No, she's not alone. And no, she's not one of *them*. As far as I can tell, she's human."

Creena shifted her gaze to Aggie. Whatever was going on, she didn't like it at all.

"No, she's just a kid and she's got a robot named Aggie, too. Yeah, a *kid*. No, I'm definitely *not*. You can't make this stuff up. Why don't you catch the next plane and come see for yourself?"

Jenkins hung up, chuckling for a moment before focusing back on Creena. "I'll bet you don't have the slightest idea what's going on, do you?" Creena shook her head. "Let's just say it's not very often that a flying saucer actually lands around here."

He laughed as if it were a very bad joke. "Usually you extraterrestrials won't let us near you with an insulated barge pole, unless you've crashed and you're dead. How come you're different? The impetuousness of youth?"

Most of what he said didn't make sense, but one thing came through loud and clear. "You can't help me, can you?" she asked, "You really can't. We've told you why we're here, you can see we're not dangerous, and since you can't help, I think you'd better let us go. C'mon, Aggie, let's get out of here."

She forgot about the restraints until her attempt to rise faltered, bringing the collective rattle of readied weapons. Jenkins waved them away and directed one of the guards to remove the handcuffs. Creena rubbed her wrists, not sure whether to thank them or not. What a bunch of snurks.

Jenkins was watching her closely, a look of concern slowly creeping into his eyes. "Okay. Creena. I really want to believe what you're telling me, but you have to understand how out of the ordinary it is for someone to arrive in a, well, like you did. I hope you can understand our position."

"I understand that your technology is way behind ours. *Way* behind. I can't believe you actually use wheels on your ground vehicles or those noisy engines in your flyers. But we really aren't here to hurt you. All I wanted was some help to get home." She thought about telling him that they wouldn't have even landed except something was wrong with their ship, then decided against it.

"And I want to believe that," Jenkins said, sounding sincere. "Would you be willing to undergo a test that can tell us if you're telling the truth?"

She swallowed nervously. "What kind of test?"

"It's what we call a polygraph or lie detector test. We'd hook you up with some electrodes, then ask you a few questions. Your reactions would tell us whether you're being truthful or not."

Creena sighed, amazed they had to actually attach something to her in order to read something so basic. Such detectors were everywhere at the Academy on Mira III and didn't even require that a person stand still. But as long as they didn't hurt her, she didn't have much to lose. "I suppose," she agreed.

"Get the polygraph specialist in here immediately," Jenkins ordered, after which the sergeant, who was still standing in the back, saluted and left. While they waited, Jenkins sat down and started writing something out on a piece of what she later learned was paper. Creena tried not to stare, but couldn't help it—he was writing with his left hand.

As far as she knew, she and her father were the only left-handed humans in the universe. Except the ones on Esheron. She swallowed hard, recalling the horror stories 'Merapa had told her about his *naterra*. If this planet was the same way, embroiled in continual wars, she was in even bigger trouble than she thought.

The pointers on the timekeeping devices had moved to the next numeral, the colonel impatiently postponing various meetings by the time someone knocked on the door. It turned out to be another guard with a bearded man, whom he introduced as the polygraph specialist from the Ogden police station. The man's hair was disheveled, he wasn't in uniform, and the collar on his shirt was all askew, giving the impression he'd just awoken from a bad dream.

"Where's ours?" Jenkins asked, eyeing the man with some degree of suspicion.

"On leave, sir."

"Great," Jenkins muttered, then got up and shook the man's hand, after which he gave him a quick explanation of the situation, including a strict admonition with regard to the sensitive nature of the situation and need for silence as a matter of national security. He ordered the man to swear, hand raised, that he wouldn't reveal any of what was about to transpire or anything else relative to the incident. After that, the man's eyes widened even more as they locked on Creena with an incredulous stare.

Formalities complete, Jenkins took off his jacket and hung it on the back of his chair, then escorted them down the hall to another room with a large machine on the far side and a soft chair beside it. While the bearded man got the machine set up, Jenkins directed her to sit down. She complied, noticing that there was now only one guard watching her, along with Colonel Jenkins.

"Where's Aggie?" she asked nervously.

Colonel Jenkins looked her over pensively for a moment, then directed the guard to get the 'troid.

Meanwhile, the man from the police station held up a handful of wires, which were connected to the machine at one end with small, round patches at the other. "We'll just place these on your arms, head, chest and back. You won't feel a thing. Your reactions will be recorded on that roll of graph paper over there. Okay?" He was looking at her as if she were a space alien or something, like one of the psetoras on Verdaris.

Creena swallowed. Where was Aggie, anyway? Jenkins seemed to sense her concern and looked toward the door. It opened a moment later and Aggie was escorted in, still in chains and flanked by guards.

"Is it okay if my 'troid checks it first?" Creena asked. "She'll just check it with her mechaniscan and let me know if it's really safe. It won't hurt the machine."

Jenkins was leaning against the far wall, arms folded across his chest. He looked more relaxed, but still clearly in control. He pursed his lips and wrinkled his brow. She could tell he wasn't entirely comfortable with the idea, but nonetheless eventually nodded consent.

She got up from the chair, greeting Aggie with her best attempt at a smile. "Can you tell if that machine will hurt me in your current mode?" she asked, pointing. Aggie moved her ring in the affirmative.

"I can assess something that simplistic with my olfactory sensors alone," the 'troid replied, sarcasm apparently lost on the others.

"Okay. Go ahead, Aggie," Creena prodded. "Make sure that thing won't hurt me."

Aggie rotated her ring in the better part of a circle, noting how many people were in the room. "I need some space," she said curtly, fixing her stare on the guard who'd carried her in. "And I can't work with these chains. They interfere with my sensors. Your weapons, too."

After a short hesitation Jenkins told the guard to remove the chains and wait outside along with the ones who had brought her in. Nonetheless, the colonel eyed Aggie with newly aroused suspicion and abandoned his relaxed stance against the wall. Slowly he dropped his arms to his sides, left hand resting on a small weapon attached to his belt as he assumed a posture on full alert. His gaze locked on Creena and she met it knowingly, but remained silent.

Once freed, Aggie shook her ring and unfolded her arms dramatically, joint by articulated joint, seemingly oblivious to Jenkins. Creena couldn't help but wonder if she would have missed his subtle shift if she were in *Survival* mode. The 'troid assessed everyone with pulsing red photoreceptors, pausing briefly on Jenkins before turning back to the job at hand. Then she focused her scanners, which had changed in color to a vibrant green, on the subject machine across the room.

The next instant the room filled with an intense flash of green light. Jenkins yelled and grabbed Creena, securing her tight against his chest as he drew his side arm and pointed it at Aggie. Alerted by the racket, guards burst through the door, all weapons aimed straight at athe 'troid's sensor ring.

"Would you people calm down?" Creena yelled, trying to wiggle free. "I told you she was going to scan it! *Snurkles!"*

Colonel Jenkins let her go and ordered the men at ease. Creena rolled her eyes and resumed her seat, then followed Aggie's gaze as, once more, the 'troid rotated her sensor ring and looked slowly around the room. With a sense of exaggerated digital drama, she again assessed the nervous expressions, tense postures, and hands poised for another quick draw, clearly checking them for threat potential. Then, for a moment, her photoreceptors flickered, and Creena was sure the 'troid was going to laugh. She stifled a nervous giggle of her own by covering her mouth, as once again the room flashed green, this time without undue reaction by those present.

"It looks okay, Creena," Aggie said. "It measures your body's electrical potential, which changes based on your thoughts and emotions. The worst it could do is give you a mild electrical shock, if there was a short in one of the electrodes."

"Are you okay with that?" Jenkins asked. Creena nodded. "Good. Then let's get this show on the road."

The bearded man stepped over, smiled nervously at Creena, and picked up the electrodes. "You'll need to open up the top of your flight suit," he said, seeming to calm down, now that he was doing something familiar. "We're going to measure your skin temperature, pulse rate and respiration while the Colonel asks you some questions."

Creena unlatched the top of her Code Orange uniform. The electrodes were a little cold, but other than that, she felt nothing. The bearded man flipped a switch and the machine hummed to life. Several stylus-like arms, one for each electrode, lilted back and forth on the paper, which had started to move slowly beneath it.

"Okay, Creena," Jenkins said, reaching over to place a plastic cassette in something which was apparently a recording device. He pushed one of the buttons, waited a moment, then said, "State your full name."

"Carinae Brightstar. But everyone calls me Creena."

"Where were you born?"

"In the city of Nada on Mira III."

"Where exactly is Mira III?"

"The Perseus arm of the galaxy."

"That's a different section than this one, correct?"

"Yes."

While she was responding, she noticed that the man who'd hooked her up was making small marks on the moving paper with a shaky hand.

"You told us you got separated from your parents when you blasted off a starship in an escape pod. Is that correct?"

"Yes," she said, emptiness swelling inside as it always did when she recalled that fateful day, when the last people she wanted to be around were her family.

"Where did the escape pod land?" Jenkins continued.

"On Verdaris," she said. "That's where I found Aggie."

"So you never saw Aggie before Verdaris?"

"No," she said, shaking her head in emphasis.

"And how did you leave Verdaris?"

Creena recounted the story of how they'd lured the pygmies into the comcenter and gassed them. When she finished, everyone was staring suspiciously at Aggie again, Jenkins and the guard poised once more to retrieve their weapons.

"Could Aggie use similar aggression techniques on us?" Jenkins asked, eyes narrowed.

"Not in her current mode," Creena said. "She's coded for *Mechanical/Communications* right now. She can only do that in *Survival*, or in her work mode, as an agricultural 'troid."

Jenkins looked at the bearded man for confirmation, who nodded. Everyone in the room visibly relaxed. The last few questions addressed why they'd landed on Earth and what their intent was. When they'd finished, the man turned off the machine, but left the electrodes connected until after he talked privately with Jenkins in the corner of the room. After that, he collected the sensors and left.

"Well, Creena, it looks as if you're telling us the truth," Jenkins said.

"It's about time you people believed me," Creena muttered, somewhat disgusted. "Since you can't help me, *now* will you let us go?"

"It isn't safe for you to go out there, even if we'd let you," Jenkins said, motioning her and everyone else toward the door.

"What do you mean?" Creena asked as they headed back to Jenkins' office. "Are you at war or something?"

"No, we're not at war. At least not here," he replied, taking his seat again behind his desk. He gestured toward the chair she'd occupied earlier, clearly expecting her to do the same.

Creena ignored it, standing while she focused on what he was trying to say.

"What I mean is you're probably the number-one historical event for the century," he went on. "Possibly the history of the world. They're not going to let you go that easily." He smiled, even as a new intensity glinted in his grey-blue eyes. "And neither am I."

Creena glowered at him as righteous indignation overtook the last of her fear. She stepped over to his desk and flattened her hands on its smooth surface, leaning toward him, eyes locked on his.

"You can't help us, but you won't let us leave in our own ship? What kind of place is this, anyway?"

"Technically, you invaded us, little lady," he said, leaning back confidently with folded arms. "We have the perfect right to seize you and your craft. I imagine we'll let you go, eventually. Like when we're through reverse engineering your ship. And the robot, too."

"What do you mean, reverse engineer?" Creena asked suspiciously. "What does that mean?"

"Yes, precisely what *do* you mean?" Aggie echoed.

He favored the 'troid with a thin smile, eyes distant. "So far we haven't been able to build a practical manned spacecraft that can go beyond our own solar system. We've been to the Moon a few times, but that's it. We can learn from yours in a month what would take a half century or more on our own."

Creena wasn't sure what a month was, but something told her it was a long, long time.

"I think you'd better let me go," she said. "Aggie, too." Jenkins didn't budge.

"I don't think so."

"Why not?"

"Because you're not going anywhere, at least not for a while."

"What?"

Creena's mind boiled with rage. They hadn't hurt a thing. Clearly, they shouldn't have landed, but there was no reason why they shouldn't be allowed to leave and be on their way. Her thoughts were disrupted by Aggie pulling quietly at her sleeve, so she turned around to see what she wanted.

"Code me to *Survival*," she whispered, barely loud enough for her to hear, "and I'll see what I can do."

Creena paused, then turned back to the colonel, ready to give him one more chance. "What am I going to do?" she pleaded. "I need to go to Mira III and get some help for my parents!"

"About the best I can do right now is offer you something to eat before debriefing the Pentagon at oh-one-hundred. Are you hungry?"

Question answered, she turned back toward Aggie. "I guess we're stuck here," she said, giving the 'troid's midsection a subtle glance while making sure she blocked the colonel's view. Understanding, Aggie stealthily released her control panel and waited.

"I don't know what they're going to do with you, Aggie," she said, feigning an innocuous conversation as she tried to remember the code for *Survival*. Her mind was a blank. Was it two-five-dash-H-six-four-nine-eight?

No.

Two-H-two-dash-nine-eight-six-four?

No. What was it?

"Are they going to separate us?" the 'troid asked, continuing the artificial conversation.

As the seconds ticked away her heart sank. She needed the instructions, that was all there was to it. She gritted her teeth against a scream with frustration.

"I don't know, Aggie," she answered, this time with double meaning, emphasized by a desperate look at her slot. She probably couldn't do the coding right now because they were getting suspicious, but at least she'd have it when the opportunity arose. The 'troid responded sooner than expected and, while she intended to grab it inconspicuously, she missed, allowing it to drop with an ear-splitting clank. Creena cringed at the shuffle of weapons and stole a sheepish look at Colonel Jenkins.

"Well, what have we here?" he said, coming over from behind his desk to snatch it up. He examined it closely, then dropped it in his jacket pocket, giving Creena an all-too-knowing smirk. She glowered back silently, mentally kicking herself for not listening to Thyron. Snurkles, was he ever right.

[Promptings come and promptings go
I hate to say I told you so.]

Creena ground her teeth as Thyron's familiar voice and scent echoed through her head.

"Which planet is this, anyway?" she asked, scowling up at Jenkins. If nothing else, she'd report their hostile behavior to her uncle when she got to Mira III.

His expression assumed a guarded smile. "Welcome to planet Earth, little lady. Welcome to planet Earth."

<table>
<tr><td colspan="3">CALMANAC: High Opps/Peak -94 Days</td></tr>
<tr><td>Temp: 46C/115F</td><td>PVs: 38%</td><td>Quakes: 50%</td></tr>
</table>

Probability

Sigma3/Epsilon

After the morning meal, Dirck roamed around the ballome, as if movement could speed Zinni's course to its lowest declination, cooling it down enough to resume work outside, at least until Zeta 's position elevated enough to start the cycle again. He'd long since disposed of his old anoia uniform for some simple, lightweight clothes he'd found on the trade table at the SD, but his hair had gotten horrifically long and he felt like a slob. He glanced at 'Merama, working on the latest information for the Barterboard.

"Hey, 'Merama, how 'bout a haircut?"

She didn't even look up. "I can't. I traded off the clippers before you and your father got back from Verdaris."

Various implications lurked behind her words and his gut tightened. "So you can't cut our hair anymore?"

"Not until we can afford another pair."

"Holy holocubes, 'Merama—." He stopped in mid-gripe, cringing at another self-imposed reminder of his part in Creena's disappearance. Eventually, new frustrations invaded his thoughts until, tired of pacing, he sat down by the comcon and called up their account. He smiled as he viewed the latest transaction: =C20C= from Jen Brightstar for a "wager." Deven and 'Merama had posted *The Regionists' Guide to Edible Plants* on the bulletin board four days before, and already they'd brought in =C700C=.

And that wasn't all. Win had found him several water-tight containers and every day he filled at least three and took them to the SD. So far, he hadn't had any trouble getting =C150C= per liter. Their total for all trading was =C15700C= and growing.

That was the good news.

The bad news was that his father had finally settled on a preliminary design for the heat exchanger. His original expectations had been too optimistic. They'd be lucky if they could maintain an inside temperature of 37C/99F, which represented a delta-T, or difference in temperature, of 64C/115F from the average outdoor High Opps temperature, which sounded impressive, except the majority was coming from the ballome's climate control system. How much they could depend on it not to degrade when its limits of 66C/150F were exceeded was unknown, with it possible it could fail entirely, in which case they'd be dead.

Even the slight but critical reduction the heat exchanger could achieve would require a duty cycle of a hundred percent, meaning it would be running constantly, which of course required more power, plus put more stress on the components. They'd use hydrated ammonia as the working fluid in what was called an absorption heat removal system. But even with the compromised temperatures, they had to have a compressor. The system couldn't keep up with the relentless heat load without it.

So far, the listing of parts and components they needed had over a hundred line items and amounted to an expected cost of over =C60000C=s. At the rate they were rolling in, thirty days before High Opps, which would barely allow time for the actual construction, they'd have approximately =C32500C=.

He had no idea how they'd make up the difference. Another =C225C's= came in as he watched, from a liter of water and one *Guide*. Maybe sales would pick up. And maybe they wouldn't.

'Merapa had decided to accumulate enough credits to buy the compressor first. There was only one at the SD and he was afraid someone else would get it first. Win had hidden it in the back, but that was still no guarantee. The remaining parts were relatively simple.

'Merapa had explained how the system worked so many times he knew it by heart. It was all a matter of transferring heat energy from one place to another. Liquid ammonia would absorb the heat in a network of pipes. The hot liquid would flow to larger tubing, where reduced pressure would allow it to evaporate, storing the energy in a gaseous state. A fan would cool the tubing, the working fluid would change phases again by condensing back to a liquid, and this time release energy which the fan would dissipate. Then the compressor would re-pressurize the liquid, and it would start the cycle again.

It was deceptively simple. And awesomely hard. In fact, their predicament illustrated why the interface between science and engineering, *i.e.*, theory and application, had tried men's ingenuity since time began, a wide gap typically separating the two.

At least he was going to meet Win when he got off work at the SD. He wasn't sure what they were going to do, but it was still a break and visiting with someone around his own age sounded great, even though it would definitely cut into what was supposed to be his sleepzone. He knew Win had gone to a Miran academy, had worked at the SD since the settlement was organized, and that was it.

Undoubtedly it would be an interesting evening.

* * *

When Dirck got to the SD, Win was alone, sorting through the day's trade items. He released the gate in the workdeck and Dirck joined him in the rear. And there, nearly dead-center on the trade table, was a familiar pair of clippers. Win stopped beside him when he reached over to pick them up.

"These were ours," Dirck explained. "I was just asking my mother today for a haircut, and she told me she'd traded them off."

"What d'ya need a haircut for?" Win asked with a smirk.

Dirck laughed. "Habit, I guess. How much to get them back?"

Win shrugged. "Nothin'. Just take 'em."

"What d'ya mean, just take 'em? My mother traded them in for something, and I oughta trade something back."

"Nah, what for?" Win scoffed. "No one keeps track of this stuff. Just take 'em. Consider them a present from our friends in those comfy subterres in Cira City."

Dirck studied the clippers longingly. "Tell you what. Take a liter of water from my next delivery, okay?"

Win shrugged indifferently. "If you say so." Dirck secured the clippers in his thigh pocket, not as elated as he'd expected with his dubious purchase.

"C'mon, let's lock it down and go," Win stated. "I'm sick of this place."

They secured the doors, activated the alarm, and headed for the rear exit, Dirck longing for numerous items he saw strewn along the way. Win palmed out, activating a heavy bolt that secured the back door with a resounding clunk. A slight breeze had come up, typical as Zeta rose above the horizon.

As High Opps drew closer, neither sun would set, but continually circle the sky at varying degrees above the horizon. Eventually, their respective apogees would ascend to directly overhead, until High Opps, when the two would chase each other around the sky, one or the other overhead continually. Then, gradually, Zinni would recede in distance as well as disappear below the horizon, such that night would finally return, allowing the ground to cool. Shortly after that, Zeta would disappear as well, for twice as long as

Opposition season, except then they'd be subjected to incomprehensible dark and its inevitable cold.

As far as Dirck was concerned, how they'd deal with that was moot until they got through High Opps, though at this point anything cold sounded mighty good.

Directly outside was Win's 'cruiser, beaten by zetalight. Dirck strolled around it slowly, reminiscing. It was older than his had been, not quite as low, and the front grating bars were custom built, extremely heavy and close together, making him wonder what Win used it for to require so much reinforcement. It looked as if the canopy was broken, but when Win palmed the lock the crack sprang to life as a spindly, long-legged arachnid scampered across the nose to the ground and disappeared in a hole.

"That's my pet crack spider, Scratchy," Win explained. "He's taken a liking to the canopy and is there every time I come out." He waved Dirck around to the passenger side. "Any place in particular you'd like to go?"

Dirck shook his head. "I haven't seen much of anything outside of here and home."

"I'll show you around, then."

The 'cruiser coughed to life, shuddered, and died. Win coaxed it back, waited for the impeller to stabilize, then banked toward the wilds behind the SD.

Most of the terrain was the same rolling hills, scrubby vegetation, and red rock mesas Dirck had already come to know and hate. Sulfuric pools bubbled beneath them, steam scattering in the 'cruiser's impeller wash and nadiric breeze that occurred when at least one sun was low. The settlement faded behind them and ground gradually flattened, vegetation sparse, the dust-ridden sky a massive orange dome overhead. A few more kilometers and a canyon stretched before them that reached the distant horizon. Its surface was flat, decorated by fractal-like trenches that wound this way and that above bottomless gorges, some hundreds of meters wide. Dirck couldn't imagine what geological forces could have formed it, its design too delicate for either water or seismic action. His interest waned with the realization the 'cruiser was making some mighty ominous sounds.

Win made a quick pass over the edge, then, much to Dirck's relief, banked and returned to solid ground a few meters from the edge. The impeller sputtered then died, and the 'cruiser sank to the dirt below. Win released the canopy and the two of them got out, gazing across the spectacle before them

"I like it out here," Win said. "I can't see anyone or anything, and I can pretend the entire planet's mine, starting right here at Guipure Canyon."

"Whoopee," Dirk said. "You can have it, as far as I'm concerned." As if in protest, a gust of wind rose from the gorge, lifting his visor from his head.

Win laughed as he lunged sideways and achieved a lucky catch before tossing it in the 'cruiser. "I know what you mean. But some mighty powerful people feel a lot different. Have you kept up with the bulletins?" Dirck shook his head. "You should. There's something going on, but I haven't quite figured out what."

"Like what?" Dirck asked.

"Since I do the ordering, I see what comes in and when. Whenever a starship comes in, it shows up on the logs. For people, there's a population indicator. For cargo shipments, the planetary inventory index increases. That's what drives prices. If the planetary inventory is low, prices go up.

"So," Win continued, "all these ships have been coming in, big ones and more than usual, yet the population doesn't go up by more than a thousand, and the planetary inventory doesn't change, either. I don't know what they're bringing in, but it doesn't make sense that all those ships would be here for maintenance. And that's not all."

Dirck's glimpse of the future onboard the *Cosmos II* blared as Win continued.

"People have been disappearing. I've known some of them, too, from the SD."

"How many people belong to our settlement?" Dirck asked.

"Around eight thousand."

"Who do you know that's disappeared?"

"It's probably better if I don't give names. But they were good people. A lot like you and your family. They worked hard, got a good flow of =CC=s coming in, were improving their property and their land. That's why I'm telling you this. You're doing some pretty neat stuff. I just wanted to warn you that maybe you ought to slow down a little, or maybe be a little more discreet. Don't put so much on the Barterboard, that kind of thing."

"But we need the =CC=s," he protested. "We have to get that compressor so we can finish up the heat exchanger before High Opps."

"If you don't slow down, buddy, you might not need to worry about High Opps or anything else. Just be careful, okay? I'll keep you posted if I hear more than they release in the bulletins. But think long and hard about anything you do and if anyone might be watching."

"Okay," Dirck promised, then sighed. The outing had hardly been the break he'd planned. "I probably ought to get back. My mother is pretty paranoid since my sister got lost." Dirck frowned to himself, wondering again where she was and if they'd ever hear from her again.

When Win didn't answer, Dirck wondered if he'd heard him until, unexpectedly, his friend broke the stillness. "Be glad someone cares, buddy," he said. "Just be glad someone cares."

Dirck looked at him questioningly, but Win's attention was back among the lacy contours of the canyon. Zeta was descending from apogee, Zinni throwing long dusty rays from behind. Nifeir, the planet's single moon, watched overhead, a dark band marking the area on its surface unaffected by either sun. Beyond that and barely visible through brown haze hovered the shimmering reflection of CSF-1, where he and his father had docked what seemed so long ago.

Eventually, they climbed back in the 'cruiser and returned, Dirck absorbed in silent contemplation until Win dropped him off outside the SD. As he stepped inside the transport a while later, he gave into another sigh, then entered the ballome's coordinates. Any doubts he'd had about a bleak future were gone.

When the transport reached home, he was surprised to see his father waiting outside rather than cylled out.

"There's a notice in the bulletins you ought to know about," he said. "The regional government has demanded the voluntary surrender of all weapons."

Dirck stopped, Miran compliance training clashing with what he saw in his father's eyes. "What are you going to do?"

"What do you think?"

Dirck nodded. "You're not going to like what I found out tonight much better."

When he told him what Win had said, 'Merapa didn't comment, only shook his head before starting for the ballome. The clippers bumped a reminder against his leg and he took them out, still less than proud of his acquisition.

"Where'd you get them?" 'Merapa asked.

"The trade table at the SD. Whoever got them before must have decided that, compared to eating, haircuts weren't that important."

"I'm inclined to agree."

"Yeah," Dirck sighed. "I guess my perspective has changed a little, too." He took off his visor and pushed his hair back as they entered the ballome. "But as long as we have them, I still want a haircut."

His father forced a smile. "I suppose I do, too," he said, then squeezed Dirck's shoulder affectionately before disappearing inside his sleeproom.

Dirck got a drink before retiring to his own, wondering if their situation would improve. The answer came sooner than he would have liked.

* * *

Territorial Tower
Cira City

An unexpected technical breakthrough advisory glowed in ominous green from Augustus Troy's comcon, the result of a developmental test done on Nifeir. His team of scientists and engineers had learned long ago not to report failures, tending to exaggerate progress instead. But the TBA reporting the result was clearly authentic, the signal found accidentally in a sideband, resulting in a breakthrough that couldn't be faked.

His researchers had just discovered that they'd inadvertently acquired the girl's psi frequency when she'd been discovered in Cyraria's local spacetime. It was unintentional, but amazingly fortuitous, the resolution rough, but viable. The signature wasn't unique to her, but it did narrow the possibilities to a short list of a few thousand individuals galaxy-wide with the same spectrum. It was a silhouette compared to a detailed portrait, but still useful for tracking her whereabouts. The odds were good that no one within that spectral range would be on the same planet, much less specific locale.

All she had to do was communicate with someone telepathically and they'd know exactly where she was. They still couldn't decipher exactly what was being communicated, other than what the aura bandwidths provided, *i.e.* the basic mood and emotional thrust behind the message, but that, too, would come in due time.

With the long-term objective of their research mind control the researchers still needed to know more. Much more, especially for those they wanted to control individually. A frequency range was sufficient for the general directives given to the masses, but key individuals required more specific commands. Now they had her psi frequency, but her individual mindprint was what would provide positive identification and the needed key for covert intrusion.

INTEGRATION's ultimate goal was to psimit using an individual's mindprint in a way that mimicked the person's own thoughts. Doing this convincingly enough for the person to mistake the input for their own ideas was still a long way off. When they could accomplish that, the person would yield complete control without even being aware of the invasion. They weren't there yet, but they were getting close.

Technological advancement was an iterative process where researchers often didn't know what they needed next, much less how to obtain it, until reaching a particular milestone. Innovation was full of surprises and unpredictable. Their current speculations assumed that to obtain a person's mindprint they had to be in close proximity, on the order of a few meters, to assure no interference from other sources.

Ultimately, all thoughts, including those exchanged via psi, wound up in the collective consciousness where they lost all identity as they merged with the mental energy permeating the cosmic soup. If there were enough thoughts of the same energy, they could congeal from the chaos and precipitate into events, but most simply dissipated. The goal of INTEGRATION was to generate enough psi energy that such events would not only transpire, but be embraced by enough individuals, to achieve critical mass. That, in turn, would be the tipping point with full dominance the natural consequences. Having important individuals under their control before that time was essential to avoid any sort of rebellion or resistance, which was where Brightstar and his daughter fit in.

Unfortunately, the girl had slipped away from Cyraria before the needed technology had been fully developed. They got some information, but not the necessary level of precision. Mindprint acquisition required higher resolution, even at close range, much less across vast stellar distances where it was subject to interference from the collective. Psi could travel instantaneously anywhere in the universe and perhaps beyond, but the ability to identify one specific signal out of the cosmic soup would probably always belong solely to the gods.

Her last known trajectory indicated she was on a planet where intragalactic traffic was highly restricted. Actually, that had advantages, given that rescue from other sources was thereby limited, providing a high probability of reaching her first. Thus, he wasn't particularly worried, especially since now they could determine her location. Worst case, after refining the techniques using test subjects, they would slip into the Terran system and obtain the girl's data. Unfortunately, the technology simply wouldn't be advanced enough anytime soon to obtain it any other way.

No matter. They had her psi profile, which was unique enough to find her. And any place in the galaxy she could reach, he could, too. She was gone for now — so what? There was one thing he'd learned from the girl's father long before: there was no such thing as a bad break. You simply made them into whatever you wanted. Being away from her family fostered independence and prevented separation issues later, when he had her in custody.

In lone celebration, Troy removed a packet of Lemitini from his workdeck's secured compartment and unwrapped it slowly, savoring its aroma before lounging back in his chair and indulging in its euphoric effects. The implications of the latest data point joined the sweetness and when the last vestige of flavor faded, he dropped his feet to the floor, latched the top of his uniform and summoned the INTEGRATOR. The response was chill and he could tell he'd disturbed him.

Troy smiled. *Good.*

"The psiveillance equipment detected a strong psimission source," he said, making no attempt to stifle the satisfaction.

<<I wasn't informed it was operational>> the INTEGRATOR replied.

"The data were obtained as part of beta testing but subsequently confirmed. While the girl was in Cyraria's local spacetime we obtained her psi spectral signature. One that implies she has even more to offer than we thought."

The INTEGRATOR paused as the new data element was sorted, filtered and analyzed. <<Telepathy?>> he concluded, clearly pleased.

"Yes."

The silence that followed reflected the devious concentration of a superior mind. <<That introduces an entirely new factor. Telepathy indicates a psi rating of five or higher. She may be more valuable than we realized. Or more dangerous. It's possible it may not be worth getting her back.>>

"I disagree," Troy said. "She makes an outstanding pawn. Furthermore, as long as the family is separated we can use it to coerce both her and her father to see the advantages of joining our team." He laughed nastily. "That is if they ever want to see each other again. Together they'd make quite an asset."

<<True.>>

"For now, the main point is we've successfully obtained data that allows us to determine her exact location the next time she makes any sort of telepathic contact."

<<Excellent. Has your Terran contact been notified?>>
"Yes."

<<Any problems?>>

Troy resumed a more relaxed pose, eyes in distant focus. "None whatsoever," he said. "Terrans will do anything for the right price."

Debits and Credits

The haircut and a decent sleepzone relegated Win's dismal news and the weapons bulletin to no more than a dim threat, such that the next morning Dirck didn't give it a second thought. Right now, he had too much to do and there wasn't much he could do about it, anyway. Before he'd even ex-cylled, his father had gone to the SD, for what he didn't know, but did know that he would be expected to not sit around awaiting his return.

The main chore on their list for the day, other than the usual project work, was to check out whether or not they could use the pubescent crawler as insulation material. It would certainly make it an order of magnitude more appealing if they could at least reduce its awful smell, which could supposedly be done using atsna root. So today they were going to find out.

Deven, as usual, was already up and about by the time he'd had his morning ration. When Dirck told him what they were going to do, the boy was delighted and anxious to help, so off they went, boxcart in tow, low-hanging rays of Zeta rising and lounging Zinni confusing the shadows before them. They found a thick patch of what they now referred to as p-crawler about a hundred meters from the rock formation near Enoch's den, realizing when they got there that this was not going to be pleasant work. Regardless of how careful they were, the stench still manifested with a vengeance, as if trying to consume them in a toxic cloud.

Holding their nose with one hand and gathering with the other simply wasn't efficient, the only other option trying to set their jaws against constant retching and watery eyes.

"This isn't working," Dirck finally admitted as he finished yet another gagging fit. It was early enough when they left that he'd forgotten his visor, but now Zeta's glare was adding to the assault on his senses. His brother nodded agreement, eyes wide and runny, face fiery red from holding his breath. They moved a safe distance away to a small stand of rocks where they sat down to catch their breath.

"We need masks, like 'Merapa and I had on Verdaris," Dirck said at last. "I wonder if they have any in the SD?"

"I'll bet we could make some," Deven suggested. "If atsna root really takes the smell away, it seems like we could line it with that."

As always, Dirck was amazed by his brother's talent for innovative solutions and wondered why he hadn't thought of that. Clearly, the boy had been fully endowed with their father's problem-solving skills and mother's creativity. "Fantastic idea," he said. "I say we go back and see what we can do. Doing it this way will kill us, before we ever have to worry about Peak Opps."

Intent on their new mission, the pair trooped back to the ballome, gathering additional atsna root along the way, a job easily accomplished with a firm tug which encountered minimal resistance from the dry, sandy soil. When they got home, Dirck found an old Academy uniform he clearly wouldn't be wearing again anytime soon and removed the side pockets. It didn't take long for 'Merama to wonder what they were up to, and then pitch in enthusiastically to help grind the atsna and provide the remaining materials to fabricate crude, but viable, filter masks. While the trio sat at the counter in the galley/living area admiring their work, Dirck got the idea to attach it to his visor and then found an old hat to do roughly the same for his brother. By now, the heat outside had increased significantly, but their enthusiasm to test out their invention compensated such that they once again grabbed the boxcart and set out to complete the day's task.

When they were within a few yards of the p-crawler patch, they donned their masks and moved slowly forward, step by step, assessing whether or not they'd conquered the insidious odor. Deven tripped and fell right in the middle of a thick cluster and Dirck instinctively sucked in his breath and waited for the wave of nauseating odor which was sure to follow.

After a moment, he slowly inhaled, relieved to only detect the mint-like fragrance of atsna. Deven scrambled to his feet, the two exchanged a triumphant Miran grip, then set to work gathering the long, scratchy vines until their arms were full. Not thinking, they dropped the first load a few yards from the ballome and started back, only to hear 'Merama yelling at them from the rear door to get it farther away until it was treated. Dirck waved a sheepish apology and complied, then set out for more.

After completing enough p-crawler runs to accumulate a huge, putrid heap, Dirck filled the tank with water, which they'd fabricated from left over still material, and threw in several liters of ground up atsna, which his mother and Deven had prepared the night before. The water turned purple as it mixed with the powder, deepening in color as they added the p-crawler, which floated uncooperatively. Using one of the discarded atsna branches, he worked at submerging it until the tank's odiferous contents were invisible. They were counting on its insulating effects, one way or the other, but it would certainly be better if it didn't stink. And hopefully, deodorizing it wouldn't compromise its insulating properties and render it entirely useless.

Dirck wasn't sure how long it had to soak before the deodorizing effects Enoch had told them about would work. The bin was leaking—not fast, but steadily—the dark liquid slipping a small trench through the dirt at his feet. Hopefully, by the time it ran dry the job would be done. He pondered the leak a moment, knowing water was too precious to waste. Grabbing a nearby piece of leftover pipe, he dug a shallow ditch to where they were setting up the growing chamber.

While waiting for the atsna to do its job, he decided to dig the planting area a little deeper and considered what supplies they'd need to recycle the ballome's grey water from the shower and galley to use on the future garden. The seedlings Deven had planted were already sprouting by the front door and nearly ready to be transplanted to their permanent home.

While Dirck was still occupied with the growing chamber and tending the atsna bath, he heard the transport bringing 'Merapa back from the settlement. When he disembarked, Dirck gestured for him to come admire his work, but his father simply waved back, clearly dismissing his request as he disappeared inside. Dirck shrugged it off and kept working. A few hours later, the water had drained, so he dragged out the vines to let them dry. So far so good. When he cautiously lifted his mask, he couldn't smell anything other than the cool scent of atsna.

By the time he set the last ones out, the first few were dry. They still didn't smell, so he gathered up an armful and dragged them inside. Merama looked up from the table and started to protest, but he waved her off.

"It's okay," he said. "The atsna worked great. I thought it would be more comfortable to weave them in here."

"Good idea," she agreed. "In fact, if we do it in here, I can help. I wanted to talk to you anyway."

She started straightening each vine on the floor while he went to get more. It didn't take long to bring it all inside, but untangling it did.

"If only Creena were here," 'Merama said. "She'd be good at this." Dirck looked up at her, not sure what to say, but her eyes were fixed on the p-crawler, so he didn't respond. As they picked their way through the intertwined stems, a heavy silence fell between them, his thoughts turning to his sister and where she might be. He still couldn't understand how 'Merapa could send her away like that.

"So, how was last night?" 'Merama asked finally. "Did you have fun with your friend? What's his name, Won?"

"Win. Yeah, he took me for a ride in his 'cruiser and showed me around a little. Did you know there's a big canyon a few kilometers out from the settlement?"

She dropped a vine to her lap, face clouding. "You didn't fly over it, I hope."

"No, of course not. Win's smarter than that, 'Merama."

"Good. So what happened with you and your father last night that put him in such a foul mood?"

Dirck kept his eyes on the vines. "What d'ya mean?"

"He's been grumpy ever since last night, but he keeps telling me it's nothing. If it was nothing, he wouldn't be upset. I would think he'd be in a better mood since I gave him a haircut. He hates it when it gets all scruffy. So what is it? You two have a fight?"

"No," Dirck said honestly, adding less convincingly, "I have no idea what's wrong."

His mother stared at him in silence so long he finally looked up. "Really," he said, holding her gaze until she sighed and returned her attention to the vines. He felt horrible lying, but didn't know what else to do. If 'Merapa didn't want her to know, it wasn't his place to tell her. After a while, Deven joined them and they wove vine after vine together until it was large enough to cover the ballome. When they were done, Deven fetched 'Merapa to show off their work.

"Looks great," he said. "Let's plan on installing it tomorrow. I picked up a broken fan from the SD that they were going to throw away, but I just about have it fixed. We can use it to ventilate the ballome during dual perigee. With the insulation on the roof, it should help keep it a little cooler. It's worth a try."

Then he returned to his sleeproom without a backward glance. He was talking too fast and avoiding their eyes. Usually when he was upset, he faced it directly or hid it so well there was no room for suspicion. But they weren't on Mira III anymore and his emotionless façade was long gone. Dirck's eyes met 'Merama's, which were trying to read his expression. He shrugged, beginning to wonder himself if it was more than the weapons confiscation order that was bothering him. Without comment, she went into the galley to start supper, worry lining her face like Win's crack spider.

Deven went outside to remove more dirt from the growing chamber and Dirck powered up the comcon to check the bulletins. His father had deleted the message about the weapons, as expected. Several new ones had come in, but nothing important. He switched over to check their =CC= balance.

At first he was ecstatic to see =C-882870C=. Then he looked again—the balance was negative. Stunned, he checked the transaction log. Captain Troy. His heart fell as defeat washed over him in a dismal wave. =C708000C= for TL-87 repairs, and =C220000C= for Lemitini. There'd been =C45130C= in their account when it hit.

He switched off the comcon and stole a glance at his mother, who was busy preparing bowlbush root. He tried to swallow the lump in his throat, then walked to his parent's sleeproom door and knocked softly.

"What?" 'Merapa answered.

"It's me. Can I come in?"

His father lifted the door, noted his expression, and let him in. "I take it you saw our =CC= balance," he said, pushing the door down behind him.

Dirck nodded.

"Any suggestions how I can break this to your mother?"

Dirck collapsed on the bench by the workdeck and buried his face in his hands.

What a waste.

A total, utter, complete waste.

"I got through to Troy from the comcenter early this morning," 'Merapa explained. "He won't negotiate. He said the best he could do was set up a schedule of minimum payments. As long as we pay at least =C1000C= per day, we keep the ballome. If we go under that, we lose it. I raised the water to =C200C= per liter. That will help a little, as long as the demand doesn't go down."

When silence followed, Dirck dropped his hands. His father was leaning against his cyll, arms folded, staring into space. A profound sadness rose within him as he tried to match the man before him with the one he'd known on Mira III. Both his parents weren't anything like before, from their infrequent smiles, to their posture, to the way they walked. The thought that none of this would have happened if 'Merapa had acted like a respectable Miran shot through his mind so quickly he hardly noticed, except for the additional weight accumulating in his chest.

"I found out something else," 'Merapa continued tonelessly. "Troy's our regional governor and that's the only possible source of appeal. Put simply, we're a mere step away from slavery."

"What about Jen? Can he help?" Dirck asked, hoping his father's brother could possibly do something.

His father shook his head "I talked to him, too. They had a storm, one of those pressure vortices. The PV caused extensive damage to their ballome and destroyed most of the others. They're okay, but lost almost everything. To make it worse, the people up there can't pay for medical services until they're back on their feet, too."

Again, memory flared of their comfortable existence on his *naterra*. "Did we leave anything on Mira III we could sell, through Kranston or someone?" he asked. "And what about

Kranston? Could he do anything?" Certainly 'Merama's influential brother back on Mira III could do something, or he wouldn't have sent Creena back there to see him.

His father shook his head again. "Even if we could contact him, we sacrificed all our assets when I relinquished my citizenship. And Kranston would have no jurisdiction here, anyway, even if I could get him a message packet, which I can't. A negative balance restricts our activities substantially, including limiting communications to domestic only."

Dirck pondered his words a moment, knowing something wasn't right. Gradually the conflict dawned and his face darkened. "If Kranston has no jurisdiction here, then why'd you send Creena to Mira III?" he asked.

His father closed his eyes and sighed with the realization of what he'd let slip. "Because I didn't want her here," he said. "She's safer there with him and his family. Maybe, in the long run, he can do something to help, but probably not."

They both jumped when the door opened and 'Merama stepped inside. She stopped, eyes growing fearful.

"What is it? Is it Creena?" Her voice was a hoarse whisper.

Dirck and his father shook their heads in unison. 'Merapa tried to explain, but wound up making helpless gestures with his hands instead. She sat beside Dirck, face pale.

"What happened?" she persisted. "Is it Jen and Para? The bulletins mentioned their region had a storm."

"They're okay. Some damage to their ballome, but no one hurt," 'Merapa said.

"So what's going on? If it's not about Creena, and Jen's family is all right, what is it?"

'Merapa crouched down in front of her, hands resting on her knees. "It's our =CC=s, Starry. They're gone. We've lost everything." He sighed heavily, then spilled out the rest.

By the time he finished, the only visible reaction was a small disturbance in her brow.

"Did we lose the ballome?" she asked.

"Not as long as we can keep up the payments."

"Can we do that?"

"Probably. But I don't know how we'll do that and have a compressor, too."

Her eyes widened suddenly with understanding. He sat down beside her and took her in his arms. "It'll be okay. Really. We'll figure out something. C'mon," he said, pulling her to her feet and heading toward the galley. "Let's eat."

Dirck called Deven in from the growing chamber, then they all sat down for their evening mealzone. It was the same dish as the night before, bowlbush and wiittiins, which tasted good, except Dirck's appetite had fled with the =CC=s. When they were finished, Dirck invited Deven to play a game of tysa in their sleeproom, knowing his parents needed to talk. He smiled at Deven weakly through the games holographic images as they sat between their cylls, floor warm beneath them.

"What's wrong?" his brother asked. "Why's everyone acting so funny?"

"What do you mean?"

Deven's face clouded and a rare frown pulled at his brow. "C'mon, Dirck. Something's wrong. I can feel it. You and 'Merapa and 'Merama are really upset about something, and I want to know what. I'm part of this family, too, and I want to know so I can help."

Dirck reflected on how much he'd done already, including communicating with the bnolar. "You're right, Deven," he replied. "Something's wrong. Really wrong. We lost all our =CC=s and have to pay a bunch back for the ship we used to look for Creena. We won't be able to get the compressor now, so we're worried about how we'll get through High Opps."

Deven's face drew into an even deeper frown. "Why? The bnolar don't have =CC=s, or compressors, and they get through High Opps."

Dirck smiled weakly at the child-like logic. "I wish it were that simple, Deven," he replied sadly. "I really wish it was."

"It *is* that simple, Dirck," he said. His expression cleared, as if the problem had evaporated, like water in the still. "C'mon. Let's play. You can have the first move. I used to beat Creena all the time. I can hardly wait to see if I can beat you, too."

Dirck stared at him a moment, oscillating between annoyance and disbelief, eyelids heavy with fatigue. "Okay, Deven," he sighed. "Let's see what you can do."

* * *

CALMANAC: High Opps/Peak -64 Days		
Temp: 50C/123F	PVs: 42%	Quakes: 52%

It took Dirck a while to figure out what the source was for that silent, ongoing tension he could feel building up between his parents. Obviously coming to Cyraria was not working out as expected, an understatement too ludicrous to express. However, it was more than that, and all he could figure was it had to do with 'Merapa sending Creena back to Mira III. Clearly, his mother was having second thoughts, or so it appeared, since it was after that when he first noticed it. It was subtle but different than any behavior he'd ever seen in her before, such as that faraway distant look she'd get or the way her shoulders slumped whenever Creena was mentioned.

It finally heated up enough that 'Merapa told her about the timebump and their glimpse of a grim future, back when they were searching for her. He left out Win's observations, however, and of course the lasomag, which on top of everything else, was now illegal. Conversely, Dirck felt it was time she knew the whole story, so the next time she and Deven went to see Zahra, leaving him and 'Merapa alone, Dirck presented his case, once and for all.

His father had been working on an efficiency factor for the p-crawler so they'd know how much they'd need to insulate the ballome. He'd been holed up in his sleeproom most the day, but when he came out for a drink Dirck cornered him by the sink.

"'Merama has a right to know," he said. "She's taken everything we've told her just fine. If anything, she gets more upset when we don't tell her things. She's going to find out anyway. Zahra probably knows a lot." So far his father had listened with no more reaction than that stiffening in his jaw that he'd noticed far too often since leaving Mira III.

"And she also has a right to know about the lasomag," he went on. "Especially since we're violating territorial law."

'Merapa finished his water and drew some more, then put the tumbler down firmly on the counter beside him. "Listen," he said, "Number one, you owe it to your sources to protect them. If your mother knew Win was leaking information, she might let that slip to Zahra. Don't forget, as a regional employee, she works for Troy. She could be a plant."

Actually, she's a jendak, Dirck thought wryly, but wisely kept silent.

"We need to compare anything she gets from Zahra to what Win says," 'Merapa went on. "Most of it is probably gossip. The last thing we need is to add to it. Most of all, you can't jeopardize Win. Or trust him too much, either. He's a government employee, too, remember? To access the data he does requires at least a low level security clearance. So be careful."

'Merapa took another long drink, paused for a breath, then finished it in another greedy gulp. With that, he straightened his shoulders, set his glass in the basin and pointed at Dirck's face. "And as far as the lasomag is concerned, you stay out of that issue, period. I never should have let you know I have it."

Dirck backed up a step and swallowed. "Yeah, well, I wish I didn't know, too. But I do. And having that thing around jeopardizes the entire family. If you're not going to comply, then the least you ought to do is hide it, somewhere away from the ballome."

His father's dark eyes held him like a vice. "Right. A commando shows up to haul us away, and I ask him to hold on so I can go dig it up. That defeats the whole purpose! What do you mean, it jeopardizes the family? It protects the family! Not all compliance is good, Dirck. The wrong kind can cost us our lives. And if you can't see that, then you haven't learned as much as I thought."

Something inside urged him on, even though he felt guilty arguing. It was contrary to everything he'd been taught about respect, and he really did respect his father. He was even beginning to understand the delicate balance between choices, blind compliance, and higher laws. But somehow, this was different, and he found himself pursuing it, regardless.

"I think you ought to sell it," he said, trying not to raise his voice. "I know Win has connections and we could sell it, then use the credits for the compressor."

"You think that's not against the law?" 'Merapa replied. "Selling a weapon on the black market is worse than having one! Trafficking in weapons, oh, yeah, great idea. Wake up, Dirck! And we don't know Win is clean. Troy validates his compensation voucher. Can't you get the picture?"

"All right, all right," Dirck muttered in angry defeat. "I never said it was the perfect solution. And I can even see keeping it. But I still think you ought to get it out of the ballome. I just have this really bad feeling about it, 'Merapa. A really bad feeling."

After that, several days passed uneventfully, except for the nearly-visible tension still between them. They'd added a total of six layers of p-crawler to the ballome and set up the fan in the roof to bring in the cooler air when both suns were low. They talked, as necessary, when working, then fell to silence at meals and in the evening, avoiding each other. 'Merama asked repeatedly what was wrong, but Dirck denied having any disagreements, as he was sure his father had as well, blaming it on worry about the =CC= situation.

That evening at supper, one of the few times when the entire family was together, 'Merama brought up her visit that day with Zahra.

"She was acting differently, even a little strange," she said.

"She's a jendak, Sharra," 'Merapa said dryly. "They're always strange."

"No, it's more than that. She really helped me when Deven and I were alone. She tried to send messages to you in Troy's ship, and helped me trade for the highest =CC= value when I was trying to keep food in the ballome. She's my friend. I know she is."

"So what did she do that makes you suspicious?" Dirck asked.

"I mentioned that we'd probably have another item for the Barterboard soon. I didn't tell her what it was, but I was thinking of the p-crawler. I knew we'd have to apply for the slot and wanted to get it started, but Zahra was evasive."

'Merama sighed, scowling. "She said we shouldn't put so much on there. When I asked why, she said that sometimes the smartest thing you can do is play dumb. I can't imagine why we shouldn't post anything else. She knew we owed Troy, which I didn't tell her, and told me we should be careful—*very* careful—and compared him to a sweeper."

Dirck thought of the direct assault of the yraglian lizard as opposed to sweepers. Birds of prey, they'd capture a fuzzball, an indigenous rodent, then taunt and tease it, letting the creature think it was getting away, before finally grasping it in its sharp beak, tossing it in the air and swallowing it in a single gulp.

"But the creepiest thing she said didn't even make sense," 'Merama continued. "She's always had this uncanny ability to predict the future. I've never known her to be wrong. Today she told me there would be a 'double dark of endless days' which would bring 'violent storms of nature and man.' She said the conqueror and destroyer were opposed in evil mansions, which was very, very bad. I have no idea what she meant, but she really scared me, Laren. A lot."

"Don't worry, Sharra," 'Merapa said without looking up from his food. "You know how superstitious they are. I'm sure it's nothing."

But even as he said it, he glanced over at Dirck with a strange look of his own, and Dirck could tell he'd taken it more seriously than he'd let on. Later, when his mother and Deven went for a walk, he approached him again. He was at his usual place, working pressure calculations with his c-com.

"I still have a really bad feeling about having that thing in the ballome," Dirck said. "I really do. Especially after what 'Merama said about Zahra." He braced for a lambasting that never came.

'Merapa looked up and sighed. "I do, too, son," he agreed. "I've been thinking about what you said, and I'm trying to figure out how to secure it, even for a while. If you have any ideas, let me know."

Dirck stared at him in disbelief. "Okay." He nodded, relieved. "I will."

Then he checked the comcon. Another bulletin had been posted. Weapons of any sort were to be surrendered immediately to a repository set up near the comcenter. Again, it cited problems with the local culture and environmental concerns. It assured regionists that government storehouses had more than adequate provisions and that there was no need to hunt to provide food, given that there wasn't much out there, anyway, and that the primary danger they faced was from the weather.

"Hey, 'Merapa, look at this."

His father joined him from his workdeck and read it, several times. "We better move on that project first thing in the morning," he said. "I don't like the sound of this at all."

"Me, neither," Dirck said, his father's grim acceptance far from relieving his anxiety.

But as it turned out, morning would be too late.

The Lasomag

Dirck had almost gotten used to the nightmares. They'd started when Creena disappeared, then come regularly ever since. Not every night, but nearly so, but he'd gradually adapted enough that he could wake himself up, cast away the horrific images, then go back to sleep.

But this time when he awoke, he had no memory of a bad dream, only the feeling of one, as a nearly palpable imprint of danger festered around him like a toxic cloud. It reminded him of how he'd felt when Creena disappeared, only an order of magnitude worse. He sat up in his cyll and looked around, the sleeproom filled with the harsh orange glow of Zinni's rays creeping through the shutters. Deven was sound asleep across the room, breathing soft and even.

The fan in the living area was silent, a vibration in the ballome's structure resonating and buzzing periodically. Dirck set his feet on the floor and listened. He thought of what Deven had said, about understanding the bnolar with his heart rather than his ears. That was where the sensation was now, but it was a feeling of indescribable peril. Gradually it grew audible, then louder. A distant whine, dirt particles bombarding the ballome. The massive PV he'd seen from the shuttle, the type of storm that nearly destroyed Uncle Jen's ballome, sprang from memory.

He bolted to his feet and peered out the window. It wasn't a storm. It was worse. An armored transport had stopped outside. Seven commandos, maybe more, stepped from its confines, each in shielded yellow armor, hostile in

Zinni's searing light. He tried to will himself awake. Tried again. What had worked successfully so often failed. This wasn't a dream. Panic jolted through him like electricity as he flew through the sanicube to his parents' sleeproom.

"'Merapa!" he whispered, "'Merapa! Wake up!"

His mother stirred and turned toward the wall. He grabbed his father by the shoulder and shook him, hard.

"'Merapa! Get up! We've got trouble! Big trouble!"

By the time his father got up, three unwelcome guests had jumped the lock and entered the living area. One had a sensor box secured to his waist and held a detector probe. He was shorter than Dirck, even with the helmet, but his shoulders were nothing to contend with, neither their arsenal of weapons. Their face plates were down, prepared for full military assault.

"What's going on?" 'Merapa demanded.

"Confiscating weapons," the tallest one said, voice warped by the amplifier.

"What weapons?" 'Merapa said, face instantly locked in Miran façade.

"Are you refusing compliance?" the commando replied.

"Of course not," he answered. "Only asking what makes you think I have any."

The commando straightened, voice hardening. "If you won't comply voluntarily, we'll do a search. It would be to your advantage if it didn't come to that."

'Merama appeared in the sleeproom entry, spontaneously alert when she spotted the intruders. Dirck stepped over and put a protective arm around her shoulders.

"What do they want?" she whispered.

"Confiscating weapons."

"Oh, that," she said, relaxing. "Then there's nothing to worry about."

Uh, actually, 'Merama, there is, he thought, but remained silent, mouth in a grim line. Now was hardly the time for the truth.

The stocky commando with the scanner slipped his hand through the probe strap and started sweeping the living area. The walls, the ceiling, the floor, the doorways. 'Merama bolted for his and Deven's sleeproom. In less than a second, three lasomags were trained on her back.

"Hold it right there, ma'am!" the commando ordered.

"Leave my bondling out of this!" 'Merapa yelled.

She gasped and froze. "I'm, I'm a, just going to get my, my son," she replied shakily. "He, he's just a, a little boy. You'll frighten him."

The leader waved one of his compadres to accompany her. She came out holding Deven's hand while he rubbed his eyes sleepily with the other. Dirck moved beside them. As the man with the scanner entered Dirck's sleeproom, the leader herded the three of them together in the corner of the living area. The commando with the scanner exited a short time later. Dirck swallowed hard. His parents' sleeproom was next.

Everyone jumped when the scanner went off, a high-pitched, rude, electronic scream. Dirck glanced at his father whose eyes were closed, the rest of his expression blank. Objects were hitting the wall as the commando searched for the source. Moments later, he joined them, displaying 'Merapa's lasomag. Dirck looked at his mother who was searching her bondling's face for an explanation in wide-eyed horror. The lead commando pulled 'Merapa's hands behind his back and clamped on wrist-wring restraints with a single deft motion, then shoved their prisoner toward the door.

"I have clearance for that," 'Merapa said, an edge in his voice. "Check your records. I have clearance."

"You're mistaken, Brightstar," the lead commando replied. "Any clearance you had was revoked."

"No. Check you records," he repeated. "I have clearance. Permanent HIO clearance."

"No, you don't, Brightstar. You don't have clearance for anything."

"Yes, I do," he insisted, stepping back evasively.

The commando grabbed his arm and hauled him toward the door. "Shut down, Brightstar. C'mon, let's go."

"Can't I at least get dressed?" he asked.

"Don't worry, you won't need clothes where you're going," the commando replied and shoved him outside.

"Wait!" 'Merama screamed, face blanched with terror. *"No! What are you doing? You can't take my bondling like that!"*

No one acknowledged her plea, just continued outside. 'Merapa remained silent and deathly calm. No goodbyes, no last instructions, no anything but the bump of the door as it dropped closed behind them. 'Merama slammed her hand on the activator and dashed outside in the dust-ridden air. Amazed by his own calm, Dirck took his brother's hand and followed. The blinding light of Zinni high overhead and Zeta lingering beyond distant hills was somehow incongruent with awakening in the middle of a sleepzone, adding to the surreal image of the armored transport lifting off.

"No!" 'Merama screamed. *"No! Don't you dare leave me again, Laren! Don't you dare!"*

The transport faded to a dot, then vanished, oblivious to the devastation left behind. 'Merama covered her face with her hands and fell to her knees, sobbing. Dirck squeezed his brother's hand as together they walked up behind her. He rested his free hand on her shoulder, felt the emotions of abandonment ripping through her.

"You're not alone, 'Merama," he said. Deven walked around in front and gave her a hug. She pulled him close and wept into his embrace. "You're not alone," Dirck repeated. *"We're* alone."

Zeta broke cover from beyond ragged peaks, blasting already parched ground with increasingly deadly infrared radiation. Dirck squinted toward the sky, watching as a sweeper soared overhead, its direction keen. Its speed increased as it headed downward, eventually disappearing as its path took it below the rise.

The shaking in 'Merama's shoulders gradually changed to a heavier rhythm. She let go of Deven and pushed her hair out of her face. The Cyrarian climate had decimated the last of its curl and most of its shine. At last she stood, the emotional mix in her eyes horrid to behold.

"Why didn't he tell me?" she asked hoarsely. "Why?"

Dirck's gaze returned to the distant horizon. No answer came to mind.

* * *

The transport's stifling heat was calculated to further subdue prisoners while their captors watched, comfortable in climatized armor. One light panel was out, another flickered, unnoticed, as Laren, nearly crushed between two troopers, stared straight ahead to the vehicle's other side, features frozen. Sweat dribbled down his temples and neck, suffocating heat stifling every breath. His mind, however, raced, undecided who he was angrier with, Troy or himself.

He should have known. How could he be so stupid? He'd always prided himself in his ability to anticipate events, the one trait that advanced him more than any other. Minor details escaped, but never the whole, his foresight astounding, especially on Mira III. Yet, for all his digs at Dirck, here he was, victim of circumstances he should have avoided. What was the matter with him? He knew better, a thousand times over.

The fact they came in the middle of their shifted sleepzone in itself was startling revelation. They'd been under surveillance, probably through the ballome's internal control systems.   When they'd changed, he'd smugly thought another of its benefits would be to avoid just such an encounter. How could he be so naïve?

He caught his jaw tensing and ordered it to relax. Behavior now could affect treatment later. All they'd need would be the smallest excuse. He'd messed up enough. Had he ever! He turned his head enough to fix his eyes on the rear hatch window toward home, staring past dust suspended in a dagger of zetalight as self-deprecation resumed.

Was he so accustomed to predictability that a crisis destroyed all reason? Was he that spoiled by Mira III's comforts, particularly lack of worry? Had he forgotten how to think? It was bad enough when it took so long to wise up about Troy on the *Cosmos II*. He'd become so single-minded about bringing Creena home he'd slid deeper and deeper into the trap. Then the urgency of securing the ballome against High Opps did it again. Dirck probably thought he was a complete idiot. And with good reason. At least his son had come a long way. Good thing. Now he had it all to deal with alone, while his foolish father figured out how he'd get out of this one. At least he'd have the c-com, if he thought to use it.

Sharra's protests rang from memory, racking his cramped and sweaty frame. Even as they'd hauled him out the door, he couldn't look her in the eye, apology aching in his heart. Yet he'd seen, albeit felt, her every move, every expression, every emotion.

Sweet Benefics, what have I done?

He blasted himself again, incredulous still that his ability to function in contingency mode was so marginal. He'd juggled crises before, done it well. Never had he messed up so much, never had the consequences been so grim. Was his objectivity and training totally negated simply because his family was involved? He chided his jaw once more to relax, even as heat and emotion stung his eyes.

Apparently so.

* * *

Territorial Tower
Cira City, Cyraria

The prisoner manifest wasn't long, but Troy's satisfaction soared as if he'd conquered the universe itself. Everything had gone exactly as planned. How would Brightstar's arrogant self-righteousness serve him now?

Data collection activities upon his arrival at the prison had been fruitful. Data needed to derive his mindprint had been recorded, something they'd definitely need later, and they already knew more about him physically that the prisoner knew himself.

Interrogation techniques had advanced exponentially since those early efforts with Project Spectra. Specific emotions were now detectible, their intricate array of electro-chemical releases radiating unique signatures which were read as easily as the spectrum of a star. Any Miran façade, no matter how formidable, was now rendered entirely transparent.

Articulated thoughts remained veiled, but valuable emotional cues manifested, allowing weaknesses to be found and exploited. While their ultimate goal of mind control wasn't complete, it wasn't far off. In the meantime, they could gather the data necessary to define a tremendous quantity of targeted and rather unpleasant input.

Troy's patience strained, eager to apply the technology to a purpose he'd awaited so long, yet knew the timing wasn't right. At this point, Brightstar would expect it, his resistance high. Anger alone would sustain him for days. It would be far more effective to let him rot for a while. Humble him a bit. Let him worry about his precious family and whether he'd ever see them again, whether they'd survive the hottest period of a 45 year cycle. That alone would do wonders. Use tried and true methods for preliminaries, then move in with the *coup de grace*.

Troy's smile hardened. Through cunning he had acquired the ultimate test subject.

Patience.

It would be worth the wait.

Colonel Jenkins

Terra Day 1

Milton Jenkins examined the device ejected from the robot, noting the plasticized metal casing with its odd three-dimensional reflective quality, behind which floated various glyphs. He had no idea what it was, his first thought that it was some sort of weapon, perhaps an explosive device; then again, probably not, unless it was selective enough in character to spare the girl and her electronic crony while disabling everyone else. Convincing himself it wasn't dangerous, he dropped it in his pocket and turned his attention back to the moment at hand.

The polygraph test results bombarded Jenkins' mind with such force that, for the moment, everyone else in the room virtually didn't exist. It wasn't so much that he'd thought the girl was lying but more a matter that the incredulous nature of the incident was beginning to register. Momentarily, he met the gaze of what was turning out to be an amazingly assertive and potentially dangerous girl. A mixture of emotions he hadn't experienced since liberating the Nazi death camps after World War II surged through him as he attempted to assess the situation. Her eyes held fear, defiance, vulnerability and intelligence to a degree he intuitively knew matched his own. In spite of appearances, this was no ordinary girl.

For all his experiences in the past thirty-plus years as a career Air Force officer, this one topped them all. Never in his wildest dreams had he ever imagined calling upon the contingency procedures specified for this particular type of incident. If there was one thing to be said about military training it was that repetition coupled with well-defined procedures worked. The entire base would have dissolved with panic before his very eyes if someone hadn't already thought about how to handle such a situation, or perhaps experienced it.

Perhaps? Yeah, right. What was he thinking? Of course they had, the evidence quietly shrouded in secure bunkers in a variety of bases around the country. While he'd never been inside the ones at Wright-Patt, like the infamous Hangar 18, he knew what was in them. Base commanders were provided Top Secret data such as that with reports like Project Blue Book required reading, based on the assumption that someday they may need to know. Even three-star generals weren't trusted to fly by the seat of their pants in situations like this, a fact he was more grateful for than he cared to admit.

He looked away from the girl to the numerous individuals in the room with whom he was sharing this incredible experience. If nothing else they could confirm it wasn't a complete illusion, but for now, they were all looking at him anxiously for direction.

In spite of his usual level of preparedness, this particular event comprised details which had not been addressed in any manual, training or briefing he'd ever heard of, much less seen. First of all, an alien spacecraft was in their possession because it had deliberately landed, right in their lap. It hadn't crashed, it hadn't been captured, but simply landed, after asking permission to do so.

The first thing that came to mind was *spinnst-du*, a German expression he'd picked up during his long tour at Ramstein, which roughly translated meant *Are you spinning tales?* Actually, to be more accurate, it had been drilled into his head by numerous superior officers, whose admonitions had frequently been prefaced by a forceful *"Spinnst-du, Lieutenant Jenkins!"* Truly the expression had a plethora of applications, including the implied translation of "Are you a complete idiot?" which fit the perpetrators of this one to the proverbial "T."

The incident had fried the brain of every controller in the tower. Chatter from pilots who'd seen a UFO was one thing; one requesting permission to land, in their own language, no less, was quite another. Debriefing the tower guys in the morning would undoubtedly be one of the most memorable and possibly entertaining meetings of his life, one where numerous cups of morning coffee would not be required to maintain an appropriate level of attention.

But for now, he had to decide what to do. At a loss, he continued to organize the facts mentally, hoping to arrive at a plan of action. All eyes were still fixed on him, awaiting orders. Clearly, he had to do something, even if it was wrong, or lose all credibility as commander.

"All right," he said. "Guards, continue with the impound ops, including the mechanical subject at hand."

"Yes, sir," the pair replied in unison, and proceeded to place the chains back on the robot, which met with numerous protests from both it and the girl.

"You can't do that!" the girl cried, working her way protectively in front of her electronic cohort.

"I'm afraid I can, little lady," he replied, cringing with the realization that he sounded like something out of a John Wayne movie. "And if you pull any more tricks, like whatever that last thing was," he said, patting his jacket pocket, "you'll be next."

A look of horror flashed across the girl's face, followed by total defeat as she stepped back compliantly, arms folded. Except for the girl, he herded everyone out of his office to their respective destinations, ordering the guards to stand watch outside, though he regretted that decision almost immediately. It wasn't that he was worried about her being dangerous, but rather the fact there was something intimidating about being alone with her.

No one, including himself, had ever anticipated that such a thing could even happen. The odds of a UFO landing were crazy enough, at least a Hill, but having a *de facto* captain, who was a young, human girl, defied imagination. Except, of course, in Hollywood, which excelled in coming up with entirely fantastic, unrealistic stories. His wife always got so frustrated when they'd watch such shows on TV Sunday nights, when he'd provide a critical commentary of everything that was either entirely wrong or utterly impossible from the science and military point of view. *Ha.* Maybe he should have paid more attention, because what he was dealing with now had apparently been addressed by Disney while entirely off the radar of the United States Air Force.

Yes, this was where the instructions in the contingency plan failed. There were procedures for impounding the spacecraft and any alien lifeforms, alive or dead, including defensive and offensive measures to employ as required, ignoring the fact that most would be ineffective against such superior technologies. But the bottom line was that the omniscient manual was entirely silent when it came to how to deal with a human, female adolescent, who also happened to be an alien from another world.

He glanced down at the girl beside him, whose eyes were fixed straight ahead with a look of forced composure, displaying control far beyond her years. There was something ironic about that orange flight suit, which looked almost too much like an astronaut costume for Halloween. If he hadn't seen the evidence himself, he would have thought it all an elaborate hoax or practical joke, a possibility he filed away in the back of his head, in case it might come in handy later.

But apparently, she was telling the truth. Somehow he believed that, which was ludicrous, yet somehow fit the entire situation, which was otherwise beyond the realm of reasonable probability. While never substantiated by fact, he was enough of a science fiction buff to recognize the remote possibility that she was some sort of shape-shifter, perhaps some lethal lizard-like lifeform, intent on hijacking the planet. In some respects, that actually was more believable than what he had before him, if for no other reason than it had been thought of before. But somehow, he felt an odd connection with this girl, one that was so strong that he believed he could actually feel her emotions. Even before the polygraph test, somehow he knew she was telling the truth.

But now what? Intuition had served him well all his life, and lacking instructions, it was all he had. He was on his own, at least for now, at 0300 when sane people slept. While he'd been in touch with the Pentagon, they were as bewildered as he was, and placed full decision-making power back on his shoulders, at least in the near-term. This was probably not the show of confidence it seemed, but rather a diplomatic sloughing of responsibility so if anything went wrong, he would take the fall. They were trying to oust officers of his rank to retirement all the time, and if he messed this one up, he'd be out before he could say lickety-split.

"Sit down," he ordered, pointing to one of the chairs by the small round conference table beside his desk. She glared at him and didn't budge. "Please," he added, getting up to pull the chair out for her. She sat down heavily and folded her arms.

Jenkins couldn't help chuckling. "Wow, you're quite a handful. You sure your parents didn't deliberately ship you off on that escape pod?"

Much to his surprise, rather than a sarcastic retort, his little charge locked huge, brown eyes on his, like a frightened doe in the sights of his 30.06, and bit her lip as her eyes filled with tears.

And at that very moment, the term "disarming" took on a whole new meaning, and Jenkins knew he was toast.

All objectivity fled and, like it would for any other respectable male in the Milky Way galaxy, military training or not, his only concern became doing whatever it would take to stop those tears from flowing, which had already melted his heart.

"Hey, don't do that, Creena," he said softly, sitting down in the chair beside her. "It's okay. We won't hurt you, really."

And as is often the case, as he should have known, the kindness removed her defenses and unleashed the waterworks faster than harshness ever could, and within moments, her heart-rending sobs filled the room. Before he could say or do a thing, a knock came from the door.

"Come in," he said, trying unsuccessfully not to sound as helpless as he felt.

Expecting the guards, he was pleasantly surprised to see the bobbed blond hair and smiling hazel eyes of his briefing officer, who was fortunately a female and able to instantaneously assess the situation. The woman was far from what he'd classify as good looking with her prominent nose and eyes somewhat too close together, but at that moment, she was the most beautiful sight in the world.

The woman snatched some tissues from the box on his desk and handed them to the girl as she sat down beside her at the table, smiling sympathetically.

Creena took them, wiped her eyes, blew her nose and looked the woman straight in the eye. "Thank you," she said simply.

"You're welcome. So. I hear you've had a rather interesting night. Hi. I'm Major Harrington." She smiled and held out her hand, which the girl took somewhat hesitantly, but at least appeared to be amazingly back in control, almost as if she'd been trained to do so. "You can call me Harrie. Are you hungry?" The girl nodded. "Okay. Colonel, why don't I take her down to the mess and see what we can find?"

Jenkins hesitated less than a second before agreeing enthusiastically. Perfect. The Major had just earned her next promotion by giving him the time he needed to figure out what to do next. He saw them out, dismissing the guards posted outside. He had no doubt Harrington was all he needed from here. Better yet, if there were two of her.

He returned to his desk, remembering he had a press conference at 0700, less than four hours away. Harrington put those things together, got approval from Public Affairs, which in this case would also involve the Pentagon, and all that bureaucratic military crap he hated. Did he want her to stop what she was doing, so she could do that?

No. Of course not.

He rolled his eyes and shook his head in disbelief, again acknowledging that nothing in life, whether by training or experience, had prepared him for this.

But base commanders didn't have the luxury of losing it, so he sat down behind his desk where he stuffed a sheet of paper in the typewriter, which he found much more reliable than that infernal computer they'd forced upon him, with all its ridiculously complicated control code commands and clumsy dot-matrix printer.

By the time the major and the girl returned, he'd already stuffed four hastily typed outlines in the burn-bag, still at a complete loss what to say, other than the obvious: A UFO landed peacefully at Hill and the pilot was in protective custody. Dismissed.

He wished! Such honesty would never fly, anyway, even if it weren't contrary to procedure. He'd been around long enough to remember the Roswell debacle, with its constantly changing stories, until the Air Force became a complete laughing stock. If nothing else, the USAF learned from their mistakes, such that the first line of defense in this situation was to use the weather balloon story from the git-go, except the cargo on this one was a bit harder to explain.

The two females chatted quietly at the table while the girl devoured with considerable relish what looked like a two day-old ham sandwich from the vending machines.

"Colonel?" Harrington asked, and Jenkins looked up, trying not to look as weary as he suddenly felt.

"Have you already arranged for where Creena will be staying? I assume it won't be the brig," the woman asked.

As always, he appreciated her dry humor. He smiled as he leaned back in his chair, watching the girl finish up a bag of what had to be very stale Oreos. "Correct, as usual, Major," he replied. "I have not."

"I was thinking, we could get her a room at the VOQ, and I could stay with her, of course, until we figure out what to do in the long haul," Harrington suggested.

Jenkins raised his eyebrows and quickly assessed the suggestion. There was absolutely no reason he could think of that such a plan wouldn't work. After all, the girl was technically the captain of her ship, so qualified to use the Visiting Officer's Quarters as an officer. "I like it, Major," he replied. "Why don't you do that?"

Harrington smiled. "Yes, sir," she replied. "I'm glad you approve." With that she impishly held up the key, the deed already accomplished, then ushered the girl off with a comforting arm around her shoulders, as if the two were off to a slumber party.

Once again, Jenkins sighed with relief at the click of the door. Taking her to the VOQ was pure genius. Thank God for Harrington. Would the truth be known, his brain had officially stopped operating when the girl started to cry.

With all that feminine emotion removed for what would hopefully be hours, Jenkins was finally able to think clearly enough to take action. First of all, the press could wait. He picked up the phone and left a short message to that effect in the public affairs office. There were more important logistical steps to cover first. Then he dialed the Wing Commander. First thing he needed to do was get the vehicle secured and on its way, probably to that place down by Nellis, which was closer than Wright-Patt. Getting that thing out of there was of primary importance. Regardless of how many people saw it set down, if they couldn't get a close look at it in the light of day, it would be a lot easier to convince them it was something else.

He laughed.

Like a weather balloon.

The man on the other end assured him the vehicle as well as the robot were in the process of being boxed up, the transport on standby until they were ready. The ship had to be disassembled, at least to some degree, in order to fit the cargo compartment, which was turning out to be more challenging than expected. They couldn't find any fasteners and so far hadn't been able to breach the metal through any of the usual means. Their only other choice was to upend it on a trailer, but at roughly eight yards in diameter would be too tall to make it beneath the various overpasses along the usual route.

Thus, a team familiar with such a situation, was being assembled to the south, which would arrive by early afternoon. Meanwhile, they'd keep it secured, out of sight in a hangar, until the fuss died down, maybe as long as a week. All they'd need was for those reporters camped outside the gate to see it leave, hanging over the sides of a flatbed, headed for Nevada. Deniability would be impossible in the light of that kind of implied evidence. Flying it out in a C130 was undoubtedly their best but, at this point, possibly impossible choice.

Satisfied that all was under control, at least as much as he could expect, he set about preparing the necessary paperwork. By the time he'd finished up and glanced at the clock on the far wall, it was just after six, the base coming to life as civilian employees and personnel who lived off-base came to work. He smiled at the thought that those who hadn't seen the news reports the night before would be in for a bit of a surprise. But the smile didn't last long.

Now that he recognized that the best approach was that the entire incident officially never happened, he realized he had yet another huge problem.

The girl.

The realization that they'd want to get their hands on her for heaven knows what test or, heaven forbid, experiment, hit him like a nuclear blast, punctuated by the vision of those doe-like brown eyes. While the public only saw the vehicle, hundreds on base had seen her disembark in that bright orange jumpsuit. However, where she wound up was clearly above the rank or need to know of the majority of witnesses, leaving few options.

Jenkins had not gotten where he was by disobeying orders. He forced himself to be objective and consider national security. After all, it was clear she was an alien. Again he was assaulted by the idea that it was some sort of clever disguise, intended to play upon his sympathies. For all he knew, she *was* a flesh-eating lizard or some other predatory species sent there to hijack his planet. Nonetheless, his gut feeling was that she was exactly what she appeared to be, in spite of how incomprehensible that was. Somehow the flesh-eating lizard would have been easier to not only believe, but to deal with. A clear enemy would have simplified matters considerably.

His conscience flared as he realized she was now stranded for what could turn out to be years, more likely forever. As an adolescent, she could undoubtedly adapt to Earth life, but it was unthinkable for her to be institutionalized or treated as a scientific curiosity for her entire life, which would undoubtedly be the case once government authorities got a hold of her.

There was also the possibility that her parents or home world would stage a rescue that would hurl them into a galactic conflict Earth was sure to lose, and for a brief moment, he wished he could just let her have her ship back so she could leave and be done with it.

At this point, too many people, more specifically the bureaucracy, knew, the situation far too complex for simple solutions, but before he could ponder the dilemma any further a huge explosion rocked the building, sirens and klaxon alarms blaring a heartbeat later.

Immediately his phone rang and he grabbed it from the cradle, mind resuming its marathon race for reason.

Friends and Foes

Creena lay facedown, nose hard against the scratchy floor covering, vaguely aware that Harrie was bodily shielding her as a variety of building materials crashed all around them. Stunned and breathless, she wasn't sure if the explosion had thrown her from the bed or Harrie had pulled her to the floor, but that was where she was now, wondering what had happened.

When the initial blast faded, she could hear the muffled sound of sirens, men yelling and vehicles arriving somewhere beyond the rubble. Everything sounded funny; her ears hurt and felt as if they were plugged. She opened her eyes and lifted her head cautiously. Harrie stirred above her then knelt down beside her in the dimly lit room, the first light of dawn streaming through a cloud of dust where the window used to be. Debris covered the bed and the floor, including a large wooden beam, which now lay where she had been trying to sleep but minutes before.

"Are you okay?" Harrie asked, helping her sit up.

"I think so, but what about you?" she replied, pointing to a trail of blood staining the woman's blond hair and slowly dribbling down the side of her face.

The woman frowned as she reached up and felt the sticky trail with her fingers. "Yeah, I'm okay," she said, then slowly and somewhat painfully rose to her feet, surveying the damage around them. The inside walls and most of the ceiling had collapsed in a dusty heap sprinkled with broken glass, but the outer wall remained intact, or at least appeared to be. "C'mon, we need to get out of here."

Creena started to reach for her outstretched hand, then withdrew decisively.

"C'mon!" Harrie prompted.

"No. I don't think we should," Creena said. "I feel as if we should stay here. It's not safe out there. Not yet." The puzzlement in Harrie's face lasted but a moment before fading to agreement. "I think you're right," she said softly, sitting back down cross-legged beside her. "What do you think happened?"

"I don't know," Creena whispered, "but something tells me it's about me."

"Was there someone pursuing you in your ship?" she asked, eyes wide.

"Not that I know of, but they tried to keep us from leaving Cyraria, so maybe someone was."

"Wow," Harrie replied, eyes locked on Creena's. "Do you think they're trying to kill you?"

"I don't know."

"Well, clearly you're in danger, one way or the other. We need to get you someplace safe. Apparently, whoever it is knows exactly where you are, which is scary. The only one who should have known was the Colonel. I need to get to a phone and let him know you're all right and find out what to do."

They both jumped when a loud thumping came from the door, followed by someone yelling.

"Harrington? You in there?" It was the Colonel.

"Yes!" Harrie yelled back. She scrambled to her feet and ran into the other room of the apartment, stepping nimbly over the scattered wreckage, Creena close behind. A huge pile of wood and sheets of some chalky substance blocked the door, which the two of them kicked out of the way enough to crack it open.

"Stand back!" the Colonel ordered, and the two of them moved to the side as an ax split the wood in a thousand pieces, which were quickly ripped aside. He stepped over the rubble and surveyed the two of them solemnly with a sigh of relief.

"I need to get you out of here," he said, looking at Creena. "I don't know if it's you they're after or what, but nothing's going to happen to you on *my* watch!"

* * *

Terra Day 2

Creena paced the room like a caged animal, footsteps silent on the plushly carpeted floor. It felt soft, yet unresponsive and dead beneath her feet, unlike the biosympathetic surfaces and wall-hosted holographix on Mira III. She never thought she'd miss a thing about her *naterra,* but this primitive world was providing a hard dose of appreciation for the comforts she'd taken for granted her entire life. Such a surge of emotion would have triggered an instantaneous response designed to soothe and comfort until she was calm again. But here, trapped in the upstairs room of the Jenkins' home, there were no soft tones or calming aromas, just the harsh light of Earth's brilliant, yellow sun, shining through the window and leaving a bright splotch on the floor, another oddity that left her strangely unsettled, having come from a fog-shrouded world.

After the explosion at the base, Colonel Jenkins had decided that the safest place for her was where no one would ever expect her to be—his personal home. If there was anything she didn't feel it was safe, from that moment she'd seen the chase planes escorting them to the ground. Everything had gone from bad to worse ever since, from their confiscation of Aggie and the explosion, to now being locked up in a house made out of what appeared to be wood. How that could be safe she had no idea, though the concept of being somewhere no one could find her did seem to make sense. But then, how did anyone know exactly where she was on the base in the first place?

She'd always hated the endless procedures and zones on Mira III, but at this point she'd give anything to know what was going to happen. She didn't have time for this nonsense. Following 'Merapa's instructions as quickly as possible was essential, especially if he was in trouble. She thought of her family for a moment and felt a sudden pang of utter abandonment. At least they had each other. They were together, no matter how miserable. Except for Aggie and Thyron she was alone, and at this point she didn't know where they were, either.

Nothing was working the way it should. Everything was going wrong, no matter what she did. She clenched her fists at her sides and gritted her teeth against a frustrated scream. She had to do something, anything, to get out of there.

The Earthlings certainly weren't any help. At least not as far as helping her leave the planet was concerned. The fact they couldn't be trusted was obvious, even without Thyron's insights. Being locked up was the basest of indignities, far worse than any punishment administered for non-compliance reports, *i.e.*, NCR's, on her *naterra*. At least then she understood why.

She sat on the edge of the bed and stared vacantly at the shaft of morning sunlight streaming through the curtains from a brilliant blue sky, remembering the sultry purple one on Verdaris. The dangers there had been from nature itself; at least so far, there had been no psetoras or comets. Aggie had saved her there without a doubt. Who would save her here, where the greatest threat was her own species?

Something about the window jarred an idea and she got up to examine the frame. As expected, it was made of wood, a substance so rare on her *naterra* that it was only found in museums, yet here it was a building material, like on Verdaris. Trees were plentiful here as well, removing it from the realms of interplanetary trade tariffs. Unless the earthlings were intelligent enough to export it, which undoubtedly was not the case.

A strange, twisted mechanism was attached to the frame between the two panes. After tracing its coils and turns with her finger, she discovered that it not only moved, but released the lock. The bottom half of the window raised easily, leaving metal mesh between her and the ground below. The roar of a primitive motor roared through the open window, its source a small wheeled vehicle driven by a man who appeared to be cutting the grass, much as Aggie had sheared the weeds on Verdaris. Its fresh scent reached out to her, the impression increasingly forceful.

[Are you beginning to get the impression you made a rather large mistake landing here?]

"Thyron?"

[Yes.]

"What happened? Why are you talking normal?"

[I beg your pardon. This may be your usual pattern of speaking, but it surely isn't normal. Actually, it's sub-standard. But until we get off this inferior world, I'm stuck with it, because there's less carbon dioxide in this planet's atmosphere.]

"Where are you?"

[Still in the ship. They're trying to figure out how to break it into pieces small enough to box it up and fly out of here. I suppose if they find me, the Earthlings will pick and stick and kick me sick.]

"Why? Why are they doing this? We need to get out of here, Thyron." She moved from the window back to the bed, where she'd spent a miserable morning. By the time Harrie got her there, she was exhausted and tried to get some rest, but it was the same ridiculous sleeping arrangements as the base. To think these people were so primitive they didn't even have cylls. She may as well have slept on the floor, since every time she moved, she felt as if she'd fall off, anyway. Getting off this horrible planet was the only option.

"When are they going to give our ship back?"

[I'm afraid it's going to take a while.]

"How long is that?"

[It's hard to say. If I learn anything I'll let you know. For now, just follow your instincts and I'll keep in touch.]

She bid him a reluctant farewell and collapsed amid the wrinkles on the bed until a light rapping came from the door. She sat up as the dead bolt slithered out of place. No palm latches, either. No wonder their technology rating was so low.

"Creena? Would you like some breakfast now, dear?"

Colonel Jenkins' wife wore maroon slacks that blended with the room's flowered wall covering, her short, gray-streaked hair carefully in place.

"All I want is to get out of here," she grumbled. "How much longer are you going to keep me here? Why won't you people let me leave?"

The woman spotted the open window, giving it a pensive look, then closing it, before sitting down beside her. "Oh, Creena. I'm so very, very sorry," she said, putting her arm around her shoulders. You have no idea how I wish I could help you, honey."

Fueled by frustration Creena's anger smoldered, growing until it threatened to consume her. How could they flagrantly ignore every law of interplanetary diplomacy, with no warning? 'Merapa would have an absolute fit if he knew she was being held like this. How could she get him help when she couldn't even help herself? She opened her mouth to argue but the woman's soft, grey eyes were filled with kindness and Creena suddenly realized the uselessness of her behavior. Especially if she alienated one of the people on the planet who really seemed to care.

Her throat burned with emotion and tears pooled in her eyes. She tried desperately to blink them back, not wanting to make an even bigger snurk of herself by bawling, like she had at the base. She bit her lip, hard, but it was useless and the next thing she knew she'd collapsed into Mrs. Jenkins' arms, again crying her heart out.

The woman held her, rocking and smoothing her hair, telling her not to worry, that everything would be all right. She felt so helpless, so tired of fighting. If only they'd let her leave. As comforting as it was to be held, it reminded her even more of how much she missed her own family.

"Oh, Mrs. Jenkins," she whimpered. "I can't stay here, I just can't." The woman handed her a tissue from the nightstand as the sunbeam blurred again. As hard as she tried, she couldn't stop the new rush of tears, especially when Mrs. Jenkins looked as if she might cry, too.

"We'll figure something out, dear," she said, then gave her another hug.

For some reason she felt a little better. Something about the odds of a Code Orange Miran girl against an entire, stupid planet hadn't been very comforting. But somehow she knew that beneath Mrs. Jenkins' velvety exterior there was an iron will.

An abrupt buzz ripped the silence, startling them both. It sounded like a malfunctioning recharge unit, though why one would be at the house escaped her. Whatever it was, there was no mistaking the worried expression it brought to Mrs. Jenkins' face.

"That's the doorbell," she said, face solemn. "Stay here while I see who it is." When she fumbled with the key, Creena felt the indignity of incarceration churn inside her again.

"Do you have to lock it, Mrs. Jenkins?" she pleaded. "I won't leave, I promise. Where would I go?"

"It's not that, honey," she replied. "It's more a question of someone getting in than you getting out. It's for your protection." Then she put her finger to her lips and slipped out, bolting the door behind her.

Creena stood looking at the closed door for several moments. Being on Earth, taking her ship, and confiscating Aggie and Thyron were bad enough. But to lock her up and say it was for her protection? If whoever wanted her could cause an explosion like the one at the base, surely a simple wooden door wouldn't keep him out. Clearly their logic here was flawed as well.

She couldn't stand it. What was going on? Resentment rekindled, again she paced the floor. If she could only get out, see who was there, what they wanted. But that awful, stupid lock. And it wasn't even electronic, only a solid piece of metal clamped into a hole in the door frame. Their technology was truly pitiful.

Pitiful. And therefore vulnerable to advanced technology. Slowly her mouth curled into a grin.

In less than a second, she had her pocket laser out of her boot, energized and sliding through the bolt, erasing her feelings of entrapment with one effortless swipe. At least they hadn't gotten that, too. She slipped into the hall and crept to the landing, where she sat cross-legged on the floor, making sure she was out of view as Mrs. Jenkins opened the door.

"Hello, Lieutenant Carlson," Mrs. Jenkins said. "What brings you out here?"

"We've had some more problems at the base, Mrs. Jenkins," he said. "The Colonel thought I ought to come out and check to make sure everything is all right."

Creena scowled. She couldn't see him, but she knew that voice. Whoever it was, his brain dimensions were obviously small. *They* had problems? What about *her*?

"Come in, Lieutenant," Mrs. Jenkins said nervously. "What's wrong? Another bomb?"

"Not exactly, but not much better," he replied, stepping aside so she could close the door.

Creena leaned forward, catching a glimpse of a slender man with short brown hair in a blue uniform whom she quickly recognized as the same one who'd given her and Aggie such a norfy look the night before. He sounded as worried now as then, but it was obvious that now he had good reason.

"Someone got past gate security again, who was clearly looking for the girl," Carlson went on. "This guy meant business. He knocked out a couple guards with some sort of energy weapon and injured several others. We're assuming it's the same guy who bombed the VOQ. He kept demanding to know where she was until he finally got the picture she wasn't there and took off. He grabbed himself a hostage, which allowed him to get away, but he let the guy go, one of the mechanics, just outside the gate, then virtually disappeared. The Colonel is busy trying to explain to his superiors, including the Pentagon and the FBI, why she's here at the house. But his biggest worry now is her safety, as well as yours."

"Oh, no!" gasped Mrs. Jenkins, leading him toward the sitting area to the side of the entry. "What should we do?"

"We're not sure. It's unlikely that whoever it is would ever figure out she's here. We have plain clothes guards posted throughout the area, which will eventually be replaced by the FBI, but we need to take every precaution, just in case."

"I would think so!" Mrs. Jenkins replied.

Creena's heart pounded as the pair slipped into the parlor. She moved down a few more steps, listening with ravished curiosity, wondering who could possibly know she was there and be so determined to find her.

"The lab hasn't finished the forensics on the explosion, but their preliminary report is that the residue is different than anything they've ever seen before. Between that and the fact this guy had some sort of exotic weapon definitely tie them together. And as if that's not bad enough, now we have another problem." Carlson sighed heavily before going on.

"Apparently the polygraph guy from the police station talked to someone who told the press and who-knows-who else about the girl," he continued. "So there's a bunch of reporters hanging around out front again, wanting to know what's going on. The Colonel finally convinced them she was from Earth, but had been kidnapped and hypnotized by aliens. Given that kids can tell all sorts of wild tales, that wasn't as interesting as the prospect that she *was* an alien, so they had just started to back off when that guy showed up. Now they're on a feeding frenzy. They know something's up, which isn't rocket science. Since the Colonel's been the public affair's contact for the entire incident, he's afraid one of them might come out here to harass him — or you — for answers."

Creena's frown deepened, wondering what the press would do, or what it even was. They'd mentioned that the night before as well, but she wasn't ever able to figure out who or what it was.

"You know what a bunch of cannibals the press can be," he added. Creena froze, visions of Sapphirans flashing in her head. *Cannibals?*

"But that's only part of it," he went on. "On the slightly less exciting side, the Department of Social Services has been out to the base all morning. It's apparent the lie detector guy tipped them off, for sure."

By now Creena had scooted down to the bottom, hoping the banister rails would hide her since she was right outside the parlor door.

"Social Services? Why?" Mrs. Jenkins asked, then groaned. "Oh, no. Let me guess. They think they should be looking after Creena."

Carlson snorted. "You got it. They decided they were responsible since she's obviously not an adult. They want to put her in a foster home because now she's considered an orphan until they can find her parents."

What a brainless bunch of snurks. Unable to hold herself back another second, Creena burst into the room.

"Who's an orphan?" she stated angrily, hands on her hips.

"Creena! How'd you get out?" Mrs. Jenkins asked.

"I know exactly where my parents are," she continued, ignoring the question. "They told me to go back to Mira III and if they'd let me have my ship, I could get off this crummy planet and find someone who could actually help!"

Both adults stared at her in silence for several seconds until Mrs. Jenkins finally looked away and walked to the window, gazing at the rolling lawns, the towering trees, the neatly cropped shrubbery. The house was set back from the street, their nearest neighbor fifty meters away. Creena looked past her to the alien scene, homesickness rising again. No one had individual dwellings on Mira III, much less living plants as ornamentation.

"I know this is hard to understand, Creena," Mrs. Jenkins finally said. "It might take some time, but we'll get it all straightened out, we really will." She turned from the window with a strained, tight smile. "Eventually."

Creena buried her face in her hands in frustration, then looked up pleadingly. "But you don't understand. I have to go *now*. Why are they treating me like I'm some kind of sub-human? Jendaks have it better than this. At least they don't keep them in a cage. Snurkles, I was better off on Verdaris, with the stupid Sapphirans." She collapsed on the couch, arms folded, as a series of looks passed between Carlson and Mrs. Jenkins.

"We're doing everything we can," Carlson said. "Our main concern now is to keep you safe."

Creena glowered even harder. "Safe. Right. I was perfectly safe until you forced us to land. And what have you done with my ship? Why can't I have it back? Now!

Then you won't have to worry about me at all, because I'll be gone."

Carlson started to say something at least three times before he finally rolled his eyes with his own frustrations. "We can't give it back yet. We want to check it out and learn from it. Which will take a while."

"But you stole it from me! Where is it? I want to see it and make sure it's okay."

"You can't," Carlson replied. "It's, well, it's being taken to a safe place where they can, well, reverse engineer it."

"What's that?"

"Uh, well, kinda like, take it apart to see how it works."

"Are you kidding me?" Creena gasped. Even without knowing exactly how complicated her ship was she, knew it was so far ahead of anything they had here that they wouldn't have a clue.

"What if they *never* get done? Or get it back together? You people are probably too stupid to ever figure it out. You haven't even progressed beyond the wheel! I might be stuck here for the rest of my life." She folded her arms and sighed angrily, trying to defy the terrified, empty feeling swelling inside as the seriousness of her predicament deepened even more.

"Colonel Jenkins has enough pull to make sure it doesn't come to that," he insisted, but it sounded more like he was trying to convince himself.

"Ha!" Creena snorted, giving him the dirtiest look she could muster. "He's the one who kept me here in the first place. He could have let us go once he knew I was telling the truth."

Carlson looked away and didn't answer. For a long time no one spoke, leaving an uncomfortable silence that clung to the air like Miran fog, cold and thick. The only noise was the ticking of the clock on the mantle, each stroke a loud, mechanical hiccough. Carlson started tapping his foot, as if activated by Creena's searing, brown eyes. Mrs. Jenkins sat in the big wingback chair by the window, then shot to her feet a moment later.

"I think I've got it!" she said.

"Got what?" Creena asked.

"Trust me," she said, turning to Carlson. "Do you have to get right back to the base, Lieutenant?"

"No. The Colonel told me to stay and make sure everything was okay. I'm supposed to make sure the guards are fully replaced by the FBI before I leave, if then. Why?"

"If you can stay and, well, keep Creena company, I'd like to run into town to pick up something else for her to wear. That orange outfit she has on is a dead giveaway."

Creena eyed her grubby uniform, which had been abused beyond the ability of its nanofibers to eliminate all the dirt and charcoal smudges, especially since she hadn't been out of it for days. No wonder they were calling her an orphan. Carlson picked up the telephone on a table and entered the code for the base on a wheel-like device. After a brief conversation, he handed it to Mrs. Jenkins. "Here. The Colonel wants to know what's going on."

So do I, thought Creena. How much she could trust Colonel Jenkins was still questionable. If it weren't for him, she'd be on her way home, right now. But then again, he hadn't turned her over to those social people, whoever they were, and was left handed, just like herself and her father, so maybe he wasn't so bad, either. Time would tell.

Mrs. Jenkins took the receiver. "Milt, we can't discuss it on the phone. Just get home early, before three. Okay?" She paused, listening, then added, "Do the best you can. I'll see you later, sweetheart," and hung up.

"I'll only be gone an hour or so," she said, grabbing her purse from the hall closet beneath the stairs. "Have a nice visit, you two."

Creena heard the vehicle in the garage growl to life, then fade to silence. Wheels—how stupid. Carlson sighed and sat down beside her.

"Well, Creena," he said. "How do you like Earth so far?"

She replied with a staunch, dirty look. What a stupid question. Only as much as genour. Or psetoras. Or storms. Or Sapphirans. Or having to spend time with some Earth-snurk, second only to the head snurk himself. Even Dirck was better than this guy. Dirck, who was comfortably situated with the rest of her family without a worry in the world, a thought that angered her even more.

Carlson blinked, apparently aware he'd said something incredibly stupid as he seemed to shrink from her glare. Was it her imagination, or was he actually a little hurt? She swallowed, looking away to watch a black car park across the street. She marveled again at how boxy and clunky the vehicles here were, unlike the sleek, smooth lines of even the oldest air cruisers on Mira III. Dirck's had looked better than that. But again, that wasn't surprising, considering they still used wheels. Carlson followed her gaze, then got up nervously and walked to the window.

"What do you use for transportation on your planet?" he asked, eyes fixed on the car. He was trying hard enough. Maybe she should cooperate. If he got mad, he might send her back upstairs. Even this was better than that. Taking an impatient breath, she uttered a curt, cold reply.

"Air-cruisers."

"Air cruisers?"

"That's right."

"What are they like?"

Creena shrugged. "I guess they're like a combination between a car, like that, and one of those funny, little air vehicles where I landed. But they don't run on fuel, they're magnetic."

"You mean the chase planes?"

"I guess."

Carlson shifted his gaze from the window to her and laughed painfully. "Somehow I doubt the Colonel ever thought of our F-16s as funny little air vehicles," he said, casting a casual glance back outside. Instantly his entire posture turned to stone. Chilled by a cloak of fear, Creena joined him at the window. A dark, heavy-set man with wavy hair and a uniform similar to Colonel Jenkins' was standing on the lawn, staring at the house.

"Who's that?" Creena asked warily.

"I don't know. He's got government plates, but I know all the colonels, the generals, too, even those at the Pentagon, for that matter, and I've never seen that one before."

All Creena knew was whoever or whatever it was out there gave her a bad, bad feeling, like the one she'd felt in the tunnel leading to the escape pod onboard the *Aquarius*. By comparison, the pygmies were benevolent and Jenkins her long, lost hero. Her mind filled with darkness, consumed by the same mysterious imprint of evil she'd felt too many times before. Who was it? *What* was it? Why did it keep following her around? She gripped Carlson's arm in terror as the man started toward the house with long, deliberate strides.

"You'd better get back upstairs and lock yourself in," Carlson said, handing her the key. "I'll find out who he is and what he wants."

Creena took it and darted up the stairs, breathless with fear. Something was wrong, all right, since even Carlson could sense it, snurk that he was. At the landing she froze, staring at the severed bolt on the bedroom door. *Good move, Creena,* she berated herself and dashed to the other three bedrooms. No locks. She headed back to the stairs, not knowing what to do, when a knock thundered through the house. Carlson was at the door, hand on the knob. She jerked around wildly. The bedrooms were out, the bathroom was out, downstairs was out.

Carlson hesitated, scowling up at her expectantly. Another knock exploded from the door. Both her hands flew to her mouth in panic as she looked around frantically for somewhere to hide. The only possibility was the bifold doors of a storage closet behind her. She yanked one open and ducked inside, pulling the louvered doors closed behind her. It was stuffy and crowded with boxes and linens, but at least she was out of sight. She crouched down, straining to see through the cracks as Carlson opened the door.

Carlson saluted and the man nodded. "Can I help you, colonel?" he asked.

"Yeah, probably you can," the man said, face contorting with a sinister smile. "Is this the Jenkins'?" Carlson nodded. "Is Mrs. Jenkins here?"

"No."

"What about the colonel?"

"He's at the base," Carlson replied.

"So why are you here?"

Before Carlson could answer he was engulfed in a green burst of lasomagnetic energy that dropped him to the tiled floor in a crumpled heap. Creena's mind reeled. The soldiers at the base didn't have lasomags, but some primitive type of projectile weapon.

But whoever was pursuing her did.

Pursuit

Paralyzed with fear, Creena peered through the louvered doors as the man stepped over Carlson's limp form, eyes directed upstairs while whispers of a cryptic connectivity flashed through her mind. That feeling in the pod's ingress tube, escaping Cyrarian airspace, and the explosion at the base all shared the same dark feeling. There was no doubt whatsoever that some cosmic evil force was personified by the man beside Lieutenant Carlson's still form. He wasn't a man-eater in the same sense as the Sapphirans, but a cannibal nonetheless—a consumer of souls.

Her limited view ended abruptly when the man veered left of the stairs into the kitchen. She sighed with momentary relief that he hadn't come directly upstairs, while great crashes and the slamming of doors raged from below. Escaping down the stairs was impossible, likewise the second-floor windows. The only possible way left was through the floor. She tried to remember what was below; probably the kitchen. Her only hope was to drop through the floor as he was coming upstairs, as he surely would at some point.

She shifted carefully, trying not to make a sound. Boxes cluttered the floor, giving her precious little room. She moved them aside as quietly as possible, glad he was making such a racket the he probably wouldn't hear anything, anyway, plus it let her know where he was. Set with a plan, she got out her pocket laser. The louvered doors allowed strips of light to enter her hideaway, providing just enough for her to switch it to manual and eliminate spoken commands; that done, she activated its blade.

Nothing happened.

She pressed its switch on and off, again and again. Still nothing. Her heart pounded harder as panic ensued. She set it to maximum and tried again. The feeblest excuse of a glimmer weakly emerged. Oh, no. It needed a charge. Great, simply great. Now what? Then she remembered what Aggie had said about using the planet's magnetic field to recharge, but didn't have a clue how to do it. She froze when a muffled bump came from below.

Oh, someone! Please help! she thought, then directed her hopes back to the laser, willing it to work with every fiber of her being. *Please, please, please! Work, oh, work, oh, work! Please work!*

Stretched by fear, time ground to a halt, her mind flaring with her last conversation with 'Merapa when she'd said, "But I don't know what to do!"

"I don't either," he'd replied. "All we can do is trust the Universe to show you the way."

It certainly didn't seem as if the Universe was on her side so far, even though she had to admit that something must have intervened which allowed them to escape the starcraft's grasp as they left Cyraria. If the Universe could do that, then it could recharge her pocket laser. But maybe she had to tell it what to do.

Her mind traced through what she knew about the laser's energy sources and how it worked. For an instant her mind shifted to a different mode, and she almost understood what needed to be done. It vanished as quickly as it had come, but the taste of insight boosted her confidence enough that she suddenly knew with a little help she could make it work.

Walls rattled around her as the cannibal pounded up the stairs, then down the hall; more slamming doors and the crash of furniture hitting the walls.

Again she closed her eyes and directed all her energy, physical, emotional and mental, to the object between her palms and pleaded for cosmic help. The effort was exhausting and it felt as if she'd either explode or pass out. Then suddenly, the energies merged, surging through her with a soothing sense of peace and assurance that illuminated every fiber of her being. Her body relaxed and panic receded, leaving her with a total sense of wellbeing, in spite of her predicament. She tried the switch again. The orange blade was steady and strong.

Thank you! she mouthed silently, then set to work. The laser slipped through the carpet easily enough, acrid fumes scorching her eyes and throat as she cut three sides of a square, which would hopefully be large enough for her to fit through. The burning precursor to a sneeze ticked her nose. She grabbed a towel off the shelf and buried her face in it, muffling it the best she could.

The racket down the hall stopped. "Where are you, you little space brat?" the man yelled from the Jenkins' bedroom.

She held her breath and didn't move. Noise resumed a moment later. Quickly but carefully, she pushed back the carpet and directed the laser into the floor. A moment's resistance and it was through. With a determined hand, she traced the square's perimeter as again footsteps rumbled down the hall, toward the bedroom where she'd spent the last of the night. She pushed the laser along its path until it stuck on something on the far side, vibrating angrily until she forced it through.

A door slammed, more footsteps, closer this time. From down the hallway came more ruckus as objects struck the walls, then a huge thud of something big and heavy. She pushed on one side of the cutout. It wouldn't budge.

Quickly she carved notches in each side, large enough to get a finger through, first one, then another. The accumulation of smoke taunted her throat as she pulled with all her might. It was heavier than expected, but finally came loose with a squawk of protest. She squinted inside the opening, a dark shadow in the dim light, and marveled that she'd dodged the heavy beams on either side. The opening was unexpectedly dark. Then she realized she was only through the floor; the downstairs ceiling remained.

She straightened enough to peer through the door's slats, across the landing to the bedroom where the noise was accompanied by abrupt, shadowed motions on the floor. Sunshine poured through a window at the end of the hall, rays dusted with telltale smoke drifting in silent betrayal. Urgency escalating, she bit her lip with determination and returned to task.

The surface beneath was smooth, too much so to be wood. What could it be? At least she was reasonably sure it wasn't cement, like everything on Mira III. She would have been in a fine fix then! Leaving the blade on manual, she turned on its sensor and swiped it past. The display pronounced *gypsum* and indicated a minimal setting. Then she recalled the debris at the base after the explosion and those chalky pieces of wallboard.

Good. She set it on low power and traced another square, then hollowed out two more finger notches as more smoke gathered in a choking cloud. Chips and particles clattered below as she pulled the piece gently upward. It squealed, then creaked and broke in half. She set the two pieces aside and held her breath while footfalls, not a meter away, rumbled to the bathroom, which shared a wall with the closet.

All she could see below was a dim perimeter of light. She reached downward until her hand brushed something smooth and flat. Then slick contours, cool and metallic. A careful sweep of her hand revealed the rest of the shelf was empty.

She turned around, bracing herself on her elbows as she lowered her feet through the opening, toeing for something solid. Finding the top shelf, she gradually worked her way down to the next one. It was unexpectedly shallow, space consumed by cans. She eased herself down some more, elbows even with her shoulders, as she felt for another. It squeaked beneath her weight, a can tumbled to the floor with an impolite *clunk*.

A raucous electronic scream sounded suddenly from above, pulsing in alarming beats of smoky fury. Footfalls thundered closer, stopped. The closet doors flew open, flooding her precarious situation with unwelcome light.

"Hey! Hold it right there!" the cannibal yelled.

Creena screamed, tightened her grip on the top shelf, let her legs dangle free, then dropped heavily to the floor, landing hard. The tight space kept her upright, her back wedged against the door. She felt behind her, quickly finding the doorknob. Light flared in her eyes as she burst for freedom, precisely as two huge feet came through the hole in the ceiling, occupying where her head had been an instant before.

She paused a second to get her bearings. She was in the kitchen, as expected. Impatient sounds of struggling and alien curses swelled from the pantry, followed by the thumping and pounding of a futile squeeze. Scuffling, grunts of struggle, then the eventual clamor of footsteps on the stairs.

A doorway beckoned to her right. Panic swelling, she slipped into a small, narrow room with two large and unfamiliar metal cubes with hoses of various sizes snaking from the rear. Heaps of clothes occupied baskets, suggesting a connection she couldn't quite make. She lifted the lid, hoping for a place to hide. Inside was an enameled tub with a center post, certainly not enough room for her. She pulled open the front door of the other, cringing at its metallic *pop*. More clothes. Aha, so they were some sort of laundry device used before the invention of self-cleaning nanofiber.

Stupid, primitive Earthlings.

Another door opposite the machines caught her eye. She dashed through it as footsteps pounded toward the kitchen. Now she was in the 'cruiser cranny or what they called a garage—big, empty, and no place to hide. Mrs. Jenkins had left the big door open, but trying to out-run the cannibal to safety didn't exactly seem like a good idea.

She looked up desperately. Rafters spanned the ceiling, some partially hidden by the open door. She scrambled up on some plastic boxes, then to the top of a huge metal cylinder. It hummed and gurgled as she scrambled from its top to the closest beam, wincing as a splinter jabbed her hand. Hearing a squeak, she froze, terrified. Slowly she turned her head back toward the house as the cannibal stepped into the garage.

If he looked up she was dead.

He ran to the open door, muttering. She held her breath, not sure whether lack of air or fear would smother her first. Her head felt light, the rafters swayed. Closing her eyes, she gripped the beam in front of her in a death grip while everything became a blur of dizzying grey. She gritted her teeth, certain capture one nauseating turn away. The cannibal mumbled something under his breath, poked around by some boxes, then returned inside, slamming the door behind him.

Creena heaved a giant sigh of relief and luxuriated in a few deep breaths. Balance secure again, she crept cat-like along the crossbeams until she was hidden from below by the garage door. Carefully, she maneuvered into a sitting position, feet on one beam, behind on another. Just as she settled back on her haunches something hit the raised door with a thud. She glanced down, watching her pocket laser rumble along the door, then crash to the concrete and roll some more until it stopped, glistening in the sun, only too ready to betray her.

Before she could figure out how to retrieve it, a car shot inside and stopped, its silver hood gleaming directly below.

Mrs. Jenkins screamed as Creena landed on it, then rolled off and yanked open the car door.

"Back up, Mrs. Jenkins!" she said. "Back up, back up, back up!"

The woman looked at her as if she'd lost her orbit, but obediently eased the car into reverse. Creena grabbed her pocket laser, then jumped inside the car, precisely as the cannibal tore into the garage.

"*Lock your door!*" Mrs. Jenkins yelled.

"*How?*"

The man grabbed the handle, the latch clicked. Mrs. Jenkins jammed the accelerator to the floor, leaving him staring at his empty hand. The car flew backwards to the street, twisted into position and jerked forward, wheels spinning with an ear-splitting screech. Mrs. Jenkins glanced in the mirror above their heads and accelerated.

"Are you okay?" she asked. Creena nodded.

"I'm fine, but I don't know about Lieutenant Carlson."

"*What happened?*" Mrs. Jenkins gasped, eyes wide with shock.

"Right after you left, this guy showed up, blasted Lieutenant Carlson with a lasomag, and came looking for me!"

"*Oh, no!* Who do you think it was?"

"I don't know, but he's gotta be the same person who bombed the base."

Creena shivered at the import of her own words, then dismissed it for later consideration. The crisis was far from over. The man's black car was in pursuit and gaining, less than a hundred meters back.

"He's catching up!" she cried. "Can't you go faster?"

Mrs. Jenkins responded by slamming on the brakes and turning sharply to the left, inertia flinging Creena and the clutter on the dash hard against the passenger side door. Miscellaneous objects fell to the floor and Creena struggled upright, noting an unpaved road bumped beneath them, dust and gravel spewing in their wake.

"What are you doing?" Creena screamed, hanging on desperately. Cruisers on Mira III were guided by Central Control, making such erratic movements impossible. Mrs. Jenkins gave her a wry smile and accelerated again.

"Taking a short cut to the freeway," she said. "Are you okay?"

Creena straightened in the seat and nodded.

"Hang on, honey. I'm going to turn again. Put on your seatbelt!"

Before she could figure out how the restraints even worked, the car left the dirt road entirely and thumped through a stand of weeds toward a short rise straight ahead, above which a paved roadway buzzed with four lanes of traffic. By the time the car merged into the first lane, Creena figured out the seatbelt, then looked back at the dusty trail they'd left behind. So far there was no sign of the black car.

"Hand me the mike, will you, dear?" Mrs. Jenkins asked, pointing to a communicator of some sort dangling from a coiled cord, similar to the one in the van at the base. Creena complied, bracing as the car edged over to the inside lane where it leveled off at high speed, only separated from traffic going the other way by a metal rail.

"*This is an emergency!*" Mrs. Jenkins said urgently into what was apparently a radio. "I need to speak with Milton Jenkins! *Now!*" Creena crossed her fingers, never dreaming he could be a welcome sight. A male voice rough with interference replied from the device between them.

"Sorry, ma'am, he's in conference."

"I don't care if he's in conference! This is Edith Jenkins, his wife. Put me through! *This is an emergency!*"

"I'll check to see if we can reach him, ma'am." Another pause, then, "Sorry, ma'am, he's left the base."

Mrs. Jenkins frowned as she replaced the mike on a hook beside the receiver. "Great, just great," she groaned.

She turned to Creena to say something, but her comment was lost in the scream of tortured metal.

The black car!

The cannibal had not only caught up, but was now beside them on the right, readying for another strike. Creena closed her eyes as another heart-stopping thump thrust them toward the guardrail. The car whipped and strained, Mrs. Jenkins struggling with the wheel. He hit them again, harder, pushing, shoving, and grinding them closer and closer, until they were precariously close to what had become a steep embankment.

Mrs. Jenkins flattened her foot to the floor and turned hard to the right, clipping the front of the other vehicle. The engine roared as the car plunged forward, leaving their foe struggling for control as it headed for the shoulder. In a dusty squeal, it swerved back on the divided highway, gaining again as easily as a space fighter. Mrs. Jenkins pulled into the right lane, the cannibal moving in on the left. A slow moving car loomed before them, coming up fast. She swerved around it on the shoulder, then back to the pavement. Moments later, the black car was back, buffeting them some more.

Scraping, grinding metal, screeching tires and the swirl of green-brown vegetation orbited around them. Weeds crackled and thumped beneath the tires in another breathless skid. Creena couldn't think past that moment, the repeated jolts, the screaming of metal and rubber. Beyond Mrs. Jenkins' tense profile, a furious blur tumbled toward them for another strike. The man looked enraged to complete lunacy. For an instant, their eyes met in a blood chilling moment of truth. Driven by forces beyond reason, one of the universe's vilest emissaries was determined to stop at nothing short of her complete destruction. And she didn't even know why.

She couldn't tear her eyes away, as if something were invading her mind. It reminded her of that tree on Verdaris, that overwhelming feeling of being controlled. When he gave her the rankest, most gut-wrenching sneer she'd ever seen, a split instant of understanding flashed deep inside. But before it rose to consciousness, the man's face took on a startled horror of its own.

Directly in front of him was a huge, slow-moving truck.

Instead of dealing what would have surely been the final blow, he veered the opposite way, skidding, swerving, spinning, a frightful cyclone of black metal. She could only stare after it wide-eyed, too paralyzed to scream as it bumped off the pavement, then dove over a concrete abutment toward oncoming traffic below. At the bottom, its nose smashed against the guard rail, rear wheels blurring uselessly as a puff of steam belched from under the hood. Creena relaxed, thinking they were safe. But the expected quiet wasn't there, a harsh scraping sound wailing insistently from the front of the car.

"What's that?" she asked.

"I think the tire's rubbing against the fender," Mrs. Jenkins replied. "We'd better get off at the next off-ramp."

Creena nodded, trying to read a green sign that stretched across the roadway, the lettering completely unfamiliar. Even though Mira III and Earth shared a common spoken language, apparently the written form had gone in different directions.

"What does that sign say?" Creena asked.

"Next Exit, One Mile."

"How far is a mile?"

"Quite a ways, if you have to walk," Mrs. Jenkins replied grimly.

The car jiggled and jerked, then started to vibrate violently, Mrs. Jenkins' arms shaking as she tried to hang onto the wheel.

"What's wrong?" Creena cried, alarmed even more when Mrs. Jenkins pulled off the road and stopped.

"We have a flat tire," she moaned, resting her head on her hands.

"A what?"

"A flat tire. When the air goes out."

"Well, come on!" Creena said. "Let's fix it!"

They spilled out of their respective doors and then stood staring at the tire beneath the passenger side fender. It was flat, all right, at least on the bottom, its casing ripped and dangling like a jendak's tail. Mrs. Jenkins grabbed the keys from the ignition to open the cargo bay in the back. Another tire was inside, yet a frown creased her forehead as she picked through an assortment of tools scattered throughout the compartment.

"No jack," she said, half to herself. "Wonderful."

Creena stared at her, waiting for an explanation, until she explained they couldn't change the tire without one.

"Maybe we can fix it where it is," Creena suggested.

Mrs. Jenkins shook her head. "You don't understand. How could we get it to hold air again? Look at it!"

In reply Creena got out her pocket laser. It wasn't fully charged anymore, but would probably work on soft material, especially with the sun recharging it. She crouched down by the tire and swept its sensor past the casing. It didn't recognize the material, but suggested medium power. Creena set it to the correct level, then pushed the severed flaps together, fusing it the best she could while Mrs. Jenkins watched with wide, questioning eyes. After several moments, the women threw a cautious glance down the road as several cars whizzed by.

"Uh, oh," she said.

Creena turned around, spotting the man just visible in the distance, alternately running and walking along the side of the road. Mind flaring with renewed panic, she struggled to mend the tire as quickly as possible. When the last of the rip had melted into place, Mrs. Jenkins attached a can to a small valve at the top and air rushed inside. Gradually the flat part disappeared and the tire looked almost the same as the others. But rather than being pleased Mrs. Jenkins groaned.

"Look!" she said, pointing to a sharp edge on the mangled fender invading the wheel-well. "It's going to go flat again as soon as we move."

Creena yanked out her laser again, hoping simply to cut off the offensive metal, but the laser was spent and merely hummed. She pushed the dial to maximum and tried again, but all it did was complain louder. Finally, the fender melted ever so slightly, but by then the laser's last joule of energy had been exhausted and it went completely dead. Whether the Universe would help her draw energy from the Earth to recharge it this time seemed doubtful.

Another frantic glance down the road; the cannibal was so close she could see sweat dripping down his livid face.

"Either we can lock ourselves in the car and hope someone stops to help, or run," Mrs. Jenkins said grimly.

Creena looked from their pursuer closing in faster than she cared to consider, to the flustered woman at her side. There was no way Mrs. Jenkins would last long running. But before either of them could move, a sudden blast of energy shattered the car's rear window, sending glass fragments soaring through the morning air in a lethal wave of sparkling terror.

Escape

Mrs. Jenkins gasped, covering her head with her arms. *"What was that?"*

"Some kind of lasomag," Creena replied.

"A *what?*"

Creena ignored her, aware only that they didn't have a chance. Even if he wanted her alive, he could switch the weapon to stun and ground them momentarily. Convinced it was over, she jumped in startled alarm when a tan car skidded to a stop in front of them, passenger door flung open.

"Edith! Get in!" the driver yelled.

Mrs. Jenkins grabbed her by the hand and dragged her toward the vehicle, where the pair dove inside, Creena barely pulling the door closed as the car tore off in a spray of dust and pebbles, leaving the man behind. Apparently consigned to at least temporary defeat, the hand with the lasomag dropped to his side, even as he glared after them in cold, frustrated wrath.

"Oh, Milt," Mrs. Jenkins sobbed, burying her head in her husband's shoulder. "Thank God! How did you know? When you weren't at the base, I didn't know what to do!"

He put his arm around his wife, looking at Creena with perplexity seldom seen in uniform. "Someone somewhere apparently cares quite a bit about our little space alien, here."

"Who?" Mrs. Jenkins asked, sobs instantly transformed to curiosity.

The colonel swallowed hard, as if hesitant to explain. "This silent voice," he said finally, "It kept repeating *Creena's in trouble, Creena's in trouble*, and I, well, saw this stretch of highway in my mind. It was so intense I couldn't ignore it. I actually walked out of my own briefing to check it out! I'm not sure whether I'm relieved or not that it wasn't my imagination." He sighed in disbelief as he glanced at Creena, then back to the road, shaking his head. "What happened to Carlson, anyway?"

"That rotten snurk knocked him out," Creena answered.

"Great. We'd better go back and see if he's still alive," Jenkins said.

Creena gulped, wide-eyed at the thought he might be dead. Snurk or not, he'd been trying to protect her.

"What happened to the guards I posted there?" he went on.

"I don't know," Mrs. Jenkins replied. "I didn't notice them, at all."

When they pulled up in front of the house a short time later, Creena sighed with relief to see Carlson sitting on the front steps, holding his head. He struggled to his feet as they exited the car, salute a disoriented wince.

"Are you all right?" the colonel asked. Carlson nodded. "Do you realize how close these two came to being killed?" he continued, louder.

Carlson stood at awkward attention, eyes straight ahead. "Yes, sir. I mean, no sir. I, uh, I'm sorry, sir."

"Sorry doesn't do it, Carlson. What happened?" Jenkins demanded.

"I don't know, sir."

"Indeed. Maybe we ought to send you back to basic, lieutenant, so you can learn how to pull off a simple job of guard duty. Do you think that's a good idea, lieutenant?" Jenkins glowered at his subordinate, awaiting a reply. "Well?"

"No, sir!"

Jenkins sighed impatiently. "We're going back to the base, Carlson, as soon as I find out what happened to those guards. I want you back there, too. We've got enough blasted paperwork to do to fill a C-130."

"Yes, sir."

When they entered the house, Jenkins gave no apparent notice to the open pantry with cans, cookware and broken pieces of wallboard strewn across the floor, instead heading directly down the hall to his den, where he had a direct line to the base. While Creena and Mrs. Jenkins surveyed the damage in the kitchen, renewed anxiety coursed through her as she realized how close she'd come to being captured. Before they could check upstairs, the colonel was ready to go and clearly impatient to be on their way. He tromped across the debris without so much as a glance and was in the car with the engine running by the time they joined him, car in reverse as soon as she shut the door.

On their way, Creena explained what had happened, including the details of her escape. Colonel Jenkins' expression assumed the same look of bewilderment as when she'd first met him at the base. Only now, his questions took a different track, not of suspicion, but concern.

"Do you have any idea who this person might be?" he asked.

Creena shook her head, wide-eyed. "No!" she replied.

"So it's not your father or someone he sent here to get you back?"

Her jaw dropped, horrified. "No! Absolutely not! Even if 'Merapa could get here, why would he act like that and try to hurt me? Or send someone like that? I'm supposed to get *him* help, anyway. I don't know what's going on there on Cyraria, but he's in some sort of trouble. And whoever that cannibal is, he gave me a really bad feeling, even before he hurt Lieutenant Carlson and burst into your house. I know a bad feeling when I have one, and that was the worst one I ever had!"

"Okay, that's what I thought, but I needed to be sure. I get the feeling that maybe whatever trouble your father's in may be behind this. It's apparent that whoever this guy is, he has access to advanced weapons, so he's not the typical, garden variety kidnapper. While that's always a concern, this guy is obviously more than that. And dealing with him is a significant challenge, given the superiority of his weapons."

Jenkins sighed and shook his head pensively. "What are we going to do with you, little lady?" he said, face etched with deep concern. "It's a cinch you can't stay here. Your pursuer, whoever he is, will undoubtedly be back. And worse yet, he has an uncanny ability to find you, when no one should even know where you are, yourself included."

"That's why I wanted you to come home," Mrs. Jenkins cut in. "I've got it all figured out. She can stay with my sister in Cache Valley. It's remote enough, plus no one should even know she's my relative. They're even licensed foster parents, so there shouldn't be any problem with Social Services, either. It couldn't be more perfect."

Creena scowled to herself. *Yeah, it could. Give back my ship and let me find a way home. That would be perfect.* Nonetheless, she couldn't help but notice how things had turned around so dramatically, from seeing her as a threat one moment to someone to be protected the next. If nothing else, she felt less alone, that maybe she'd be able to find help on this backward planet after all.

"Sounds good to me, Edith," the colonel agreed. "You're one step ahead of me, as usual. Except with the latest security problems, Social Services can't know. Let's check in at the base, then I'll make arrangements to get us to Janet and Tom's. This has to be done right, so the location remains classified. Are they expecting us?"

"Yes. I called them. From a pay phone."

"Good girl. And it's a great idea. No doubt Creena will be a lot safer up there. Happier, too. The Pentagon wants to send her to Cheyenne Mountain, which is in that general direction and thus a great cover. It won't be that hard to make it look as if that's where we're going."

During the long, boring wait at the base, they found out that the guards had left at the command of the mysterious man, who'd fooled them all with the fake uniform and counterfeit government vehicle. It was obvious by the colonel's serious expression he wouldn't be taken by surprise again by the sophisticated means being used to abduct her. This time, her transfer would be carefully disguised as a training exercise, heading for the location that everyone else on base thought she was going.

They waited in the colonel's office, which had an entirely different atmosphere than the night before. She and Mrs. Jenkins sat around the small conference table, eating something called a hamburger that Harrie brought from the cafeteria. It tasted good, even though everything about it was different than anything she'd ever had before. She wondered what exactly it was, yet didn't care enough to ask, mind racing with the events of the day.

She was still trying to grasp that now she was being protected. The shift in energy was a comfort of sorts, that the strength and power of the military was now directed at her safety. It reminded her of how she always felt around her father, though of course they couldn't begin to replace the emotional component. 'Merapa would probably be pleased to know his only daughter ranked such backing, even though progress toward obtaining help from Mira III was obviously undergoing significant delay. A surge of fear enveloped her as she thought of their last conversation and the urgency in 'Merapa's voice. What was going on that was so threatening that he wouldn't even let her come home? What if by the time she got help it was too late?

"Are you okay?" Mrs. Jenkins asked, breaking her thoughts.

"I think so," she replied, coming back to the present. She gave Mrs. Jenkins a weak smile, then took the last bite of her hamburger and washed it down with a fizzy drink. Rather than get her thoughts tangled up in too much speculation that made her stomach hurt, she proceeded to tell Mrs. Jenkins everything that had happened back at the house. The woman marveled at how somehow everything had worked out, even though it had been far from easy. Indeed, if Mrs. Jenkins hadn't returned when she did, there could have been a far different outcome.

"Why did you come back so soon?" she asked, wondering if Mrs. Jenkins had experienced an impression similar to her husband's.

"I forgot my credit cards," she replied. "But don't worry. I'm sure they'll have something that will fit you up there."

"Oh," she replied, not entirely sure what she meant. Having worn nothing but a color-coded uniform for years, the thought of anything else was a foreign and somewhat uncomfortable prospect.

Several hours later, the three of them left the office for a secure hangar where she as well as the others dressed in drab olive fatigues like the soldiers wore the night she'd landed. Hers were way too large, even over the top of her own, the sleeves and pant legs rolled up in bulky rings around her wrists and ankles. She and Mrs. Jenkins sat on a bench in the huge enclosure, their escape vehicle crouched before them, heavy and formidable, a conglomeration of bulges and scoops in a shade of green similar to their clothing. The cramped passenger compartment was topped by a massive impeller that drooped from its own weight.

When Colonel Jenkins joined them a short time later, he handed them each a set of bulky ear covers. "It's going to get noisy," he explained, nevertheless looking at the vehicle with obvious pride.

"What's it called?" Creena asked, nodding toward it, having never seen anything like it in her entire life. The propulsion systems on any air vehicle she'd ever seen were entirely enclosed and unrelated to generating lift through direct air movement. Rather, they used electromagnetic or gravitational energies, which were not only more powerful, but a lot quieter.

"It's a helicopter," he replied. "We call this particular one a Huey. Pretty soon, we'll have an even bigger and better one called an Apache, which will kick this one's butt." He smiled. "I can hardly wait."

"I've never seen an air or space vehicle that was so open and unprotected," she mused out loud. "It seems so, well, primitive. Or unfinished."

"These were designed for combat, so comfort wasn't as important as speed. We rather save the weight for payloads, such as weapons, ordnance, or more people."

He stepped over to it and opened one of the doors, gesturing toward a sling-like seat on the bulkhead behind where the pilot would be. "You two go ahead and get settled. I'll be with your shortly." Creena and Mrs. Jenkins took their seats and pulled on the harnesses. The seat was suspended fabric, the straps fastened to the metal frame too high to be comfortable, obviously designed for adults. Mrs. Jenkins tried without success to adjust them, leaving Creena no choice but to feel as if she were hanging in midair, her rear end barely touching the seat.

Great, she thought, hoping she wouldn't be tossed about, swinging in the breeze when they took off.

Shortly after they were settled, the crew arrived, who were momentarily occupied with Colonel Jenkins inspecting the vehicle from top to bottom before the Colonel, pilot, co-pilot and four guards in full battle gear, joined them inside. All assumed their posts, the Colonel on Creena's other side, sandwiching her between him and his wife, the pilots in front, and two guards on each side by the open doors, who readied the vehicle's weapons mounted on metal frames outside the doors.

Even though she knew they were protecting her, Creena felt a wave of fear and intimidation. These soldiers knew what they were doing and had the means to inflict lethal force, if necessary, even if the technology was less advanced. She pondered her first impression of Earth as a horribly primitive and backward planet with a glimmer of new respect. Maybe their technology was inferior, but they were certainly operating to their maximum capacity, nonetheless. These people were not nearly as stupid as she thought at first, and would undoubtedly catch up eventually. She tried not to think about the fact that if her pursuer had a lasomag, he could also have access to a means of pursuit that would be impervious to such weapons.

Her thoughts returned to the present when Colonel Jenkins showed her and Mrs. Jenkins how to secure their oxygen masks, which he said they'd need later. The engine roared to life with a deep, pulsing roar, and she quickly donned her ear protection as the hangar's two huge opposing doors gradually opened, allowing the vehicle to proceed slowly outside, tarmac hot in the midday sun. After a short warm-up, the pilot continued to check the instrument panel as he fired up the impeller amidst a tremendous, clanking roar.

Much to her surprise, the vehicle's two side doors remained open as the vehicle lifted slowly in a clatter of mechanical fury. Two vehicles like their own flanked each side with another one in the rear. Once they'd risen high enough that the buildings and aircraft below looked like toys, an F-16 escort joined them, just like the one that had forced her ship to the ground. The racket made it impossible to talk, lacking the headset the colonel and other crewmembers used to communicate.

As the pilot directed them toward the mountains, Colonel Jenkins pointed out where he'd picked them up, not an instant too soon. Mrs. Jenkins' car was gone, but she could still see skid marks, beaten down weeds, and smashed fence, beyond which the black car still listed in the ditch. She shuddered at how it would have turned out if he'd gotten to her, back at the house.

With conversing impossible, Creena's thoughts gradually merged with the noise and scenery below. The impeller's clatter changed pitch as the pilot banked to the side, turning away from the mountains and following the length of the valley. The space between homes lengthened until they nearly disappeared entirely, replaced by endless fields and neatly ordered trees. As the valley rose toward steepening hills, he turned again, circling back toward where they'd come, except now he was heading toward a large body of water in the distance. A white expanse of plain surrounded it and stretched to the horizon, its desolation similar to what she'd seen of Cyraria.

Yet, where the Jenkins lived it was lush and beautiful, giving her hope that Cyraria had similar diversity, especially with 'Merapa's training and experience in terralogy.

Their altitude began to increase steadily, the inside getting colder. Creena started to feel light-headed and dizzy, even nauseous. Colonel Jenkins was watching her and indicated for her and his wife to don their oxygen masks, as he did the same, which helped immediately. The ground remained entirely featureless. Eventually, they closed the doors and turned back toward the mountains, but at a point far from where they started. Vast peaks merged into view and the ground beneath changed from desolate white plains to massive patches of green and tan. A few dwellings dotted the landscape as well as huge complexes of odd shaped buildings. Cars were specks, people invisible.

A range of gentler mountains gradually rose beneath them, not as rugged or high as the ones by the base. The chopper turned again, following the peak's edge. How pretty and peaceful they'd appeared from her ship. In spite of their obvious climb, the ground drew closer as they crossed what had grown once more to towering peaks crested with snow. An occasional glimpse of highway broke the monotony, winding like a concrete serpent with steep, rocky zeniths on either side.

It was pretty, but frightening, the rugged beauty but another on a long list of threats. If she'd only known, only listened to her feelings or Thyron. He'd surely been right about Earthlings, yet something told her that her greatest danger wasn't from this world, but another. She wondered where he and Aggie were, if she'd ever see them again. In all the excitement the sense of abandonment had fled, but returned now, cold and empty, as she realized she was horribly and permanently alone on an alien world, whether they were trying to protect her or not.

Any sense of direction she might have had earlier was long gone, and she had no idea which way they'd come from. Undoubtedly, their circuitous path was intended to assure no one was following them. Of course, there were other means for tracking air vehicles, but hopefully whoever was after her couldn't access them.

Suddenly, the mountains diminished and a lush valley flattened out below, its elevation apparently higher because the ground was closer than before. Endless fields stretched below, filled with what looked like lofty, broad-leafed plants whose tops waved golden tassels. The rows fell away like soldiers in formation, following their airborne path. Her memory slipped back to Verdaris, the rupture of stalii playing through her mind.

They flew over a small city centered around a stone building with towering spires, a huge complex high on a hill, more towns with streets in orderly grid-like clusters arranged along the mountains' base, then fields again. The helicopter blades changed pitch as they started to descend, skimming increasing rises that wrinkled into hills before lifting into mountains again. Homes were few and far between, all surrounded by a variety of crops thriving in various shades of green.

Forward motion slowed suddenly, and the choppers dipped toward the ground, kicking up a cloud of dust along a dirt road that led to the front of a two-story home with several large buildings in the rear, function unknown. The Huey settled gently to the ground, blades still turning, as the escort continued on. Colonel Jenkins shed his mask and harness and quickly directed her and Mrs. Jenkins to do the same.

"*Go!*" he yelled, pushing her gently toward the open door where they jumped to the ground, then dashed toward the house twenty meters away, bent under the blades' thundering turbulence.

The escorts were fading from sight where they hugged the ground up ahead, the chopper they'd forsaken quickly joining them until they rose once more in unison above the mountains beyond. In spite of the ear protection, the sudden absence of noise left her ears ringing as Colonel Jenkins herded them up on the porch, then inside the front door.

"Okay, little lady," he said, managing a smile in spite of the exertion of their uphill run. "This is it—your new home."

Aftermath

Dirck's mind hadn't stopped racing since the arrest. Why were the only dreams that came true nightmares? The ballome was too quiet. Too empty. There was so much to do, and he didn't know where to start. Lost and confused, he sent a comcon message to Uncle Jen. He didn't even know what to say. Finally, he settled for *Problems – 'Merapa arrested.*

Short and far from sweet.

'Merama had surprised him. Within a few hours, there'd been no more tears. But it wasn't composure. It was a quiet, malignant despair. She hardly spoke, and said the rest with the distance in her eyes. She refused to eat, but insisted he and Deven have their usual breakfast. Again, genour was getting low.

She wanted to go to the comcenter, but had to wait several long hours until normal work shifts began. Dirck hadn't been there since he and 'Merapa arrived onworld. She insisted on seeing Zahra and he didn't want her to go alone. He and Deven had barely finished eating when she summoned the transport and directed them outside to await its arrival in the rising heat. Her shoulders drooped and expression drew tighter as she stared at the horizon where the transport had disappeared hours before. Since that moment, she'd aged considerably.

Her urgency didn't make sense. Sure, she and Zahra were friends, and he wanted to talk to Win, too, but he couldn't forget his father's admonition. Both were government employees whose livelihood depended on Governor Augustus Troy. And conversely, their befriending the Brightstars could be construed as aiding and abetting the enemy. Worst case, their friends' caring could jeopardize their own safety. Best case. . .there wasn't any. Or were they working for Troy in other ways as well?

The transport arrived in a dusty cloud. Dirck slouched down in the seat and pulled his visor over his eyes, hoping to erase the throbbing image of the raid. He couldn't. Why'd 'Merapa have to be so stubborn? Not listen to his warnings? For all the trouble they'd had so far, why couldn't he see? What was the matter with him, anyway?

When the transport shuddered to a stop in the compound, he and 'Merama each took one of Deven's hands and walked to the comcenter, Dirck thinking back to the day they'd arrived. Any news they'd receive today wouldn't be any better.

The door was secured, comcenter not yet open for the day. The single window in the hunched, composite building was tinted against zetas' harsh light, making it impossible to see inside. Zeta was high in the turbid sky, Zinni sauntering along the lowest point of its increasingly lopsided path. At long last, the public access time arrived and the door responded to his touch.

Zahra was at her post by the comcon, almost as if she was expecting them. She watched solemnly until they reached the counter, then approached slowly and stepped up on the booster rail. Her expression indicated she already knew.

"So sorry I be," she said softly with her gravely, nasal voice. "He not be one only. There be five taken, in nights last."

Emotion returned to 'Merama's face, her eyes glazed with tears.

"Is there someplace we can talk? In private?" Dirck asked, glancing around at an even mix of humans and jendaks.

Zahra nodded. "You be gone out to door front. Be there meeting you."

Back in the heat, Dirck swatted at pinflies and watched other regionists enter and leave, for what felt like a long time. Eventually, he cast his gaze across the street to a similar throng patronizing the supply depot. Already depressed, dismal thought after dismal thought trudged through his mind like a funeral cortege. The weight of responsibility had fallen like lead. As if losing 'Merapa weren't bad enough, now he'd have to take care of the family. If he didn't, his father would kill him.

If he ever came back.

And then there was Creena. He'd never forgiven himself for his part in that. His sister's disappearance had taken a hearty toll on 'Merama, compounded by the time he and 'Merapa spent chasing around the galaxy and beyond. At least they knew she was okay. For now, anyway. One family member missing at any given time was certainly enough. If there were any way that she could find help, now would certainly be the time. Then he remembered what 'Merapa had said about only sending her to Mira III for her safety, quickly dashing that hope as well.

If only he'd been more insistent about getting rid of the lasomag. He'd known, with every fiber of his being, that it meant trouble, from the first time he'd laid eyes on it, back on Verdaris. Why hadn't his father listened? Did 'Merapa still think he knew nothing, was only a kid? And now, kid or not, he had to take care of everything. Absolutely everything. And for a flicker of time, he wished they'd taken him, too.

Legal processes on Cyraria were ill-defined. Regional governors had more power than he could comprehend. It wasn't like Mira III, where things were black and white, clear and defined, organized and predictable. If only they'd never left. If only 'Merapa had complied. If only he knew what to do. If only he could talk to him, even for a few minutes. What would happen to him now? Where was he? Would there be a trial? Sentencing?

His heart caught in his throat. An execution?

Unable to face the harsh speculations, he shifted his thoughts from the unknowns to the knowns. He had to finish the heat exchanger and ensure they were prepared for High Opp's torturous heat. Since the compressor was no longer an option, 'Merapa had redesigned the system. Dirck knew he'd expanded the evaporator and condenser sections and lengthened the run of liquid ammonia. The primary change had been to enlarge the system, but the amount of fluid needed hadn't been determined.

Trial and error would be all he had without his father's engineering know-how. The design wasn't even finished — every time it came close, they couldn't find components certified to the right specifications, so he'd have to modify it some more, based on what was available. Plus, he needed more parts. Critical parts. Pressure transducers, regulators, check valves, and more relief valves, which would necessitate questionable transactions with Win, plus the ammonia itself. 'Merapa had planned on manufacturing it, but never said how. And what if it didn't work, period? His father had said repeatedly there were no guarantees. And how would he ever dig an underground safe, the usual defense against High Opp's heat, all by himself?

Maintaining the =CC= flow was essential. Would they even be allowed to keep the ballomestead, =CC=s or not, with 'Merapa arrested? What if the answer was no? The thought generated a chill down his spine in spite of Zeta blazing overhead.

He was spared further inference when Zahra joined them from around the side of the building. 'Merama ran to meet her then they stood and held each other, his mother stooped over with her head resting on Zahra's. Until then, Dirck hadn't realized the depth of their friendship and hoped with all his heart she could be trusted. The two of them were talking now, so he left them alone a while longer, then took Deven's hand and walked over beside them. He had some questions he hoped she could answer, but knew from 'Merama's improved posture alone that the most important reason for the visit had already been accomplished.

'Merama was asking about Zahra's last prediction as he walked up. "Is this what you meant by darkness in the endless days?" she asked.

"Not," the jendak replied. "That be more, planet be, much trouble. Sign to come, two, very rare. Zeta, Zinni blocked, one then other. Bondling yours, different mansion be. Much mula, path of many troubles."

"What about me? What do you see for us?" 'Merama asked anxiously.

Zahra looked from 'Merama to him and Deven, dark purple creases crinkling her massive brow. "Shravana. Troubles, but with uttara bhadra. Ahir Budhyana assist be, ruler to water and darkness. Much to come."

"Will we survive?"

"Not be to tell. Vishnu no reveal one or not."

"Can you tell us anything else? What should we do?" 'Merama asked pleadingly.

"Cannot cheat by karma. Cannot tell, must you deciding. I tell, I be to karma. No more. Wall be blank. No be more."

A heavy silence fell, Zahra obviously uncomfortable with whatever it was she saw or perhaps didn't.

"What do you know about regional law?" Dirck asked, changing the subject to more mundane concerns. "What will happen to my father? Is there some way to contact him?"

Zahra squinted up at him, her height only slightly taller than Deven's. "Be hard saying," she said. "Violation be territorial, sentence determined be by other factors. Region, conditions, all important be. Could seriousness, could let free be happening. No be knowing."

"How can we find out?" Dirck persisted. "Is there anything we should be doing?"

"Authorities may notifying be, direct or by comcon. Or silent be. They choosing."

The jendak rubbed her eyes, large ones designed for dimmer environments. "Must inside be. I watch. Will be telling what be founding." She gave 'Merama a final hug and turned to go.

"One more question," Dirck called after her. "What about the ballomestead? With 'Merapa arrested, what will happen? We should be able to keep the =CC=s coming in, but is the property still ours?"

"It be lucky being, it not be of father. When mother here first be, she ballomestead property, so land hers be. No lose."

Dirck nodded thanks and waved as Zahra scurried back around the building and disappeared. His mother's face was flushed with heat, gaze fixed on her departing friend.

"Let's go to the SD," he said gently. "I'll get you a drink from our =CC= water."

She didn't answer, just followed across the clearing and into the SD, but her chin was higher, tears gone. He gestured for her and Deven to sit on some shipping cartons inside the door and looked for Win. Crjlx-IM stepped over and scanned him with his *videra*. The multiple eyelids which controlled light input moved slightly as they adjusted on his face.

"Where's Win?" he asked.

"Not here," Crjlx-IM replied, the origin of the sound deep in his chest.

"Will he be later?"

"Not know," the Erebusite replied, then walked away to resume work in the back.

Dirck's heart pounded with apprehension. Where was he? What if he'd been taken, too? He glanced at 'Merama watching him vacantly and tried to stifle his agitation as he pressed the transport summons near the door, then ushered her and Deven back outside. The transport's arrival was mercifully swift.

"Will they ever let 'Merapa come home, Dirck?" Deven asked.

Dirck had thought of little else since seeing the commandos outside their ballome in Zinni's harsh light. He pulled his visor over his eyes to avoid Deven's searching stare and the realization that now he was responsible for the boy's well-being.

"I don't know, Deven," he said. "I don't know."

* * *

Dirck returned to the SD right before closing, using delivery of the day's =CC= water as an excuse when 'Merama asked where he was going when it was time for their modified sleepzone. Exhausted but hyper over Win's fate, he had to know, one way or the other. When he got there, he entered slowly, bumping through the door with the boxcart of bottled water, mind paralyzed with his most gruesome fears. No one was at the counter so, terror rising, he looked to the back and to his great relief saw Win, stocking bins.

"Hey, Dirck, what's happening?" he asked. "Crjlx-IM told me you were in early, looking for me." Dirck met his eyes but couldn't speak. Win glanced over his shoulder and lowered his voice. "What's wrong? Something happen last night?"

Dirck nodded, searching for words. "He's gone," he forced out, sound catching in his constricting throat. "Commandos. They took him."

"*Who?*" Win asked.

Dirck's rising emotions precluded an answer.

"Not your father!" Win gasped.

Dirck swallowed hard and nodded. His friend uttered what sounded like an alien curse, then came out from behind the workdeck, yelling over his shoulder to Crjlx-IM to lock up, that he was leaving, even though the shift wasn't over.

"C'mon," he said, steering Dirck outside. "Let's go for a ride."

Dirck was so embarrassed, he wanted to die. He was too old to cry and now Win would think he was either a wimp or an idiot. He followed him out back reluctantly, wiping angrily at the moisture leaking from his eyes. Win palmed open the canopy on his 'cruiser and pushed him inside.

"W-where were you this morning?" Dirck asked shakily, trying to be cool. "I didn't need a scare like that, you know."

Win coaxed the 'cruiser to life. "I was late to work. 'Cruiser broke down, halfway in. Blew the impeller."

Dirck nearly choked on the irony. "I blew one once, back on Mira III," he said.

"How'd you fix it?"

"I didn't. I replaced it." He didn't know whether to laugh or cry as the memory rushed back of when he'd pilfered 'Merapa's, only confessing such a short time ago.

Win eased the 'cruiser around the corner of the storage building in the rear, then took off in the same direction as before. Several kilometers of dry, red earth passed before Win broke the silence.

"How can I help?" he asked.

Dirck sighed heavily. "I don't know where to start. Everything's on me now. Everything. The heat exchanger, digging a safe, 'Merama, Deven, Creena, helping 'Merapa, you name it. I wish they'd taken me, too."

"Hey! Don't talk like that! No, you don't. Don't even think things like that!" His tone softened. "Don't look at everything at once. Take it one thing at a time, okay? Just like when you're building something. What's most important?"

"Find my father and getting him back."

"That may take a while. Be realistic. What's next?"

"The heat exchanger. I need parts. Important parts. Without them, it won't work. And you know our =CC= situation."

"Aha," Win said triumphantly. "With that I can help."

"How? You think someone's going to barter them in, like the hair clippers?"

"Hardly. There are other ways. You can trade directly, you know. There's a certain degree of risk to both parties, but it can be done. Everything's supposed to be processed through the system so they can track and tax it, but like the clippers, we have workarounds. What do you need?"

"Some 'ducers, regulators, check valves, that kind of stuff. And ammonia. We were going to make it, but he never got around to telling me how."

"Not a problem," Win said, smiling. "I may even be able to find you a compressor. I've been working on that, anyway. How soon do you want it?"

Dirck looked solemnly at his friend. "Hold it, Win. I don't want any more trouble. I've lost enough people to last a lifetime. I feel responsible for what happened to my sister, and now my father. I don't want to feel responsible if something happens to you, too."

Win pulled back on the controls and settled the 'cruiser to the ground, canyon before them bathed in dust-provoked reds and pinks as Zeta rested just above the horizon.

"No, *you* hold it. You didn't ask me to do a thing. I volunteered. And I won't get caught. I do this all the time. It's fun, gives me something to do besides stocking bins. So don't worry. Where'd you learn to worry so much, anyway?"

Dirck smiled weakly. "Probably my mother."

"Well, unlearn it, the sooner the better. Nothing will hold you back more than fretting over stuff that may never happen. Just do what you have to, one step at a time. Hear me, pal? One step at a time."

They got out and stared across Guipure Canyon where it faded in atmospheric haze at the curvature of the horizon. Even though he'd been there before, the impact of its unexpected beauty remained with the odd twists and turns of its lacey gorges. The main branch with its numerous tributaries lay before them, like a huge fossilized impression of a delicate fern. Something about it made his problems seem almost insignificant, at least manageable. No wonder Win liked it there. Coming here was a good idea.

The wind was rising, sweeping through the gorges and vast plateaus, disturbing the desiccated dirt in swirling eddies of evening change. It whistled through dry vegetation, propelling a rattle of flockweed to another location, back toward the settlement. The gusts intensified, and Dirck barely rescued his visor as it lifted from his head as it had before. Movement caught his eye and he stopped, squinting into the distance at a quivering light. It was growing larger. And closer.

"Hey," he said, grabbing Win by the arm. "What's that?"

Win responded with the same curse he'd uttered earlier. "Could be a patrol veke. It's probably past curfew."

"Curfew? Since when do we have a curfew?"

"Two days past. C'mon, let's get outa here."

Dirck hopped into the 'cruiser and pulled on the straps, hoping it had enough power to get back before getting caught. Mercifully, it started on the first try. He wanted to believe that Win's 'cruiser was no more than an anonymous bleep on the veke's scanner, but instinct told him otherwise. More likely, they'd already been identified by the transponder code required on all privately owned vehicles. They were as good as dead.

"Hold on," Win said, "I know how to lose these guys."

With that he set his mouth in a grim line and banked sharply toward the canyon.

* * *

Epsilon Territorial Prison
Cira City, Cyraria

Of the many challenges Laren expected of Cyraria, languishing in a territorial prison wasn't one. His cell held contrasts similar to everything else on the planet, at once a crude dungeon and technological marvel, with a hole in the floor for waste and door that concealed itself in the adobe-like wall so effectively it defied detection. He studied it for days on end, conclusions swaying between fact and illusion, holography and mind implants.

The worst part was the stench. It permeated everything, from the air to the walls, the rancid food, the prison greens. Its reek was foul, a homogenous mix of everything from dry, scorching heat to the worst aspects of alien diversity present in the prison population. His olfactory nerves should have long since surrendered, rendering it to no more than background noise — or smell, as the case may be — yet so far he hadn't been so lucky.

He didn't know what level of the complex he was on, but sensed it was closer to the surface that the depths. They moved him frequently, usually to a cell putrified with waste from the previous occupant. Enough to make him long for the meager comforts of their decrepit ballome.

It hadn't taken long for the anger to fade, replaced by something worse. At least rage generated energy; worry consumed it. And there was certainly enough to worry about. Not that he wondered what was going to happen. Quite the contrary. He knew. The likes of Troy were predictable. Even the timing: long enough for his caution to stall, soon enough to assure incomplete preparations for High Opps.

Images of the ballome etched his mind, indelible, like singed retinal nerves clinging to tracings of lasocular weapons fired in the blackness of space. His last remaining hope was that this time Jen would intervene. If he only knew that much, that they were safe. With that, he could handle anything. If this was his fate, so be it. But so recklessly abandoning his family was unforgivable.

Petitions to the cosmos became repetitious, somewhere between sacrilegious bore and divine insult. He cut back to periodic, short appeals for strength. Assurance. That his oft-repeated plea to watch over his family had been heard.

No answers.

Worry expanded to fill the void. Sometime later, he laughed out loud. Of course not, why would the Universe care? On safe and predictable Mira III he hadn't even thought once to ask for guidance or help. He didn't need the Benefics then and they didn't need him now. He was on his own.

And so were Sharra and the boys. Here he was, stuck in a wretched cell little more than two meters square with a plank to sleep on while his family awaited Peak Opps ill-prepared. Clearly, his spiritual life had spent too many years in silence. Now, he'd have to wait accordingly for answers. Or perhaps he'd forgotten how to listen.

The days were long and unpredictable, the artificial lighting but another vehicle of torment. Whatever circadian cycle it was set to, it certainly wasn't human. Light and dark came at seemingly random times, some long, some short, but never expected. He debated between adapting and setting his own schedule, finally settling on the latter. So far his routine consisted of meditation, exercise and worry, usually in that sequence. He'd try to generate some hope and assurance; workout to maintain what he could of his physical strength; then, exhausted, slip back into worry.

He tended to worry more about Sharra and the boys than Creena, somehow sensing she was in better hands. However, any chance that she'd get to Mira III and back again in time to bring relief was too remote to entertain. Besides, the main point had been for at least her to be safe.

He had few regrets, actually only two. One, that he'd been caught before the family's safety was assured, and two, that he hadn't told Dirck more about the Order. Then again, maybe not. Membership was undoubtedly synonymous with hardship. From distant memory, one of his father's oft-repeated sayings came to mind: *Show me a Ledorian with an easy life and I'll show you one who has no idea what the Order means.* As a child, the statement hadn't made sense. Now it did. Was it any wonder there were virtually none on Mira III?

So, knowing that, did he really want his son a part of it? Yes, he did. Overcoming hardships were what brought out what you were capable of accomplishing, albeit by force. He should have done it. He had sufficient authority to do so, but now it was too late. At least for him. Hopefully Jen would take care of it. That and everything else.

He'd always counted on his brother's help, at least for Peak Opps, arrest notwithstanding. It would take a miracle for the heat exchanger to work, even for a few weeks. The entire project had been strictly to give Dirck a hands-on experience in self-sufficiency, never a long-term fix. He probably should have told Jen, but never had, knowing their welcome was assured for any time and circumstance. Surely his brother would know to look after them now.

Yet a nagging fear persisted that perhaps counting on Jen was naive. When he and Dirck had been looking for Creena, he'd counted on it, too. There was no telling what circumstance could dictate, especially when someone of high station had your number. His amended hope was slightly more realistic—if Jen could, he would.

A lump of fear thickened in his gut as he remembered finding Deven and Sharra destitute in that hideous ballome, their only recourse the Esheronian Contingency Law through which their bonding would have been dissolved as they joined Jen's family. He'd come so close to losing them both. Since leaving Mira III, he'd tried to be true to his beliefs, the strongest of which was looking out for his family. In retrospect, every act reeked of sheer foolishness. Instead of preserving them, they'd most likely perish. Maybe already had. What if it came to that again? He closed his eyes and sighed with resignation, his only petition at this point for their survival.

His own was another matter. It had been easy to refuse Troy's offer before, based on integrity alone. Now it was more complex. As a member of the Order, it was no longer choice, but obligation to refuse. No matter the consequences. The Order and the INTEGRATOR were not on the same side. Once Troy understood his initial refusal stood firm, irrefutable and unconditional, he was as good as dead. A death that wouldn't be quick or painless, HIO convention or not.

He sighed, wincing as the odor's amplitude rose. His belief in life after death helped. The war prisoner training he'd received in the Space Force didn't. Knowing what to expect was not conducive to optimism. He suspected the Cosmos wanted him to live, yet knew in short order he'd want to die. The misery he'd seen so far was nothing. He knew it was coming, only a matter of when.

And degree.

Serendipity

Win had no sooner headed for the canyon, when what had been a distant flickering light became a disk-shaped craft, ten meters off their tail. It was compact, but powerful, blue and amber lights tracing the perimeter in an illusion of green, a uniformed pilot and copilot visible inside the encasement.

Vekes were the height of civilian technology; going up against one with an aging 'cruiser was insane. The 'cruiser plunged downward, Dirck's heart and stomach already far below.

They were dead. There was no doubt. None whatsoever. Absolutely dead.

The sordid thoughts matured, then exploded in his face for the selfish folly they were. He thought of 'Merama, what it would do to her, and was consumed by remorse. All his moaning, wishing they'd taken him, too, was all but reality. As requested, he was about to die. His death would be quick and painless, hers slow and excruciating, the demise of a broken heart. She and Deven were both doomed. What if 'Merapa found out? The thought of his father being hopelessly disappointed in him hurt the worst, and he silently cursed his foolishness, anger, shame and fear battling for control.

The 'cruiser leveled out, then dove again, jerking his thoughts back to the present. What was Win thinking, anyway? Vekes, the name derived from Vacuum Certified Vehicle, or VCV, were equally maneuverable in atmosphere or out.

"You don't actually think you can out-run that thing, do you?" he asked, teeth clenched as g-forces flattened him against the seat.

"Of course not," Win said. "But I can outsmart him."

"Yeah, right." Dirck folded his arms with an exasperated sigh. What kind of an idiot was he, anyway?

"I can. Really. I know this canyon." Win's eyes were fixed ahead with laser-like intensity. "But it wouldn't hurt if you'd quit worrying and generate some positive energy."

Dirck found himself relaxing, whether from Win's overblown confidence or acceptance of their fate, he didn't know. "How?"

"Pray."

Dirck frowned. Funny he should mention that. First of all, Win didn't seem like the praying type. And secondly, he'd thought about it a lot himself lately, about whether or not the Benefics could possibly be in charge of the universe. The concept was barely tolerated on Mira III, only by a few fringe groups, but his father had told him, not that long ago, of its predominance on Esheron. On worlds out of control, it was the only stability they had.

Pray? Why not? It would take the Benefics to untangle this.

The 'cruiser plunged into another steep descent. Pink and brown sandstone raced by an arm's length away, walls darkened by shadow and deepening hue. When it leveled out, Dirck checked the rear—the veke was close enough to be in tow.

Win gave it full power and pulled up the nose. Sandstone flashed a kaleidoscope of changing color. The plateau again, ablaze in Zeta's low-cast light. Skimming scrub vegetation, random rocks, an occasional atsna, a spickle tree. Zinni spun wildly above them as Win found another gorge and initiated another dive. This one had tributaries, branching off at every angle and all directions.

He jerked the 'cruiser around to follow one, took a sudden turn, and plunged into another breathless descent.

How long the 'cruiser could take such abuse he hardly dared guess. Designed as generic transportation, the structure wasn't built for maneuvers like that. It was starting to rattle, yet power was holding, the impeller still strong and responsive.

For now.

Win left the gorge with an erratic climb, slipped over the wall between fractals, then down through another. Dirck had no idea where they were or where they were heading. All he knew was that he'd lose either way, either as a smear on a canyon wall or in a territorial prison. Still, the veke held their tail, as if it were attached with synthetic adhesive. The receiver crackled, a voice demanded surrender. Great. They'd identified Win. The next statement threatened force, whatever necessary for compliance.

Dirck gasped. "Are they going to blast us?"

"They might," Win replied, eyes fixed ahead. His mouth tightened. "I guess it's time to quit playing with these guys."

Playing?

Dirck knew he was dead. There were no doubts. He wouldn't have to worry about Peak Opps, the heat exchanger, his father's fate, 'Merama, Deven, Creena or anything else, because in a few minutes he'd be dead, and that would be that. He closed his eyes firmly and prayed with all his might.

Benefics, if you're there and if you care, now would be a really good time to help out. I know I'm not worth much trouble, but it'll kill my mother if anything happens to me. She's had enough. Please. Help us get through this alive.

When Dirck opened his eyes, the 'cruiser was zigzagging down a wide channel. The next thing he saw was a lasoclear blast. It missed, leaving a gaping hole in the canyon wall. The next one came closer. Win's intensity evolved to dead seriousness. Not scared, just intent, as if focusing his entire being. Dirck tightened his grip and prayed some more, sweat droplets falling from his temples as he wondered what it felt like to die.

The trench narrowed suddenly, cut to the right, the left. *And ended!*

The 'cruiser leapt upward, over the lip between stony fronds, straight for a massive rock formation. Dirck screamed and covered his eyes, his terrorized body relinquishing all control. Win veered sharply to the left, so close Dirck could hear impeller spray peppering its surface as he braced for impact that never came. The veke was less fortunate, its dodging attempt vain. It tumbled with a faulty braking maneuver, entered a pitch-axis spin, then slammed into the rock in a shower of sparks, encasement taking the brunt of the collision. It rebounded, bounced, flipped, then thumped back toward the canyon's edge, coming to rest upside down a few meters from the gaping gorge, skid trail smoking amid orange dust in Zeta's lengthening rays.

Win decelerated and banked toward it, then set down about twenty meters away and waited. Dust and steam billowed from it, caught and redirected by the stiff canyon breeze. Zinni hovered above the horizon behind them, washing the ground in purple shadows.

"Think. . . they're. . . dead?" Dirck asked in panic-driven gasps.

"Hmmph. Can't imagine they're not." He looked at Dirck and wrinkled his nose. "Oh, no," he said. "You didn't."

Dirck smiled sheepishly. "Sorry, man. I was really scared."

"Apparently." Win shook his head then grinned, blue eyes victorious. "I told you I could outsmart them. Exactly as planned."

Dirck's jaw dropped, words smashing his perceptions as immovable stone had the veke.

"What. . .are you. . .talking about? You mean. . . that wasn't. . .luck?"

"I make my own luck." Win opened the underseat stowage and pulled out several items, including two pairs of heavy, well-worn work gloves and two breath masks, handing one of each to Dirck, along with a box of wipes. "Here, get cleaned up, then let's see what we've got. Hurry!"

Dirck climbed in back and took care of business, then donned the gloves gingerly, wondering at their need and where they may have been.

Win smiled, reading his look. "You don't want to know," he said. "Since you're obviously new to this, just do what I say. Crash scenes are dangerous. Composites produce nasty stuff when they burn. Especially boron. Bad for the lungs. Real bad. Looks like magnetic tape. Flutters in the wind like dead leaves. With no fire, we're probably okay. But then, in this case, there's gonna be biohazards—blood and body fluids aren't much better. So stay back. We should be fully suited, but by the time we did that, our window of opportunity would close. So, c'mon. Let's get on with it."

With that, Win shoved open the canopy, heat hitting like a wall as they crept toward the lifeless craft, Dirck following cautiously a few paces behind. Damage was less than expected. The passenger encasement was gone, shattered on impact, but the composite structure had taken the impact well. There was one large deformation from the initial impact and numerous fractures, but that was it.

One occupant had been thrown from the wreckage, body a misshapen lump among a grouping of phynques, shadows lengthened by Zeta's lowering rays. The other was still inside, evidenced by a lifeless arm visible between the overturned veke and the ground.

Dirck froze, startled by the gut-wrenching smell of death, organic and electronic. Mere minutes before, they'd been alive. The bodies weren't even cold yet. When someone died on Mira III, it was usually expected, allowing the body to be whisked off and disposed of by authorities while relatives paused for a moment of remembrance, then got on with their ordered lives. Death was nearly invisible, yet the unknowns of what it really meant had always given him the creeps. He could barely think about it without hyperventilating, and now two corpses were literally within reach.

His jaw clamped hard against nausea, sweat covering his face faster than it could evaporate while his hands fumbled to get the mask over his face before pulling on the gloves. He looked away and took several shallow breaths, the medicinal smell of the mask not much better that what it professed to hide. He knew he had to do something to fight the wall of darkness quickly encroaching on his brain or he'd pass out and again look like an idiot, besides being of no help at all. Taking a few slow, deep breaths he gradually coaxed his racing thoughts back to coherence via denial, until a dull, empty calm took over, directing his mind toward the next logical action.

"Hey!" Win hollered, "Get the tool box over here!"

Their eyes met and locked, minds moving in devious sync. Dirck ran back to the 'cruiser, grateful for the distraction, breathless from the heat as he detached it from the back panel, control returning by the time he joined Win.

Being upside down was perfect to extricate the veke's guts. Win demagnetized and then pried off the power chamber faring and tossed it aside. Then he started to laugh. And dance. And slap Dirck on the back. And dance some more. He was laughing so hard he was crying.

"Hey," Dirck said, the entertainment value of his friend's behavior rapidly depreciating. "Don't you think we ought to do what we have to and get out of here, before they send another veke?"

Win dropped down on a rock, still howling with laughter, and wiped his eyes with his arm. "Yeah. You're right." He cackled some more, then, "Yeah. Okay. C'mon. Let's get to work."

Win called for tools like a surgeon, removing component after component, finally ditching the bulky gloves. The extent of their bounty was beyond anything Dirck could have ever imagined. Storage batteries, power units, even most of the zeta cell array tiling the brim would be usable. Their only limitation was what would fit in the 'cruiser.

"Too bad it blew the cryo line," Win commented. "But you'll be happy to know what's attached to it looks okay."

Dense shades of purple and red smudged the horizon's circumference as Zeta reclined to its lowest point and Zinni culminated by the time Win finally hefted out a bulky, tank-shaped assembly and handed it to Dirck. It was some kind of pressure vessel of a compact size that defied its weight. Dirck took it, groaning with effort, and edged toward the 'cruiser.

"What. . .is. . .it?" he panted, grabbing harder as its slippery surface slid against the gloves.

Win pushed his hair out of his face, tilted back his head and howled with a new cycle of hilarity. "Y-you mean you d-don't know? You *really* d-don't know?"

"No," Dirck said, scowling defensively. "Should I?"

"Yes! Yes, you should!"

"Well, I don't," Dirck retorted, annoyance rising as he set it in the back of the 'cruiser.

Win shook his head, bringing himself to the edge of control. "I'm sorry," he said, battling a grin. "I didn't mean to hassle you like that. I, uh, couldn't help myself."

He put his de-mag spanner on the tool box and sauntered over to the 'cruiser, where he rested his hand on Dirck's shoulder and spoke directly in his ear.

"It's. A. Compressor," he whispered. "A *com-press-or!*"

The words fell on Dirck's consciousness like a Cyrarian PV.

For the second time within minutes, his jaw dropped, then he smiled in spite of himself. "I thought you said you didn't believe in luck," he said dryly.

"*Luck?* What luck? You think that was luck?" Win laughed again, but this time it was devoid of humor. "The only luck was you coming along at the right time. You think I don't know this place well enough to know when those vekes are on patrol? No, no, pal. My plan worked flawlessly, that's all. Luck? Nah. No such thing."

Dirck was speechless. "You've done this before?"

"Not exactly. But when I have a requisition from a valued customer, I fill it. You asked for a compressor. But you didn't have any =CC=s. So. Order filled."

"We could've been killed, too, you know. Or caught."

"Yeah. But we weren't. That's what counts. There's a risk to anything worth doing. You got your compressor. At worst, I'll be on the wanted list for a while, but I can take care of that. Meanwhile, let's finish up, shove that thing over the edge and get outta here."

Dirck could only stare, again speechless. "Thanks," he finally said. "For more than the compressor. You helped more than you know."

"Not a problem," Win replied. "What are friends for?"

After that, Win removed the transponder and lidar systems for "personal" use. When everything usable was tucked away, Dirck attached a tow strap to part of the veke's exposed frame so Win could drag it to the edge, then give it a final shove with the 'cruiser's heavily grated nose. It tipped over slowly, the patroller's body swinging limply in its straps as the eviscerated vehicle bumped and crashed against the canyon walls, echoes eventually still.

Win got out of the 'cruiser and replaced his work gloves with a rubber pair, prelude to the worst yet to come — dragging the other patroller's body to the ledge to do the same. Renewed guilt and horror tugged at his throat, faintness smothered solely by his own will to survive. After giving the body a final shove, Win demonstrated how to remove the gloves so they were inside out and likewise tossed them over the side.

"Remember one thing, okay?" he said. Any and all humor had fled, his eyes hard. "Remember we're in a state of war. It may be undeclared, it may be covert, but it's war. Them against us. If you doubt that, just remember what they did to your father. They didn't even have the decency to come when you were awake. This is war, pal. *War.* And we just won our first battle."

"I know," Dirck replied. "But it still doesn't seem right."

"It's not. But freedom of choice is a universal right. When someone or something tries to take it away, we're justified to fight back. I don't know what you prayed for back there, pal, but I assume it was answered. If what we did was wrong, I doubt we would have gotten that little bit of help we needed."

He met Win's stark-blue gaze and held it. Something about it reminded him of his father's explanation of the Ledorian Order and that he'd been charged to fight the INTEGRATOR. And thus they had done. While Win knew nothing of his father's position, nonetheless he was on the same track.

With that, his guilt evaporated, never to be had again, at least not as far as their true cause was concerned. This was undoubtedly in that range of "higher law" 'Merapa had also mentioned. It was all starting to make sense. He smiled slowly and offered the Miran grip. His friend returned it firmly, the gesture's meaning, "all is well in unity," providing appropriate closure to the deed.

Back at the 'cruiser, Win opened the side panel and located the transponder. He pulled the wires, removed the transmitter and put it in his pocket. Disconnecting it was illegal, the devices usually contained in a heavy, black box that couldn't be accessed. Obviously, Win was no stranger to evading the authorities.

"I should have done this before," Win said, "but I wasn't planning this operation for a few days. It needs to disappear off their scanners until we get any record of tonight erased. Then I'll hook it back up." He gestured to get in. "Let's get out of here and get you home before your mother worries herself to death."

Zinni was dropping toward the horizon and Zeta stirring when the 'cruiser finally settled behind the ballome.

"I want you to come in and formally meet my mother and brother," Dirck said. "I'm going to level with her about what happened, and I want you to back me up. You're also welcome to stay. Under the circumstances, you probably shouldn't go home."

Win studied him solemnly, eyes steady in the console's dim light. "Thanks," he said. "I'll think about it. And I'll be honored to meet your family."

They exited the 'cruiser just as 'Merama came out the back door, arms folded, just like a mother. "In your father's name, Dirck, where have you been?" she demanded, invoking her right to speak as head of the family. "You take off to make a simple water run and don't come back for hours. If your father were here. . ." The sentence hung, unfinished.

"I'm sorry, 'Merama," Dirck said. "I know. I can explain. By the way, this is Win."

"Pleased to meet you, ma'am," he said, offering a hand that she took with obvious reserve.

"What's that awful smell?" she asked.

"We need to talk," Dirck went on, ignoring her question as he followed her inside. "You need to know everything that's going on. Unless you don't want to. Your choice. Tell me, okay?"

She stopped by the sink arms folded, green eyes weary and rimmed with red, but unwavering as they locked on his. "I've been frightened since leaving Mira III. But hiding from it doesn't make trouble or danger go away. Your father tried to protect me, Dirck, he really did, but it only left me unprepared. That made it worse. A lot worse. Please, Dirck. Don't do that to me. No matter what, I don't want any more secrets or surprises. Okay? I need to know what's going on, so I don't get caught off-guard like that again."

He noted the trust resident in her eyes, swore to himself he'd never betray it. It didn't take a genius to know that, no matter how justified morally, his actions during the preceding few hours made him a principal in the destruction and theft of Epsilon property. And incriminating evidence was no farther away than the rear door, in a 'cruiser with an illegally modified transponder.

"We'll tell you everything, I promise," he said. "But right now we have some things we need to do. Trust me, 'Merama."

He could tell she wanted to protest, but didn't, and left to check on Deven. Taking advantage of her absence, he quickly stepped to the comcon and called up the offender list. It was long. The last entry was Win Sendori, wanted for questioning by the Regional Patrol.

"You're on here," Dirck said grimly.

"Already?"

"Yeah. But only for questioning."

"We've gotta get the 'cruiser out of here. Fast. Transponder or not, the S3's have motion and infrared detectors. 'Cruisers have their own signature, and there aren't that many."

S3's were components of the Satellite Surveillance System. Before Zinni had stationed in its ascending spiral to High Opps, Dirck had watched them in the evening, multiple points of reflected light. Infrared images actually improved when both suns were low and temperature variations steepened, so even darkness wouldn't cloak their actions.

"Is there anything we can use to disguise it?" Win asked.

"P-crawler ought to work," Dirck stated. "There's some outside, in the bin. C'mon. Let's go."

The Bensons

At first, Creena balked with the realization that the room before her held a herd of people. Besides the two expected adults, there was a bunch of kids, and every single one was a blond, shaggy-haired boy.

Tortured memories of her life with Dirck, complete with his role in her current situation, closed in like a bad dream and her heart sank. After the events of the last day, she never imagined things could go from bad to worse, but so it appeared. Yet, something inside chided her that the past did not determine the future. There was more before her than mortal eyes could see.

One boy, about Deven's age, edged forward and stared at her with wide, blue eyes.

"Gee, Mom," he said. "It's only a *girl*!"

Mrs. Jenkins turned and smiled at her again. "Ready?" she asked, then at Creena's somewhat reluctant nod, guided her forward with a gentle arm to make the appropriate introductions. "This is my sister, Janet Benson, and her husband, Tom," she started.

The woman's brown hair was shoulder length and curved gracefully around her face. She was taller than Mrs. Jenkins, but Creena could see the resemblance between them, especially around the eyes. The woman held the youngest child on her hip, who buried his head in her shoulder shyly when she prodded him to say hello.

Creena swallowed hard and tried to smile, but the kindness in Mrs. Benson's eyes reminded her too much of her mother. Mr. Benson was only a little taller than his wife, but had broad shoulders and a bronzed face that almost matched his hair. He reached down and took her hand in a firm, friendly grip.

"Welcome to our family, Creena," he said.

A bolt of familiarity shot through her, an odd feeling, as if in some weird way or twist of fate she knew these people. It was as if they'd met before. Impossible, of course; yet, for an unexplainable instant, how it felt.

The sound of choppers clattered in the distance and everybody froze. The next thing she knew, she found herself in Mrs. Jenkins arms hugging her goodbye, the colonel affectionately rumpling her hair.

"Take care," Mrs. Jenkins said softly, then kissed her on the head. She held her at arm's length a moment, smiled, eyes glazed with tears, then hurriedly followed her husband out the door.

The group crowded onto the porch to watch as the two escorts surged forward, the center chopper dropping to the ground long enough for the Jenkins' to climb onboard before resuming its position. Once all three Hueys were airborne, they banked in unison back toward their original heading to maintain the façade that they were taking her to the military outpost at Cheyenne Mountain.

Creena bit her lip as if it could stop the unexpected emptiness filling her heart. Whether or not she could trust Earthlings had been questionable from the start. Colonel and Mrs. Jenkins had restored some hope. She'd only known them a few days, too short a time to have grown so attached. But she had, and now they, too were gone. Then, that silent voice chided her again, and something told her not to fear.

By the time the choppers' din faded to silence, rational thoughts intruded again. Had she done the right thing, coming here instead of availing herself of the safety and security of that other base? The Jenkins had allowed her that choice. Neither matched her heart or mitigated her frustration at being stuck here when she had a mission to accomplish. As frightening as the cannibal was, however, being a virtual prisoner deep within a mountain hadn't felt right. It was more that she rejected the base, rather than deliberately selected the Bensons'.

The choice had a different flavor, now that she was here. There was a certain "meant to be" quality, though she had no idea why. It was as if she'd stepped into a different world, dreamlike yet real.

Mrs. Benson resumed the introductions where Mrs. Jenkins left off, interrupting her ponderings.

"Creena, this is the rest of our family," she said, nodding toward the first in the line-up of boys. "This is Allen, our oldest, at least here at home." Much to Creena's dismay, he looked about the same age as Dirck. He had that same bored, uncomfortable expression that her brother always wore when compelled to do something he didn't like. Loneliness struck again, its force doubled by how much she wished it was her family there instead. Then, oddly enough, she met the boy's stare and that feeling came again, that this *was* her family.

"Then David, who's fourteen. . ."

David looked an awful lot like his older brother and almost as bored. The one who'd accused her of being "only a girl" was Jimmy, who was ten, and the toddler in Mrs. Benson's arms was Billy. And then, they all stood there and stared, like a bunch of rejects from a 'troid factory.

"Are you part Indian?" David asked. "You look kinda like a Navajo kid I know at school."

Creena frowned. "I don't think so." At this point she didn't quite know who or what she was, the eerie sense of familiarity fogging her brain.

"Of course not, dummy," Allen said. "She's from another planet!"

"How was I supposed to know?" David said.

Allen rolled his eyes. "'Cause Mom and Dad told us, before she even got here! Don't you ever listen?"

"Whatever," David grumbled. "From what she's wearing, she looks like some kind of commando."

"Stare hard, retard!"

Creena turned in the direction of a youthful, female voice. A freckle-faced girl, a year or so younger than herself, was coming down the stairs, giving the boys a look punctuated with a dramatic eyeroll. One of the boys murmured an appropriate retort, then they all laughed and shuffled away in several directions. The girl came over to Creena with a winning grin.

"Don't mind them," she said. "Brothers can be such a pain. And boy, am I glad you're a girl! If there's anything I don't need around here, it's another brother!" She introduced herself as Tammy Benson, twelve years old, and grabbed Creena's hand in greeting with a grip that rivaled her father's. Again, the contact tingled, heart burning with some hidden awareness.

"Come on," she said. "Let's find you something else to wear and then you can help me do chores." She led her back upstairs, stopping at a closet in the hall to rummage through a few boxes before pulling out a pair of shorts and shirt, similar to her own.

"Here," she said, handing them to her. "These cutoffs oughta fit. They were David's, but he's outgrown them and won't care. The one's I have on were his, too, so don't worry about them being boys'. I like 'em better, anyway. They don't wear out as fast."

With that, she directed her to the sanicube and waited outside while Creena got out of the fatigues as well as her Code Orange uniform underneath, which had become uncomfortably hot once the chopper had descended to the ground. The clothes fit reasonably well and it only took her a moment to figure out the zipper on the shorts.

"That's better," Tammy said, smiling, when she finally came out and showed her where she could leave her other clothes in one of the rooms off the hall. Then she led her back down the stairs, through the kitchen and out the back, screen door rebounding behind them.

The girl broke into a run across lush, sheared grass in long, bare-legged strides, reddish blond ponytail trailing behind with Creena in close pursuit.

"Where are we going?" Creena called after her.

"To feed the calves," she called back over her shoulder.

"The *what*?" Creena asked, head spinning with the dizzying combination of high altitude and confusion.

"The calves. We need to feed them with a bottle. It's one of my chores."

Aha, she thought. *Chores must be like zones.* "What's a calve?"

"A calf. A baby cow."

Creena couldn't bring herself to ask what was probably another stupid question, so simply followed Tammy around the outside of the house, then toward a large shed, figuring she'd find out soon enough. She paused by the doorway to catch her breath while Tammy kicked the door open and disappeared inside. The dust-laden light triggered memories of her first encounter with Aggie, a thought that tugged at her heart, again feeling lost, yet somehow found, on another strange world.

Gradually, her thoughts slipped back to Tammy, who had scooped some coarse, white powder from a large sack into a bucket, then filled it with water from a tall faucet. After making sure it was all dissolved, she poured the creamy liquid into six, gigantic, bottles with a nipple on top. She set each one carefully in a small wagon, then pulled it to another wooden building in the rear. The inside reeked with a pungent, unfamiliar odor. Creena wrinkled her nose, wondering what it could be.

Odd rustling sounds came from several small, fenced-in compartments on either side of the walkway. She crept up behind Tammy and peeked inside. A pair of huge brown eyes stared back from one of the strangest animals she'd ever seen. It didn't look threatening, only big, but Tammy didn't show any fear at all as it poked its black and white head out between two slats, trying to lick her fingers with a massive tongue. Others competed for attention with a sound that reminded her of Dirck studying relativity theory.

"Here," Tammy said, handing her a bottle. "Give this to the one at the end."

Creena took it gingerly, then watched Tammy from the corner of her eye to see what to do. The girl held it out and the calf latched on eagerly, guzzling down the milk in a few hearty gulps. It snorted with pleasure and shook its head, splattering stray drops across the straw-littered floor. Still not entirely sure, Creena held hers out hesitantly, looking into its dark, trusting eyes. It jerked on the nipple, nearly pulling it from her hand. She squealed with surprise, then laughed as Tammy joined her, babbling on about how old each one was, especially the one that was her very own to raise.

There were six small ones to bottle feed, then several others that were quite a bit larger. Tammy showed her how to give them a few chunks of this scratchy green stuff she called alfalfa, then led her back to the house.

"I never saw anything like that before," Creena said. "What are they called again?"

"Calves," Tammy said. "You don't have them where you're from?" Creena shook her head. "What do you have instead?"

"We don't."

"Do you have other animals?"

"No."

"So you don't have meat?"

"A little. It's brought in from other planets and costs a lot."

"Wow. That's weird. We've got enough of them around here."

When they returned to the house, Tammy took her back upstairs, stopped by the bathroom so they could wash their hands, then entered the sleeproom where she'd left her clothes. This time she noticed that it was obviously a boy's. Dark plaid hung from the windows and covered the beds, walls paneled with wood similar to the outside buildings. Cold fingers of doom seized her again as she eyed two beds, like the one at the Jenkins'. Compared to the security of a cyll, Earth beds were scary. And the thought of a boy in the same room didn't help, either.

"This is my brother, Terry's room," Tammy said. "But, he's up in Idaho, away at college, so you can use it."

Trying not to show her relief, Creena walked over to the dresser and picked up a postcard with a picture of a village. It had narrow streets crowded with odd cows which had strange horns and long, floppy ears, nothing like the Bensons'. The animals were drawing primitive carts amongst hoards of people that vaguely resembled Erebusites, but with thick black hair. She flipped it over, nearly choking when she saw the back. The left side was filled with a scrawled version of the Earthling's language, as well as four lines of it on the right. But printed along the top were characters that looked just like Miran. Her attempt to read it failed, as it didn't say anything she could pronounce, only a jumble of meaningless sounds.

"Where did this come from?" she asked.

"Terry sent it from India. He was there for a year as an agricultural exchange student."

"Where's India? Is that another planet?"

"No! Of course not," Tammy replied.

"Then why is it so different than here?"

"Because it's on the other side of the world!" Tammy exclaimed, wide-eyed.

"Really? But that doesn't explain why it's so different. Was it colonized by a different planet or something?"

Tammy just stared at her, mouth open, as if such a question was impossible to answer. Clearly, the people on Earth were so isolated from each other that they hadn't attained a homogenous society such as the one on Mira III, which had been in effect for thousands of years.

"I was just wondering, because their writing is similar to my planet, but I can't read it," Creena explained. When Tammy remained speechless, she quietly put it back by the mirror.

The tension quickly dissipated as Tammy took her down the hall to her own room. The first thing she saw was something tan and furry curled up on the bed. She stopped, wondering if it was alive or even belonged there. Her unspoken question was answered when Tammy walked over and started to pet it. The creature moved a little, then stretched lazily before laying down again and turning over so Tammy could scratch its belly. Creena stared at it, wide-eyed, at the thought of an animal of some sort in the house, much less on her bed.

"This is my cat, Dusty," Tammy said, scratching behind his ears. "You can pet him if you like." Creena stepped over slowly and reached out her hand, surprised at the softness of his fur. He was much friendlier than the calves and made a strange noise in his throat when they ran their hands down his back. "He does a good job of catching mice in the barn," Tammy added. "Don't you, Dusty?"

Creena held her breath, wondering if the creature would answer. "Does he talk?" she asked, staring into round, wise eyes the same color as his fur, realizing she wouldn't be surprised if he did. After all, Thryon did.

Tammy laughed. "No, silly, he just purrs and meows when he wants to eat. He makes a bunch of other sounds, too, but they're not words." She cocked her head pensively. "But you know something weird? I know what he means, so I guess it *is* sorta like talking."

Creena wondered what it would be like to learn another language, something which had never been necessary on Mira III. A short time later, Mrs. Benson called them for supper and she followed Tammy downstairs. The entire family sat around a large oval table, which held several dishes of steaming food. Again, the hazy image of being there before, perhaps in her dreams, flashed before her, as Creena realized how starved she was. All she'd had all day was that hamburger back at the base, what seemed a lifetime ago.   That had actually been quite an improvement over genour, but what was before her now looked like a veritable feast.

There was a steaming chunk of meat that smelled wonderful, a nest of crisp, green leaves mixed with a variety of round, colorful slices and wedges, and a plate with large yellow cylinders covered with knobs packed together like buttons on a control console. Back on Mira III, their servatroid had prepared some pretty impressive meals, considering they only had dehydrated imports and sporadic biodome yields to work with. But never anything even close to this.

When her plate was full, she studied the strange eating utensils, watching and then mimicking the others as they started to eat. The food was delicious, the flavors intense and fresh, especially what she learned was called strawberry pie, which they had for dessert. After they were finished Tammy beckoned her outside again.

"It's Allen's night to do the kitchen. First, I need to grab a flashlight from the barn, then we can go up the hill, to the tramp."

Creena followed, wondering if they spoke the same language after all. She knew what a hill was, but a tramp? They followed a well-defined trail past the buildings in the back, beyond a fenced enclosure which contained several full-grown cows. Creena wanted to stay and watch, but Tammy prodded her on, across a large field that was scratchy and damp against her ankles.

"We'll be mowing this in a few weeks," Tammy said.

Creena couldn't figure out why, since it didn't seem to be in the way, like the grass and weeds on Verdaris. "What is it?"

"Hay. It's what we fed the calves, only before it's cured and baled."

"Oh. How do you get it inside, with 'troids?"

Tammy laughed. "You'll find out soon enough."

Creena gave her a puzzled look, but didn't pursue it, grateful for Tammy's easy manner. At least it didn't seem as if anyone was going to force her into some stiff routine of forced compliance. So far, everything felt amazing easy and peaceful, a natural, even flow. It lacked the rigidity of Mira III's zones, yet appeared to maintain some level of predictability.

At last, they reached the edge of the field where three strands of wire with sharp twisted barbs separated them from parched, boulder-strewn hills.

"There's a gate farther down, but this way's shorter," Tammy explained as she showed her how to squeeze between them, after which she led the way down another well-worn path, dried vegetation crunching beneath their feet.

"We brought it up here on the hay wagon," Tammy explained. "It's really neat. It's like you can jump clear up to the clouds. Or stars."

Her words didn't make sense until they reached a broad ridge, mountains towering in the back with the valley stretched out below. There, among yellow wildflowers and pungent smelling weeds, was a rectangular mat the size of a small room suspended from a frame with several coiled springs. Tammy didn't waste any time before scrambling onto it and starting to jump. The mat rebounded, sending her upward as if gravity had released its grip. After a little while, she coaxed Creena to join her and showed her how to drop to her knees and bounce back, then do the same thing from a sitting position.

The sensation was like a breezy version of zero gravity and reminded her of the place on Mira III where her family would go occasionally for fun, except that was real zero-g produced by an antigravity generator. The pod had been similar, but there it was constant and routine, an easy way to move around that lacked any element of fun, especially the consequences, which she didn't care to remember.

With each jump, her remaining anxiety lessened, fear and tension diminishing to the breathless rhythm. They took turns until the sun dropped on the far side of the valley, staining the Earth with red and orange that gradually faded to black. Golden light shone from the windows of the house, looking small but warm in the distance, pinkish lights lining streets far below. More and more lights filled the ground, a halo lighting the sky toward town. Stars emerged, a few at first, then more and more, until eventually they formed a spectacular show of patterned light.

Instead of taking her next turn, Tammy sat down on the mat cross-legged and stared across the valley to where the sun had dipped below the horizon.

"I'm sure glad you're a girl," Tammy repeated, beckoning her to sit beside her.

"I'm glad you are, too," Creena replied, still a little out of breath from her last turn. "I was a little worried when I saw all your brothers."

"They're really not too bad. For brothers." Tammy giggled, flopping backwards to stare at the sky above. "Did you have constellations on your planet?"

"I don't know," she replied shyly, likewise laying back on the mat. "What are they?"

"You see the way the stars kinda make pictures? We call them constellations."

"Oh. No, we didn't, at least not on Mira III. They were there but it was too foggy to see them. But they did on Verdaris."

"Is that another planet?"

"Uh-huh."

"How many planets have you been on?"

"This is the third I've actually landed on. When I get home, Cyraria will be four."

"Wow! The farthest I've been is Arizona."

Creena smiled, having no idea where that might be, as she continued to study the stars, thinking how different they looked versus out in space. The designs they formed were more apparent because they seemed as if they were spots on a gigantic dome, all the same distance away. One looked like a giant ladle, a smaller one off to the side. One slightly above the mountain tops behind them reminded her of a starcruiser, but Tammy said it was a swan, whatever that was. One looked like a psetora, the giant insects on Verdaris, another like the Great Miran Tower of Law. The one called Bootes reminded her of Aggie.

"How did you learn so much about the stars?" Creena asked, wondering if they went to schools like the Academy.

"I learned a little in fifth grade, but most of it I learned from Allen."

For some reason the answer startled her, because she couldn't imagine an older brother doing something nice. The nicest thing Dirck had ever done was give her the pocket laser, and that had questionable motives, given that according to Miran law she wasn't old enough to have one. Sighing at the discrepancy, she quickly lost herself in the wondrous world above. The vastness of the night sky took her breath away as eternities stretched before her, shrinking Earth and her troubles to mere specks in endless time. One section of sky just above the mountains beside them drew her fascination like a magnet, stars winking as if to draw her there.

"Where did you come from?" Tammy asked, breaking her thoughts.

Without hesitation, Creena pointed in that same direction. "You can't see it until later," she stated. "But in a few hours, Mira will rise over there."

The confidence she felt in its truth was strong, yet it made no logical sense whatsoever. She remembered what Aggie had said about being illogical and marveled even more, knowing it defied all realms of reason, but somehow she'd either retained some sense of direction with regard to the galaxy or her instincts were stronger than she realized. Above her head arched a trail of thousands of stars, so many they appeared smeared together.

"What's that?" she asked. "One of the galaxy's spiral arms?"

"Yes. We call it the Milky Way," Tammy replied.

"Oh. That's nicer that what we call it. It's just the Hostii Galaxy where I come from."

She turned slowly back to that part of the sky hovering above the far end of the valley, which continued to draw her attention like none other.

As if reading her thoughts or perhaps only to show off her knowledge, Tammy chimed in again. "That's part of the zodiac you're looking at right now. See all those stars that look as if they're together and moving across the sky?" Creena followed her pointing hand along a parade of constellations, their specific outlines well-defined.

"Yes," Creena replied, noting that the one that had just cleared the mountain tops resonated stronger for some reason than the others, its distinctive shape like that of an insect or animal with a long tail which curled at the end.

"What's that one called?" she asked, pointing toward it.

"That's Scorpio, the scorpion."

"What's that?"

"Nasty little things like a giant bug, but with a stinger on the end of its tail. Fortunately, there aren't any around here, it gets too cold in the winter."

"What's that red star in the middle?" Creena asked.

"That's Antares. The heart of the scorpion," Tammy replied proudly.

"What about the others. Do they have names, too?"

"Not really. They're mostly called alpha, beta, gamma, names like that from the Greek alphabet, for each constellation. Some of them only have some other designation in a star catalog. I think Antares is also called Scorpius alpha. I know they classify them according to how bright they are, or their magnitude."

"Really? A catalog? What information do they have?"

"I don't really know," Tammy replied. "But Allen has one."

Again, she couldn't explain it, yet knew beyond a sliver of doubt, that somewhere in that constellation she'd left her own heart, not long ago. A place she'd never set foot on, yet where she called home. And appropriate to its namesake, she had definitely felt its sting.

"Somewhere in what you call Scorpio is where I need to go," she said, her voice suddenly saturated with emotion. "That's where my family is." She swallowed hard and blinked against the gathering tears, grateful for the darkness.

Momentarily speechless, Tammy stared at her in awe. "Oh, my gosh, Creena," she finally said. "That's so totally and majorly cool!"

* * *

Territorial Tower
Cira City, Cyraria
Psicomm to BH9

"Our first attempt failed. Apparently she's been moved." Troy braced himself for the INTEGRATOR's reply.

<<She got away?>>

"Only temporarily. Rumor has it she's been moved to a secure facility, but one psimission and we'll know exactly where she is." He shuffled through his comcon messages hopefully, cursing silently when the awaited notice wasn't there. "Besides," he added, leaning back with folded arms, "once enough time passes, she'll be looking for us, if she thinks we can get her offworld."

<<Don't underestimate her. Or forget who she is. She's on guard, now.>>

"I know," Troy said. His brows pinched together in a frown as the negative effects failure would have gathered unbidden. "Our contact is aware of the consequences if he fails," he went on, forcing confidence. "Don't worry. Before long, I'll be telling her father she's in custody."

<<How's he adapting to prison life?>>

"Quietly," he said. "Still insisting he has clearance for the weapon."

<<He does.>>

Troy's laugh was loud. "I know. But if he wants to keep it, he'll have to play by our rules."

<<That should give him plenty to think about.>>

"Only if he's interested in seeing his family again. The readings indicate he's extremely concerned for their safety."

<<Do you plan any intervention there?>>

"That depends on how cooperative he is."

<<Except for the girl.>>

"Right. Except for the girl."

Cover-ups

It was as dark as it got, Zeta and Zinni low enough to be partly obscured by Cyraria's atmospheric haze, the time when Dirck and his father usually performed outdoor tasks while everyone else slept. The zenith was heavy with anticulminational shadow, Zinni and Zeta reclining and awakening respectively, their orange light ringing the horizon with an eerie circumferential glow. Cyraria's moon, Nifeir, rode the line between light and dark, seeming to watch as Dirck and Win stood next to the ballome, waiting for a break in the S3s skimming by overhead. They were difficult to see in the lightened sky until their declination exceeded that of the suns, at least a quarter of the way up. There were usually no less than four visible when they were lucky enough to see them at all, and it was virtually impossible to tell whether the satellites' footprints would cross their location.

Win watched one approaching overhead, Dirck tracked two from the left. While they waited, Dirck gave him a quick description of p-crawler as the insulation covering the ballome, and indicated the bin to their left, nestled against the still's frame, where they'd stored what they hadn't needed or had time to treat with atsna. Three lights crossed overhead, then diverged, leaving a patch of sky with nothing but a few weary stars barely visible in the murky sky above.

"Now!" Dirck called, and raced for the bin, lifting its lid.

"Whew!" Win gasped. "Is this all you've got?"

"'fraid so," he answered, grabbing an armful while Win stood immobilized, holding his nose.

"What is it with you and offensive odors, Brightstar?"

"I don't imagine it smells too good in prison, either," Dirck quipped, simultaneously remembering the breath masks he and Deven had made, so ran back inside to get them, along with visors, in case they were gone long enough to need them. Relieved of the stench, Win quickly pitched in and scooped some up, most of the 'cruiser's nose and canopy covered by the time more satellites came into view.

The next gap, they tied the strands to the grill and tucked them into the canopy crevices. One more load would be enough to cover the cargo bay, but Dirck wanted the compressor out first. Clear again, Win dug it out; Dirck stashed it in the bin, covered with a few scraps of p-crawler.

Finally, the 'cruiser was ready. Neither knew how they'd appear in infrared, but hopefully it would either look like a 'troid or some type of ag implement, depending on their movement. How much the satellites had already relayed was left unsaid. When the sky cleared once more, Win pulled away on low power, running lights dark, impeller exhaust peppering the ballome.

"Which way?" he asked.

Dirck waved in a direction east of the bnolar's cave. The never-black sky was distressed with rocky silhouettes and folded hills spiked with vegetation. The next wave of S3s was thick. No stopping, just an erratic path, mimicking a 'troid harvesting bowlbush.

About a kilometer from the ballomestead, Win zigzagged to the base of a towering arch flanked by huge boulders and pulled the 'cruiser into a thick stand of scrubby vegetation. He retrieved a portalume from door stowage, then each got out slowly and stood beside it, waiting. The evening silence rivaled the canyon, broken only by the cry of a sweeper and a gusty breeze as they watched for the next break.

"This will have to do while we scout around for something better. Hopefully somewhere under those rocks," Win said. "*Clear!*"

With precision borne of desperation, they rearranged the sagging p-crawler, separated, then scouted the immediate area until the next wave was upon them moments later. They froze as close as possible to some sort of cover until starting the cycle again. Meter by meter, Dirck circled the huge base, a stiff breeze slapping his face, undoubtedly the same one that had worn its windface smooth and coated with powder.

The steep hill behind it was littered with brush and rocks. Dirck took a few steps down it and froze, not for approaching S3s, but an eerie, greenish light. It floated a short distance from the ground, a shapeless mass, tossing in the breeze. The air was still hot, his shiver the chill of unknown fear. The next wave of S3s passed. Slowly, he descended the embankment, wincing with every scrape and shuffle of dirt and stone. At the bottom he stopped, staring hard. Lines were visible within the glow amid tiny, flickering shadows. He crept forward, heart pounding, caught between fear and necessity.

Its form lacked definition, the movement slow and ethereal, yet failing to translate its location. He crept a few steps closer, jumping when a twig snapped beneath his foot. A gust of wind fired past him, dust burning his eyes, as he squinted at the image, poised for a rapid retreat when relief washed over him in a single swell.

It was only a bush, its phosphorescent branches and leaves glowing softly in the dusky night. He'd seen them before, numerous times, but there was nothing unusual about them in the full light of day. He broke off a small twig to see if the glow persisted—it did. He returned to the stone base, noticing a deep indentation marred it at the very bottom, a few meters beyond where he'd descended. He stepped over to it to see if he could tell how deep it was, but it was too dark to tell. The opening was easily wide enough for the 'cruiser and the inside wall felt smooth, sired by the same process as the arch.

"Hey, Win," he called. "C'mere. Bring the light."

Win's boots crunched against rock as he slid down the embankment.

"Whatcha got?" he asked then froze, crouched against the ground. "Incoming," he whispered.

Dirck saw it too, the same flickering of blue and amber they'd seen at the canyon. Both crept toward the opening and backed inside.

"Looking for us?" Dirck whispered.

"Hard to say. They're moving too fast for a detailed scan. It should be the next shift by now."

The veke's trajectory didn't deviate and was soon a distant point of light. Turning toward the opening's depths, Win turned on the portalume and swept a wide arc. It was a cave, as expected. The ground descended gently for about ten meters before widening to a flattened area in the back.

Win turned off the light. "Perfect. It won't get any better than this."

He stepped back to the entrance and waited until four pinpoints of light had dispersed above, then scaled the incline with a few well-placed strides with the 'cruiser safely inside by the time the next array passed overhead. He secured the canopy, then walked it down one more time, leaving with obvious reluctance.

Dirck climbed to the front of the arch, eyes trained on the sky in what was fast becoming a rhythmic game of stop and go. Nefeir had lowered to the lighted band, not far from Zeta, face lit by Zinni on the opposite horizon. What they might encounter in the shadows darkened his mind as they paused beneath some brush. He didn't remember seeing any spickle trees, at least, and hopefully yraglian lizards weren't active in the dual suns' sallow glow. He looked skyward. CSF-1 and a few stars shuddered overhead, the S3s momentarily gone.

"You said you could take care of the wanted lists," Dirck mentioned as they started for the ballome. "How?"

It was several paces before Win replied. "I need access to the terminal in the SD. But that will be the first place they'll look for me, except for home. If I log in, it'll send off an alarm, with that alert posted. Worst case, they're tracking me now, by satellite. It all comes back to how much they know."

So getting Win off the hook wouldn't be nearly as simple as he'd made out. And Dirck was hardly desirable company himself, considering they'd just hauled off his father on a weapons violation.

"I should've gone by the SD on the way back and taken care of it when it posted," Win mused. "Then we could've just gone on, business as usual."

"But if it had already been posted, you'd have been dead."

"Yeah. Good point."

They'd reached a thick stand of atsna, spreading branches occulting the ground from the searing gaze of waxing opps when Dirck heard a subtle scraping of gravel. He hesitated, startled when something grabbed him around the ankles.

"*Hey!*" he yelled, looking down to see the muscular coils of a huge snake, only a small fraction of its length holding him bound while the rest drew in slowly and encircled his feet.

"*Don't move!*" Win whispered. "It's a shackle snake. They strike when you go down or struggle. Just stay still."

As long moments crept by, Dirck held his breath, wincing as the viper tightened. His toes went numb, legs cramping, pain weakening his knees. He swayed slightly, looking for something to hold on to. The snake's head swayed, watching.

"Don't move!" Win hissed. "It needs to think you're a tree or something not worth eating."

Dirck braced himself against accelerating pain. "How much longer?"

"Shouldn't be long. Stay still." Win bent over slowly and picked up a rock, tossed it in the brush. The coils relaxed and the snake slithered off, disappearing toward the noise. Dirck and Win bolted away, unmindful of anything save distancing themselves as far and fast as possible. A cluster of boulders cast more sinister shadows ahead, and they climbed among them, waiting breathlessly for the in-progress passing of five more S3s.

"You're lucky we were moving slow when he hit," Win explained. "They usually throw you to the ground, then you're gone. Their venom paralyzes in seconds. You would've been no more that a lump in its digestive system in no time."

"Thanks," Dirck stated. "Must be my lucky day."

They moved on carefully, gravel-accented steps breaking the silence. "So where were we?" Win asked. "Oh, yeah. Access to the SD."

"We'll figure out something. Speaking of business as usual, though," Dirck said, "I better make my usual water run in the afternoon or we may not make our =CC= quota. Obviously, that last haul never got logged."

Win's eyes lit up, his face oddly flushed in the evening's sultry glow. "That's it! You go in right before lunch, when Crjlx-IM's anxious to leave. You come up with some crazy contingency—something real time-consuming—he gets reeked and leaves you alone. Then you get into the terminal."

"Think he would?"

"Yes, I do. He always gets upset if I'm not there right on time. He goes home every day at the mid-shift break and if he's late his *rakii* gets mad. From what he says, she sounds like a nuclear nag. Anyway, if you tie things up somehow, there's a good chance he'll leave. He'll assume I'm in trouble when I don't show up, especially if the Patrol goes in and starts asking questions. It would implicate you more if you didn't go in. You know, sometimes the smartest thing you can do is play dumb."

Dirck stepped carefully around several large rocks, eyed the sky for S3s. Still clear. "When I take in the water, you always check it in, liter by liter," he said. "He'd have to do that, right?"

"Right."

"So there's water there already, plus I'll be taking in more. I go in late. Maybe miscount it, too, that kind of thing."

"Yeah, that would work," Win agreed, face shadowed against Zeta's increasing light brightening the horizon.

"How much does he care? Is he pretty tight with procedure?"

"No, not at all. He hates the place and hates the governor. He wouldn't help us directly, because he wants to cover his own tail. You know they have one, don't you? Yeah, a short one, but a tail anyway. So where was I? Oh, yeah. He'd turn his head in a second." Win laughed, then pointed overhead and the two ducked for cover beneath a stand of atsna. "Especially with me gone, he'll be real busy, anyway," Win went on. "And in an *extremely* bad mood."

Dirck rolled his eyes. "Is he ever in a good mood?"

"Not very often."

"So what do I have to do at the terminal?"

"You need to get into the system for the Planetary Law Enforcement Database, or PLED, then delete the offense." He shrugged, eyes on his. "Simple."

Dirck wasn't so sure. "Won't the locals get suspicious if it just disappears?"

"Are you kidding? With all the bribes and local corruption, they'll just figure I knew the right person and got off."

"Even when two members of the local patrol were, well, deleted?" Clear again, the two resumed their path.

"They probably don't know that was intentional, remember?" Win said. "For all they know, those guys defected or were goofing off, which actually happens a lot. The region hasn't had vekes that long and they love to take them out to see what they can do."

"And it doesn't take long for a bad pilot to become a dead pilot," Dirck interjected.

"Exactly. The veke is over the edge and we pulled the transponder. Right now I'm only wanted for questioning. They know they're missing, have possibly figured out there was an accident, but it's extremely doubtful they know it was a set up."

"We can always hope," Dirck said, then slapped his friend on the back. "Okay. Looks like a plan. So how do I get in?"

With the ballome just over the next rise, Win sat down on a rock, expression intent. "Okay," he explained. "Here's what you do. . ."

It was far more complicated than expected and by the time he'd finished, Dirck had forgotten how to log in. His memory had always been sharp on Mira III, but stress and lack of necessity had driven it into withdrawal. The worst was the exit routine, which would assure the invasion couldn't be traced. If done correctly. If not, it would trigger an intrusion alarm. As expected, Win wasn't satisfied until Dirck repeated it back, flawlessly, over a dozen times.

"Okay, you're ready," he finally said. "Let's go brief your mother and get some rest."

As they got up to leave, Dirck glanced up at the sky and promptly stopped dead in his tracks.

"Holy holocubes, what on Wimba's Moon is *that?*" he asked, pointing toward what appeared to be a dark shadow creeping across Zeta's rising disk. He set his visor in place against the glare, able to see it was definitely not a cloud or other obstruction, such as a massive spacecraft.

"Whoa!" Win exclaimed, dropping his in place as well. "You don't see *that* very often! Must be an eclipse."

Dirck had heard of such things, but never seen one, eyes and mind entranced by the eerie coincidence with everything else that had happened the past day.

"A dark of endless days," he muttered, shivering as a chill crawled up his spine.

"What are you talking about?" Win asked.

"Holy holocubes," he breathed. "Wow."

"It's only an eclipse, man," Win said. "Rare, but what's the deal?"

"Wow," Dirck muttered, still transfixed.

"Hey! What's the deal? What am I missing here?"

"Wow," he mumbled again, awash in the implications that Zahra had been right.

"Are you going to fill me in here or not?" Win asked, annoyance edging his voice.

"Yeah. Sure," Dirk replied at last. "You know that jendak at the comcenter? Zahra?"

"Yeah. She seems pretty smart, considering. What about her?" Win asked, puzzlement covering his face in his own eclipse of understanding.

"Well, only a few days ago, she told my mother this would happen. In fact, it sounded as if there would be two of them. She said they were rare and extremely bad omens of some sort, that they indicated storms, both natural and man-made. My father dismissed them as superstition, but gave me a pretty funny look when 'Merama wasn't looking. Given the events of the last few days, I would say she was right."

"That's for sure," Win agreed. "Even knowing what's causing it, it's pretty weird. As far as I know, they only happen every thousand years or so, when everything like position and distance is lined up precisely."

"Even weirder that Zahra knew." He shuddered, remembering the other things she'd said, when they went to see her after the arrest.

"Well, as far as being a bad omen is concerned, that sure doesn't take any cosmically enhanced intelligence," Win replied, voice saturated with cynicism. "All you have to do is look around and know we're headed for trouble. She probably knew about the eclipse already and just added that other stuff. She probably sees every message that goes through that place and knows what's going on. Jendaks are known for making up myths and all sorts of tall tales."

"Maybe so," Dirck agreed. "But she warned my mother about putting too much on the barterboard, just like you did."

"See what I mean?" Win said smugly.

"I suppose," Dirck agreed, yet wasn't entirely convinced. "I wonder if my mother's watching? In a way I hope not, it may scare her to death. She was pretty shaken up by the prediction."

"We'll find out soon enough," Win replied, and hastened his pace toward the ballome.

When they got there, she was standing outside, eyes wide, as she ran out to meet them. "Did you see that?" she asked, grabbing Dirck by the arm. "That's exactly what Zahra said was going to happen! It didn't make sense before, but does now. How could she have known that? Do you think she's right, that it means bad things are coming?"

Dirck sighed, unsure of an answer. His logical Miran mind told him to side with Win, yet something inside pulled the other way. Besides, bad things were already there.

"She probably knew an eclipse was coming, working in the comcenter like that. Whether that other stuff is true or not, well, I suppose we'll know soon enough," he replied, borrowing Win's practical approach.

"I suppose so," she agreed, calmer as she changed the subject. "I moved Deven in with me," she explained, leading them in through the back door and into the living area. "That way, you two can have the sleeproom to yourselves." She sat on the floor, motioning for them to join her, then hugged her knees to her chest and looked him square in the eye. "All right. I want to know what happened. All of it. Including where you've been for so long."

Dirck took a deep breath and started in. She listened attentively, asking a few questions, her face lined with weary solemnity by the time they finished. She made it clear she didn't like dishonesty, but understood the realities of survival. When Win explained his philosophy of war, the distance increased in her reddened eyes.

"Everything makes more sense then, doesn't it?" she agreed, stared straight ahead for a while, then excused herself and retired to her sleeproom.

As soon as Dirck was sure she wouldn't be back, he checked the comcon again. The listing hadn't changed. He and Win sat and talked for a while after that until, unable to stay awake, he directed Win to the shower and then Deven's cyll. Once his friend was settled, he rinsed off as well and finally cylled out, mindful of every subtle adjustment of its cushions as his mind and body begged for relief from a day saturated with anguish. Within moments, Win's breathing was deep and even, louder than his brother had ever been.

A morbidly familiar orange glow was firing the walls and he glanced at the time—exactly when the commandos had arrived the night before. The brutal reminder agitated the loss, the guilt, the burden, beyond what his weary body could stand, and he sank almost unwillingly into a dark and dreamless sleep.

The PLED

Dirck sat down at the workdeck, Win beside him, where he used to sit next to 'Merapa. He located his father's notelog in one of its compartments and started perusing the information on the heat exchanger, finally bringing up the system schematic. The details were sparse, futility hitting him like Zeta's heat at culmination.

"He must have had everything in his head," he said, scowling. "This is way too sketchy."

He buried his face in his hands, wishing he could tap into his father's brain, then looked up with a start, realizing that maybe he could.

"I wonder where he kept his c-com?" he thought out loud.

"His what?" Win asked.

"His c-com. Cerebral Companion. Clever little device he got on Esheron. It operated with a psi link where you input what you knew about something, asked questions, and it would augment and store all the information. If we can find that, we may be all set."

"What does it look like?" Win asked, glancing around the cramped and cluttered room.

Dirck was already rummaging around the various compartments in and around the workdeck.

"Like this," he said, holding it up triumphantly. The device fit in the palm of his hand, smooth and seamless, with no obvious means for activation. "Now we just have to figure out how to access the data."

He cupped it between his hands, thinking of his father, where he might be and whether he was okay. It was as if he could feel his presence emanating from the c-com, almost as if he were being whisked away to where he was. Startled and slightly spooked, he set it down, looking at it warily.

"What's the matter?" Win asked.

"I don't know," he replied. "It was weird. It felt as if it was going to talk to me or something."

"Maybe it was. Do you know how it works?"

"No, not really. I know 'Merapa spent a lot of time with it, though. If it works on psi, it may be coded only for him. We might not be able to get in."

"I don't think so," Win speculated. "He knew he was at risk. He probably knew this could be the only thing you'd have if he was gone."

"Good point." Dirck picked it back up, heart racing with anticipation as he held it almost reverently between his palms. Moments later, a feeling of connection flowed through him, centered in his chest.

'Merapa? he thought tentatively, as if speaking through his heart—

—which nearly stopped when his father's voice came into his head.

Win's eyes were locked on his, which he was sure were wide, nodding his head in affirmation that something was working.

> *Dirck, if you're hearing this, then obviously I'm not around for one reason or another. I've stored a lot of key information in here that you'll need to know. I've secured it so that you can access everything. There are also parts for your mother, Deven, and even Creena, in case I never come back. It will be up to you to decide when that may be.*
>
> *If the heat exchanger isn't finished, everything you need to know is here. You can download the specs to the notelog for easier reference. Every*

version is here, from the original concept to the final. You can call up any of them using keywords. If you need to make additional modifications, you can request help. Be sure to listen to all the instructions, including any risks and hazards which need to be mitigated or controlled. You can store your thoughts and data as well in a specific sector I created for you. Use it like a chronograph, to record what happens each day, not only your technical endeavors, but everything else, as a record. You never know when you may need such information.

I hope you realize that I love you and have confidence in your ability to fill my obligations to the family. However, you should also maintain close comm with Jen, in case you need additional help. You know I'll do everything in my power to return, but if I don't, it's all up to you.

Dirck set the device down on the workdeck, his father's words still echoing inside his head.

"Well?" Win asked. "Did you get in?"

"Did I ever!" he said. "Everything we need should be here, we just need to figure out how to download it on the notelog."

"Didn't he tell you how?"

"No, so it shouldn't be hard, or he would have."

He set the notelog in front of him and picked up the c-com again, commanding it mentally to transfer data for the latest version. The notelog came alive, schematics, parts lists, working fluid volumes, quantities, pressures, and so forth, flashing across its screen at the speed of thought. Moments later it was still, indicator blinking at him from standby mode. He picked it up and scanned through the data, holding it so Win could see.

"Excellent," he said. "Following that oughta be like downing Lemitini."

Dirck looked up, surprised, knowing he'd never mentioned how he and 'Merapa had used it to advantage sometime back. But then, everyone in the known universe knew about Lemitini. He left the schematic and found the parts list. He committed the few things he'd overlooked to memory, and turned off the notelog.

"Until we can get the 'ducers and such, we may as well work on something else," Dirck said, folding his arms. "We have fifty-nine days until Peak Opps sets in and we haven't put in enough food yet, plus we'll want to get that storage area on the roof done. If nothing else, we could start collecting p-crawler. What were you going to do during Peak Opps, anyway?"

Win shrugged, avoiding his eyes. "There's a safe at the SD. I was just going to move my stuff in there. During High Opps, it's only open once a week, in case people need emergency supplies. Most of them can't even get in, since the transports shut down."

Dirck didn't respond until his friend met his gaze. "Why don't you move in here?" he said. "I could use the help and I'm sure my mother and Deven won't mind."

Win's eyes were serious for what seemed a long time until a hint of his usual smile reappeared. "Maybe I will," he said. "I have the 'cruiser to go in, as necessary, and could bring my genour, plus anything else that might be useful. I have a case of opps cloaks I stashed that would be good to have."

"What are they?"

"Insulated capes. Then you can go outside during the less severe parts of Opposition. At least until Peak High Opps, when you can't breathe anymore."

"That'd be terrific," Dirck said, going into the galley for a drink. "What do you do during the worst parts?"

"Then you can't go out without a full-up oppsuit with eye protection and breathing gear."

Dirck frowned, still not comprehending how it could get any hotter. "Let's load up for the water run and go over that PLED routine one more time. It's almost time to go."

They filled the containers with water from the storage tank, loading the boxcart to capacity plus eight larger ones, which they lugged to where the transport always stopped. It took three trips to get them all moved and Dirck wondered how he'd unload them all in time when he got to the settlement, knowing from experience that the vehicle departed as soon as its last passenger had disembarked.

"The transport stops right outside," Win said. "Just stand in the door and yell for Crjlx-IM." He laughed. "It'll be a fine start to getting him to leave you alone."

Dirck laughed. "Does he always go home at the same time?"

"There's only been three times he hasn't since I've been there and I've been there since the end of Spring Down. That's about two standard years."

"Why didn't he go then?"

"They had company." Win laughed. "His *rakii's* mother was there."

Dirck laughed, remembering how his father used to quietly disappear whenever 'Merama's family was around. His mood grew more serious, however, after he'd summoned the transport. When it arrived, they loaded the water, then joined hands in a heartfelt Miran grip.

"Good luck," Win said.

Dirck smiled, remembering what he'd said the day before about luck. "Thanks. Now it's your turn to pray."

And he prayed, too, the entire time until the transport stopped in the settlement compound, where Dirck did exactly what Win had suggested.

"Hey, Crjlx-IM!" he yelled. "Get out here and give me a hand!"

Not surprisingly, the Erebusite didn't appear.

"Hey, I need some help!" he hollered, wondering if the term "hand" was meaningless to a three-fingered Erebusite. "Crjlx-IM! You there?" He strained to see inside, but glare washed it to darkness. A few minutes later, Crjlx-IM stepped outside and stared him down with his *videra.*

"Hey, help me with this water, okay?"

The Erebusite didn't move. "C'mon, will ya?" Dirck shouted, genuine anger rising. "I need some help here!"

"I busy," he said, and disappeared inside.

"Get over here, *now!*" Dirck yelled, surprised himself by the statement's authority. "Send Win out or something!"

Crjlx-IM came back out and walked slowly to the transport. Dirck handed him one of the larger bottles, purposely taking his time. "You not know where is Win?" the Erebusite asked.

"No, of course not," he lied, handing him another one. "Why would I know? Didn't he come to work?"

"Not come work, not comcon work," Crjlx-IM growled. "Busy day. Crjlx-IM need help. Must soon leave, or *rakii* angry. Not good if *rakii* angry. Hmmmph." He turned around and stepped inside the SD to set the two bottles inside, then returned for more.

Dirck handed him another two, then stooped over and set the last four on the ground, next to the transport. After that, he carefully guided the boxcart out, deliberately taking his time. Crjlx-IM passed him on the way and beat him back inside with the last four, one in each three-fingered hand and another under each muscular arm. By the time Dirck got inside, the Erebusite was holding the workdeck open.

"You fr'end at Win. You help Crjlx-IM," he said, and dropped the workdeck in place, trapping Dirck inside.

"Hey, I can't. I've got things to do, too. Like finding Win. Where do you think he is?"

"Not know. Maybe 'cruza broking. You find when done help." The Erebusite tapped the bench by the terminal with a three fingered-claw. "Sit. I show how loggin' water."

"Hey, man, I gotta go."

"*Sit!*"

Dirck complied, trying not to smile as plan merged with action. Slowly and deliberately, Crjlx-IM showed him the procedure.

"Now you," he ordered and Dirck slowly entered the first bottle. "Good," he said. "Will go. Not leave 'til I back."

And he was gone. Dirck watched until he got on the transport, then entered the rest into inventory at lightning speed. The SD's cooling system was finally operative, and a cool draft struck the back of his neck. He shivered, trying not to think about what he had to do. Truly, the linearity of the mortal mind, that focus limited to the task at hand, was all that kept him functional during the events that followed.

From the core system, he called up the first routine. It would remain in memory to code the changes and be the first control they couldn't be traced. Then, he began the process of logging in. He waited. Before long, the space before him filled with the holographic green, yellow and cyan logo of the Planetary Law Enforcement Database.

The door of the SD opened. Blinded by backlight, all he could see was a silhouette. The door closed. A uniformed Regional Patroller stepped over to the workdeck. Dirck yanked his attention away from the telltale projection, grateful for the back panel that prevented the holo from being compromised every time someone entered. So Win had been right about logging in betraying his whereabouts. Hopefully they wouldn't ask why he was in the system with Win's credentials.

"Can I help you?" he asked hollowly.

"Maybe," the patroller stated. His hair and skin were dark. "You Win Sendori?"

"No."

"So where is he? Is he here?"

Before Dirck could answer, another patroller entered. This one was taller and heavier, but had light-colored hair.

"I don't know," he replied. "I haven't seen him since yesterday."

"You see him often?" the patroller asked.

"I come in every day, and he's usually here," Dirck replied. "Crjlx-IM, the Erebusite who works here, said Win didn't come to work and asked me to fill in." The cold air blasting his neck felt cold on the gathering sweat.

"So who are you?"

He met his eyes. "Dirck Brightstar."

Both patrollers froze. Neither spoke for what seemed a very long time.

"So where were *you* last night?"

"Home, with my mother and brother. Why? Is there a problem?"

The dark one shifted his weight. "Do you have any idea when Sendori might return?"

Dirck shook his head. The patrollers exchanged another look.

"Mind if we look around?"

"No. Of course not," Dirck replied, hoping his relief wasn't too apparent that the PLED had timed out and was no longer visible.

The two split up and walked every aisle of the SD. One went out the back door, setting off the security alarm which screamed through the hollow building in an ear-splitting shriek.

"What's in here?" the dark one yelled from the rear.

Dirck went back to see what he was talking about, holding his ears. It was an ominous looking metal door with a cipher code lock. Probably the safe Win mentioned. "That's the safe," he hollered.

"Open it."

"I can't. I'm just helping out today. I don't know the code," Dirck shouted truthfully, the last of his answer louder than necessary when the alarm suddenly fell silent.

The light-haired one joined them. "Nothing out back," he reported, giving his partner a look that seemed to convey it was all clear.

"All right, thanks," the dark one said. And the pair left.

Dirck exhaled hard, holding his temples while his mind pounded with veke components and dead, distorted bodies. The reality of what he and Win had done skidded through recent memory, then halted in reality. This was their only shot at not joining his father. He had to do it, and do it right. And time wasn't on his side. He took several breaths, slow and deep, then forced his attention back to the PLED.

So far everything had worked, exactly as Win had said, including the fact that the pause necessitated by the patrollers' had timed out the connection, which had been a good thing. He logged in again, hoping it wouldn't set off another alarm.

A few commands later, the criminal history of the entire planet and beyond spread before him. Another deep breath, relief this time. He ran a search using Win's name. Response time was slow. After what seemed like forever Win's name, description, *naterra,* and just about everything, including his scores from an academy on Mira III, displayed on the terminal.

Dirck filtered the data for unlawful activities, criminal charges and arrests. Every field was clear except the *Suspected Violations* field. All it said was *curfew* with the decimalized galactic date of the previous day. Other than that, Win was as clean as a newborn babe, or so it appeared.

Of course. Win knew this routine a little too well.

He erased *curfew* using the edit function. Win had told him that deleting more than twelve characters would trigger an audit. No worry here.

Satisfied there was nothing else in Win's record, he called up his own, curious. His adventure with the truancy scanner back on Mira III came up. It had even retained the fact he'd been remanded to Uncle Jen. But that was it. He looked up his grades, debated changing a few with the six characters he had left, then decided against it. If there was anything that no longer mattered, it was his mediocre academic record. He went back to the directory, noting there were quite a few Brightstars. He stared at them for some time, trying to figure out if he knew any.

And felt so incredibly stupid he almost fell off the stool.

He could check on 'Merapa! Find out once and for all, not only what the charges were, but where he was and anything else he could possibly want to know. It was too perfect. He half-wondered if Win had intended for him to find that out, too, then decided it didn't matter. His hands shook as he entered his father's name. The search was long, much longer than for himself and Win together. When the record came up, it was huge. He filtered it. Minutes passed, so many he was scowling impatiently when the criminal portion graced the screen.

It was longer than his grades transcript for his entire school career.

Every imaginable offense spilled across the projection: 'cruiser airspeed infractions; military malfeasance; stealing government property (the *Cosmos II*); grand larceny (the Lemitini); and even noncontiguous juncture, legal jargon for illegal time travel (the TAS). The latest charge, as expected, was the weapons violation. He panned across the screen for more information.

The regional ordinance number was there; criminal rating (treason); time and place of arrest; arresting officials; indictment number; storage locker number and code where the evidence (lasomag) was in storage; and on and on and on and on and on. A field called *Attainder* was highlighted and Dirck made a mental note to check the meaning before exiting.

Four fields revealed the information he was looking for: Cira City, Territorial Containment Facility, Block eight-forty, Cell twenty-nine-fifteen. He memorized the information, glancing at the digichronometer long enough to realize Crjlx-IM could be back any moment. He exited from his father's record, barely remembering to check on *Attainder,* which turned out to be the removal of civil rights due to extensive criminal activity. Quicker than consciousness, another lifeless body brandished his mind like a strobe, its identity repressed by denial.

He took a deep breath, refusing to believe what he'd seen as he exited to the core system, so rattled he almost logged out directly, but caught himself just in time, instituting another surge of panic at what the consequences would have been. He took several deep breaths, closed his eyes to clear his head, and then carefully entered and executed the code sequences, which would post the changes to a datafile and upload them anonymously.

The =CC= menu came up at the same instant Crjlx-IM walked in the door.

"Win's fr'end here still," he commented. "Water loggin'?"

"Just finished," he mumbled.

"Win not back, you work?"

"Win'll be back," he responded. "I'll bet he's back before the day's over."

The Erebusite nodded, the horizontal slits in his *videra* opening as they adjusted to the dimmer light. "Crjlx-IM thank Win fr'end for good help."

"Yeah, no problem," Dirck said, releasing the gate. He stepped outside, temporarily blinded, and walked toward the transport stop. A few people were waiting already, featureless shadows in the midday sun. A familiar roar rose to his right, and he hastened his steps, mind blaring with facts too horrific to behold.

"Dirck!"

He squinted into the glare toward the sound, seeing his brother, then his mother's questioning eyes. "What are you two doing here?" he asked, startled to see them.

"I came to see Zahra, tell her I saw the eclipse," she said. "What's wrong? You look as if you've seen a corpse."

I have, he thought, then yielded to a higher law, one he'd never thought he'd understand.

"Nothing, 'Merama," he said solidly, "Everything is fine."

Chores

Terra Day 42

The Sun had barely cleared the mountains, yet was already hot, morning freshness nearly gone. Snow, which had topped their peaks when she'd arrived, had long since melted, delivering its icy remnants as irrigation water through a system of canals, similar to what she'd found on Verdaris. Allen and David were moving sprinkler pipe, Tammy on the other side of the garden, picking peas. Meanwhile, Creena weeded the row of feathery growth which would eventually produce carrots, wishing she could recapture the peace she'd felt stargazing several nights before.

Allen had a telescope and several nights a week they'd go out and look at the stars and other planets that shared Earth's system, which had somehow made home feel a little closer. Using his star catalog, they'd looked up all the stars in Scorpius, finally deciding that Cyraria had to be part of the star system known as Xi. Reading about it and being able to see it in the telescope somehow helped her maintain the hope that someday she'd be there, looking back at Earth. She wished they could see Cyraria itself, but just knowing the direction helped a lot. She'd picture each of them looking back as she told them she loved them and would get help as soon as she could. Crazy as it sounded, it provided a sense of connection she desperately needed.

Today, however, that comfort was far removed as the vague feeling of nervousness and gloom returned. Logically, it didn't make sense. Every precaution had been taken to keep her location secret and there had been no sign of the cannibal since her arrival. But something inside told her it wasn't over.

Fear had become her constant companion, murmuring in the background like low frequency vibrations on a starcruiser, below awareness yet always there. It fluctuated between two equally unpleasant unknowns: First, would the cannibal find her again; and second, when would she get her ship back so she could leave? Even then, she'd still have to get to Mira III. She thought of her family, especially Dirck, in the sheltered security of home, then forced her attention back to the garden and the task at hand as the thought became too much to bear, never dreaming that things on Cyraria were far worse than she could imagine.

Gradually, the rhythm of rural life was becoming natural. The rigid zones on Mira III and onboard the pod had forced the days to a militant formation of marching time. Getting to Earth had been quick by comparison, but loose and sloppy, her sense of time blurred by boredom and its sagging structure, random activities lacking time tags for reference. At the Benson's, however, the days blew past, their gentle discipline and schedule as comfortable as David's old cutoff jeans and t-shirts were, compared to Code Orange or those Air Force fatigues.

Yet even though the days played forward in an easy, peaceful flow, every dawn she awoke with a jolt to the muffled sound of the compressor in the milking parlor thinking it was the *Cerulean Nimrod* coming to take her home. Each day brought more disappointment when they not only didn't arrive, but there was no word from Thyron, either, her only escape the fact she was able to stay busy, usually in the garden. Not that it was horrible, just not where she really wanted or needed to be.

Everything felt familiar from the moment she'd arrived, and now it felt as if Mira III and everything else, from the *Aquarius* to Verdaris, were from another lifetime.   The feeling she was there for a reason persisted, often reinforced in simple but forceful ways.

Sometimes in the evening, Mrs. Benson would play the piano and the family would sing songs. Earth's music was one thing she would always be grateful for, not only the beautiful melodies, but lyrics which often touched her heart. There was this one that talked about being separated from your father which of course had immediately gotten her attention, but when it said *"for a wise and glorious purpose thou hast placed me here on earth"* it had not only given her goosebumps, but brought tears to her eyes, especially when it also mentioned being a stranger on the planet. It was as if its message were specifically for her, and she wondered what the composer had been thinking when she wrote it. She pondered the song's lyrics on a regular basis and often hummed it softly, which never failed to bring a sense of peace.

For a moment, she recalled the random tones of Mira III's grafix, which never coalesced into anything even close to a melody, but simply provided a slightly refined form of background noise. It wasn't distracting, but it also lacked meaning. Or, as she'd discovered here, messages. Messages that touched her heart and soul.

Nonetheless, getting home was forever on her mind, her homesickness a component in yet another increasingly uncomfortable dichotomy. She missed her family terribly, loss gripping her heart in a cold, steely grip, yet her pain was muddled by the fact it was beginning to feel strangely comfortable here, as if she belonged. Why would Earth feel more like home than Mira III? It didn't make sense.

It was everything that Mira III wasn't, from the Sun's warm caress to the stars piercing gaze, from the awesome food, to the easy balance between work and play, schedule and freedom. Tammy was even left-handed, both David and Allen, also, and she couldn't help but blush with awkward pride whenever Mrs. Benson complimented her for her regal profile, dark, expressive eyes, or rich chestnut hair, whatever a chestnut was. Tammy thought she was beautiful, not a mutant, half-breed alien, and no one ever accused her of being illogical, either. No one even seemed to think of her as strange, except for the ironic fact she was from another planet.

David had shed even more light on the issue when he explained about left and right sides of the brain. Aggie had mentioned it, but in a way that made it sound like a liability, while he'd done a science project on it and even went on to name several famous Earthlings who had been left-handed. Einstein, Michelangelo, Benjamin Franklin, Walt Disney, Mark Twain, and a host of others, none of which meant anything in her void of Earth-based history, but she sensed their importance and relished the information, regardless.

Maybe they'd all hailed from Esheron, like 'Merapa. But whether or not that was true, most important had been his assertion that left-handed people were nearly all right-brained, which meant they relied more on intuition than logic. Right-handed people, at least on Earth, tended to be split between being left and right-brained, those that were left-brained using logic more than intuition.

It was amazing how such a simple bit of information could make her feel so good, as if a sudden source of brightest light had evolved in her mind, illuminating parts of herself that had previously been not only an unpleasant mystery, but cause for self-doubt and discomfort. David had convinced her that there really wasn't anything wrong with her after all, only that her mind operated differently.

It almost seemed too good to be true, yet its truth had felt more like distant memory than revelation. Whether it was her newly gained comfort with the idea or not she didn't know, but her intuition had definitely increased. She nearly always knew what someone was going to say before they actually said it, and had even been able to tell when one of the cows was going to have difficulty giving birth and require assistance. The only thing she didn't know was how much longer she'd have to wait before she could leave. Or maybe she was afraid to probe that particular issue for fear of its answer.

She looked up from her garden reverie at the sound of a tractor choking to life and took a moment to watch it lumber toward the field behind her, Mr. Benson high in the cab. The alfalfa had grown a lot since her arrival, from ankle length that first time she'd trudged through it on the way to the tramp, to well above her knees. The implement's enormous wheels trudged slowly forward, a contraption in tow behind it. She watched as it passed into the area enclosed by the barbed wire fence, jumping when something inside the attachment started to move. As Mr. Benson followed the fence line, severed plants fell behind in ordered rows, remembrance of Aggie flaring as she recognized it as a mower.

Where was Aggie, anyway? Where had they taken her and, worse yet, done to her? They'd certainly been suspicious enough of her capabilities back at the base. How patient would the Earthlings be with that temperamental streak? And what about Thyron? Had they found him onboard? Could they hear him, like she could? As if in reply, a whiff of freshly severed vegetation wrapped itself around her.

Thyron? she thought, closing her eyes, summer sun warm against her face.

Doesn't it smell good?" She opened her eyes, finding Tammy in front of her. "I love the smell of freshly cut hay, don't you?"

"Y-yes," Creena stammered, mind slipping from memory to real-time.

"I'm going inside to get a drink. Would you like one?"

"Yes, thank you. I can't believe how hot it is already."

"At least we'll be done soon," Tammy called over her shoulder. "Maybe we can go tubing in the canal this afternoon."

Creena got up and slowly walked to the fence to stretch her legs. The tractor was at least a hundred meters away by now, a neatly shorn wake strewn behind it. The fresh, green aroma was heavy around her still, the association too strong to deny.

Thyron! she thought with deliberate concentration. *Thyron! Are you okay?*

Ever so subtly, the character of the alfalfa changed, its sweetness suddenly magnified with discernible intelligence.

[I'm fine. How's it with you?]

Thyron! I'm fine, too! Where are you?

"Here, Creena. All we had was water. I hope that's okay. Allen finished off the lemonade, as usual."

Creena opened her eyes and tried not to sigh, wondering if the brief encounter had been truth or illusion. There was something about it that didn't feel quite right.

"Thanks," she said, forcing a smile as she accepted the glass. She chugged it down, surprised by how thirsty she was, then leaned against a fence post as David approached from the barn. Anyone could tell he and Allen were brothers, but his hair was lighter and eyes more blue than green.

"Here comes David to weed the lettuce," Tammy said. "It's time for me to go to 4-H. I wish you could come, too."

"That's okay," Creena replied. "You can tell me about it later." With that, she returned to task, but changed rows. It wasn't long before she noticed David giving her a funny look.

"How come you speak English?" he asked abruptly.

Creena perched back on her heels. "I don't know. I suppose Earth was colonized by us or something. Your writing is different, except for the way they write in that place, India, where your older brother was. Don't you know who settled your planet?"

David looked so thoroughly norfed she had to bite her lip to keep from laughing. "Adam and Eve, I suppose," he finally replied.

"Who were they?"

"The first man and woman on Earth."

"So which planet did *they* come from?"

His eyes widened and jaw slackened until he finally shook his head in frustrated ignorance.

"Maybe your brother can find out while he's away," she suggested.

"I don't think so," David muttered, then resumed weeding in silence. Creena shrugged and turned her attention back to the weeds, wondering why he wouldn't know something that should be a simple historical fact.

That evening at dinner, David mentioned their conversation, so when they were finished, Mr. Benson got out a big book and read what they referred to as the "creation story." The language was somewhat awkward, but she could follow generally what it meant. Once it got past the part where night and day began, and the waters were gathered together, the story had a fairly familiar course.

"And God said, Let the earth bring forth grass, the herb yielding seed, and the fruit tree yielding fruit after his kind, whose seed is in itself, upon the earth and it was so," read Mr. Benson, pausing for a moment to sip his glass of water. Then he continued, referring to more plants and animals populating the earth.

"That's what my father does," she commented.

Every eye in the room fell on her as if she'd just said something decidedly horrible, even worse than the time she'd suggested reprogramming Dusty so he wouldn't claw the furniture. The silence expanded to a near vacuum before Mr. Benson asked softly, "What exactly do you mean, Creena?"

"That's what he does, for his compensation. He's a terralogist. They heat the core of newly formed planets until the land is how they want it, then they stimulate the atmosphere, assuming it has one, to produce weather patterns. Once it stabilizes, they design the right plants and animals to live there, let them get settled for a while, then auction off the planet so anyone who wants can add people."

"Your father makes planets?" David gasped.

"No, not exactly. The planets are already there. They just fix them so people can live there. And they can't do it to just any planet. It has to be in the right location in the star system to have a good climate, plus the planet itself has to be quickened."

"What's that?" Allen asked. Creena couldn't help but notice he was the only one in the room whose expression showed interest instead of horrification.

"Kind of like alive, I guess. I'm not sure, exactly. From what 'Merapa said, I think it radiates in some exotic emission band or something, but they can tell. If it's not alive, they can't do anything with it. It won't respond or something. Mira III is like that now. Stars burn out and die, so I suppose planets can, too."

"What about where your family is now?" Tammy asked. "Did he help with that planet?"

"Not yet. Whoever set up Cyraria didn't do a very good job, and that's why he was transferred, to help fix it. Except something must have gone wrong, because now they're mad at him and he's in trouble or something. That's why I need to get back to Mira III."

"So do you believe that someone like God made the planets?" David asked.

"'Merapa never said who made the planets, only what he did to make them livable. Otherwise, it could take thousands of years or even longer. They just speed things up. Don't you do that here?"

"Not on that scale," Mr. Benson answered. "We take care of our land the best we can, but in some places on Earth they don't and actually make it worse. Once it won't grow things anymore, there's not much we can do."

"That's what happened on Mira III. Now it won't grow anything, except in the biodomes, a process my uncle helped develop. He's the one I need to see when I get back."

Mr. Benson continued reading, finally including the two people David had mentioned earlier, when they were weeding the garden. And he was right, it definitely didn't come right out and say where they came from.

"They had it easy, compared to going to a planet that's not quite finished," Creena commented. When he got to the part about the serpent, she shuddered with remembrance of the decarachnid on Verdaris, then realized a far greater threat had attended her numerous times, more specifically the cannibal and that bad, bad feeling he provoked. She shuddered at the memory, hoping that he was gone for good.

When the people in the story were thrown out of the garden, she couldn't help but think that was pretty harsh for eating a piece of fruit. Nonetheless, having grown up on Mira III she could generally relate to the fact the pair had earned what was apparently a very serious NCR, like she used to get when she didn't follow the rules. If Dirck had had his way, he would have thrown her off the planet, too.

After the story ended, she swapped a troubled look with David.

"What's wrong?" he asked.

"I'm not sure. I'm just wondering if whoever it was that threw those two out of their garden might be the same one who made us leave Mira III."

The entire family stared at her, aghast, apparently too taken aback to even venture a guess, but the similarity troubled her for days.

Hauling Hay

Terra Day 46

Snurkles," Creena puffed, struggling to heft a bale of hay onto the pickup's tailgate. It was time to deal with the alfalfa Mr. Benson had mowed several days before, introducing her to yet another aspect of farm life. It was mid-afternoon and they were almost done, much to her relief.

"It sure would be nice if they'd at least give Aggie back."

"Who's Aggie?" Allen asked, glancing over from where he was stacking bales in the back of the truck.

"My 'troid. She could do anything. I wonder where she is and what they did to her. Dumb snurks. . ."

She picked some dried alfalfa from her hair, then scratched her back against the tailgate, stopping when she noticed he was smiling at her. Not a sneaky, snurky smile, like Dirck used to give her, but a real smile topped by a pair of wide, blue eyes and sun-streaked hair that shone like an aura of gold.

"I think it's absolutely cool that you've traveled in outer space," he said. "When I watched NASA send a rocket to the moon and men actually walk on it, I knew that was what I wanted to do someday, no matter what it takes. At the very least, I want to be an engineer and build stuff that goes into space, even if I can't go myself."

"Your planet certainly has a low technology rating," she replied. "We didn't see anything when we came in, except a few satellites. No major space stations or intragalactic traffic to speak of at all."

"Actually, we have a space station. It's called Skylab. It has three astronauts onboard who conduct various experiments. Is that cool or what?"

"Oh! So that's what that was," Creena commented. "Right before Aggie and I landed, we saw a small satellite with people in it. When did they send someone to your moon?"

Allen pursed his lips and looked pensive. "I'm pretty sure the first time was nine years ago. I know it was summer, because we were listening to it on a portable radio while we hauled hay, just like we're doing now. They went a few more times, then started building a new vehicle they're calling the space shuttle, which will let us go into space all the time. It won't be done for a few more years, though. It should be up and running about the time I graduate from college. I can hardly wait."

He held her gaze a moment, excitement evident in his eyes, then he jumped down from the truck and sauntered off for another bale while she crossed to the next row, pondering how exciting he thought going into space would be. As far as she was concerned, it was a monumental bore. But she'd grown up with it, making it one more fact of life that didn't impress her in the slightest. He probably wouldn't believe how far behind Earth was technologically, even if she told him what was normal for her.

Yet, it seemed strange they were actually so backward given the fact she and Aggie had definitely seen a few intragalactic spacecraft in the vicinity. Clearly, they were being watched or something, probably because they had such a nice planet. No telling.

She glanced up at the sky, still amazed at Allen's enthusiasm. It was hot, several hours of daylight remaining, though the sun was leaning toward the western horizon. Sweat dripped from her temples and down her back.

Snurkles, did hauling hay itch. But the discomfort was purely physical, her reserve dropping like a barometer before a storm. The Bensons almost made work fun. They did most things together and simply accepted it had to be done. They seldom wasted time or energy on arguments or complaints.

Up ahead, two-year-old Billy was hanging out of the truck window from his mother's lap as she guided it slowly across the field rutted with irrigation channels. Creena waved and smiled, wondering how Deven was doing on Cyraria. Her little brother would fit in anywhere. He was always the model of compliance, yet there were certain directives within him that he'd follow, whether they defied logic or not. He was the perfect blend of Miran and Esheronian, never noncompliant, but willing to follow his instincts when it wasn't forbidden.

He hated it when she and Dirck argued. She wondered if he missed her, then instantaneously knew that he did, a lot. She almost felt his presence, in a warm but strange way, and wondered what he was doing on Cyraria. Everyone else, too, for that matter. Since it was primitive, maybe they were doing some of the same things.

"What's it like to travel in space?"

Allen's voice barely carried above the roar of the pickup as Mrs. Benson shifted into gear and moved forward several meters. Creena returned from her thoughts and stared deeply into his questioning eyes. They were the color of the sky, so alive against his well-tanned face. He kicked at a broken bale, then stooped over to pick up two pieces of twine and roll them into a ball.

"I'll bet it's neat," he prodded, staring expectantly at her again. Creena met his wistful, so-blue eyes.

"I suppose," she shrugged. "Actually, it's really boring. Like being locked in your room for weeks and weeks with nothing to do."

"I think it's pretty boring here. I wish I could go with you, when you leave." He hopped into the back of the truck to stack the most recent additions, expression blocked by sun's glare. When he jumped down, the truck lurched forward again, and Creena walked briskly for the next row of bales, Allen matching her stride.

"You mean you'd leave your family, just like that?" she asked.

He sat on the nearest bale to catch his breath and scratch his neck. "Oh, I don't know. I guess."

"I thought you people liked each other."

"We do. It's just I get sick of it here. All summer we help Dad work the farm, then all winter we go to school. There's always something I *have* to do. I'd love to get away from it all for a while."

Creena tried to laugh but couldn't. "I used to feel the same way."

"But not any more?"

"Not really. I'd give anything to be back with my family right now, boring or not. I might even be able to stand my snurky brother, Dirck. *Maybe.*"

"You have a brother?" Allen asked, eyes wide.

"Two. Deven's pretty cute. He's about Jimmy's age, maybe a little younger. But Dirck's a total snurk."

"How old is Dirck?"

"Your age," she said quietly, stifling a smile.

"Is that so?" Allen laughed. "So what makes him a snurk?"

"Because he hates me. All he does is pick on me and tease me, make me look stupid and remind me I can't do anything right."

"Do you hate him, too?"

"Yes!" Creena snapped, but something inside her wrenched and she walked evasively toward the last block of hay. Allen's voice was behind her a moment later.

"I'll bet he doesn't really hate you, Creena," he said gently.

"Ha!" she argued, refusing to look at him as she tried to work her fingers beneath the scratchy twine. "Then why does he treat me like an asteroid fungus and act so mean all the time?"

Allen shooed her back so he could grab the bale himself. "Because—that's—the—way—brothers—are," he panted, moving toward the truck. "And I'll bet he's really sorry now. Really, really sorry."

"Ha! How would you know?"

He dropped the bale and sat on it, expression different than any she'd seen before. "Because I used to be a *snurk* to Tammy all the time," he said. "Just ask her! Then last winter she got real sick, and we had to take her to the hospital. Her appendix had ruptured and for a while we weren't even sure if she'd make it. Thinking she might die made me realize how much I cared about her. I never cried or prayed so hard in all my life. And I promised God that if she got better, I'd never be rotten to her again. And I'll just bet that Dirck feels the same way about you."

Something about his words rang true. Thinking she might die probably would make Dirck change his mind about her, especially since he had that thing about death. Maybe he did miss her. As much as she hated to admit it, she missed him. A lot. And the evidence was gathering that she may not ever see him again.

Much to her complete mortification, tears flooded her eyes. She whirled around to wipe them away, almost angry when Allen lifted her up from behind and boosted her into the back of the pickup. Still refusing to look at him, she leaned forward against the stack of bales behind the cab, gaze fixed straight ahead as she continued to battle her persistently leaking eyes. David scrambled in beside her and Mrs. Benson turned the truck around and accelerated for the dirt road leading to the hay barn.

"What's the matter?" David asked.

Creena looked away, catching Allen's *shut up!* gesture with the corner of her eye. The pickup bumped forward and she braced herself against the wheel-well, letting her mind bounce through Allen's words like the truck through the fields. It felt so right her heart filled with hope she hadn't felt in a long, long time.

Or maybe it was only because she wanted it so much to be true.

A few moments later the old pickup shuddered to a halt in front of the barn.

"Your dad and I are going into town to pick up a few things," Mrs. Benson said as she got out of the cab, gathering Billy into her arms. "We need to run by the feed store and post office to mail a package to Terry. We'll pick up Tammy at 4H and take her with us. Think you can handle things okay?"

"Sure, Mom," Allen said, jumping lightly to the ground. "C'mon," he said, turning to Creena. "It's time to feed the cows."

Creena followed him and David, who swung open the barn's huge double door, and the three of them entered, but Creena lingered near the entrance to the milking parlor, looking at a picture of a funny-looking, two-wheeled vehicle. Allen stopped beside her to gaze at it longingly while David went to the last stall to get started from the other end.

"You have them on Mira III?" he asked.

She shook her head. "The only thing on wheels is 'troids. What is it, anyway?"

"A Honda 250 dirt bike," he replied. "I've been saving for one for over two years. The stupid price goes up as fast as I can put it away. I'd give anything to get it this summer. All I need is another two hundred bucks." Then he grabbed a bale in each hand, hauled them over to the feed bin and rummaged through his pockets until a rare scowl creased his forehead.

"Great," he grumbled. "I must've lost my knife haulin' hay." He tried to pull the twine off the bale but it wouldn't budge, only scratched stubbornly at his knuckles.

"Great," he mumbled again, sucking them angrily.

"Here, let me" Creena said, taking out her pocket laser. First she guided the material sensor near the twine, then severed the cord, ragged ends smoking in the dim light.

"*Wow!*" Allen exclaimed. "Can I see that a minute?"

She handed it over, then kicked the bale apart as she'd seen him do, and proceeded to throw the flakes over the railing while cows crowded the feed trough in a black and white press.

"What's in there?" he asked, pointing to a small door on the handle.

Creena's eyes met his questioning stare, squinting at her against an incoming ray of late afternoon sun.

"Just a compass," she replied. "It should indicate the four cardinal directions."

He handed it back and watched her flip it open. The digital readout read a steady zero when she pointed it north and progressed appropriately through the other directions as well. It worked perfectly.

"That's weird. It wouldn't work on Verdaris at all," she said. "I thought maybe it was broken, but I guess not." Then again, Aggie had said this planet had a good magnetic field.

She put it back in her pocket and headed for the barley scoop, stopping when Allen leaned against the railing and sighed, one foot on a salt block next to the trough.

"You know what really bugs me, Creena?" he asked. "You keep telling me all this super-neat stuff, and I can't even tell anybody. And when you're gone, no one will ever believe me." He grabbed another flake and tossed it in the feed bin, scowling.

Creena smiled. "Maybe some day I'll come back, with my family." She scattered barley on the hay with a flourish, pondering the possibility. Dirck would simply *love* hauling hay.

"Tell me what it's like on your planet," Allen said. "I want to know everything about it."

"Like what?"

"Everything. What's a normal day like. Did you go to school?"

"Unfortunately. It was called the Academy. We had different levels, which were color-coded. I was Code Orange."

"Ah, like your uniform, right?"

"Yes. We had to all dress alike within our own Code. And people above you always looked down on you and made you miserable, any way they could."

Allen laughed. "That happens here a lot, too."

"Yeah, well, if they got caught they'd get an NCR."

"What were they?"

"Noncompliance Reports," she replied grimly, remembering all too well. "And when you got one, they'd put it up on the Board so everyone could see."

"That must have been embarrassing," Allen said, turning momentarily to grab another bale. Creena smiled and handed him the pocket laser. He smiled back, looking at it in surprise.

"Here, let me show you," she said, demonstrating how the material sensor did most of the work.

"That is *so* cool!" Allen replied, admiring his work. "Tell me more about the Academy. Did you have books?"

"No, everything was in my e-log."

"What's that?"

"An electronic tablet that had all the information you needed stored inside. You'd attach it to the terminal in class, which would show you were there, and then download the information for the day. The next day, it would make sure you did the assignment correctly and record it. If you made too many mistakes, you'd get an NCR."

"And it would go on the Board?" he asked.

"Yes. I got a lot of them," she admitted. "Actually, I did well on assignments, but I got them for other stuff. And it would really embarrass Dirck."

"He didn't get any?" Allen asked, kicking the bale apart.

"Yeah, he did, but only academic ones."

"There were different kinds?"

"Yes. You got them for behavior, too. Like if you asked too many questions the system couldn't answer." Creena sighed and rolled her eyes. "I sure don't miss any of that."

"What about your friends," Allen prompted. "How did you communicate with them? Did you have telephones like we do?"

"Not exactly. Everyone had personal communication devices or PCDs. We could use them to talk to anyone we wanted from anywhere or send them notes or look something up we needed to know. You could play games on them, too, but if you did that at the Academy and got caught..."

"You got an NCR," Allen finished for her.

She laughed. "Exactly."

"So someone was watching all the time and you had to follow all the rules or you got in trouble," he concluded.

"That's it," she answered. "I don't miss it at all."

"I can see why," he agreed. "The technology sounds really cool, but not if you're watched all the time. Even if you don't do anything wrong, that doesn't seem right. Could they read your thoughts?"

"Not really, but they could come pretty close. They could kind of figure it out, by what you were doing on your PCD. If you complained too much or played too many games, you could get labeled as a problem and they'd watch your every move."

"Wow," Allen replied. "That's scary."

"I suppose. It was how they kept order."

"That sounds like a pretty high price for order," he said.

"Hey, look. Someone's coming."

She looked up with a start at the sound of David's voice, almost forgetting he was there. Sure enough, a tell-tale cloud of dust was just visible, some distance beyond the house. The Benson's couldn't possibly be back already. The three of them gathered at the corner of the barn, the car's billowing dust backlit by the lowering sun.

"Who's that?" David asked. Allen shrugged; Creena, however, was frozen with fear.

Allen touched her arm. "What's wrong?"

"That's him!" she gasped.

Return of the Cannibal

Who?" Allen asked, a puzzled look claiming his features.

"That snurk who bombed the base and ran me and Mrs. Jenkins off the road! Th- the cannibal!" Creena stammered, panic surging.

"How can you tell? We can't even see the driver yet."

"I can just feel it," she replied frantically. "I would know that feeling anywhere. What am I going to do?"

Allen's eyes widened. "Stall him, David! Stall him!" he yelled, grabbing her by the arm and nearly dragging her back into the barn.

"Be careful!" she yelled over her shoulder. "He has a lasomag!"

"A *what?*" David answered.

"A lasomag! A laser gun!"

David's wide-eyed look of horror didn't exactly inspire a lot of confidence. Allen dragged her around the corner, out the back door and into the hay barn, past Mr. Benson's office where he kept the dairy records, and all the way to the granary at the far end, a huge, wooden box with dimensions the size of a small room. It was taller than she was and Allen, too, making it impossible to see inside it from the floor. The pulley creaked and swayed as Allen pulled the rope to lift the lid then quickly secured it on a hook.

"Get in!" he said, helping her up the make-shift ladder nailed to the side. The bin was only half full, the current year's harvest destined to fill it back to the top later that

year. She swung each leg over the top, sat a moment to get her balance then jumped, landing in the grain below with a slippery thud.

"Dig down as far as you can," Allen instructed, peering over the side. "Once you're covered, don't move or make a sound. We'll just pretend we never heard of you. How did he find out you're here, anyway?"

"I don't know, I don't know!" she replied frantically, dropping to her hands and knees and starting to dig as mice darted frantically for the corners. Clearly Dusty wasn't doing his job very well.

Try as she might, she got nowhere. As soon as she'd push a handful aside it would slide back, no matter how fast she tried to dig. Clearly the grain lacked friction, at least enough to allow her to create a decent-sized hole.

"Forget that, just wiggle down inside," Allen said, a frustrated edge in his voice as he pointed to the back. "There's a small hole in that corner, a foot or so down. You can use it for air. Hurry!"

Outside in the direction of the house, a car door slammed, her heart jumping with fear. She worked her feet down as far as she could, then squirmed and pushed, wiggling her way beneath the grains until they were as high as her chest. It felt smooth and warm against her bare arms and legs, reminding her of the sleepskin she'd used to adhere to the escape pod's cyll and sleep in zero gravity.

The dust and chaff she'd generated were now burning her eyes and nose, which both began to run profusely. A sneeze was inevitable, regardless of how hard she tried to stifle it. And sneeze she did, spraying everything in sight with an explosive blast. She wiped her nose on her sleeve then glanced up sheepishly at Allen who was frowning sternly over the side with a finger across his lips.

Finally, her feet hit something solid, but her head was still above the surface. She swiveled back and forth, bending her knees to shrink her height, gradually working herself down, little by little, until she had barley up to her chin. She kept at it until the grain reached her lips then stopped abruptly when a surge of claustrophobia struck with unprecedented panic. She recoiled instantly, exposing her entire neck again in a single motion. "I can't do it, Allen," she said frantically. "I just can't!"

"You have to," he said. "We don't have time to go anywhere else. You don't want him to find you, do you?" He disappeared and she wondered if he'd abandoned her until he reappeared a moment later with an old bucket, its bottom partially rusted through.

"Here!" he said, tossing it over the side. Her arms flew above the grain just in time to catch it. "Put that over your head. And don't make a sound or move an inch!"

Then the lid slammed shut and it was dark, except for a few strips of light between the boards. Memories of being trapped in the access tunnel to the escape pod closed around her, filling her with the same, ominous feeling of dread she'd experienced then. In spite of the warm grain against her skin, she felt cold as deep, thick darkness enveloped her in a suffocating cloud. The urge to break free struck again, her heart pounding and lungs heaving in heavy gasps as the walls closed around her.

Then she heard voices outside, coming from the other end of the barn.

She held her breath abruptly and commanded her body to be still. She put the bucket over her head with shaky hands and pushed her arms back down beside her as, once again, she wriggled from side to side, scooting down until barley covered her chin. Another claustrophobic swell rose inside her and again she fought the urge to burst free. She leaned back slightly so she could look up, relieved slightly by the dim light coming through the bucket's holes. Gradually panic resolved to survival mode and she worked herself down as far as she could until, once more, grain reached the bottom of her chin.

Dust stung her nose, bringing on another sneeze. She brought her hand up slowly from the grain and squeezed her nose, muffling it the best she could, then keeping her hand by her nose instead of burying it again. Voices grew louder until they were right outside the wall.

"Listen, mister," Allen was saying, "You've been all through the house. You need to believe me. There's no one here, but me and my brother. What d'ya want, anyway?"

"She's here somewhere, has to be," a man's deep voice growled.

She knew that voice. Panic surged again. It was definitely the same person who'd blasted Lieutenant Carlson and tried to capture her at the Jenkins'.

"*Who?*" Allen asked, footsteps crunching toward the calf pens.

Their voices faded, barely audible as they entered the other building. Doors slammed and young heifers lowed above muddled voices. Another slam, voices growing louder. Still muffled as they entered the milking parlor, louder in Mr. Benson's office, then louder still.

They were there.

"Open it up," the man growled.

Pulleys squeaked, light poured through the bucket's holes. Creena closed her eyes and held her breath, fearful tears running down her cheeks as heavy feet fumbled on the makeshift steps. She bit her lip to contain a sob, unable to keep from trembling.

"See? It's only grain," said Allen. "What makes you think she's here, anyway?" Creena hoped with all her heart that the man couldn't hear the fear in Allen's voice.

"It's none of your business, kid," the cannibal said. "I have my sources. All I know is that UFO girl is here. All I want to do is talk to her. Why don't you make it a lot easier on both of us by telling me where she is?" The grain rustled as a hand sifted through it. "Listen, sonny" he went on.

"Cooperating is really your best bet. Believe me. Besides, I'll even make it worth your effort."

Allen sounded even funnier now. "What d'ya mean, mister? She's not here, never was. *Really.*"

There was a thump as the man returned to the ground, then a different sound, like crumpling paper. "Here," the man barked. "How 'bout a hundred bucks, kid? Where is she?" Silence, then more crumpling. "Okay, look. Here's three hundred. You drive a stiff bargain, kid. How 'bout four?"

All Creena could see was that picture of the dirt bike on the milking parlor wall. On Mira III, compensation was based on a person's abilities and performance, their resources and wealth distributed by government decree in predefined ways. Earth economics were obviously quite different.

"How 'bout a thousand, kid? How long would it take a kid like you to make a thousand bucks? Couple of months? A year? Well, here it is, right now. All you gotta do is tell me where she is."

From nowhere, Thyron's words blared through memory in an unwelcome burst of déjà-vu:

[Humans on this planet are
not trustworthy very far.]

More hot, fearful tears spilled from her eyes as she waited for the words that would betray her. The next sound was Allen's raspy laugh.

"I'd love to take your money, mister," he said.

Creena stifled a sob with her hand as her heart sank.

"Thing is, I don't know what you're talking about," Allen finished.

She sighed with relief, then fear rose again that perhaps they'd heard her. It was quiet for what seemed a very long time. Had they? What was going on out there?

"Well, kid," the cannibal finally replied. "You're either mighty stupid or telling the truth."

The granary's lid slammed shut and Allen laughed again, this time more naturally. "I told ya, mister. I don't even know what you're talking about. All I know about that girl is what's been on TV. Whatever gave you the crazy idea she was here?"

Their voices faded, it seeming like forever before she heard the car start and crunch away down the dirt road. Only then did she take the bucket off her head. Moments later, the lid creaked open and Allen beckoned her out.

She stood up, grain tickling the back of her neck as it slipped down her shirt. "Is he gone?" she whispered. Allen nodded as he hopped into the bin and helped drag her out the rest of the way, then boosted her up so she could climb over the top. He followed a moment later, taking her hand as soon as he landed on the ground with a thud.

"I got the license number of his car," he said, dragging her toward the door. "Let's go call the cops."

With her free hand, Creena pawed at the dust clinging to her nose and lashes, further smearing the grime muddied by tears.

"Oh, Allen!" she cried, spontaneously throwing her arms around his neck. "Thanks for not telling. Thank you so much!"

When self-consciousness hit, she let go, relieved he didn't seem embarrassed at all. If anything, he looked pleased.

"C'mon," he said softly.

Creena didn't move. "Is that another car?" she whispered.

Allen rushed to the door. "It's my parents. C'mon!" They ran outside, getting there as David spilled out what had happened.

"Should we call the cops, Dad?" Allen asked.

Mr. Benson shook his head. "No, son. I'm afraid we can't."

"Why not?"

"It's simple. Creena's being here is highly classified. The Jenkins and maybe a few high ranking Air Force people are the only ones who are supposed to know. I'll let Uncle Milton know, of course, but other than that, it would cause more trouble."

"But. . ."

"No *buts,* Allen," Mrs. Benson added. "If that man believed you like you say, we shouldn't have any more trouble. To report it would only bring more unwanted attention or even verify she's here."

With the matter quickly but unhappily settled, Allen proceeded to unload several feed sacks from the back of the car while Creena followed Mrs. Benson, who was carrying a bag of groceries, into the house. Neither of them said much, but as Creena helped tuck the various cans and boxes away, her panic was gradually replaced again by a warm feeling of peace and belonging.

She could hardly believe that Allen had refused all that money just to protect her and wondered if her own brother would have done the same. If only she could forget her own family, staying there would be simply great.

* * *

Territorial Tower
Cira City, Cyraria

After the holographic image disappeared, Augustus Troy stared at the interference bands left behind for several moments, unable to understand why it was so difficult for some people to follow simple directions. They couldn't have been more explicit, the girl's location always within a radius which never exceeded a few hundred meters. It had taken a while to triangulate her new location, but the moment she sent another psi signal it was immediately captured. Sending those teaser signals had worked perfectly.

He shook his head with disgust and frustration. How hard could it be, intelligence level of Brightstar's daughter notwithstanding? Furthermore, what was that idiot thinking, going during the day? Stealth and surprise would have been so much more effective, but now they were on full alert and might even move her again. Why did he think he'd been issued a lasomag, if it weren't for tactical purposes? Worst case, some collateral damage was expected, and the least of their worries. Surely, the fool didn't actually think he'd get caught? Even if he did, he would have been rescued accordingly *if* his assignment had been successful. Which, of course, so far it hadn't.

It wasn't as if she were in a secure military installation, she was in a private home! How hard could it be! How could he have gotten within the gate of a military base and come so close, then not been able to complete the assignment with no guards or protection other than a couple teenage boys? They'd reprimanded him for the explosion, which could have injured or even killed the target, but never said he couldn't do what he had to otherwise, as far as others were concerned. Troy rolled his eyes again with disgust. What an idiot. No wonder Terrans were still stuck within the bounds of their own solar system.

The worst part was the report he'd have to provide to the INTEGRATOR. His superior would not be pleased. Troy would undoubtedly be held accountable for this latest fiasco for choosing such an incompetent accomplice, which he had to admit he deserved. Obviously, the people on that planet who were willing to perform such deeds were not the brightest stars in the galaxy. The way things were going so far, maybe he'd have to do it himself, a prospect that elicited mixed emotions.

A trip to Terra held certain appeal. After all, he hadn't taken the Cosmos II out for a long time, not since Brightstar had used it. Getting offworld for a short jaunt held tremendous appeal. For the most part, Terra certainly had a better climate than this infernal Cyrarian furnace. Maybe he should go and stay until Peak Opps was over. Certainly there was business he could conduct, see how things were progressing. Too bad he had too many things going on, like dealing with Brightstar, or he'd use his TAS privileges to manage time and spend a few days on Terra, then stretch it out for the duration of the heat season. Terra's technology was starting to finally take off, though they still had a long, long way to go. At least they were finally getting into space. It took them long enough.

According to HIO Convention, interference in the form of technological help had to be approved, but that wasn't much of a threat, considering the power accruing through INTEGRATION. Minerals on Terra were abundant, a fact that made the place a significant galactic resource for millennia. Gold, silver, diamonds, copper, a plethora of random minerals and elements were in generous supply, as well as plenty of salt water and a strong magnetic field.

The fact Terrans hadn't figured out yet how to harness energy from either was absurd. Its abundance of open water alone made it a frequent logistics stop for interstellar craft, along with a high concentration of hydrogen, which was processed for fuel. Mining operations had been conducted in concert with various civilizations in the distant past, all connected through a global communication and energy grid which had benefited the indigenous people as much as the visitors.

Then greed set in, war quick to follow, wiping out Terra's residents as well as those selfishly exploiting their host planet, which eventually resulted in it being declared off-limits by the HIO, to allow the natives to stabilize. Meanwhile, the planet continued to evolve, albeit slowly, until they started figuring a few things out for themselves which had been helped along at a moderate pace as approved by galactic authority. The appearance of numerous manmade satellites and a few trips to their moon indicated they were on the verge of becoming a spacefaring civilization at last.

So, maybe taking care of business himself was his best bet. He had always believed if you wanted something done right, you had to do it yourself, and this was apparently no exception. It would be better this way, especially if he could convince her to go willingly. Knowing what she was capable of, if it were by force, there was no telling what could happen. Psi technology had come far enough to use coercion, if necessary, as well as the usual inter-dimensional cloaking to avoid detection.

And if she refused to come willingly, rather than force the issue, he would do everything in his power to make sure she was stuck there for the rest of her life.

Prepare and Beware

As soon as Dirck got back to the ballome from the SD, he said he needed to check something and went around back as his mother and Deven went inside. A short time later, he climbed up on one of the storage bins and gestured through his sleeproom window for Win, who was chilled out with the notelog, to meet him outside, assuming he'd make sure his mother was occupied before joining him. After he got down, he leaned against the still's frame, suddenly breathless, as the glaring landscape dimmed. Moments later, his knees failed and he slid to the ground, heart pounding as darkness closed around him. The next thing he heard was Win's voice somewhere far away.

"Put your head between your knees and breathe easy," he said. The next words were louder and a hand rested on his shoulder. "Take it easy, pal. Everything's going to be all right. Just relax, okay? Breathe slow, real slow. C'mon, pal, you're okay. Slow. Real, real slow."

Dirck complied, one breath at a time, overcome by his father's criminal record as well as the memory of a canyon scarred by death. Both were indelibly etched on his mind, whirling dizzily before him with their respective consequences. Win's soothing calm continued, talking him back until, ever so gradually, the panic ebbed.

"Okay now?"

He took another deep breath and opened his eyes. "I, I guess." Win crouched down in front of him, eyes fixed steadily on his face.

"Good. Now stay cool, relax, and tell me what happened."

Dirck sighed heavily. "Okay. Here goes." Dirck tipped back his head and rolled his eyes as a cool trickle of sweat slipped down his back. "Okay. Everything went fine at first. At least with Crjlx-IM. Exactly like you said. He was beggin' for help, so that was no problem. He couldn't get out of there fast enough. But I'd no sooner gotten into the PLED, than I had company."

Win's eyes widened. "Who?"

Dirck drew a breath, unwelcome hot air catching in his chest. "Two patrollers, looking for you."

Win froze. "Terrific. I was afraid that would happen. What did they say?"

"Not much. Just wondered where you were last night, who I was, if I knew anything, looked all around, that sort of thing."

An edge of urgency overtook the former calm in Win's voice. "So what was in the PLED? Did you fix it? What did they have on me?"

Dirck sighed, lighter this time, but adrenaline still fired every cell, fright and flight battling for dominance. "Nothing much." He took another breath and wiped his palms on his shirt, forcing calm he didn't feel. "The curfew violation, that's it. It's gone. Erased, like you told me. Everything worked fine. You're clear. Completely clear."

Win stopped pacing and leaned against the ballome. "Really?" Dirck nodded. "That's better than I'd hoped for. Now I'm glad I didn't disconnect the transponder first. If I had, they probably would have had the entire region after me. As it was, we were a local problem they thought they could handle." He laughed. "Not!"

Dirck tried to smile, but couldn't.

"So what's wrong?" Win asked, relief short-lived. "They didn't get you on something, did they?"

"No." He looked away, avoiding Win's eyes as the truth closed in with merciless clarity. "But I saw something else."

"What?"

"What they have on my father."

For a moment, Win looked as if he'd been slapped. "Oh. I hadn't even thought. . . Hey, I'm sorry, man. I was so busy worrying about myself, I didn't think."

"Yeah. At least now I know." Dirck covered his eyes and swallowed hard, a lump unrelated to heat rising in his throat.

"At least that means he's still alive," Win said, trying to sound optimistic. "Otherwise you wouldn't have found a thing. Really. There would have been nothing. He wouldn't even exist anymore."

Dirck couldn't respond. Couldn't move, couldn't talk, and once the first sob erupted the rest followed, hard and fast, as the reality of the past two days hit, full force. He had no idea how long the meltdown lasted until, at last, he looked up cautiously, half hoping Win would be gone. Instead he was sitting on the ground a few meters away, propped against some heat exchanger components with his wrists propped limply on his knees. Gradually, his eyes lost their distant focus and he scrubbed his face with his hands.

"I'm really sorry, man," he said quietly. "Really, really sorry."

Dirck sighed heavily then cleared his throat. "Sorry? What for? Listen, I'm the one who dragged you into this, and now you're in as deep as I am."

"Nah. As long as you fixed the PLED, I'm no worse off than before. You didn't touch any of, uh, your father's record, did you?"

"No. I didn't dare. I figured it'd have security triggers all over it. I'm sure they're watching him closely, anyway, and if anything happened to his record, like it disappeared or something, they'd know."

Dirck wasn't sure whether to tell Win or not that his father had tampered with his record before, and had obviously been found out. Big time. He had to assume Win had the method perfected. But he couldn't help but wonder how he knew so much.

"Okay. Good." Win scrambled to his feet and brushed himself off. "Looks like we're okay then. So. Let's get the 'cruiser and get on with it."

Dirck nodded, but couldn't bring himself to offer the Miran grip. Instead he cleared his throat one more time and called their plans inside to his mother before setting out for the arch.

* * *

Sharra watched them leave from her sleeproom, the window's oxidation rendering them to little more than shadows. She shifted to keep them in view, Zeta's glare surging briefly, then waning, the gait and stature of the one she knew was her son suddenly familiar. She'd never seen his father in him before, only in Deven and Creena, and the observation surprised her. The feeling it evoked wasn't pride or comfort, however, rather an increased sense of melancholy that Laren wouldn't be coming back, and her thoughts shifted inward to their usual haunt.

Where was he? Was he okay? Even alive? What had really happened? While she'd never actually known he had the lasomag, somehow she wasn't surprised by that as much as his arrest. He'd been nearly omnipotent on Mira III. He'd never actually broken any of *The Laws*, yet always maneuvered expertly around them. Actually, through them. He was respected, almost revered. What could he have possibly done to bring such a complete reversal? He hadn't even seemed surprised. *At all.* What else wasn't he telling her?

She left the window and sat on the cyll ledge, staring vacantly at his workdeck. How many hours she'd spent like that, watching him work, content just to have him there. How could she have been so naive to think he'd never leave her again, by his own will or otherwise?

Yet this time something was different. A certain numbness. Perhaps she was getting used to it. Either that, or shock. Or entering another phase of depression. In either case, the pain wasn't as acute as she'd expected. She was sad, scared and lonely, but not frantic. Dirck and Win had done a tremendous job taking over, but that alone didn't account for it. It was more like a buffer of sorts, a comfort zone that seemed to shield her from the harsh realities around her. She could see them, understand them, but didn't feel them. Oddly, it wasn't resignation; she'd felt that before, and this was different. Less painful. Like she were under some kind of emotional anesthetic.

It wasn't that she was optimistic. If there was any hope left for either Laren or Creena's return, she dared not search hard enough to find it, for fear of opening herself to the devastation of disappointment. What it really felt like was too illogical to acknowledge, enough to make her wonder if, at long last, she'd finally reached the limits of sanity.

Everything around her was falling apart, literally and figuratively, her life so askew she no longer recognized it. There was no question that every expectation she'd had for her life a year ago had corroded as completely as the aluminized mylar that constituted her pathetic home.

It made absolutely no sense at all, that with everything as bad as it was, and no immediate hope of relief, that she could feel like this. But she also knew she couldn't deny it. It was somehow real. As real as the harsh realities which were somehow being kept at bay. It still made no sense whatsoever. But what she felt was more than peace or even detachment. It was a deep, incredible sense of love.

Maybe Zahra could explain it.

"Deven?" she called. "Are you here?"

"Yes, 'Merama," he answered, coming in from the living area and looking up at her expectantly.

"Get your visor and let's go," she said. "I need to talk to Zahra."

* * *

"You're right about them triggering the record," Win stated, eyes on the path ahead. "But there are still ways it can be fixed. It just takes patience. You can't go into something like that and erase it in one session. But it's not impossible."

Dirck laughed cynically, encapsulated once more in Miran composure as they walked leisurely across the withered terrain. "It looked pretty impossible to me. Even if we could erase everything in the PLED, how would we get him out of prison? It'll be a miracle if we ever see him again."

"Miracles are often no more than serving someone's purposes with high rank."

Dirck pondered that a moment, then stopped in the shade of an atsna tree. "Can I ask you something?"

"Sure."

He lifted his visor momentarily so he could look his friend in the eye. "How did you know how to get into that database? I can't imagine why it would have anything to do with the SD. Unless your job entails a lot more than I'm aware of."

Win likewise lifted his visor, gaze steady in return. "My unofficial duties are another story. *Real* unofficial. I'd have a record that would make your father's look like docking violations if I ever got caught."

"So who are you working for?"

"No one."

"Then why? Why are you taking such a risk?"

Win looked for a moment as if he shouldn't even utter the words. He replaced his visor and resumed walking in silence until they were almost where the shackle snake had grabbed him the night before.

"I suppose you're in deep enough I can level with you," he finally said. "I used to work for one of the deputies to the territorial general. The guy was sloppy and lazy. I was only a clerk, but he took a liking to me, thought I could be trusted, and had me do a lot of the scut work he should've been doing. You know, stuff requiring a higher clearance than mine, that I had no business messing with."

"Like the PLED?"

"Yeah. Among other things. But it was real obvious after a while that a high percentage of the stuff in repositories like the PLED was fictitious. It's all political. If some guy with rank likes you, you can do no wrong. If they have it in for you, well, you've seen the result of that. I got sick of it, that's all. I asked for a transfer. I knew I was condemning innocent people, yet had no way of knowing which ones were legitimate and which ones weren't. It got to me after a while and I finally got switched to the SD."

"So you're doing it out of the goodness of your heart? To be one of the good guys?"

Win laughed. "I suppose. I have this strong sense of justice, or something, and don't like the way a few have so much power. Especially when they use it to destroy people."

"Is that what happened to your family?"

"Pretty much. My father got sent off on a bogus charge he couldn't buy his way out of. My brother made so much noise about it, he finally disappeared, too, and my mother basically gave up and died within the season. I decided to fight in more covert ways. Crjlx-IM feels the same way. So, we bend the rules and do what we have to. He's generally more careful, though, since he has a family.

"So now it's my turn," Win concluded. "Will *you* answer a question?"

"If I can."

"How's your family learned so much in such a short time about how to survive here?"

Dirck knew that would come up sooner or later and didn't know how to answer. He finally decided that if he answered indirectly he could defer the rest until Deven could tell him about the bnolar.

"Well, my father's a terralogist, so knows a lot of stuff. He used to recommend which newly discovered planets were the best candidates for colonization and come up with plans to make them habitable. He knows a lot about mineral surveys and that kind of stuff. If there are marketable resources, he suggests an economic plan to utilize them, and also determines what, if anything, can be raised or mined commercially. That, and he did planetary engineering analyses, to figure out how to make marginal planets habitable."

They reached the arch and slipped down the embankment. Puffs of dirt swirled here and there, the plain beyond cloaked in dust-ridden haze. Win went inside and leaned against his 'cruiser, eyes reflecting the fruits of contemplation, even in the cave.

"A terralogist, huh? That certainly explains why Troy has it in for him so bad," he stated abruptly.

"I know Troy wanted him to work for him, but 'Merapa would rather die."

"Exactly. If Troy can't have your father working for him, he's going to make sure no one else does, either. Regional governors are very competitive. That's how they get promotions to the territorial level. There's a lot of pandering. You know, running down the other regions, that kind of thing. That and more covert stuff."

"Like what?"

"Everything from falsifying planetary research data to blatant assassinations."

"You think Troy's doing this to blackmail 'Merapa into working for him?"

"I'd bet my life on it," Win replied "He's obviously been watching him since Mira III."

"What will happen if he still refuses?"

"The charges in the PLED will take their natural course."

They talked quite a while longer, comparing notes and sharing information before they finally climbed into the 'cruiser to return to the ballome. Win brought it to life and eased outside, light and heat hitting like a wall, plastiglas canopy darkening in response.

Red soil skimmed by below, Dirck's only awareness the reappearance of the heart stopping feeling he'd had when he'd seen his father's record in the PLED.

"Let's assume your theory's correct," he finally went on. "How long do you think it'll take Troy to make his offer?"

"People like Troy have more patience than I've ever seen. He's going to make your father sweat, make you sweat, too." Win scowled, eyes fixed ahead. "Things will probably get worse before you see any sign of them getting better. So I doubt he'll do anything, until either during, or maybe even after, Peak Opps."

When he and Win reached the ballome a short time later, 'Merama and Deven were just getting off the transport. His mother seemed calmer than before, panic gone from her eyes.

"Zahra put me through on voice com to Jen. He told me we can stay with them, if we need to." She paused, watching his reaction. According to Esheronian Contingency Law, she could lay claim on her husband's brother for support, but it would require disavowing her current bond. Dirck knew she'd been offered that option before, but refused, preferring poverty to admitting 'Merapa wasn't coming back. He couldn't bring himself to ask, wondering if somehow she knew.

Her green eyes locked on his, searching. "I told him no, but it made me feel less like we're on our own," she went on. "Besides, now that we're domiciled here, we could go as visitors."

"Not the ECL?" he asked quietly, stifling the sigh.

She sighed. "No. I could never do that. Never. But, you know, in a way this is worse than when you both were gone, looking for Creena. I knew then, deep inside, that you'd both make it back. I just knew it, deep inside. This time I'm not so sure."

Dirck avoided her eyes, thoughts darkening again with visions of the PLED.

* * *

CALMANAC: High Opps/Peak -43 Days		
Temp: 64C/147F	PVs: 49%	Quakes: 60%

The day started like any other, the list of tasks a continuation of the day before. Win continued to work at the SD, commuting alternately with the transport or 'cruiser while Dirck gathered needed data from the c-com to fabricate the heat exchanger. It was hard work, mental exertion some days feeling as if he was developing a brain hemorrhage, but he gained confidence each day as understanding grew. The simple fact 'Merapa believed in him prodded him on, his mother and Deven cheering him on as well, when confidence waned. The c-com was loaded with data and he'd only gotten through a small fraction of what was there.

When he encountered something he couldn't understand, he'd take a break so he could digest it, usually grabbing his visor and an opps cloak and taking a quick walk around the ballome's perimeter. If nothing else, once outside, the heat's looming consequences motivated him to stick with it until he could figure it out. Typically he would note Zeta's and Zinni's respective positions and how their declinations changed each day, more from habit than anything else.

This time Zeta was high, nearly directly overhead, Zinni listing in her eastern bed of atmospheric haze. He looked again. Something wasn't right, the glare far less than usual. He squinted hard toward the horizon, hoping it wasn't a dust storm or, worse yet, a PV.

And realized it was happening again.

He activated the back door and stepped inside. "'Merama! Deven! C'mere! Guess what!"

They arrived together, expectant looks on their respective faces as they gathered by the now permanently darkened plastiglas. He pointed to the sky where, only slightly obscured by persistent haze, Nifeir was darkening Zinni's face, producing another eclipse, just as Zahra had predicted.

Deven was grinning as if it were the coolest sight in the known Universe, but 'Merama looked as if she'd seen a ghost.

"I wonder how she knew," she said solemnly. "And whether they'll bring as much misfortune as she predicted."

"Win said they only happen every thousand years or so. I wonder if they ever bring anything good?" Dirck replied, chilled again by the implications.

"They sure haven't so far," his mother sighed. "I suppose time will tell."

* * *

Epsilon Territorial Prison
Cira City, Cyraria

The wretched routine of prison life grated against Laren's nerves like tectonic movement. Treated like an animal, shifted cage to cage, taunted by sporadic lighting and temperature variations, then provided with slop that generated fond memories of genour. There was nothing to see except rough, colorless walls, nothing to hear but incidental low frequency vibrations. While moves broke the monotony, each time the quarters got more cramped, conditions more extreme.

Reviewing everything he'd ever learned since he was Deven's age occupied several days, not only distracting him from fretting about the family, but preserving his sanity. Then periodic tables, laws of physics, thermal and orbital dynamics, multivalent bonding schemes in organic chemistry, sub-atomic particles, the world of quanta, non-location. Mineral formation, atmospheric pressure variances, galactic navigation, gravitational relativity. Fluid and solar dynamics, electromagnetic flux equations. Project Spectra made an appearance, quickly retreated at his command, but not before reminding him why he'd walked away.

Much had changed since then, technology racing forward at a pace he was wont to grasp. Psychology had changed as well, collective knowledge and experience advancing theories of the human mind. If they were that close to controlling it then, it was frightening to think where it could be now, particularly in the wrong hands. Like Troy's.

Again he pondered that first day at the prison, the impressive array of sensors they'd almost seemed to flaunt as he was admitted. Ordinarily a palmprint would have sufficed, yet he'd recognized the reflective properties, the odd delays, the resonant sounds, all indicative they were probing him in invisible ways. He examined the fading bruise inside his elbow where they'd injected him with something. The needle had been huge, its contents unknown other than the fact that immunizations were done with infusion patches. At the time, he'd been so distracted by rage and worry it had skimmed his consciousness, another oddity in a hostile environment, strangely out of context. Now he wondered. Probably a nanoscale transponder in case he escaped.

Or worse.

As his memory rebounded from Spectra, however, a dark and ominous dread fell upon him, that the incarcerated guests of Epsilon's Territorial Prison were more than simply detained.

HIO conventions forbade such practices, but Sigma obviously didn't recognize them or his clearance would have justified possession of the lasomag. Perhaps Troy had already given up, realized, perhaps, through some mentally intrusive technology, that his refusal to lend his talents to INTEGRATION still stood. Was imprisonment no more than revenge, pure and simple? The slow, unpleasant road to death already begun?

His senses sharpened, perception more astute. As much as it appeared he'd been forgotten, instinct told him otherwise. Another revelation materialized, that beyond the usual variations, the temperature rose when he exercised and fell when he slept, maximizing his continual discomfort. He tried fooling it with isometric or stretching exercises, by feigning sleep. No difference. Within the day he was certain they were watching every move. Why and their intentions remained the equation's unknowns.

Answers didn't come immediately. But, as if triggered by observation, conditions after that definitely got worse.

* * *

CALMANAC: High Opps/Peak -30 Days		
Temp: 66C/150F	PVs: 54%	Quakes: 68%

The ballome was at its thermal limits, inside temperature already increasing to an uncomfortable range with only thirty days left until Zeta and Zinni would unleash Peak Opp's killer heat, leaving no time for self-pity or revenge. Already Zinni was tracing an increasingly higher loop in the sky, heat increased with the angle of incidence. Zeta's arc likewise was rising toward the zenith, outside temperature intolerable and there was much to do. 'Merama and Deven built up their food supply while Dirck and Win worked the heat exchanger. The plans and information in the c-com were so detailed that once they had all the components, it only took ten days to assemble, which would have been shortened considerably, except for the need for frequent breaks from working in the heat.

The compressor assembly they'd garnered from the veke had cryo fluid inside the reservoir, as Win had suspected, so there was no need for ammonia; what the change in phase mediums had done to their system specs never entered their minds, other than that they had gained efficiency and could shorten the lines. The zeta arrays and storage cells, also salvaged from the veke, were set up for the extra power they needed. In short, everything was as ready as it ever would be for their first test. Dirck held his breath as he turned on the compressor. It made more noise than expected, probably why his father had designed it to be outside, though he did wonder how much it might be affected by the heat.

The system hissed as air evacuated and cryo fluid began to flow. Then the labyrinth of lines sighed and breathed, wheezed a few times and gradually came to life. The question was, would it work? And if it did, would it work well enough? Gradually, the hissing stopped. Win cracked a valve. The tubing gurgled as the last of the air purged and the two-phase mixture entered the condenser.

"Hey, there's moisture on the condenser coils!" Win said. "They're cold...they're icing up a little...what's going on down there, Dirck? Is anything getting back to the compressor?"

Dirck felt the line entering the compressor. It was warm. He kept his fingers on it, taking its pulse, until eventually it was too hot to touch. The compressor stabilized as the flow returned and the system fell into sync.

But did it work?

A few minutes later, 'Merama and Deven burst out of the ballome, yelling and screaming. For all the fuss, Dirck wondered if something had blown up. Then, within all the ruckus, he heard the words he'd been waiting for.

"*It works!*" she yelled. "*It works!* There's cool, and I mean *cool* air coming in! I haven't felt anything like that since the *Aquarius*. It's great! You two did fantastic!"

Win climbed down from the roof and they all went inside. Dirck didn't believe it until he felt it himself. When at last he felt cool air blowing in his face, he didn't know whether to laugh or cry. He thought about all the work his father had done and how his detailed instructions had made it all possible. He wondered what the temperature was in prison, looked at 'Merama and knew she was thinking the same thing.

Cool air continued to spread, dropping like a rock in the hot ballome. Dirck turned toward Cira City and closed his eyes as their greatest concern for surviving High Opps disappeared with the hot, stifling air.

"Thanks, 'Merapa," he whispered. "Thanks."

Beneath the Surface

Dirck knew the official start of Peak Opps was based on Cyraria's celestial coordinates, but for him it began when he couldn't make it to the transport with the =CC= water without stopping every few steps to catch his breath, even with an opps cloak. Zeta now swept a high and scorching loop overhead that was still lopsided, but its apogee was now at its most powerful declination while Zinni mirrored the effects, commencing its ascent as Zeta declined, each only slightly below the horizon at perigee.

Besides being antithetical to his cool, foggy, Miran upbringing, he'd never thought about anything other than heat's basic annoyances before. Sweating, listlessness, discomfort, simple facts of everyday life for half of Cyraria's sixteen seasons ascribed to Sigma-3/Epsilon's 45 degree latitude. Only two were reasonably comfortable, albeit long at 1528 and 1582 days, respectively. Before they would arrive however, they would have to survive not only the remainder of High Opps, but long days of a dark and frigid winter as well as a chilly spring. And as Peak Opps became experience rather than anticipation, it was apparent the effects were more than annoying — they were deadly.

There was the heat, of course, but increased levels of ultraviolet radiation and ozone contributed as well. Timekeeping even reversed from a forward progression to one based on how many days remained. End minus one hundred thirty-six or E-136, was the first day, then counted down from there.

The worst was about two weeks away, but the heat exchanger was working so well there were times it got uncomfortably cold. It was great, their worries evaporating as if connected with the cyro fluid's phase changes.

They'd optimized the ducting inside and diverted some of the cool air to the storage area above the roof so they could move the veke components that they'd left buried in the cave. Which was just as well, since a grouping of phynques had moved in, along with thousands of bushbirds, the Cyrarian equivalent of cockroaches. The phynques would have a feast. While there, Dirck had also collected several branches from the luma plant, for when they started working on their underground safe.

In spite of their successes, 'Merama seemed quieter lately and distance was returning to her eyes. He tried not to mention his father or Creena, but could tell that was all she thought about. They were on his mind continually, too.

Comcon bulletins came less frequently and usually related to warnings regarding ultraviolet, or UV, levels and ozone concentrations. A few =CC=s trickled in, mainly for the Cyrarian plant guide, now that regionists had plenty of time to read. Those fortunate enough to have abundant =CC=s left entirely, heading for a more temperate clime, like the equatorial regions, though their turn with High Opps would come about the time Sigma3/Epsilon finished up. In Cira City, most people remained, however, since its underground design withstood the seasons' diversity and extremes. Public opps shelters were there, also, which brought in thousands unable to weather it out on their own.

With 'Merapa gone, Dirck sometimes wondered if they should have gone there, too, or accepted Uncle Jen's offer. If the heat exchanger broke down, it could be catastrophic, but so far it was operating beyond their wildest expectations, so his concerns were never more than a passing thought. Usually, such thoughts diverted to how much the prison was protected. Security-wise, it was a toss-up between being deeply imbedded in the ground or at the top, where the only escape was to the outside. Logically, it seemed the lower levels would be cooler and wouldn't be wasted on criminals.

Criminals.

'Merapa a criminal. The thought was abhorrent and he seethed every time he thought about it. Yet his father hadn't been entirely innocent, either. He certainly should have known. Especially with Troy after him. What Win had said about accidental deaths and assassinations haunted him with speculations of how Troy got where he was. He'd probably never know. Nor want to.

The fourth day into Peak Opps, or E-132, he and Win finished up the storage area and started on the safe. At least with the outside work done, they were back on the same diurnal schedule. The safe's opening was beneath the wall that separated Win's cyll in one room and his father's workdeck in the other, so everyone could access it quickly in an emergency. The worst part was getting started, when they had to cut through the floor of the ballome, which was harder than expected.

The dirt was hard at the surface, but got easier to remove as they reached the next layer, which was relatively sandy. The sides were undefined, yet it was easy to remove, at least at first. With each boxcart of dirt, visions of the mounds surrounding Cira City rose in Dirck's mind. Too bad Win couldn't "requisition" some excavation equipment so they'd be done in a matter of hours, an impossible option which he realized would have meant even more when they reached the next layer.

Riddled with rocks of all sizes, there were days they only progressed a few centimeters. Win brought a pick from the SD, which helped some, but it was still slow and frustrating work. The heavy, mindless labor gave Dirck's thoughts too much license, and they wandered freely. At first, prison conditions preyed on him with every thrust of the shovel. The heat, the food, and the unspeakable issue of how 'Merapa was being treated. Besides all that, he missed him terribly, his absence leaving a tremendous void. Then it was Creena, wondering where she was, who she was with, would he ever see her again. But as the trench grew deeper, a different emotion evolved, as if the depression and worry circuits in his mind had overloaded and were yielding to forbidden paths.

In the beginning, it was only the dimmest flicker of an idea, as speculation and bits of information fused together, the polarity negative. How many times had his father emphasized making careful decisions, thinking things through? Had he simply thrown caution to the wind, failing to heed his own advice? Or had he known this would happen? Evidence screamed for the latter, escalating the sense of betrayal. The man wasn't a fool. He had one of the keenest minds in the galaxy. The c-com alone bore witness he'd known.

Gradually, logic and reason devoid of inspiration conspired to a different slant, shifting melancholy to anger, until gradually *How could he?* assaulted every thought. His father's refusal to comply had taken them on a precarious trek that could yet end in death for them all. How could he say he loved them, yet abandon them at a time like this? What about his *Promises* to provide for them?

Dirck said nothing, not even to Win, fearing what expression aloud might release, and capitalized on the toil and dust as an excuse for his sullen introspection. And dug deeper and deeper and deeper and deeper, shovelful by shovelful, literally and figuratively, into the pit.

His darkening thoughts likewise blinded him to other factors. Heat wasn't the only threat from Peak Opps, though that was what had gripped both his and his father's attention since their arrival. The planet itself writhed from passage between its two suns, thermal effects and atmospheric turbulence created by excessive temperature differentials the least of it. Gravity had begun a relentless tug-o-war with Cyraria's molten core. Its rocky nature had saved it thus far, though the current orbit was relatively new, having only completed five full circuits, which constituted a few hundred years. How many passes it could endure was unknown, implications largely ignored.

Rumbles of protest growled within, but remained below the threshold of repeated thrusts of the shovel, hum of the heat exchanger and turmoil in his mind. But tension was building which would inevitably release.

* * *

Territorial Tower
Cira City, Cyraria

Augustus Troy observed the drama within the mammoth aquarium pensively, the black marble floor reflected in its depths. Fish and other creatures swam amongst the rocks and reefs, their predatory natures ranging from subtle to aggressive. He hadn't been told why he'd been summoned, but was reasonably sure he knew. His superior wanted a progress report.

The competition was stiff, more so than Troy had expected. Regional governors like himself were as numerous as bushbirds, each with varying degrees of talent, leadership ability and ruthlessness, to say nothing of vast differences in political ideologies. Some were democratic, some fascist, some socialist, and others a combination of several. All were appointed, however, and whether they remained an RG, were demoted, expelled, or ascended into higher ranks depended on their territorial general's, or TG's, benevolence.

Fortunately, Troy's leanings were in line with Rohtik Spoigan, the TG's deputy and economic advisor. Spoigan's dedication to INTEGRATION was firm, but the TG himself was liberal, his RGs a remarkable mix. Troy had come with high recommendations, from the INTEGRATOR himself, thus Spoigan had arranged the appointment, but maintaining his position was not as easy as he'd expected. The TG expected to see steady and honest progress, something Sigma hadn't yet produced, under Troy or anyone else. And thus his progress was stalled. Given the seasonal extremes and weak economy, it was no wonder. And now High Opps was upon them, survival the only thing on regionists' minds.

A large blue picala with orange markings lurked within the cavity of a porous rock, eyeing a cluster of smaller, fast-moving groullies. Groullies schooled, their synchronized movements intriguing to watch as they darted about as one. Nearly faster than Troy's eye could see, the cluster was reduced by three, the picala back on station for the next pass. The event's symbolism wasn't wasted and Troy considered once more why he was there.

Sigma had significant problems. The industrial base was nearly nil, the regionists largely uneducated, and the climate harsh with alkaline soil. Where there *was* soil, for the majority of land area was no more than dust covered rock. There appeared to be fairly copious subterranean water resources, which helped some, but ores or minerals to build the industrial sector were essential. Either that, or some kind of agriculture. It was no secret the planet needed to be self-sustaining, and whoever could hasten that would be assured promotion. Perhaps even beyond the territorial level.

Spoigan knew about Brightstar. Knew his talents, abilities and history. Not only as a terralogist, but other endeavors, those that few were privy to. Since Brightstar's arrest, the queries had come nearly every day. Once on board, Spoigan could assign him where he pleased. While Troy hoped to use him to develop his own region, numerous territorial openings vied for his talent. Troy wanted him to develop Sigma's potential and thus assure his own ascension. When he was promoted from RG, he'd take his protégé with him to the top.

Spoigan, however, was more ambitious on another level. His designs were on Brightstar's technical abilities, not manipulating planetary ecosystems and energy sinks. So far, he'd respected him as Troy's find, but the pressure was building. If there wasn't significant progress soon, that could change. Spoigan could even release him from prison and steal him outright if he grew impatient.

Troy watched the groullies wander among the lilting sea plants, oblivious to the picala. Whether Brightstar had been sufficiently "conditioned" to receive his best and final offer was not assured. If not, they'd simply have to turn up the gain. That nanobot implant could inflict whatever physical, emotional or mental pain necessary to bring anyone to their knees. Even the likes of Brightstar.

But, as the groullies' numbers reduced again, Troy knew time was running out. Past experience indicated it would take at least another two weeks, even with ramped up persuasion efforts, to get Brightstar to so much as listen. The only problem imaginable was that the degree required to break him could compromise that brilliant mind.

Knowing Spoigan would want a hard deadline, he lifted the flap covering the screen on his uniform's forearm and consulted his schedule. It was full, some items more flexible than others. He'd be off-world for a while, but he could be back and reasonably free by E-59. That would have to do. He dictated the time and event, watched the appointment snap into place, then closed the flap as his name flashed on the databoard. Pausing only long enough for a final wink at the picala, Troy strode confidently toward Spoigan's chambers.

Betrayed

Creena slipped into her chair at the dinner table and eyed the food on her plate with complete disinterest, mind faraway. Eluding the cannibal a few weeks before had left her in an odd state, anxiety heightened on one hand that he may indeed return, and lowered on the other, as her trust in the Bensons increased. As she'd pondered these concepts with their respective implications, she'd then begun obsessing on the fact that since her arrival not a word had been said about her ship.

Not a single word.

Her appetite vanished as she focused on facts far more important to her future than the meal at hand. Barbecued porkchops, the family favorite, disappeared off the others' plates in no time flat, but Creena's remained untouched. She watched silently as the others enjoyed the meal, suddenly jealous of the ease and comfort of their lives. Mr. Benson looked at her casually and their eyes met.

"How long have I been here?" she asked quietly.

"Oh, I don't know," he replied. "A couple months, I guess."

"When are they going to be done with my ship?" she asked quietly. "Why haven't I heard anything about it since I got here?"

All movement stopped as everyone's gaze shifted to Mr. Benson. His fork clattered to his plate, the only sound. He swallowed, eyes resting solemnly on hers as the light suspended over the table swayed in a breeze from the kitchen door. Tammy grabbed her napkin as it started to fly away, spilling her milk. No one even cracked a smile while she ran into the kitchen for a towel, bumping Creena's chair as she passed.

"Have you heard anything from Colonel Jenkins about my ship?" she asked again. Nobody spoke, the only sound the towel slapping the milk. "When are they going to be done so I can go somewhere else to find a starship to Mira III?"

Everyone continued to stare expectantly at Mr. Benson. "I don't know," he said finally with a sigh. "I guess I'll call down to Hill tomorrow and find out." Creena looked wistfully from him to his wife, who had a look on her face identical to one her mother used to get when 'Merapa procrastinated something he really didn't want to do.

"Tom, I really think you ought to do it now," she said softly.

Creena knew it wasn't their fault, but she remembered Colonel Jenkins saying they could learn more from her ship in a month than they could figure out themselves in years. According to Earth's timekeeping, they had already had it twice that long. The time had gone quickly, true. But it was time to go, especially since she had to get on with what 'Merapa had instructed her to do, which would further delay her return to her family. There was no telling how long it would take to get to Mira III and accomplish what she had to do there.

The import of everything which had happened since her arrival suddenly washed over her in a suffocating rush of uncontrollable grief. She blinked fiercely, not wanting to cry in front of everyone. The last thing she wanted was for them to think that she didn't appreciate all they'd done. Coming there was one of the most amazing things that had ever happened, from the dairy to the renewed hope about Dirck. But certainly it wasn't intended to be forever, a thought she refused to harbor.

She excused herself quietly, pushed away from the table, and flew up the stairs, two at a time. Her long, well-tanned legs carried her quickly to what had become her room, where she sat on the side of the bed, still fighting tears. The Bensons felt so much like family. She had everything she needed. Food, clothes, companionship, protection, at least for the most part. But it wasn't home. That's all there was to it, it simply wasn't home. Home was 'Merama and 'Merapa, Dirck, Deven.

And it was thoughts of her little brother that did it, a previously dammed up tear breaking free and sliding around her nose, leaving a cool track down her cheek. She grabbed a tissue from next to the bed, staring blankly at splintered rays of afternoon sunlight escaping the blinds. Suddenly, every alien fixture screamed a reminder that this wasn't where she belonged. The bed instead of a cyll, the funny light, the wood paneling, even the plaid curtains. Every item silently taunted her, its lack of response amplifying her dilemma as if mocking the fact she was a virtual prisoner on an alien world.

She thought of her family, what they might be doing. Cyraria. She'd never been there, at least on the ground, yet it was home. There were so many times during chores that she'd wondered if that was what it was like there. And maybe it was. Maybe outside, away from this Earth-type house, she'd be more at home than she realized. She dashed downstairs, slowing to a normal pace as she peeked into the dining room from the parlor. The Bensons had finished eating, the kids sprawled on the floor in the family room watching TV, Mr. Benson in his chair as they always were after dinner and before evening chores.

"I'm, uh, going for a walk. Okay?"

Mr. Benson hesitated but a moment before he nodded. "Not too far, okay?"

"I won't," Creena promised, then slipped out the back.

She wandered past the garden. Even weeding, which she actually enjoyed, held no attraction right now. Weeding was Earth and Earth wasn't home. She walked through the hay field, the dampness of alfalfa cool against her legs while a wheel-line spewed water in rhythmic pulses at the opposite end of the field. Across the canal on a wobbly board, through dry weeds toward the hills. She trudged upward until she reached the now-familiar grassy plateau, no longer green since the onset of summer heat. She plucked a wild sunflower, stopping a moment to study its golden petals. Were there flowers on Cyraria?

She boosted herself up on the edge of the trampoline, wishing as she always did that it were a literal springboard to the stars. The valley spread below in a grid-like panorama. Back-lit by the sun leaning toward the horizon a tractor chugged in the distance, coughing and sputtering puffs of exhaust as it inched across a chocolate-colored swatch where narrow green stripes of late corn were barely visible.

Maybe her original fears of being stuck there were right. Already it seemed as if she'd been there forever. Her family, Cyraria, everything was blurring into the past, like a pleasant, beautiful dream she didn't want to forget. There were times since coming to Earth that she'd felt as if her mind had turned inward, little bits of knowledge seeping into her consciousness that she'd never been aware of learning. They often touched on agriculture, tidy little facts she felt she'd need when she got to Cyraria.

It wasn't that she missed Mira III. Far from it. Her family, yes. Even Dirck. Again, she obsessed on what they were doing, what their life was like, what she would do when she got there. Her sojourn on Earth had brought other insights, too, not only about family dynamics but about people in general, civilizations, and why they acted the way they did. Mira III had been deadened by time. The people there were like the Bensons' cows. They had simple routines which they obeyed unquestioningly. Where to work, whom to marry, how many children to have, where to live. There was unending, unquestioned peace, no decisions, no worries, no cannibals. But it was a cold, gray world where, family aside, living was a void. For all the pain she'd experienced since she'd left, she'd still never felt more alive. And on Cyraria, she could have it all.

The Earthlings had been messing with her ship for over a month. They had to be done soon, had to be. If she had to stay much longer, she'd lose her orbit. Or her marbles, as Tammy would say. What were marbles, anyway?

And then her senses were abruptly bombarded by a familiar bouquet. Creena sat up straight on the edge of the tramp, eyes closed as she savored the welcome fragrance and awaited the formation of words in her mind.

Thyron! You're back! she thought.

[Your voice is dim and far away

Aloud your thoughts you have to say.]

"Okay. How's this?" she asked, complying, yet wondering if she'd changed so much that now even Thyron couldn't hear her.

[A little better but still faint

Something still your voice does taint.]

She closed her eyes and concentrated as hard as she could. "Is this better?"

[Better much, now I can hear

It sounds as if you're present here.]

"Good! Oh, Thyron, it's so good to hear from you. Are you okay?"

[As you wish my tale I'll tell

Of how I came to wish you well.

When I wilted in a heap

Then the Earthlings tried to keep

The CO2 found in their air

Higher so I'd better fare.]

"That's wonderful! So where are you?"

[Southward and a little west,

A thousand kilometers, at best

Here in Area Fifty-one

Is where they took us, all undone.

Other ships are here as well

Their fate, like ours, is sad to tell.]

"Snurkles! Aren't they done with our ship?"

[Not to add to all your woes,

But they're not done, or even close.

The ship's in total disarray

It looks like you're on Earth to stay.]

"Oh, no!" she groaned. "We can't stay here! What can we do?"

[When the time's exactly right,

I think that I can end our plight.]

"Really?" she cried. "How?"

[Earth's restricted, don't you know?

Prohibited by the HIO.]

"Now you tell me."

[That fact I tried to tell you, true,

"Shut down!" is what I got from you.]

Creena scowled with the recollection, hoping he wasn't as vengeful as Aggie. "I was wrong, about a lot of things," she admitted. "I'm sorry, Thyron. Really. So how can you get us out of here?"

[Traffic they do watch with care

Thus I'll know when one is there.]

"Can you make contact?"

[I can t be heard, comcon or not

So only if they talk through thought.]

Creena opened her eyes for fear she was imagining the conversation, her mind in a muddled whirl. A pickup bumped along the road below, reminding her of where she was and what she had to do. She closed her eyes and concentrated again.

"Where's Aggie?" she asked.

[Here, with me, she gets to stay
Components all in disarray.]

She cringed, certain she'd detected a hint of satisfaction in his silent voice. "Thyron, you have to put her back together."

[With her left electronic brain,
She has caused us lots of pain.
In her disassembled state
She can't affect our future fate.]

He did have a point, especially when she needed an attitude adjustment. And she'd certainly been obnoxious since leaving Verdaris. Creena opened her eyes and watched as a fluffy cloud exploded in brilliance as it drifted in front of the Sun. Her mind flashed back to Verdaris, the comet, the Sapphirans. Aggie had saved her life. When the Sun reappeared, Creena knew what she had to do.

"We can't leave her here," she insisted. "She's helped me out of a bunch of trouble. It's the least I can do."

[Maybe that was true before
But don't forget who opened the door.
Until then we could have departed
Before these troubles even started.]

She also couldn't forget that when they'd first arrived, Aggie had suggested a more thorough investigation. Creena had been the one who'd insisted on landing, then ignored that bad feeling.

"Never mind," she replied. "I want her back. What's it like there? Are they guarding you all the time?"

[Most the time there's someone here
  Except on weekends guards are near.]

"Is that long enough to get her back together?"

[If you think that if I do
Happiness will come to you.]

Creena smiled. "Yes. It would. So contact a ship. Then have them pick us up late Sunday night."

[What you ask may take some time

Before we leave and all is fine.]

The botanical cynicism was clear, even across a thousand kilometers. "Oh, Thyron!" she cried. "Please! I can't stay here any longer, I just can't!"

[Since it means so much to you

I will see what I can do

But Sunday next is very near

The likelihood quite null, I fear.]

A twig snapped and Creena whirled around. Two pairs of wide, questioning eyes returned her startled gaze.

"Are you okay?" Allen asked.

She smiled weakly, wondering how long he and David had been there. She'd never told them about Thyron, only Aggie, so hopefully they'd only think she was talking to herself. Or maybe she should tell them she knew her ship was in billions of pieces and was trying to arrange some other way off-world.

Maybe, maybe not.

"I'm fine," she said, jumping down from the tramp to follow them back to the house, choices still cycling. Allen *had* saved her from the cannibal. Did she owe it to him to be truthful? Completely? Before she could decide, David spoke.

"Uncle Milt said they're almost done with your ship," he said.

She looked over, mouth agape, wondering if she'd heard him correctly. David's head was down, eyes glued evasively to the trail.

[Humans on this planet are

Not trustworthy very far.]

Whether it was memory or a parting thought from Thyron she didn't know, but its pain was more than simple loneliness or homesickness, the trust and warmth of belonging shriveling up inside her like tender sprouts in the noonday sun. The confusion and hurt grew with each step, her only consolation that whatever their motives might be, hopefully she'd be gone in a few days.

But try as she might, she couldn't quite convince herself it didn't matter.

Intrusions

By the time they got back to the house, Creena was more confused than ever. If she couldn't trust the Bensons, then she was even worse off than she thought. She excused herself early, claiming her head hurt and she wanted to go to bed. Upstairs, she crawled between the sheets, aching worse than she ever had from hauling hay. At long last she fell asleep, only to be assaulted by nightmares.

First, she was being chased by Erebusites and Sapphirans, firing at her with lasomags. She rounded a corner in a dark, misty alley that ended against a shiny, metal wall. When her pursuers turned the corner, part of the wall melted, the Bensons on the other side, beckoning her through. Before she could make up her mind, she was in a steaming, sticky jungle. Carnivorous plants crowded around her, reaching toward her with spiny nodes dripping with blood and imprinted with the same evil she'd encountered too many times before.

When she awoke the next morning, she felt as if she'd never slept. Though the dreams faded, the burden in her heart didn't, with the question of why she'd been betrayed still foremost in her mind.

She did her chores with Tammy in silence, counting the days until the weekend. It was Thursday, so there were only three more days until Sunday night.

Good. Soon she'd be on her way and wouldn't have to worry about it anymore.

When Sunday night came, she was so excited she could hardly contain herself. Everyone kept commenting how nice it was to see her in a good mood again, which made her laugh even more. That night she laid awake, awaiting Thyron's summons. Funny he hadn't verified an arrival time, but then he always was a bit eccentric. She couldn't have slept if she'd wanted to. The hands on the clock progressed in a time warp, minutes like hours. The house grew still, dark and quiet.

At two o'clock, she couldn't stand it any longer. She slipped from bed quietly, got dressed in her old Code Orange uniform and knelt by the open window, watching. The waning moon was completing its path across the sky, dipping toward the mountains marking the southwestern horizon where the last throes of moonlight were shadowed by an approaching storm.

Thunderheads thickened, quickly covering the sky with snarling flashes of violent light. Before long, a volley of heavy raindrops pelted the window, smearing her view as lightning assaulted the mountains. Thunder rumbled through the canyons, amplified as it escaped its rocky containment to the valley beyond. She beheld its primitive power and beauty with detached awe, remembering her first encounter with such a storm on Verdaris and wondering if Cyraria had them, too.

Gradually, the clamor faded and the sweet fragrance of summer rain rose from the earth, thirsty vegetation welcoming the unexpected shower. The clouds broke up, but didn't clear, allowing only an occasional glimpse of a few lonely stars. An eerie stillness crept through the valley, the shower's brief interlude changing in character from refreshment to peril.

It almost sounded like thunder, as if the storm were returning, except the din was more localized, moving like a specter above the clouds. Creena watched, fascinated at first, then mesmerized by the stealthy motion of unearthly light.

Something wasn't right, foreboding penetrating every fiber of her being. The illumination was constant, a steady searching beam above high fog, until it settled on a single location above the front lawn and hovered there, waiting. The vapors parted, opening like an aperture controlled by unknown forces. The light's intensity swelled, rays spiking the ground, then the source gradually lowered through the opening, undiscernible at first, then resolving to what looked like a wedge-shaped starcraft within a globular concentration of blinding light

The terror she'd felt at the prospect of being stranded on Earth was abruptly consumed by another fear, one deeper and more soul threatening than anything she'd ever sensed before. Suddenly, it wasn't simply a matter of not getting back to her family, but a matter of being annihilated, body and soul.

<<Creena.>>

A cloak of icy fear clenched her entire body, yet she couldn't move, her attention transfixed by the surreal light dropping lower, hovering toward the house.

<<Creena. It's time to go home.>>

The call wasn't audible, but it wasn't Thyron. Whoever or whatever it was invoked the essence of darkest evil. *Who are you?* she thought, terrified.

<<We're your friends. We'll take you to your family. We know where they are, Creena. On Cyraria, waiting. Come with me, and you can join them.>>

The light was less than fifty meters from the house, its edges now defined as a brilliant ellipsoid that seized her mind in commanding attention as it lowered to the ground.

"No," she said, but even as she uttered the word, logic screamed within and without for her to obey. It would be her only chance, ever. She rose to her feet involuntarily and started toward the door. With each step, the fog of deepest malevolence invading her mind thickened. She was in the hall, outside of David and Allen's bedroom, heading for the stairs. She tried to stop and go back, but her body kept going, as if it were no longer her own.

"Help!" she screamed, but the sound never materialized beyond her will to speak. "I won't go!" she cried desperately, even as her feet started down the steps.

<<Don't be foolish. We'll take you home. We won't harm you. If we wanted to harm you, we would have long ago. You must come with us. We're the only ones who can take you back.>>

Now on the main floor, she found herself in the tiled entry, the door already open. The ellipsoid had settled to just above the ground, the light's potency fading to reveal the vehicle's triangular form, its ramp descending. It was bigger than the *Cerulean Nimrod* and far more sophisticated, vector disks entirely silent as it hovered in place. The Earthlings had lied to her, and within a few meters distance was a vehicle capable of transporting her home. To refuse was insane. Any Miran with a quark of sense would have been onboard by now.

Transfixed yet repulsed, the forces of evil closed in to suffocate her last spark of righteous will. She walked slowly through the door, stepped down from the porch, and started across the lawn still damp with rain. All she could see was the illuminated ramp as reality faded to another dimension, a bending of space and time, good and evil that warped the scene before her in twisted waves of faulted destiny.

The impulses in her mind were growing stronger, her will nearly devoid of power. It was beyond her thoughts now and becoming part of her mind, still driving her feet closer to the starcraft. As if no more than a hapless observer, her refusal couldn't stop her steps. It made so much sense to go. They would take her home. It was what she wanted, waited for, for so very long. Logic saturated her mind, occulting her instincts. If she didn't go, she'd never get home. *Never.* She'd never see her parents, Dirck, or Deven again, and be stuck on Earth surrounded by people she couldn't trust.

But going wasn't right. Something was very, very wrong. Of all the bad feelings she'd ever experienced, none had come close to this, even when she'd been chased by the cannibal. Logical or not, it wasn't what she was supposed to do. Something horrible would happen if she went. Yet, her footsteps continued, the distance closing in rhythmic, controlled motion beyond her control. Her senses were fading—the sensation of cool, damp grass beneath her feet, the smell of freshly laundered air, the rhythmic splatter of a distant sprinkler.

"Thyron!" her mind screamed. *"Thyron! Help me!"*

The interface was but steps away, her consciousness merging with a force that imposed a strange and uncomfortable sense of calm upon her frantic mind. It was over. There was nothing more she could do. She didn't know who it was that wanted her so badly, only that her will was slipping inexorably, her thoughts garbled and yielding to something outside herself. A gaping void edged in, fractured energy beckoning her through. She closed her eyes and held her breath, resigned to the inevitable.

[Creena! Stop!]

A blinding flash of awareness jolted her to attention, her bare foot only a step away from the energy field's boundary. The impulse was retreating, her mind alert, senses wrapped in a familiar photosynthetic fragrance.

[Tell them no but one more time,
Shift your thoughts from theirs to mine.]

"Thyron!" she gasped, then closed her eyes and obeyed.

<<Creena. This is your only chance. If you refuse, you will never see your family together again. No one else has the power to deliver you home with that guarantee.>>

A sliver of indecision held her fixed. Could it be true? Part of it was, she could tell, or it wouldn't have struck her heart as it had. Yet the overwhelming sense of evil she felt spoke louder, and she knew it was wrong. She stared into the strange patterns of twisted power before her, oscillating between logic and feeling.

She didn't think she could live with the thought of never seeing her family again, not if she had a choice. The technology before her was more sophisticated than anything she'd encountered since coming to Earth. They promised not to hurt her. All logic prevailed upon her to go. The only reason against it was that feeling. That same feeling she'd had in the tunnel on the *Aquarius*; that she'd had when the pygmies landed on Verdaris; that she'd had when they landed on Earth; that she'd had when looking into the cannibal's loathsome eyes. She'd yielded to logic on all those occasions, and where had it gotten her?

"No! It isn't right! I won't go, not with you!"

<<We will not force your return. But I must warn you, if you do not, your family will suffer greatly.>>

An agonizing knot of fear twisted her heart at the thought her actions could cause them pain. How could she deliberately and willfully hurt them? An unbidden vision resolved in her mind's eye, of incredible despair and grieving, of a chain of events in which she was a fateful link. There was truth there, beyond denial. The anguish stabilized in an incredible, searing hurt that threatened to collapse her heart, emotions shoving her back toward logic, even while intuition blared a strident warning not to cross the beckoning threshold.

[Creena! No! Wait!]

She swallowed hard, tears burning her eyes as she paused, debating again. The pain reached a dark crescendo, then surprisingly evaporated, releasing a feeling of peace that promised joy beyond measure. It would be okay. Regardless of what the voice said, eventually it would be okay. But only if she did what was right. If she went with them, the final outcome would be worse. Much worse. How she could possibly know that, she had no idea, only that she did, beyond a shadow of a doubt.

"No!" she stated decisively. "I won't go. It isn't right."

<<Creena...>>

"No! Go away! Leave me alone!"

A long and ominous silence followed, one that penetrated her mind with the finality of her decision. Right or wrong, her options were closed.

<<So be it. Your fate is sealed. Our course will be altered, but we will not fail.>>

Shaking with emotion, she winced as its parting words ripped through her in a chilling surge. Clarity of thought returned as the energy field faded, dimming until it eventually disappeared. The craft withdrew its ramp, again became a globule of light then rose slowly. Its glow hovered above, briefly pulsed in a blinding flash and was gone.

Creena moved forward slowly to check for any remaining signs of the visitor. Nothing. Even where she'd clearly seen the ramp descend into the grass was unscathed, the damp blades untrampled beneath her toes, the fresh fragrance deluging her senses as she returned to the porch.

"Thyron?" she called. "Are you there?"

No answer. She sat down on the porch, watching pinpoints of light flicker on the valley floor then looked up to a flawless dome of stars. The clouds had cleared, revealing the smoky band of the Milky Way.

The panic was gone, leaving only the vestige of a nightmare behind. Had it been no more than that? It was so real, yet no tangible evidence remained, not even a crease in the lawn. Only the oppressive weight of impending doom. Why did she feel so abandoned? Should she have gone? Had she somehow made the wrong choice again?

Finally, she crept back inside, locking the door behind her before going upstairs. She resumed her post by the window, calling Thyron periodically to no avail. Where was he? Had he rescued her or not? Confusion was encroaching fast, the witness of truth wilting under the harsh scrutiny of logic. Had she once again failed to make the right choice? Dawn bleached the eastern horizon, yet no answers came, and by the time the mountains were cast with the onset of sunrise, she was so overwhelmed with failure that she climbed back into bed, clothes and all, and cried herself to sleep.

When she finally came downstairs that morning, no one said anything about the late hour or her red, swollen eyes, but it seemed as if they'd never stop staring. Even Tammy kept still. But that evening, when Creena was getting ready to go to bed, Tammy slipped into the room and asked if she could sleep in the other bed. Creena shrugged, then climbed into her own and got comfortable facing the wall. Tammy didn't take the hint, but chattered on and on, but Creena didn't hear a word.

As another weekend approached, Creena's hopes inflated again, only to rupture painfully when Monday arrived on another week of milking and feeding and weeding, picking beans and shucking corn. Tomatoes were on, too, the kitchen cluttered with huge kettles and mason jars as she and Tammy helped bottle everything from pickles to peaches. She'd never seen so much food before in her life. Or work. So much that even genour was beginning to sound like an acceptable alternative.

Each day her heart closed tighter with any closeness she'd felt with the Bensons as lifeless as an expired fuel cell. Allen and David kept trying to act normal, but never said another word about her ship. A few times she'd been tempted to throw their deceit in their face, but she really didn't want to talk about it, anyway.

Thyron had been caught, she just knew it. They'd discovered him trying to reassemble Aggie and made him into a vegemal feast for Earthling diplomats. It was all her fault. She'd refused her one chance to go home and now she was stuck.

Forever.

* * *

Terra Day 77

Saturday night Creena dreamed of her cousins for the first time since she'd gotten lost. It was dimensioned as if she were there, viewing from above. There they were, safe on Cyraria, adapting to their new home with cheerful, contented hearts. They were on the periphery of a large settlement, living in a luxurious underground dwelling attached to her uncle's medical office. They played with carefree abandon, lives as good or better than they'd been on Mira III, never knowing what it was like to be lonely or hurt or sorry. Bitter tears covered her face until her jealously was abruptly quenched by a kind but forceful impression.

Envy not those whose path excludes hardship, it said. *Life's peaks and valleys bring wisdom, the gift from troubles born and suffered. Reaching the summit is only joyful for those who labored hard to get there.*

Her vision panned across kilometers of parched terrain to a ramshackle ballome, surrounded by dusty red hills beneath scorching binary suns. The obvious poverty and desolation meant nothing, smothered by the desire for one glimpse of those she knew dwelt within. The image started to fade, the ground itself seeming to rise up around it.

No! she cried. *Please! Just one look. I want to see them. If I can't go home, at least let me know they're okay!*

She strained to bring it back, realizing at last that the vision itself wasn't fading. Rather, it was within the scene itself, a pounding pillar of violence bearing down on the defenseless abode she knew was her home. The whirlwind thundered into full view, nothing visible but wind-driven dirt and debris. When at last it retreated, all that remained was parched red ground, surrounded by unspeakable silence.

No! she cried, heart rending. *No!*

She awoke with a start, the dark, heavy feeling she'd retained since the starcraft encounter evolving to unspeakable horror. Her longing to go home had blinded her mind, creating the false assumption that everything was fine. Maybe that wasn't how it was at all. Maybe, as 'Merapa had indicated, something was very, very wrong.

She sat up in bed and covered her face with her hands, silently pouring out her heart to anyone or anything that might listen. She begged for assurance, some indication that it wasn't true. No answers came. Her pleading shifted, this time for help and reassurance.

Gradually, shadow by shadow, the pall evaporated. They were in serious trouble, true. But somehow she knew they weren't dead. At least not yet. But any relief she felt was short-lived, replaced by the equally clear impression that if she went home before fulfilling her promise to her father, things would be even worse. Gradually, her fears diminished, crowded out by faith and the inbred Miran desire for obedience. Again, she sensed that everything would be all right.

She belonged on Earth, at least for now. When it was time to leave she would. Refusing to go with that starcraft was right. She wasn't supposed to go home, but to Mira III, like 'Merapa had asked. And when the time was right, she'd leave.

While a driving concern for her family persisted, her newly gained insight brought her fears to a more manageable level. She hoped for their safety and protection and that they would know she was okay; that they, too, would believe they would be together again someday.

For all the explanations and understanding and hopes she'd gained, however, one mystery lingered—why the Bensons had lied about her ship. And with that one remaining, troubling thought, she fell back to sleep.

Beating the Heat

Dirck was just donning the opps cloak to go empty the boxcart when a sudden pounding echoed through the ballome. Everyone gathered in the living area, staring at one another nervously. Dirck tuned into the humming of the heat exchanger, wondering if something was wrong.

The pounding repeated, this time obviously from the front door. 'Merama's horrified look chilled him more than the heat exchanger at top efficiency. At least Win had rigged the palmlatch to keep everyone but them out. Bracing for the worst, he herded her and Deven into their sleeproom and told Win to stay out of sight.

He opened the door to the front entry, which served as a heat lock, closing it behind him. Heat and the scent of ozone took his breath away. He peered through the window in the outer door. The silvered helmet of a full-service oppsuit was visible outside. It bore no markings. Whoever it was had arrived in a veke with no territorial crest or other identification. Shards of light reflected from its dimpled skin, a feature reserved for increased lift in rarified atmospheres. Heat closed in and dizziness began to fog his brain as he strained for a glimpse inside the helmet beyond the window. Reflections shifted and a pair of familiar eyes met his.

Gasping, Dirck palmed the lock, then burst through the inside door to the living area, struggling for air as the visitor followed. By the time he'd caught his breath, the helmet was off and the caller had him in a firm, back-pounding embrace.

"Uncle Jen!" he exclaimed, grinning.

Within moments, the others had joined him to share the hugs and excitement. Dirck introduced Win, and gradually the chatter ebbed.

"Quite a place you have here," Uncle Jen commented, looking around. "I'll say this much, it's cooler than my place, which has the best cooling system I could get in Cira City."

"'Merapa designed it, but Win and I put it together," Dirck said proudly. "So far, it's working great."

Uncle Jen was trying hard not to stare at the trail of dirt on the floor. Dirck could well imagine that, especially with the cleanliness standards he held as a surgeon, he probably was wondering mighty hard what it was doing there.

"We're digging a safe," he explained. "Not only from the heat, if necessary, but as a hiding place. We're not going to get caught in another raid, if we can help it."

His uncle nodded approval. "Good idea," he said, then turned to 'Merama. "So how's Laren?"

She swallowed and shook her head. "No one knows. We've heard nothing, absolutely nothing."

Dirck debated whether to open up about the PLED right there, or get his uncle alone. He decided on the latter, playing along with the conversation until his mother and Deven went to fix something to eat and drink.

"Come see how far we've gotten with the safe," he said, nodding urgently toward the sleeproom. Uncle Jen took the hint and followed.

"So what's going on?" he asked softly.

Dirck gave him a quick summary of the PLED. His uncle sighed, holding his temples with his fingers. "I was afraid something like this would happen. I didn't expect it to be this serious, though."

"How could he let this happen?" Dirck asked shakily. "For days, even since we left the *Aquarius,* all he talked about were choices and thinking things through. How could he leave us like this? *How*?"

Uncle Jen shook his head. "I don't think it's something we could easily understand, Dirck. He loves all of you more than life itself, I know that. But you're right, he's also never done anything in his life without full knowledge of the consequences. Nonetheless, when your father and I were on Esheron, they told us something about mistakes that's worth remembering, especially when it comes to situations like this, where innocent people get caught in the crossfire."

"Oh, yeah?" Dirck replied, somewhat defensively. "And what was that?"

"*There are no mistakes, only detours.* In other words, we'll get where we're supposed to be, one way or another. We're free to carve our own destiny and no one can stop that without our permission."

And that was as far as it got before Deven arrived with drinks, the venting a brief episode of pressure relief that prevented what could have been a devastating explosion.

"How have you been?" 'Merama asked when they'd returned to the living area. "How are Para and the children doing?"

Uncle Jen sat on the floor and leaned back, stopping as the oppsuit tanks hit the wall. "Let me get out of this thing," he said, removing his boots, unlatching the front and slipping it off. The shirt underneath was clean and colorful, a soft shade of aqua. Dirck tried not to stare, wondering what it was like to have clean, colorful clothes instead of mud-stained rags. Uncle Jen dropped the oppsuit in a heap beside him and relaxed.

"We're doing quite well, after getting over that pressure vortex," he explained. "There were so many injuries, about a hundred fifty deaths, and damage like I've never seen before in my life."

Dirck swallowed hard, the scene in his mind abruptly punctuated with other recent deaths.

"The only residences that made it through were the subterres, since they're below ground," Uncle Jen continued.

"Some of them lost power when zeta arrays blew away, but generally, they survived fairly well. All ballomes in its path were utterly destroyed. In some cases, you couldn't tell they'd ever been there, any sign completely gone."

His expression darkened with unpleasant memories as he went on. "We were just getting ready to move into our subterre at the clinic when it hit. I never heard such a racket before in my life. Ever hear one?" Everyone shook their head. "The noise is overwhelming, a deep, pulsing roar, real low pitch, almost beyond audible range. You feel it more than you hear it at first, then it gets so loud you think your head will explode from the pressure changes. This one wasn't even that big. I hear they get more frequent during Peak Opps, so be careful. Get that safe dug at least four meters deep, with good ventilation. And if you hear anything that sounds suspicious—*anything*—don't wait to get to cover. They can form in a matter of seconds."

Dirck hadn't thought of the safe as a PV shelter before, but it made sense. "Where'd you get the veke?" he asked. "Is that yours?"

Uncle Jen nodded. "You could say that. It's mine to use, however I want, but technically it belongs to the clinic. We have a mediveke, too. There's auxiliary power for surgical procedures, full life support, and so forth. It even has a holophonic sound system. We use it to transport patients to the ALSIC in Cira City, or pick them up, when necessary. It's pretty impressive, if I do say so myself."

It was obvious from the silence that followed that Uncle Jen's listeners were impressed, too. He smiled a little awkwardly, then pulled what looked like a small grafix generator from one of his pockets. "Listen to this," he said, and switched it on. No lights or graphical representation were projected, but the sounds that filled the ballome were such as Dirck had never imagined. The tones of grafix were pleasant, even soothing, but never stirring or emotional like this.

"What is it?" Mother asked, fascinated.

"Esheronian music," Uncle Jen replied. "It was illegal on Mira III. One of my patients bartered it for my services a while back. Best deal I ever made."

Dirck listened intently, wondering at the feelings invoked by the multidimensional sounds. "Why was it banned on Mira III?" he asked.

"Its effect. They were afraid of its power, that it would generate too many uncontrolled feelings and self-expression. Mira III's goal was to suppress emotion and individuality, not stimulate it. I grew up with this and missed it, a lot."

"I can see why," Dirck commented, absorbing each rising strain and sensing something he'd never felt before. "That's pretty potent stuff."

"I know," Uncle Jen agreed. "Isn't it great?"

"Yeah. I like it."

"So do I," Mother said quietly. "I think. It does get to you, though, doesn't it?"

Uncle Jen studied her a moment, then switched it off. "It can do that, all right. The entire spectrum, from joy to despair."

"So what brings you here?" Dirck asked, changing the subject when he noticed his mother was obviously shaken.

"I was checking on a patient I transferred to Cira City before High Opps. While I was so close, I felt compelled to see how everything was going. You're still welcome to join us, if you want. We have plenty of room."

His mother looked tempted, but for some reason known only to herself, she remained quiet. "It looks like you've done very well, Jen," was all she said.

His eyes held hers. "We've been lucky," he replied. "It's kind of embarrassing, actually." He looked at the floor, arms resting on his knees, as if debating whether or not to explain. "Our RG, or regional governor, Bryl Woeyel, has a niece about Deven's age who was visiting at the time and seriously injured during the PV," he went on. "I was able to fix her up. Bryl has seen to it that I've had everything I needed ever since."

Dirck didn't know whether to be happy or jealous. So that was what the other side of Cyrarian politics was like: They like you, prosperity; they hate you, prison.

"I don't suppose," 'Merama said hesitantly, "that you could help Laren?"

Uncle Jen's expression darkened. He pinched the bridge of his nose a moment then sighed. "I don't know," he said. "Governor Woeyel is the same rank as Troy. I suppose it depends on who has the most influence at the territorial level. The main problem I see is Laren's probably under regional jurisdiction. But I'll see what I can do. Don't get your hopes up, but I'll do what I can. Maybe I can at least get the charges reduced."

"What charges?" 'Merama asked quickly. "Is there something other than the weapons violation? Is there something else he's been charged with?"

"No," Uncle Jen replied quickly, trying to cover the slip. "I don't know. But I'm sure they're exaggerated, knowing Troy."

"That's better than we have now," Dirck said, slipping his uncle a look. His uncle nodded knowingly.

"How long can you stay?" 'Merama asked.

"I can't. I need to get back to the PAR. As you can imagine, this is our busiest time." Uncle Jen had been chartered to organize a Physical Assistance and Remediation Center before they'd left Mira III. His plans on Cyraria had come to fruition, but in a different region than originally intended.

"There are six times as many deaths during Peak Opps as the rest of the circuit, even when it's cold," he went on. "It's easier to insulate against cold. People don't take the heat seriously enough, much less the UV or ozone, until it's too late. If their cooling systems break down, most people don't know what to do. They usually don't have emergency plans, supplies, a safe, or other way to survive. What they don't seem to realize is that you can literally cook out there. And there's not a whole lot anyone can do if that happens."

"Can you at least stay for a meal?" 'Merama asked.

It wasn't hard to tell how badly she wanted him to stay. Uncle Jen looked at her and smiled, that patient, kindly smile Dirck remembered so well. He meant a lot to him, too. All those times when his father had been gone with work, he'd always been there.

"I'd love to," he said. "But then I'll have to go."

'Merama fixed their family favorite, wiittiin stew, and explained how she made it while they ate. Uncle Jen was truly impressed.

"Laren would be very proud of all of you," he said. "Dirck, you and Win did a terrific job with the heat exchanger. I'm proud of you, too. Keep up the good work and when your father and Creena get back, the family will be in good shape. Have you heard any more from her?"

"Not since we talked to her in the comcenter," 'Merama replied. "But I feel as if she's okay, that we'll be together again, eventually."

"You hang onto that," Uncle Jen said. "And Laren will be back, too. Just don't give up, okay?" Dirck nodded along with his mother and brother, almost believing it himself.

They'd no sooner finished eating than Uncle Jen embraced everyone, then got back in his oppsuit, saying he had something for them in the veke. Dirck waited in the heatlock while his uncle removed five boxes from the cargo bay, then carried them back into the living area.

"What is it?" 'Merama asked, child-like anticipation animating her expression.

"Oppsuits," he replied. "I thought it might be a good idea for you to have them, just in case. There's about a one-day supply of air in the tanks."

"We can refill them at the SD," Win said.

"Good. I still wish you'd come stay with us, at least until Peak Opps is over."

The smile froze on 'Merama's face. "We're fine, Jen. But thanks so much. For the suits and everything. And we'll keep in touch."

Another round of hugs, then the mood became more solemn as they joined in the Miran grip. They held hands a bit longer than usual, then Uncle Jen wished them well one more time and was gone. Everyone crowded into the heatlock to watch him get into the veke, then soar skyward and disappear. One by one, the others left, leaving Dirck alone by the oxidized window.

His uncle had his own veke. He could hardly believe it. His own *veke*. Economically, Uncle Jen's family and his own had been equals on Mira III. In fact, his father's compensation had actually been higher, by quite a bit.

But that was then. They certainly weren't equal now.

* * *

Epsilon Territorial Prison
Cira City, Cyraria

At first it was so obvious they were finally trying to break him that, under different circumstances, Laren would have been amused. His Space Patrol training had been so accurate that their techniques' origin brought more distress than the acts themselves. Pain could be dealt with. It was direct and understandable, something he'd been trained to withstand.

But it didn't take long before they changed tactics, toying with his mind. It took a while, but results came. Rational thought mingled with fantasy, neither satisfied with completion. Worst of all were the sounds, sometimes rasping and grating, others high pitched bleeps of mixed frequencies that upended every nerve.

The hallucinations were mild at first, petty annoyances compared to everything else. Focusing on reality and past training, reassuring himself it was typical, normal and reversible in such conditions, he refused to be alarmed. Knowing they were watching, perhaps in greater physical and emotional detail than he cared to ponder, helped maintain control. It was a form of winning, at the least satisfaction, that in spite of what they did, they couldn't own his mind. *Thank you, Mira III*, he thought. All those years of maintaining the requisite Miran façade were serving him well.

Further reinforcing the idea the cell had been configured specifically for him was the fact he hadn't been moved for a long time. Within a day they did, but after being dragged blindfolded through what seemed several kilometers of stuffy corridors, he was certain he'd returned to the same one. Why? Hardware installation? He searched for clues, even where the entrance faded so effectively it became invisible. Nothing.

Then, before his eyes, its rough textured walls seemed to retreat. He reached out instinctively, expecting to encounter a solid barrier cloaked in holographic illusion, recoiling quickly when nothing was there. Suspecting drugged food as the source, he ate less. Concentration wavered, his mind darting randomly, like a sped-up dream. He prayed for strength, distractions precluding proper reverence or attention. His mind shot from thought to thought, none completed, reality merging with illusion. Still recognizing the source, he slept as much as possible, feigning it when not.

Then real pain set in. Dull at first, nagging, like a nuisance sprain. The sensation wandered from site to site, limb to limb, while a dull, heavy ache persisted in the back of his neck. Sharp jabs in his ribs, his back; mouth dry, then aflame. No doubt illness prevailed in such environments, yet no sooner would he accept it as such, hope it would become the vehicle of death, and it would retreat, strength would ebb then surge, mental clarity upon him long enough to miss it when it evaporated.

Lighting no longer changed gradually, but flashed and spun, jittered and splashed. Then darkness, utter and complete, longer than any night. Time pulsed and moaned, like being stuck in a timebump, sensations gut wrenching. While he'd thought his life had witnessed the entire emotional spectrum, he found himself mistaken. Depths of despair closed in as the walls, an anguish of soul. Coherent thoughts refused to form, only fragments. Past memories strobed before him, flashes of joy blackened by the present. Reality teased, then beckoned, home likewise. Confusion dimmed, the answer clear. This could end. Would end. In one of two ways.

Still he refused, not ready for either.

Opposition

Win's 'cruiser was dead.

His posture said it all, whatever expression etched in his deeply tanned features invisible within the oppsuit helmet. They'd constructed a simple shelter and 'Merama and Deven had made a p-crawler cover for both the roof and the vehicle, but the canopy was sagging and body blistered, regardless. Dirck finished his drink and returned to his sleeproom, braced for the inevitable. Moments later, Win slammed back inside and threw the oppsuit helmet on his cyll.

"I shoulda left it in that cave," he growled, kicking the wall. "I shoulda known better than to leave it out. That was so stupid!"

Dirck sat quietly in his cyll with the c-com, trying to tune out the tirade. He'd learned that blending in with the walls was his best tactic whenever Win was agitated, so he didn't move or say a word. No doubt, the ambient temperature in the cave was likewise in a range that would be lethal for electronics, but he probably didn't want to hear it. Win grumbled some more, rummaged around for some tools, then grabbed his helmet and headed back out.

"*Hey*! Where you going?" Dirck called, jumping up to follow.

"Where do you think?" Win snapped.

"There's nothing you can do that won't take weeks. There's only so much air in the oppsuits. We might need it later, for something more important."

"*What's more important than this?*" Win yelled. "If I can get it running, I can get into the SD and get more air. Then we're not stuck here! The transport quit running four days ago, remember? And it's only E-89!" The Miran curse was muffled as he pulled on his helmet, then slammed out the back door.

Again, Dirck opened the galley window cover enough to see outside. The cruiser's p-crawler cover was scooting across the ground in a stiff breeze, Zeta glaring off the canopy from a position just low enough to dodge the shelter's roof. He watched as Win opened the nose panel and fumbled around inside. He removed what looked like the compressor switch, looked at it closely, then threw it on the ground. Dust billowed around him, sharing his fury as he stamped his foot, then came back inside, not slamming the door because the wind did it for him.

He unlatched his helmet and tossed it on the floor. "It's melted," he said. "Melted! All the semi-conductors are gone, and the circuits fused. It'll never run again. Never." He sighed with resignation and dropped to the floor, cross-legged, arms folded.

Dirck knew there was nothing he could say. He'd worked long and hard for his 'cruiser on Mira III and felt as bad about leaving it behind as any of his friends. Selling it to one of them had helped a little, as if he'd placed it in an adoptive home, but it still hurt. And Win had watched his die.

"I'm sorry," he ventured quietly. The ballome creaked and moaned in the wind, as if trying to fill the silence.

"Yeah, yeah, I know," he said, finally. "Could be worse. I didn't really want to go in, anyway. But I'd better comcon Crjlx-IM and let him know." He went into the living area, returning a few minutes later.

"Comcon's gone, too," he reported. He picked up the helmet again. "I'll take a look outside and see if it's fixable."

He wasn't gone long. "Antenna's melted," he said. "So much for that."

The wind was bad news, too. The heat exchanger cooled, but didn't filter, so they were in for another day of choking dust, even worse than the usual from the safe.

"Great," Dirck muttered. "Guess we go back to the safe, then."

In fact, the safe and the heat exchanger were the only good news. They'd finally chipped their way past the worst of the rock layer, so that now, the safe got deeper every day, plus the continued heavy exercise had resulted in an unexpected side benefit.

Dirck could feel strength increasing in his arms and shoulders, and see it in Win's. The increased sense of urgency coupled with reaching another layer of clay allowed them to consistently remove more dirt each day, but they still had a long way to go. They rotated digging during most of their waking hours, grateful to be past the worst of the rocks.

So far, it was a shaft about a meter and a half across and three meters deep. The sides were impaled with luma for light and demonstrated Cyrarian stratified geology as red clay beneath the upper sand layer and rocks yielded to brown, then nearly black. When it was time for the midday meal, it was deep enough that Win couldn't reach Dirck's down-stretched hand. A quick measurement told them they'd exceeded the four meters Uncle Jen had recommended. Now they just had to expand the sides and add supports to prevent cave-ins.

"After we eat, we can dig out the storage area and get that stuff off the roof," Win suggested. "Hopefully, it's okay." In spite of p-crawler and diverted cooling effects of the heat exchanger, the temperature had been rising steadily.

Dirck ate so fast his mother told him to slow down, but he was more anxious than ever to get back to the safe. Protecting the veke components from the heat applied to more than Peak Opps. If there was anything the Brightstar household didn't need, it was any more criminal charges.

Dirck went back in his sleeproom and tossed down the bucket box, then rappelled to the bottom, dodging luma. He chipped away, shovelful by shovelful, wishing they'd had a cache like that for the lasomag. How would things be now if they had? Alternative scenarios still played regularly, endings always lost to the demands of the present, but anger still smoldered.

The digging position got more awkward until, out of breath, he put down the shovel and stretched his cramping shoulders. "Hey, Win," he called up the shaft. "Bucket up."

His friend complied. "How's it coming? Should I start getting the stuff?"

"If you want. There's a big sack under my cyll."

"Okay. I'll be back."

Dirck kept working, Deven responding to his "bucket up" commands as he filled it several more times.

"Hey, Dirck," Deven called down finally. "The boxcart is full, and I mean *full*."

"Win'll empty it when he gets back," he replied. "I'm almost done here, anyway." He filled it one more time then sat down to rest, wondering what was taking Win so long. He was just about to climb out and suit up when he heard his voice.

"Here's the first load," he said, lowering the sack. "It's heavy. And hot, so watch out." Dirck grabbed it carefully by the fabric and set it on the ground beside him.

"What took so long?" he asked.

"P-crawler's a mess. I nearly got lost up there. The wind's blown it all over and the crawl space is almost gone. While I was sealing up the cool air duct to the storage area, all the parts got tangled up in it, plus it's hard to see, especially with the helmet. I guess no one thought to put a light on it when it's constant day."

"I guess not. Is it all over the heat exchanger, too?" Dirck asked.

"A little. I got it back on the frame the best I could, but we probably ought to do it right, as soon as we can."

Win left with the boxcart and Dirck knelt down to unload the sack. The contents were too hot to touch. He didn't even know what most of them were. 'Cruiser parts were one thing, vekes another. *Maybe someday,* he thought, thinking of how Uncle Jen's had banked effortlessly beyond the rise.

Win got back with the remainder, plus 'Merama sent down a few bowlbush roots and several containers of water. At last, Dirck concealed their contraband with a piece of leftover composite material and hoisted himself to the top.

"Let's work on the ventilation system plans after we sweep up and shower," Win suggested.

"Is that a hint?"

"No. This time I probably have you beat. Besides, how do you expect to get really dirty, like a professional, with that snurky haircut?"

"What snurky haircut?" Dirck replied. "I like it short. Yours is longer than my sister's. You know, she used to call me a snurk, too. All the time." He laughed nastily. "You know what she'd like to do?" Win shook his head as he dropped the oppsuit to the floor. "She'd like to braid your hair, like she used to do to 'Merama. I can just see it now, all these tiny, little braids, all over your big, fat head."

With that, Win wrestled him to the ground. "No one, and I mean *no one*, messes with my hair!" The two thrashed around, trying to pin each other in a cloud of dust, until 'Merama came to see what all the commotion was about.

"Look at you two!" she exclaimed. "You're disgusting! And look at this mess!"

Dust coated everything, from cyll covers to the numerous boxes Win had contributed to the tiny room.

Neither loosened his grip, but the distraction of the comment was enough for Win to pin Dirck's arm behind his back.

"Hey, no fair!" he yelled, then started to laugh.

"Say it back," Win demanded, "Say you want your hair to look as good as mine." Dirck laughed even harder. "C'mon, man," he repeated, trying not to laugh. Dirck kept cackling, until Win loosened his grip and gave in, too, the pair laying on the floor and laughing until they could hardly breathe. 'Merama was still standing in the doorway, almost smiling, with her arm around Deven.

"You two put in a lot of work" she said, once the levity and dust had settled. "I don't know what I'd do without you."

"Thanks, 'Merama," Dirck replied.

"Yeah, thanks, 'Merama," Win echoed.

"This is my new sister, *Winella*," Dirck teased. "Creena always wanted a sister, so when she gets back, she can braid Winella's hair. Whatcha think, 'Merama? Wouldn't she like that?"

"I think if Creena walked in that door right now, she'd go back to wherever she's been."

Dirck sat up and brushed the dirt off his arms, lost for a snappy retort. "I miss her, 'Merama," he said, finally. "When she comes back, it won't be like that. Really."

"Good," 'Merama replied. "I don't think I could stand it if you two picked up where you left off on the *Aquarius*." Then she shook her head and left, eyes distant.

"What was that all about?" Win asked. "You and your sister used to fight?"

"Yeah. A lot. It was kinda fun to get her mad. She'd really have a fit."

"It sounds kinda stupid to me. I would have loved to have had a sister."

"It *was* stupid. If it weren't for those fights, she'd be here right now. And we'd be living in Cira City instead of this hovel."

The statement stuck in his mind like a rock, berating him again. Then the blaming cycle shifted off center to the other players. Troy and his corrupt ambitions were a constant, but the fact that his father's own actions had put him in prison had resolved even clearer in his mind, especially after what Uncle Jen had said about consequences.

The fact he was still unable to figure out what his rationale had been fueled the festering resentment to ever increasing temperatures. Why had he been so stubborn about hiding the lasomag? It wasn't like he didn't know he was targeted. He'd known that for a long time, even before leaving Mira III. There was even that time before they left, when Dirck had claimed Creena's noncompliance had caused the transfer to Cyraria. He couldn't help cringing as he remembered his father's decimating glare.

"Dirck," he'd stated sternly. "Speculation is not a Miran trait. It had to evolve somewhere else, so you might want to examine your own behavior more closely before starting in on your sister. Besides that, your conclusions are presumptuous and, I might add, fallacious. The move has absolutely nothing to do with Creena and everything to do with me. So, if you want to blame someone—rather than accepting the status quo, like a purebred Miran would, I might add—then direct it at me. Understand?"

Dirck swallowed hard and nodded.

"Is there anything else you want to say about the move?"

"No, sir," he'd replied hoarsely, then stood at stark attention until his father had left the room.

Dirck shivered with renewed intimidation as he recalled how his father had faced down Troy on the *Aquarius*. He was used to getting his way, and usually did. Until now. If only he'd been more careful and compliant, things would be different. A lot different. Like they'd be living in a luxurious subterre in Cira City and partying instead of digging a safe.

Feeling the festering *if only's* expanding to a dangerous level, he grabbed some clean clothes and disappeared into the sanicube to shower. When he was done, Win got in, then the two of them sketched out a ventilation system for the safe.

They didn't get very far. Dirck was too tired and distracted by what might have been, and Win was no better off. A few moments later, the two of them wound up in their cylls with Dirck telling stories about Creena, including how she'd gotten blasted off in the escape pod followed by some of his experiences in Troy's TL-87.

"Now I can see even more why Troy hates your father," Win said when he finished. "Troy doesn't like to be wrong."

"I don't like to be wrong, either, but it's no excuse for throwing people in prison."

"You've got that right," Win agreed. "But if you had that kind of power, you can't be sure what you'd do. I'll bet you'd do all kinds of vengeful things to Troy, if you could."

"Yeah. Punching him in the face would be a good start."

Win laughed. "True enough, but we're not going to change much of what's wrong with Sigma/Epsilon right now. C'mon, let's cyll out. I'm beat."

Dirck closed the window cover against the perpetual light, and got back in his cyll, seething again. Weariness overtook him, regardless, and in short order he was asleep.

* * *

Epsilon Territorial Prison
Cira City, Cyraria

With time, how much he didn't know, Laren learned to cope with the pain. While still excruciating, it became bearable when he quit resisting, allowing possession, a companion of sorts. While illusions taunted his other senses, it anchored him to reality. As long as there was pain, he was probably sane. And alive.

Tuning out the psi noise and propaganda was somewhat more challenging, but accomplished, though the artificial insanity turned out to be more pleasant than the now-coherent thoughts that took its place.

At first he clung to thoughts of home, love sustaining him as memories surged. Unbidden, ever-increasing dread took their place, an unquenchable ember that something was terribly wrong. They were in danger, he could feel it, yet was entirely powerless. His need for control clawed at his guts, never more apparent than now, when there was none. He was a doer by nature, helplessness unknown, his only choice to relegate their fate, as well as his own, to the Cosmos. The answer was clear, yet he couldn't let go, guilt searing his conscience as he considered what they might be experiencing due to his neglect.

It festered and seethed like an exothermic reaction, chilling him deeper as the obsession grew, the longing for their presence a raging hunger. With its denial came loneliness, deep and soul-wrenching, quickly followed by despair, dark and destructive.

Gradually, the need to know edged into obsession. Purpose in prayer returned. No matter what the answer, he had to know. For if they were gone, nothing else mattered. If he couldn't be with them, to help and protect according to his *Promises*, indeed, if his own foolishness had caused their demise, nothing else mattered. There was no reason to live. Only to die.

* * *

CALMANAC: High Opps/Peak +61/E-81 Days		
Temp: 101C/214F	PVs: 90%	Quakes: 93%

The first time Dirck awoke, he wasn't sure why. He lay perfectly still, the only light, that which crept through where the shutters didn't quite meet. Then he heard something, but wasn't sure what. At first he thought it was the heat exchanger, then decided it wasn't mechanical. Or was it? Was it wind? Gradually, a deep rumbling far below reached audible range.

Then the entire structure started to rattle, slightly at first, then violently, as if the ground beneath the ballome were being tortured by unseen forces.

He flew from cyll to window and activated the shutters, waiting impatiently for them to separate, alert for a PV. By then, Win joined him, equally on edge as the tossing continued. The glaring landscape lacked any evidence of a storm, but a serpentine wisp rose from the ground in what appeared to be an erratic trail that stretched at least a hundred meters or so in both directions. Dirck shot into the living area, Win on his heels, where 'Merama and Deven joined them, eyes wide and terrified, as they struggled to keep their balance amid the ongoing waves.

"What is it?" she asked. "A PV?"

"If so, we'd better get to the safe," Win said, everyone instantly heading in that direction..

Dirck poised on its edge, ready to rappel down first to help the others, fighting for balance as the ground rolled beneath them. The sides were crumbling, dirt and luma hailing down to darkened depths far below. He hesitated, thinking maybe it wasn't such a good idea after all, if they'd be buried alive.

And then it stopped, an eerie stillness pervading the unsettled ballome.

Everyone froze, looking at each other as if to ask if they were all sharing the same bad dream. An aftershock rumbled beneath, lasting only a heartbeat, but long enough to confirm the cause.

"A groundquake," Dirck said decisively. "Terrific. Another gift from High Opps."

An inspection revealed no major problems inside, only a few items displaced, none broken. Dirt shaken loose in the safe turned out to be minimal, no more than what would fill a few bucket boxes.

"We'd better check outside," he stated, heading for his sleeproom to suit up, even as he spoke.

He and Win exited carefully, standing outside the backdoor and scanning the familiar landscape for change. Nothing appeared disturbed until they circled the ballome to outside the sleeproom windows. A small fissure stretched in either direction, where the wispy trail had appeared earlier, its depth already compromised by windblown sand.

"Looks like we're okay," Win said. "What do you think?"

"Yeah," Dirck replied. "Not much we could do, anyway."

"Right."

Back inside, he reassured his mother and Deven that everything looked fine and to go back to bed, he and Win doing the same.

It seemed as if he'd barely gotten back to sleep when he woke up with a start. Was it his imagination or was it getting hot? He could hear the compressor running and so was the fan. Maybe the heat was his imagination, all the work they'd done that day combined with the excitement of the groundquake.

He sighed and lay back down. Troy invaded his thoughts again, and he couldn't go back to sleep. And it was getting hotter, he could tell for sure, now. He sat on the edge of the cyll, listening.

Win opened one eye, then bolted from his cyll. "What's going on? Why's it so hot?"

"I don't know," Dirck said, getting up to pull on his oppsuit. "But we'd better find out."

By the time he and Win were ready to go outside, 'Merama and Deven were up, too. The fan was blowing hot air. He shut it down, donned his helmet and followed Win outside. Zinni was high in the sky, a screaming, yellow furnace. The compressor sounded horrible. A hollow ring echoed through his helmet, along with a banging he'd never heard before. He threw the switch and looked at Win.

"This isn't good," he muttered into the helmet mike. "Get the portalume and meet me on the roof."

The p-crawler was a bigger mess than he'd imagined. It hadn't only detached from the frame, but had dried and broken up, the long, woven strands now tufts of crumbled twigs. He pawed it out of the way and climbed inside, while Win joined him with the portalume. He turned it on and crept over the domed surface to the heat exchanger.

The clamp attaching the ductwork to the cool air outlet had come loose.

"Whew. Thank the Benefics," Win said. "I'll get the toolbox."

He returned a moment later, and Dirck soon had it reattached. When they got inside, cool air was circulating again, which actually felt even colder than before.

"Maybe it's just because it had warmed up so much," he speculated.

"Or the vent had been loose for a while," Win added.

"Yeah, maybe."

The two of them returned to their sleeproom with the intent of cylling out again, but by the time they'd entirely removed their oppsuits, it was apparent cool air had again turned warm. Then hot.

"Uh, oh," Dirck muttered, exchanging a worried look with Win as he stepped back into his oppsuit and raced outside.

Back on the roof, he checked the digital readout on the nearest pressure transducer and groaned—zero. Closer examination revealed wispy threads of steam sublimating from a layer of ice coating the condenser, the outside dripping furiously.

"Let's let it thaw, then fire it back up and see if there's any pressure," Win suggested. Dirck nodded and pushed the p-crawler aside so Zinni could hasten the thaw.

This isn't good, he thought. *This really, really isn't good.*

The safe wasn't finished, the 'cruiser was dead, and so was the comcon. Walking to the SD, over fifty kilometers away, was out of the question, oppsuits or not.

Once the ice melted, Win adjusted everything to the configuration they'd used when they'd initiated the system. When the ice was gone, he started it up, watching the numbers rise slowly, then stabilize.

"There's some, but not much," he reported. "About half what it should be."

Dirck adjusted the valves to maximize the pressure and went inside to see if they were getting any cool air. Barely. He went back out and checked the transducer output again. The numbers were descending. Dirck scrambled back on the roof, frantically ripping p-crawler out of the way so he could see the entire system. Something was hissing, audible even through the oppsuit helmet. He followed the convolution of tubing with his eyes, starting at the compressor. A tiny stream of vapor was escaping from the liquid phase line.

"Shut it down!" Dirck hollered, "We've gotta leak!"

"Don't yell!" Win snapped.

"Sorry," he muttered, remembering the helmet radio as he ducked under the frame to identify the source. Tiny stress fractures sketched a radial pattern from a nearly invisible hole, which had ruptured, apparently due to vibrations instituted by the quake.

"Hey, Win—c'mere. Look at this." A moment later his friend was beside him.

"It must have been under too much pressure," Win mused.

"I wonder why the relief valves didn't work?"

"I don't know. Let's take a look."

Win crept down to the nearest one and examined it for any signs of venting. Seeing none, he removed it from the line and looked inside. The seal was not only hard and brittle, but fused to the poppet, preventing release.

"I never saw one do this before," Win said. "It must have been the low temperature from the cryo fluid."

Dirck groaned, remembering his father's continual battle with out of spec parts, one they had ultimately lost. The extreme cold of cyro temperatures introduced factors he'd barely considered, except for the care they had to take in handling it. Apparently, some materials were subject to frostbite, too.

Even worse, neither he nor Win had so much as thought about the high pressures necessary for cryo phase changes as being too much for pipe intended for liquid water. Even ammonia would have pushed it substantially. Sometime back, Dirck had been cruising around the c-com and found his father's directions for manufacturing it by hydrolysis of calcium, which was available in limestone, except at this point there wasn't enough time.

A few hours later, they'd finished replacing the compromised line and recalibrated the system for lower pressures. It was working, but not very well. Dirck was exhausted, but at this point, he'd never get back to sleep. Win felt the same, so they searched for solutions long after 'Merama and Deven had returned to their cylls. They hadn't solved a thing over an hour later when his mother and Deven got up, acting as if everything was back to normal.

"C'mon," he said grimly to Win. "We'd better get back to work on the safe."

Since most Cyrarians survived Opposition by going underground, expanding the safe into the beginnings of a subterre became the most logical option. But by E-79, two days after the initial breakdown, the safe was only two meters square. The ground had changed textures again laterally, and progress was painfully slow. Fortunately, the ventilation system would be simple, consisting of strategically placed intake and exhaust vents, made with pipe and a small impeller. When the chamber was a little larger, they could install it, along with a water line. Meanwhile, the ballome was livable. But with the worst yet to come, the chance of making it through was rapidly diminishing.

And on E-74, only sixty-eight days into Peak Opps, probability dropped to zero.

Dirck and Win were down in the safe, which had only expanded by another meter or so, hardly sufficient to install the ventilation system much less house four people. The sound was muffled, but shook the ground, sending chunks of dirt and luma tumbling down on their heads.

Not sure whether it was another groundquake, Dirck was the first one out, grabbing an opps cloak instead of taking time to suit up. He stood outside the back door, staring up at the roof in dumbfounded horror. An explosion had blasted the heat exchanger to a convoluted mass of worthless metal.

Breathing was impossible, his mind refusing to process the visual input. Finally, Win grabbed his arm and forced him back inside. 'Merama and Deven were right there, expressions drenched with apprehension.

"We'll probably have about an hour before it gets unbearable, maybe two or three more in the safe," Win stated grimly. "By the time we have to suit up, we'd better have some idea what we're going to do. That is if we plan on staying alive."

Dirck slammed one fist into the ballome wall, twirled around then shook them both at the ceiling. "*How could he do this to us?*" he snarled, fury burning in his eyes like lasers. "*How?*"

'Merama and Win stared at him numbly, thinking he meant Troy.

He didn't.

Departing

Terra Day 86

Creena mumbled, turned over, then slowly opened her eyes. The clock read quarter after four. She listened carefully. All she heard was the chatter of a distant sprinkler and the crow of a rooster.

[Creena! Creena, wake up.]

She jerked upright, fully awake. "Thyron?" she whispered. "Where on Earth have you been?"

[Trying to penetrate the densest field of negative energies I've ever encountered. What was the matter with you, anyway? Finding a ship wasn't easy. I finally had to interrupt an HIO caucus for outside help.]

The night time shadows made the conversation dream-like, affecting its credibility, but she didn't dare turn the light on with Tammy in the other bed. She blinked hard, swung her feet to the floor. The curtains flared on the crest of a cool breeze that rattled the blinds and rustled the pages of a book Tammy had left open on Terry's desk.

"Why are you talking in normal sentences again?" she asked.

[I'm out of my environmental chamber, for observation.]

Convinced the conversation was real, a deluge of questions fired in her mind. "The starcraft that came — who was that?"

A pause, then, [Have they been back?]

"No. I just wondered who they were."

[Don't go with anyone unless you know without a
doubt who it is. What you've experienced is part of
many dangerous forces. You must be very careful,
Creena, very careful.]

"But who are they?" she insisted. A chill crept across
her skin and she shivered, wondering if it was triggered by
the breeze or recollection. "What do they want?"

[It's known as the INTEGRATOR, or one of his agents.
There are very few in the Universe in whom he
takes personal interest.]

She swung her feet back into bed and pulled the covers
to her chin. "Why would he care about me?"

[I cannot tell you any more. You will know in due
time.]

"Why didn't you come that night? I thought we
agreed..."

[I never said I'd be there that first week. Putting
motor-mouth together was a challenge, even for
me. I'd no sooner get part of her assembled and the
Earthlings would dismantle her again the next day.
But that doesn't matter now. I've arranged for a
ship. We'll pick you up tonight at twenty-one fifty-
two sidereal time, at the place we made contact
before.]

"Tonight?" she gasped, heart racing with excitement.
"What time is that here?"

[Yes, tonight. About one-fifteen, local time. And if
you hadn't changed your thinking when you did, it
would have been a long, long time before the next
one.]

"So you got us a ship, you really did."

[Of course.]

"And it'll get us to Mira III?"

[Most certainly.]

When Tammy's sheets rustled, she held her breath, watching a tree's moonlit silhouette lilt a ghostly dance on the blinds.

[What's wrong?]

"Nothing. I'm surprised, that's all. See you tonight."

[Be ready.]

"I will."

A sudden sense of deep solitude signaled the conversation's end. She slid beneath the covers, but by now her eyes refused to close, sleep far removed, as thoughts raced wildly through her mind.

Thyron had arranged for a rescue ship. *Finally*. In less than a day, she'd be on her way. It sounded too good to be true. Was that why her heart was pounding, for fear that it might not happen? Or that it would?

Normalcy had been a convenient diversion, a comfortable fit. While worries had preyed on her mind since her arrival, the daily routine had been consistent for weeks into months, providing a sense of security. Each day she knew what she'd be doing the next, creating a comfort zone she hadn't appreciated until now. Where would she be tomorrow? With whom? Would she be safer and closer to home or farther? Her errand to Mira III cut rudely into the thought queue, its vague necessity riling concern to overt anxiety. The prospect of returning to her *naterra* remained unsettling, her only consolation the fact she'd return home soon after. Hopefully.

So why the bad feeling?

The curtains billowed again, leaves of the cottonwood outside the window whispering as if to answer. She sighed nervously, trying to force her thoughts to more positive ground. Not finding any, she gradually fell back into a dark, restless sleep.

When she awoke again, the room was aglow with mid-morning light. She swung her legs over the side, groggy, until she remembered the conversation with Thyron. Why did it seem so distant in the brightness of day? She sighed and stretched. Tammy's bed was empty. It was quiet. Too quiet. She pulled on her usual faded cutoff jeans and Allen's old *Good Planets are Hard to Find* T-shirt. If he only knew how true that was! She made her bed, then trudged downstairs for something to eat. No one was down there, either.

She poured a bowl of Rice Krispies, added a handful of fresh raspberries, and covered them with cream skimmed from the gallon milk bucket they kept in the fridge. She sat down, savoring the various textures and flavors with full knowledge it would be her last. If there was one thing to be said for Earth, it was the quality of their food, which she would definitely miss, with the possible exception of zucchini.

But where was everyone?

Finally she remembered. It was Sunday. Most of them were at church. She tried to remember whose turn it was to stay home with her, but couldn't. She couldn't hear the TV, so it was probably Mr. Benson, who always sat outside on the porch and read, taking advantage of the quiet.

When she'd finished eating, she rinsed her dish, then paused a moment to stare out the window at the garden. Memories of hours spent in her favorite place on Earth, except maybe the tramp, flooded her mind. It was incredibly stupid, but suddenly Earth didn't seem so bad. When the familiar crunching of tires in the driveway scattered her thoughts, she raced upstairs to delay seeing them, even for a few moments. As expected, Tammy bounded into the room, a little too cheerfully, and plopped down next to her on the bed.

"Hi!" she said. "You feel okay?"

"Sure. Why?"

"Just wondering. You had a nightmare or something last night. You were talking like crazy in your sleep."

Creena froze. "What. . .what did I say?"

"I don't remember, exactly. Something about your ship, I think. By the way," the girl added, bouncing off the bed. "Allen wants to see you in the den. He says it's important."

She waved cheerfully, then disappeared out the door. Her footfalls padded down the hall to her room, then a few seconds later, bounded down the stairs, followed by the slam of the front door.

Creena sat on the edge of her bed, elbows on her knees and chin in her hands. Great. Allen wanted to see her. Well, she didn't want to see him. The pain from what they'd said persisted, pulling even tighter with the reminder. After avoiding them for over three weeks, maybe they'd finally figured out she didn't believe it. Otherwise, she would have been excited, at least a little happy, if her ship had really been nearly done. It was almost funny that tonight she'd leave, ship or not.

So it really didn't matter what he wanted, did it?

She set her jaw and got up from the bed, suddenly curious whether he was going to feed her more lies.

The drapes in the den were drawn against the noonday sun, steady wisps of sunshine slashing the carpet from where they didn't quite meet. Allen was slouched on the sofa, reading the comics. David was on the floor with a book, Mr. Benson in his recliner, asleep. She watched Allen steadily from the door until he felt her gaze and got up, tossing the paper carelessly on the coffee table.

Paper. It had become normal, as had books, and Tammy had been teaching her their alphabet. Would she ever see either again? Probably not.

"Let's go outside for a minute," Allen mumbled as he stepped around her for the front door.

A frown creased her forehead as she followed, heart suddenly filled with lead.

The smell of freshly-cut alfalfa was thick in the air, the late-morning sun already hot. It was quiet with a vast, pervasive stillness, as if eternity itself were holding its breath. No tractors in the distance, no bumping of pickups across rutted roads. Allen strolled around the house past the garden and stood by the fence, fidgeting with some cattle hair stuck in the barbed wire. Her heart sagged with the renewed conviction that Thyron had been right. The silence thickened.

"Well?" she said, tired of waiting.

He sighed, still looking the other way. "Uh, well, you see, uh, Creena. We weren't exactly, well, honest with you the other day. I know it was wrong, and it's really bothering me a lot." He stared straight ahead at the recently sheared alfalfa, a breeze ruffling his hair.

"I know." she replied simply.

Allen looked at her, puzzled. "What d'ya mean?"

She slipped her hands in her pockets, shifted her hip to one side. "My ship isn't almost done at all, is it, Allen?"

The shock on his face was almost funny. His eyes would probably fall out of the sockets if she told him she was leaving. Gradually, the surprise left his expression and he hung his head.

"No, it isn't." Then he lifted his chin and looked her straight in the eye. "But let me explain—"

"You know, Allen," she said, "I was just starting to trust you. When you saved me from that cannibal, I really believed you cared. You and your family were starting to seem like my own family, in a way. You were even nicer to me than my real brother. I thought I could trust you. Believe you." He looked back at the ground, kicking the soft dirt, but said nothing. "You know, someone told me once not to trust the people here," she went on. "I was just starting to think he was wrong, when you told me that."

"Creena, please. Let me explain."

She set her jaw and folded her arms, waiting.

Allen swallowed hard, holding her steady gaze. "When Dad talked to Uncle Milt, he said they had your ship completely torn apart and it would probably take at least a year, maybe more, before they could get it back together. If then. Dad thinks it may take even longer. A lot longer. In fact, he believes it's been impounded by the government and they have no intention of ever giving it back.

"Anyway, the way you felt that day, we were afraid you'd be too upset if we told you that. But we knew you were expecting to find out something, so we decided we'd kinda break it to you slowly. We were going to tell you, as soon as we felt you could handle it. We really were! It might not have been right, but we thought it was, then. We only wanted to spare you the truth, at least for a little while. We thought that, sometimes, even false hope is better than none at all."

His eyes shifted back to the alfalfa, neatly strewn piles poised gracefully before the sun. She glanced at him briefly, then, without saying a word, raced back to the house and up to her room.

Now she was really in a fix. Should she tell? What if they wouldn't let her go? She couldn't chance it, couldn't. But she had to explain, tell them she cared, or they'd think she was a sneaky, ungrateful snurk. She got some paper from Terry's desk and picked up a pencil that felt as thick and awkward as the words in her heart. Slowly, she printed her message in the alien alphabet Tammy had taught her one stormy afternoon as thunder wandered the canyons beyond the tramp.

Deer Bensons,

Thank yoo for letting me stay and treeting me like won of yor famly. You have really bin nice and made me feel at home. I am sorry I kood not tell yoo good by. I was afrade yoo wood not let me go. I cannot wate that long for my ship. I hav to go home to my reel famly. If I dint care so much about all of yoo it would be ezyer to go. Yoo are all wonderful and taut me a lot.

She read it over slowly, trying to think if there was anything else. On impulse, she scrawled at the bottom in Miran, *I'll always remember my family on Earth.*

She was just signing her name when she heard Tammy's footsteps. "Creena? Dinner's ready."

Creena stuffed the note under her pillow. "I'll be right down," she replied. Snurkles, she'd miss her. She'd always wanted a sister, and no one would make a better one than Tammy. Swallowing hard, she trudged downstairs. When they'd settled into eating, Allen glanced at her from across the table before preemptively clearing his throat.

"I, uh, told her," he said. "Everything."

Everyone froze for a moment, then the tension in the room evaporated like summer rain.

"We're really sorry, Creena," Mr. Benson said. "That isn't what we wanted to find out at all." She nodded, eyes fixed on her plate.

"Hey! Maybe you'll get to go to school with us," Tammy said, grinning. "It starts soon, in a couple weeks. We can tell them you're our cousin, from out of town."

Everyone laughed, including Creena, but a twinge of conscience caught in her throat. She wanted to tell them so badly it hurt. The rest of the meal was less strained than it had been for weeks, Allen rambling on about a meteor shower due that night, among other things.

"There are actually two of them, the Aquarids and Perseids, and it's supposed to be great. D'ya want to watch it with me?" he asked.

Creena stared at him, remembering Verdaris. If anything, it seemed such an event should be spent in the basement, not outside. "Thanks, but I don't think so," she said.

That night she lay in bed watching the clock progress as she'd done so many Sundays before. Earth clocks had fascinated her from the start, with their analog sweep of hands rather than abrupt snapping of digits. The flow of life had been like that, too, a steady, easy flow of transition, rather than sudden change.

At long last, what she'd longed for was happening. Her last night on Earth. *Her very last night.* Now it was only a matter of hours. She should be thrilled. Delighted. Ecstatic.

But she wasn't. Not at all. Not even a little.

If she were going home to her own family again, maybe it would have been different, but she wasn't. Her comfortable routine here was over and she was going back to Mira III, a world she'd always hated, *naterra* or not. That alone was not sufficient cause for rejoicing. But at least it was one step closer to going home.

After what seemed like forever, the clock indicated ten after one. She slipped from between the sheets, knowing the next time she slept it would be in a cyll. She got out her Code Orange uniform from beneath the bed and tugged it on. Mrs. Benson had patched the rip in her sleeve, even gotten the various stains out of the pants. She hadn't had the heart to tell her it would have suited her just fine to throw it out. But since she was going back to Mira III, it was probably better that she had it.

It felt strange after jeans and T-shirts, which she wished she could take instead. Even one pair of David's old, faded cutoffs and a nice, comfy shirt. 'Merapa would absolutely love the one that said *Good Planets are Hard to Find.* She grabbed it off the chair and caressed it between her fingers, tempted, but knew she should leave with what she came with, no more. She felt like a sneak as it was. A sneaky snurk, not even telling them good-bye, except in a stupid note, which she'd almost forgotten.

She took it out from under her pillow and placed it on top, hoping they wouldn't be too hurt. She turned and smiled at Tammy, who hadn't slept in her own room in weeks, sound asleep across the room. "Bye," she whispered, then tiptoed out the door and down the stairs. The fifth stair squeaked, as usual, and she froze, almost wishing someone would wake up. Nothing stirred, not even a breeze through the open window on the landing.

When she reached the bottom, the darkened family room beckoned for one last look. Rumpled newspapers littered the couch, silvered by moonlight that spilled through the south window, leaving a nondescript splotch on the floor. She could almost hear the TV, Mr. Benson telling them to quiet down, so he could hear the news. The Benson kids fought over the TV like she and Dirck had over the holovid. Especially Tammy and David. And those weird transmissions they'd watched, not always laughing at the same things, but laughing nonetheless.

Like that show that was on late, the one that the kids snuck out of bed to watch, after their parents were asleep. The main guy would dress up in all sorts of weird outfits and acted as if he was from another planet. When she'd asked if he was, Allen and David had laughed so hard that their parents woke up and shooed them all off to bed, but she could still hear them laughing in their room, until she'd eventually fallen asleep. That show called "Star Trek" had her fooled at first, thinking maybe the Earthlings were more advanced than she thought, which was more cause for uproarious laughter when she asked why the Enterprise couldn't take her home.

She shuffled to the kitchen, smiling at the memories. Besides the Bensons, she'd really miss the food. Snurkles, it was good. Especially right from the garden. Maybe, just maybe, it would be as good on Cyraria. Realizing she was hungry, she snatched a bag of Oreos from a drawer, then started for the back door, trying not to think that her next meal would probably be genour.

Allen's headset beckoned from the counter, reminding her of something else she hated to leave. How music evoked such pleasure made no sense, but somehow explained why it didn't exist on Mira III. The closest thing there was grafix, computer generated tones, colors and forms that were hollow and trite by comparison. Would he mind? Probably not, especially since his parents gave him a new one for his birthday, the month before.

She thought back to that first morning after she'd arrived, before her introduction to TV or commercial radio, when she'd helped Allen milk the cows by holding the cones attached to the milking machine while he sterilized each udder with a disinfectant-soaked rag. He had something over his ears, wired to a small device attached to his belt, and curiosity had finally prevailed.

"What's that?" she asked, pointing.

"Huh?" he asked, rather loudly, peering up through shaggy bangs.

"What''s that? On your head?" she said, pointing and raising her volume to match his.

He dropped the headphones around his neck and smiled as puzzlement crinkled her face. Small, but distinct sound pulsed from the ear pieces, such as she'd never heard before. In response Allen stood up and dropped them over her ears, then stepped back to watch. Mira's grafix were random and meaningless, its effect as moving as conversing electronically with a fax machine. This Earth sound was another story, its rhythms and cadences absorbed into her heart and soul, generating a sense of being she'd never experienced before.

"Snurkles!" Creena cried, eyes wide. "What is it?"

"Don't you have music on your planet?" he asked.

"Have *what*?"

"Music. You mean you don't have it?"

"No, only grafix. And it's nothing like this!"

"Do you like it?"

"Yes! It's, it's wonderful!"

He smiled and laughed, seeming to enjoy her obvious pleasure. "I usually leave it on the counter in the kitchen, when I'm not using it. You can borrow it anytime you like. I'll show you where I keep my tapes."

And he had, introducing her to a variety of musical styles she never could have imagined. Odd, how Earth was so behind in a technological sense, yet had something like this. And it was even more amazing when the family would sing. She'd only recently joined in and loved how it made her feel.

She slipped the headphones over her ears and turned it on, undecided, until sad country strains of untimely goodbyes intoned their message on her heart. She took it off and returned it to the counter. She'd have enough melancholy memories without that. Resisting one more glance, she grabbed the cookies and slipped out, closing the screen quietly behind her. How many times each day had she looked up from the garden to see who was coming when she'd hear it bang closed with its predictable rally of rebounds? Another simple detail of Earth life that would stay with her forever.

Moonlight cast its gentle light before her, highlighting everything from the burgeoning garden to where cut alfalfa lay in wakes of swerving shadows. She kicked through it thoughtfully, remembering the first time. A wheel-line sprinkler splattered in the distance, the only sound besides the hush of evening air tickling the stars. They quivered at its touch, bright and clear, the Milky Way a smear of light overhead. Their timelessness spanned eternities, yet for her they began on Verdaris, then followed her here. She smiled with the realization she'd see their beauty from an entirely different perspective, long before these were extinguished by Earth's dawn.

Even when a trail of light scarred the blackness above, she failed to remember the meteor shower or realize that Allen was watching from his open window. He followed her quietly, crouching behind some sage and chokecherry bushes, as she crossed the canal on a wobbly board, then finished her trek to the tramp, where she sat before the astral panorama, munching an *Oreo*. Moments later, an eerie rumbling grumbled down the valley, followed by an unearthly glow above the mountains. When it came into view, she could see it was far larger than the *Cerulean Nimrod*.

"*Creena!*" Allen screamed.

Startled half to death, she shot to her feet. Allen was tearing up the hill, the ship approaching from the ragged peaks behind her. Tears spilled freely in a flash flood of emotion as the farewell she'd tried so hard to avoid became reality.

"*No!*" she cried, backing away. "I can't stay here! I can't! I've gotta go!"

The surrounding weeds flickered with brilliant rays of red as the ship descended slowly and hovered above the ridge, a short distance beyond the tramp.

He walked toward her slowly, stopping a meter or so away, eyes fixed on the spacecraft with obvious disbelief for several moments, before his eyes met hers.

"Why didn't you tell us, Creena? *Why?*" he pleaded.

"I couldn't," she replied. "I guess it was kinda like you telling me about my ship."

"I wish I could go, too," he said, staring back at the waiting vehicle with longing far more intense than any she'd ever seen.

"No, you don't!" Creena retorted. "It's never fun to be away from the people you love." Her eyes filled again as she realized that was exactly why this was so hard.

The hatchway eased opened, emitting a blinding flash of light that slashed the darkened landscape.

[C'mon, Creena! Don't delay
Board the ship or simply stay.]

"I have to go," she said, yet didn't move as he closed the remaining space between. "'Bye, Allen."

A heartbeat later he grabbed her by the shoulders and pulled her into a firm embrace.

"God be with you 'til we meet again," he said, voice laden with emotion.

She threw her arms around him and kissed his cheek, then pulled something from her pocket and pressed it into his hand, before racing for the ship, tears blurring the way. Halfway up the ramp, she stopped and turned around for one more look. At the barn, the house, the valley with its sparkling lights, and the Milky Way overhead. Allen stood where she'd left him, hair ruffled by the evening breeze. He lifted his arm and waved, slow and final. She returned it; paused a moment, remembering, then wiped her eyes and proceeded inside, ramp hissing closed behind her.

Arrows led to the acceleration chamber where dozens of seats were empty, save for her and Thyron, Aggie clamped to a railing. She nodded at them, then concentrated on strapping herself in. A deep, pulsing whir of gathering momentum rumbled beneath them as the ship elevated sharply, mountains, valleys, fields and roads receding in night time shadows. It shifted direction toward the city, then hovered above it a short time later.

"What are we doing?" she asked, looking intently out the window strip and worried that for some reason they were going to take her back.

"Recharging," Aggie responded, explanation quickly verified by a tell-tale, low frequency vibration.

Creena watched the lights below shudder, dim and then go out entirely as the ship extracted power from Earth's magnetic field, the draw disrupting electrical power to the towns below. Moments later, they were on their way, the vehicle clearing the atmosphere and acceleration shells inflating as they merged with the stars. Earth receded in a heartbeat, its sun no more than another point of light in a sea of nothing. Once beyond the solar system, warp harmonics kicked in and blackness replaced the stars in the acceleration chamber window.

"It sure feels good to leave that obnoxious place," Aggie snorted, releasing her grip. Thyron's reflection in her window nodded agreement.

"You haven't said a word, Creena," the 'troid commented. "Are you okay?" Creena turned a tear-stained face from the glass.

Thyron shuffled over, examining her closely with wide, protoplasmic eyes, then studied her in botanical wonder, leaves fluttering concern.

[What is wrong? What did they do?
You should be glad and not so blue.]

"You were wrong, Thyron," she said, voice quivering with emotion. "The humans there aren't bad at all. At least most of them."

"*Are you out of orbit?*" Aggie screeched. "They stole our ship, tore me apart, wouldn't let us go. . ."

Creena waved her to silence. "I know you can't understand, but at least try to believe me. They weren't all bad, they really weren't, at least not where I was. They really weren't."

Choking up again, she reached inside her uniform for a tissue, the pocket laser's absence replenishing the tears. She smiled through them, trying to imagine Allen's face when he realized what she'd given him.

Thyron and Aggie looked at each other, sharing a rare moment of agreement, before leading her up the ramp to the flightdeck. Its size was no comparison to the *Aquarius*, yet dwarfed the *Cerulean Nimrod* and appeared more than capable of getting her directly to Mira III. She smiled when a cube-shaped 'troid skimmed down the passageway, the world of paper, wheeled vehicles, and food processing already fading.

"Are we on our way to Mira III?" she asked, changing the subject.

"Yes," Aggie replied. "Direct, nonstop."

"Good. By the way, how did you finally make contact?"

"Once I found out the HIO was in the area—"

[Nuts and bolts! This mouthy 'troid
Was spaced out like an asteroid.]

Aggie sniffed, indignant. "Maybe so, but we wouldn't have gotten out without me hacking the security system."

Creena looked at her, startled that she could hear him. Apparently, Thyron had enhanced her communications package while putting her back together. He nodded affirmation before returning attention to the matter at hand.

[What she says is what she did
But that was later in the bid
We did what we had to do
To make sure that we got to you.]

Creena stared from one to the other in disbelief. They'd actually cooperated? What had happened, that required them to put aside their vast differences for her benefit? There would certainly be a lot to talk about on the way to Mira III.

They entered the flightdeck, a huge circular chamber encircled by a symphony of multi-colored lights interrupted by a holographic image of the galaxy. She looked closer, finding Earth's sun with receding melancholy, then Mira, their location somewhere inbetween.

"So where's the captain?" she asked, noting they were alone. "You didn't commandeer the ship just for me, did you?"

"Below deck, updating the ship's log to reflect a few diversions, including this one," Aggie answered.

"Oh," she replied, only slightly disappointed. There would be plenty of time to get acquainted. The main thing was she was on course again. Once they took care of contacting Uncle Kranston, she'd get to Cyraria, somehow, and her family would be together again.

Or so she thought.

<table>
<tr><td colspan="3" align="center">CALMANAC: High Opps/Peak +68/E-74 Days</td></tr>
<tr><td align="center">Temp: 103C/217F</td><td align="center">PVs: 93%</td><td align="center">Quakes: 96%</td></tr>
</table>

Surviving

Uncle Jen's words battered Dirck's mind like a club, devastating what little remained of control.

If their cooling systems break down, most people don't know what to do. They usually don't have emergency plans, supplies, a safe, or other way to survive. What they don't seem to realize is that you can literally cook out there. And there's not a whole lot that can be done if that happens.

They were no smarter than anyone else, and now they were paying for it. How could he have been so stupid?

Win's first action was to block the vent in the top of the ballome to conserve as much cool air as possible. Deven and 'Merama were lowering food down to the safe. Meanwhile, Dirck wandered about aimlessly, trying to figure out what to do.

All his life his father had said that there were no insurmountable problems. It was a simple, *a priori* assumption. Nothing was impossible. *Nothing.* Yet, his father was incarcerated with little hope for release, the natural consequences of his unexplainable behavior, and his family was about to perish. It wasn't like High Opps was an unanticipated surprise. It was a natural weather cycle that they'd been preparing for since their arrival.

And for all their hard work, they weren't ready.

How could he leave them like that?

Probably the most valuable asset they'd lost was the comcon. With that, there may have been some hope. If nothing else, it would have allowed contact with Uncle Jen, who could still probably make it in with his veke. If they could get to the settlement, they could stay in the SD or maybe even find a way to the shelters in Cira City. Or if they'd spent less time on the heat exchanger and more on the safe, its loss wouldn't have been so catastrophic.

If, if, if, if...

It didn't matter, there were no options now, the time far spent.

'Merapa himself had stressed repeatedly how important it was to avoid single-point failures. Redundancy and backups were essential. One, crummy little part shouldn't take an entire system down. Of course, the heat exchanger had hardly been designed under ideal circumstances. They'd done amazingly well, all things considered. What had put it out of commission had been out-of-spec components, which had been unavoidable, and the groundquake probably didn't help, either. However, there was still no excuse for not being prepared in case it failed.

How could he? Why hadn't they dug the safe first? Why hadn't he told him to work on it, while he worked the heat exchanger plans? Stinkin' lizards, he hadn't even mentioned the safe since that first day! He and Win had been the ones who'd finally gotten it started, long after he was gone.

And his father was supposed to be some kind of strategic military mastermind. Dirck had learned in the lowly Academy Cadet Corps that the entire focus of military training was to plan for the worst, then have some recourse if it happened. It was essential to know what to do, so well that emergency procedures were second nature. Executed with little thought, no panic, and the utmost confidence.

Dirck's mind raced, reverted to Miran mode, bouncing from one idea to another, never staying with one long enough to nurture it to viability. Eventually, some of the rage retreated, blending in one pervasive thought that screamed above the others, one he couldn't shake or begin to forget:

Unless something drastic changed, and fast, a day from now they'd all be dead.

They'd be part of those statistics Uncle Jen had mentioned, of foolish people unprepared for the unexpected. Dead with the patrollers and the PV victims.

And to think Uncle Jen had even invited them to his subterre, where they could have weathered out High Opps in comfort and style. What had ever possessed 'Merama to refuse? As a property owner, she was domiciled in Sigma/Epsilon and the ECL was no longer an issue. Why was she so independent, proud, or whatever it was, that she couldn't accept help? She'd go out of her way to help others, but as far as he could remember, never accepted any herself.

Eventually, Dirck ran out of people and things to blame and found himself dead center, anger quelled by urgency, as he realized he'd wasted precious time, when he could have been trying to find solutions. Then he started battering himself. Why hadn't he this, and why hadn't he that, and how could he blame anyone when he was so stupid? No matter what his father had done, inadvertent or not, consciously or not, he wasn't there and couldn't do a thing. Dirck was, and had failed miserably. He'd been so obsessed with anger and blame that he'd entirely shirked his responsibilities. What would his father have to say about *him*?

And then he realized he'd be dead, so it really didn't matter, anyway. It would take a miracle to save them now. Yet, something wouldn't let him give up. He wandered into his sleeproom and looked around for something—*anything*-- that might spawn an idea. His mind was still racing, thoughts sprinting by before he could catch even one, the panic so fierce he was hyperventilating.

It had to stop. *Now.*

He quit pacing and sat on his cyll, face buried in his hands, then kicked up his feet and laid back, took a deep breath and closed his eyes.

Stop it stop it stop it stop it stop it.

Ideas still arced, ungrounded, in his brain, leaving no more than static. He took another breath, held it, and tried to relax.

"Are you all right?"

He opened his eyes. 'Merama walked over slowly, dodging the mess from the safe, and sat beside him. He closed his eyes again and sighed involuntarily.

"You're doing one of two things," she said. "You're either blaming yourself, or doing what your Uncle Kranston does." Dirck didn't comment. "If you're blaming yourself, don't. It wasn't your responsibility, it was mine and your father's. You've done a tremendous job filling in and you need to take credit for your successes. We wouldn't have survived this long, if you and Win hadn't worked so hard. And we're not dead yet."

"Yet," Dirck echoed grimly.

"That's right. *Yet.* Now, like I was saying, there weren't many choices to deal with on Mira III, but Kranston's position required a lot of creative problem solving. He's the one who finally came up with the idea for the biodome radiation shields and is so essential to the process, they'll never let him leave. Anyway, whenever he's faced with something formidable and everyone else is going crazy, he'll find someplace quiet and lie down. It drives his superiors and subordinates alike to distraction, but you know what happens, every time?"

"What?"

"He comes up with some brilliant solution that makes everything else seem like utter foolishness."

"Hmmmmph."

"I'll leave you alone," she said quietly, patted his hand and left the room.

* * *

Sharra returned to her sleeproom and quietly lowered the door. At least Dirck hadn't blamed her, though she was certain he remembered. That look he'd thrown when she'd refused Jen's invitation haunted her enough, without seeing it in his eyes again as she'd entered his sleeproom. She sat down at Laren's workdeck, caressed its warm surface, then rested her head on her arms. It simply wasn't something Dirck could understand.

None of the children knew that, before she and Laren bonded, she'd actually been betrothed to Jen. About a week before it was final, his renegade younger brother returned from an offworld tour with the Space Patrol. From the moment Laren walked in that room, the future had been set. It hadn't been easy to reverse the betrothal, but Jen never argued. He was good-natured, even then, his release of her untainted by bitterness. The irony at nearly becoming Jen's again under the ECL had been almost too much to bear.

Of course, now they were domiciled, and for High Opps such a stay wouldn't have invoked the ECL. Now it was something else. Her life had always held more uncertainties than other Miran's, but enough security reigned on her *naterra* to temper the anxiety with a vitalizing excitement. Cyraria was different. Here uncertainties were heart-wrenching and deadly. And deep inside, she knew if she joined Jen's household, even for a visit, she'd never be able to leave. Staying in the ballome was the only way to honor her *Promises*, even if it meant dying for them.

At the time, Dirck and Win seemed to have everything under control. Even Jen had been impressed with what they'd accomplished. No, at the time it hadn't been hard to believe she'd done the right thing.

Now she wasn't so sure.

Perspiration mingled with tears slid over her nose to her arm, cool for a fleeting moment as it evaporated. The heat inside was already rising like an early morning Miran mist. She rested her chin on her arms and wiped her eyes with her sleeve, recalling something Laren had said, not long before his arrest. Everything would be fine, that the Universe would look after them, as long as they did what was right. She hated to think that her own weakness had jeopardized not only her life, but the boys'. Maybe she'd been right, maybe she'd been wrong. One way or another, soon she'd know.

She sighed and got up with resolve, gathering what few valuables she had to take down to the safe.

* * *

The steadily warming ballome didn't help Dirck's racing thoughts. Uncle Kranston, indeed. 'Merama had probably made that up to make him feel better. The very thought of him doing anything like his uncle was ludicrous. That man was brilliant. Probably a certifiable genius, whereas Dirck placed himself at the other end of the bell curve, with the morons. He almost smiled. The notion that he'd do anything even remotely similar was downright crazy. But it was a sure bet he didn't learn it from his father, either, who did his thinking on his feet.

His thoughts wandered to Creena. It was a good thing she wasn't there, or she'd die, too. He shuddered to think of how she'd feel when she got back and everyone was dead. He'd never see her again and there was so much he wanted to tell her. Now he'd never have a chance. What if he had? What if he could get her on a voice comm, right now?

Creena, I'm really, really sorry. I've acted like a snurk for your entire life and I'm really sorry. Honest. I can't even tell you why I acted like that. It's not that I don't care. I really love you and I'm glad you're my sister. You're a cute kid. And I'm sorry I'll never have the chance to make it up to you.

I'm really glad right now that you're not here. This way you still have a chance. I don't know what's going to happen to 'Merapa. But when we're gone, you'll be all he has. Tell him I really tried. We wouldn't have made it this long without him. Tell him we all miss him, but now I'm glad he's not here, or he'd die too.

Except if he was there, he'd know what to do, plus it probably wouldn't have happened in the first place. He took another deep breath, tried to relax, refusing to think of anything, as thoughts of Creena went full circle. Maybe he could just die now and save himself a lot of trouble.

Gradually, his exhausted mind settled to a more normal rhythm, then fully relaxed to that frequency where conscious and subconscious meet. Whether it was aplomb, denial or complete surrender he didn't know, but somehow the thumping and banging of Win's frantic efforts seemed almost amusing. Usually he did well in real-time emergencies, but this time was different. Any solution to this went deeper than a quick fix. Way deeper.

He sighed and relaxed some more. Oddly enough, he felt better. Less frantic, less angry, less depressed. He was awake and alert, yet somewhere in consciousness he'd never been before. It was quiet, deep and comfortable, a place of refuge. If this was what death was like, maybe all his fears had been in vain. From the stillness words formed, stranger than he could imagine, words he knew weren't his own.

> [You often take the troubled path
> Invite misfortune's heated wrath
> Solutions now you soon will find
> Within the depths of your own mind.
> All you need to know is there
> Invite the truth to you to bear
> It can be done, you know it, Dirck
> But Creena thinks you're still a snurk.]

What?

In spite of his shock, he noticed the scorched smell of the baking ballome had been replaced with the sudden scent of freshly picked greenery, like that inside Mira III's biodomes. *Who or what are you?* he thought. *What's going on?* Or was he already dead?

> [Your parents you did think insane
> When they perceived my words to gain
> But if you have the mind to hear
> It will check your greatest fear
> Your family will not die of heat
> Your brother's words it all can beat
> Who I am it matters not
> Until this battle you have fought.]

The aroma swamped his senses again, saturating his entire being until it ended as suddenly as it had come. Consumed with awe, he could hardly wait to tell 'Merama. If his parents were crazy, now he was, too. Whoever or whatever it was obviously had some connection with Creena and wanted to help. He lay there quietly, trying to decipher the strange message, when the answer erupted. And the words were indeed those of his brother, from that time he was trying to explain why everyone was so upset about losing their =CC=s.

The bnolar don't have =CC=s or compressors and they get through High Opps.

Dirck opened his eyes and stared at the ceiling while his mind finished returning to baser realities. It was so incredibly simple. How could he ever have been in such a panic?

Then he wondered why Deven hadn't thought of it. Those were his very words. He tried to remember if his brother had ever told Win about the bnolar. As far as he could recall, he hadn't. Maybe that was it. He'd already broken his promise once and wasn't going to again.

And why hadn't 'Merama thought of it? Most of the information for the Barterboard had come from the bnolar. Had she forgotten? Or was it something else? Would she forsake survival for the sake of pride? Was that it? It certainly had nothing to do with the ECL this time.

Doubts assailed him as he sat up and swung his feet to the floor. Maybe he was losing his orbit. He sensed movement and glanced up. Deven was standing in the door. He beckoned him inside. He entered slowly, eyes too solemn for someone so young. He patted the cyll beside him and Deven sat down.

"You know what we need to do, don't you?" Dirck asked. Deven nodded. "How do you feel about that?"

"I don't know. I promised him I wouldn't tell."

"But I met Enoch, too, remember? I didn't promise anything."

Deven sighed and shook his head. "I just don't know, Dirck."

"Have you ever told Win about Enoch?" Deven shook his head again. "Why not? Because of your promise?"

"I guess.'

"Enoch is your friend. He'd want to help. If he were in some kind of trouble and you could help, you would, right?" Deven nodded. "How about you and I suit up and go see Enoch? You can tell him we're in trouble and see if he can help. Would you do that?"

Deven heaved a sigh deep enough to kill an adult. "I guess," he said. "But none of us can ever tell anybody, okay? No one."

"Okay. That's reasonable enough. Now come on. Let's tell 'Merama and Win our plan."

The heat in the living area was rising faster than in the sleeprooms and Win was still trying to plug the fan vent. He looked down from the chair and shook his head.

"What were you doing, taking a nap?" he said sarcastically. "There's a million things that need doin', you know." Win's face was red and streaked with sweat, eyes broadcasting nearly tangible fear.

"There's nothing we can do in the time left," Dirck replied calmly. "You're wasting time and energy. All it'll do is delay dying. Panic will hasten it.   There's another solution."

He ignored Win's indignant expression and stepped into his parent's sleeproom where his mother was gathering what few valuables they had to take down to the safe.

"'Merama," he said quietly. She looked up expectantly. "I have an idea. But it wasn't entirely mine. And it came, or at least the idea for the idea, if that makes any sense, came in a really strange way. Remember that cut vegetation thing you and 'Merapa talked about?" She nodded.

"That's how it was."

"You, too, now," she said. "Did it mention your sister?"

"In a way. It said she still thinks I'm a snurk."

'Merama laughed. "Was it in rhyme?"

"Uh-huh. It was really weird. Anyway, I think I have the answer."

He stepped back into the living area and asked Win to join them. His friend's face emanated all the emotions Dirck had battled earlier. He stared hard at Dirck, then got down from the chair and sat on the floor cross-legged, arms folded.

"So now what?" he mumbled impatiently. "I suppose you've come up with some brilliant plan."

"Deven and I are going to suit up and find a place to stay."

Win's mouth dropped in total disbelief, but 'Merama's face lit up with understanding.

"*Where?*" Win asked belligerently. "There's no place worth walking to, oppsuit or not. The settlement's too far and there's no one else within a hundred kilometers. And if you're thinking about some cave or something, how would we ever move enough supplies, especially water, assuming you even found one?"

Dirck got the feeling that even if he told Win about the bnolar in vast detail, that he wouldn't be overjoyed. He was technologically oriented and would think of the bnolar as primitive cave dwellers. And maybe they were. But they survived. And that was Dirck's principal responsibility, to survive.

"Why don't you and Deven go ahead and suit up?" 'Merama suggested quietly. "I'll explain your plan to Win."

Win looked at her as if she'd jumped states. "You mean you're actually going to let them go out there, alone, on some crazy whim?"

"It's not a crazy whim," she assured him. "It's the best solution we have."

Win refolded his arms, posture stiffened by frustration. "Insanity obviously runs in *this* family."

'Merama laughed. "You're probably right. Laren has walked the genius-insanity interface his entire life. But let me tell you what's going on. Have you ever wondered where we got all the information we put on the Barterboard? Or how we learned so much about edible plants?"

She waved Dirck and Deven away to don their suits and the pair left the chore of telling Win in her hands.

Deven's oppsuit was a little baggy, but a fairly good fit, considering it wasn't custom made and also allowed growing room. Dirck checked the connections in his own, then entered the living area as his mother finished briefing Win. He looked dumbfounded and more than a little skeptical.

Dirck studied him solemnly. The Win that had defied a patrol veke in the canyon and outsmarted the PLED was not the one who stared back. It was getting hot, but not enough to account for the sweat running down his face.

"Do you have any better ideas?" Dirck asked.

"No, I don't," he replied sullenly.

"All right. While we're gone, you and 'Merama get some supplies together, mainly genour. Load up the boxcart with that, and anything else we can't live without. If everything goes well, we should be able to leave as soon as we get back."

'Merama gave him and Deven a hug, then waved goodbye as they secured their helmets and exited through the back door.

Seventy four more days of Peak Opps remained, with nearly a standard year left before the temperature would drop to an even marginally comfortable range. Zeta was climbing, Zinni riding the horizon. Without the oppsuits, such a trip would have been suicide. He thought again of Uncle Jen and realized that they'd been more prepared than he'd realized all along. It was as if someone or something was watching over them, letting them go only so far before bailing them out.

Dirck took his brother's hand and followed the boy's lead, pondering how the idea had come. And what they would have done if it hadn't.

The Brightstar Saga continues in Volume III,
"A Psilent Place Below"

Find out what happened to Thyron and Aggie behind the scenes in the latest Star Trails Adventure!
"The Terra Debacle: Prisoners at Area 51"

About the Author

Inspired by science fiction stories as a child, Marcha Fox's love of astronomy eventually led to a Bachelor of Science Degree in physics from Utah State University, followed by a 21 year career at NASA's Johnson Space Center in Houston, Texas. While there, she held a variety of positions including technical writer, engineer, and eventually manager.

Born in Peekskill, New York, she's lived in California, Utah, and Texas in the course of raising her family. All of her six children are now grown with offspring of their own, providing her with 17 grandchildren and four great-grandchildren, so far.

Never at a loss for something to do, besides writing she enjoys gardening, her two Bengal cats, and keeping up with her family.

Connect via Social Media

Series Website: http://www.StarTrailsSaga.com
Facebook: https://www.facebook.com/marchafoxauthor
Website: http://www.StarTrailsSaga.com
Twitter: https://twitter.com/startrailsIV
Blog: http://marcha2014.wordpress.com/
Amazon Author Page:
http://www.amazon.com/Marcha-Fox/e/B0074RV16O/
Goodreads:
https://www.goodreads.com/author/show/6481953.Marcha_A_Fox
Author Facebook: https://www.facebook.com/marchafoxauthor